Sita's Ramayana

Text by Samhita Arni | Art by Moyna Chitrakar

Groundwood Books
House of Anansi Press
Toronto Berkeley

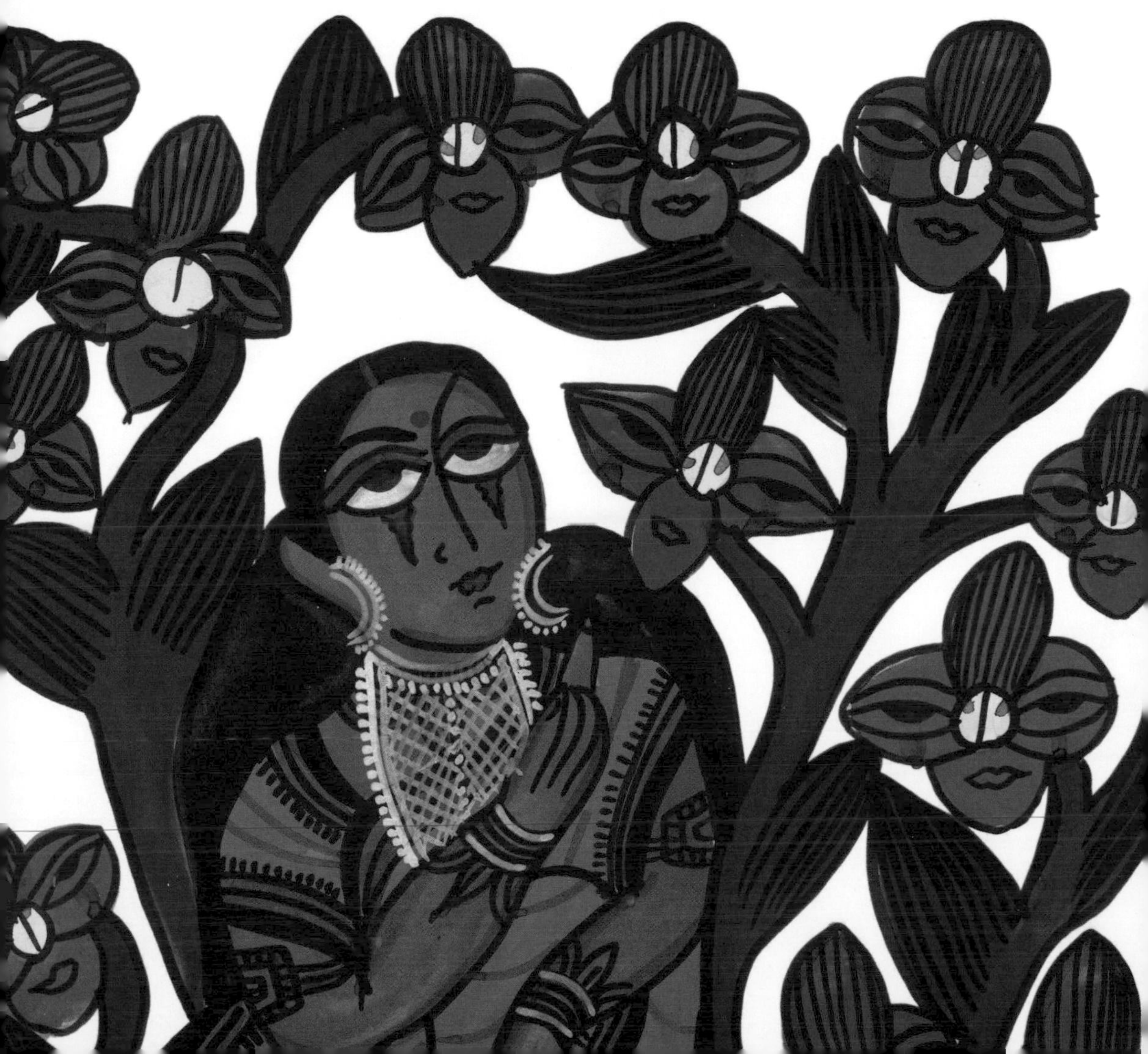

LAKSHMANA
Rama's younger brother

RAMA
Banished Prince
of Ayodhya

SITA
Princess of Mithila
and Rama's Queen

SHATRUGHNA
Lakshmana's twin
brother

LAVA
Rama and Sita's son

KUSHA
Rama and Sita's son

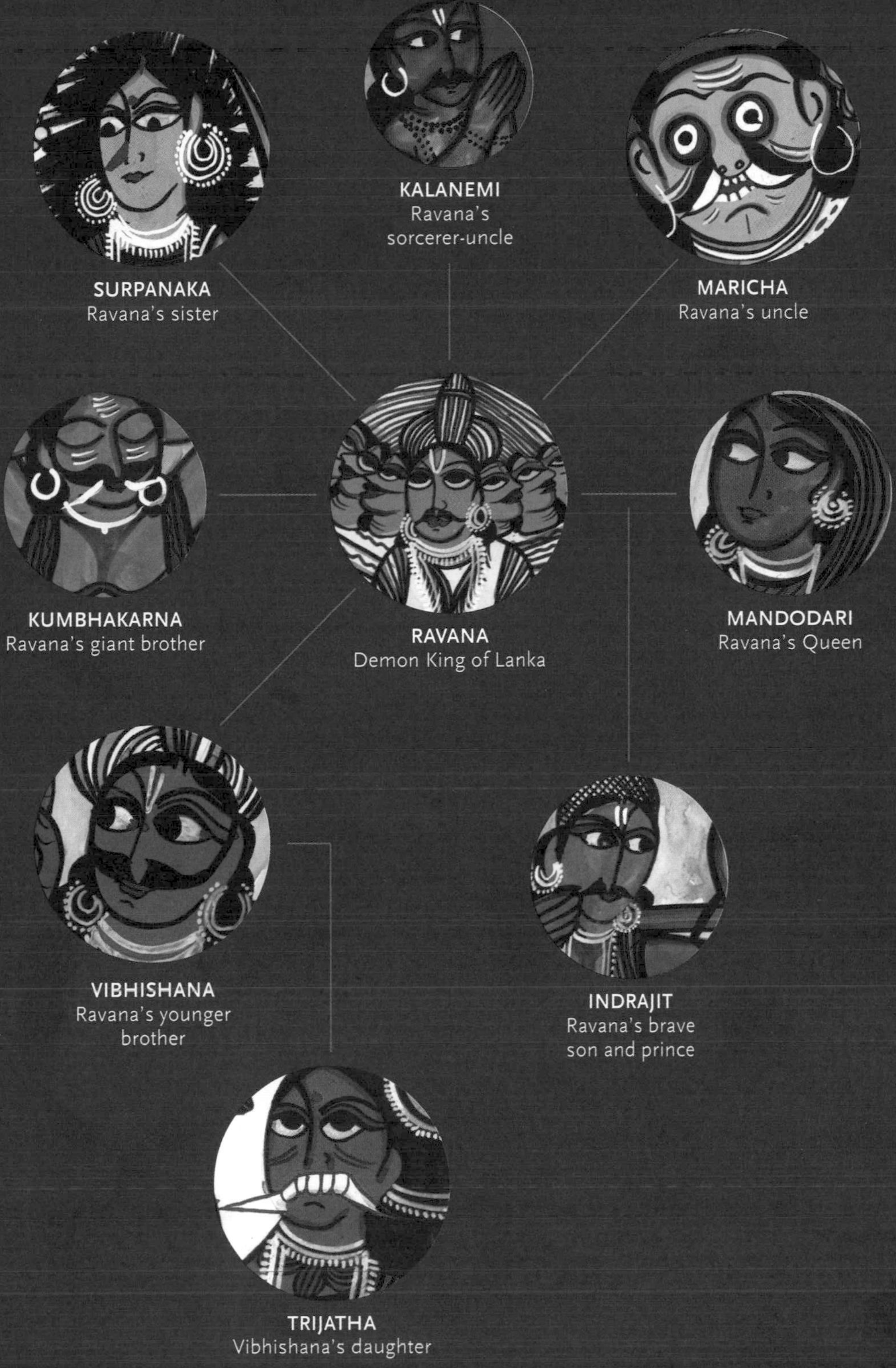
KALANEMI
Ravana's sorcerer-uncle
SURPANAKA
Ravana's sister
MARICHA
Ravana's uncle
KUMBHAKARNA
Ravana's giant brother
RAVANA
Demon King of Lanka
MANDODARI
Ravana's Queen
VIBHISHANA
Ravana's younger brother
INDRAJIT
Ravana's brave son and prince
TRIJATHA
Vibhishana's daughter

HANUMAN
A wise, brave and
ingenious monkey

SUGRIVA
Valin's brother and deposed
King of the Vanaras

VALIN
King of the Vanaras

TARA
Valin and Sugriva's wife

ANGADA
Tara's son

NALA
Architect of the Vanaras

SUSHENA
Surgeon of the
Vanara army

VALMIKI
Author of the
Ramayana

JATAYU
A kind eagle

MAHIRAVANA
Sorcerer-king of the
Underworld

GARUDA
A divine bird

AGNI
Fire god

VARUNA
Sea god

For a thousand years the Dandaka forest slept.

Until, one day, the daughter of the Earth came.

At her touch the flowers, creepers and trees of the Dandaka awoke from their long sleep.

The forest watched her, with great interest. She was no hermit's wife – beautifully dressed in priceless silks and ornaments, worth a king's ransom. She walked with pain, her belly huge with child, her ankles swollen, her delicate feet bruised by thorns and brambles.

Who was she? The forest wondered.

What was she doing here?

And why was she crying?

She knew the forest watched her, and she heard the whispered questions.

I AM SITA, DAUGHTER OF THE EARTH, SPRUNG FROM THE SAME WOMB THAT NURTURES THIS FOREST. I AM THE PRINCESS OF MITHILA AND THE LAST QUEEN OF AYODHYA.

The forest was silent, but the plants
edged closer still and the leaves bent
to catch her words.

LET ME LIVE HERE.

Sita begged.

**THE WORLD OF MEN
HAS BANISHED ME.**

And then the forest spoke:

Tell us, sister, how you came here.

And so she began —

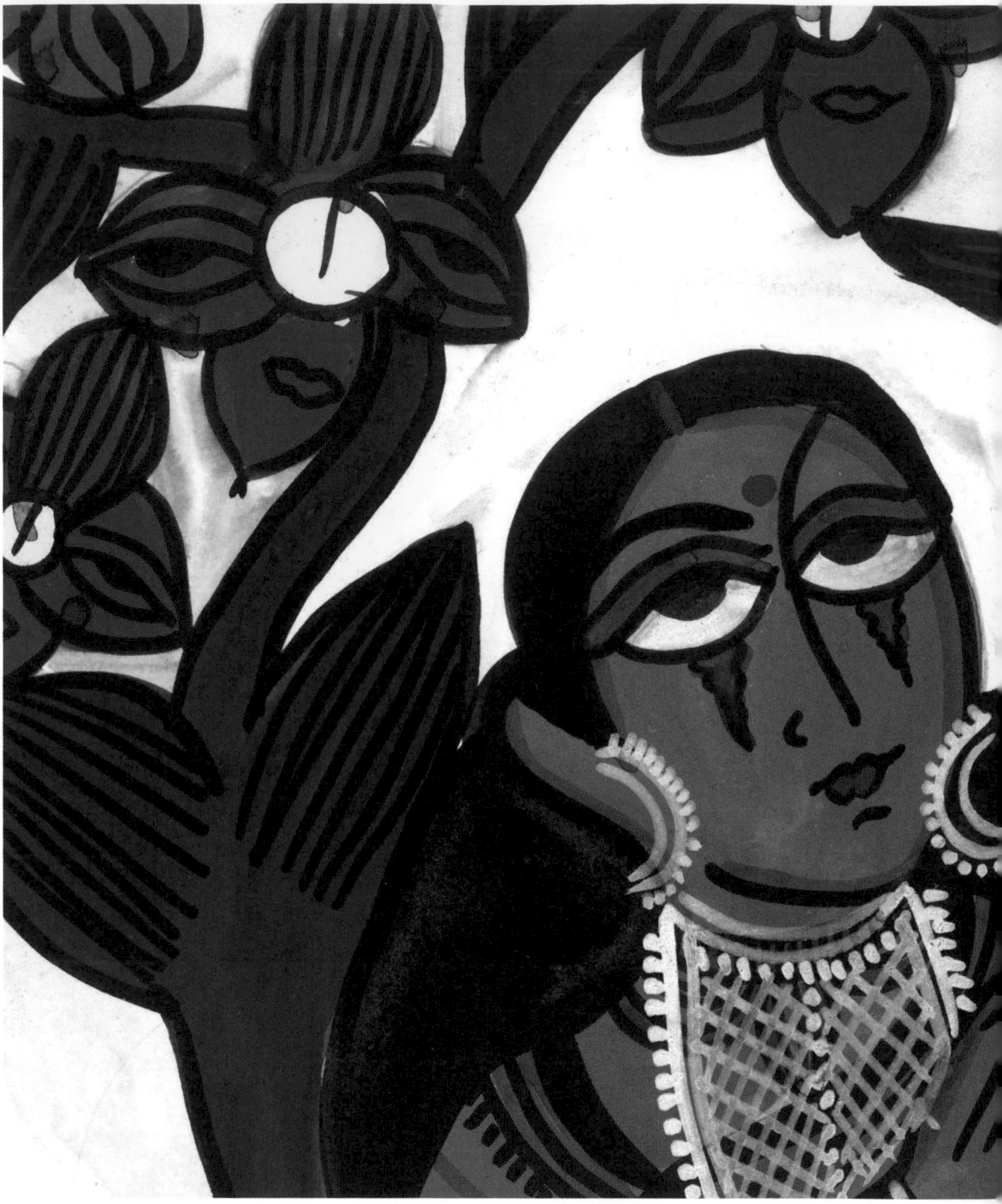

SITA'S RA

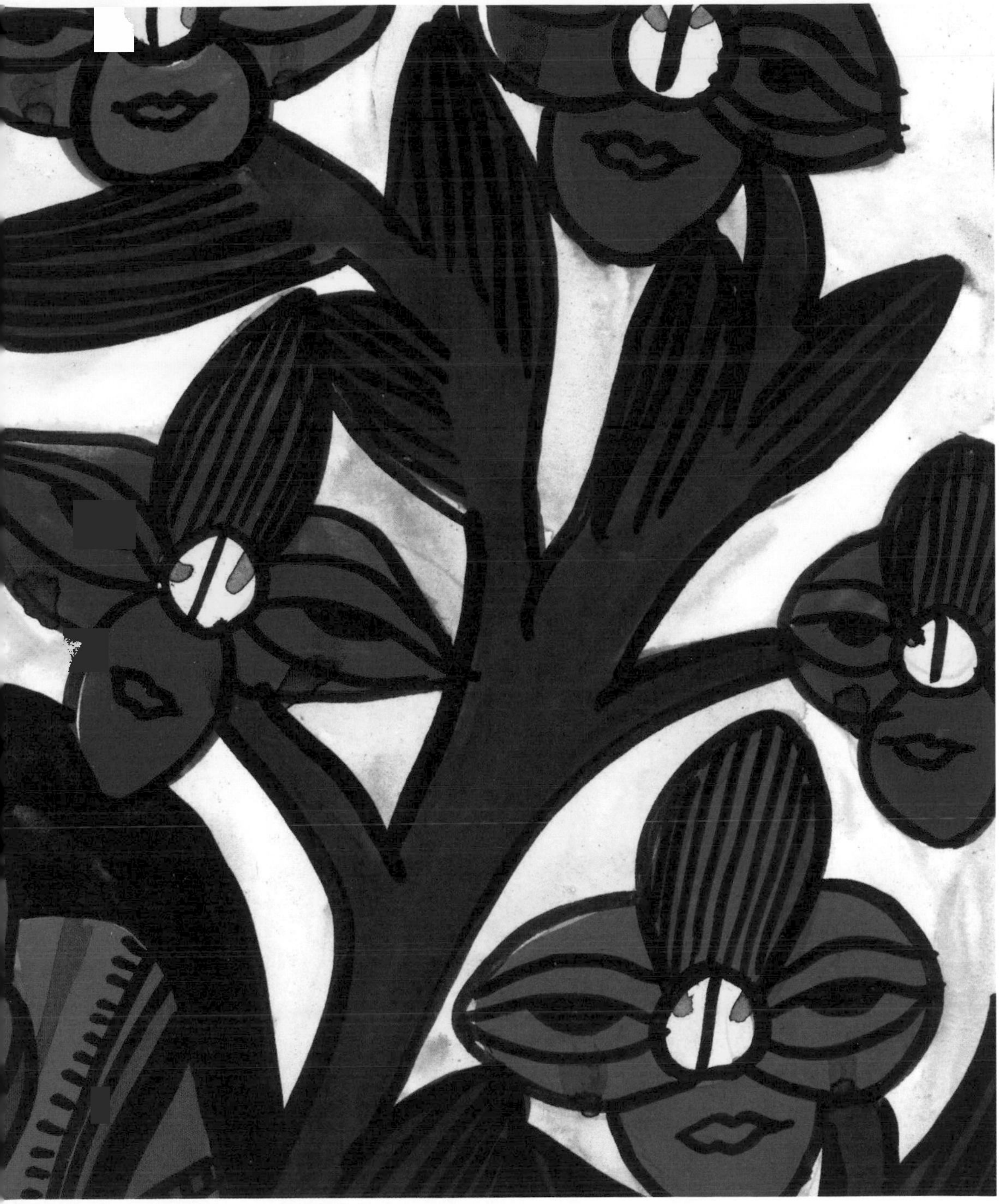

MAYANA

MORE THAN FOURTEEN YEARS AGO, MY
HUSBAND RAMA, PRINCE OF AYODHYA,
WAS EXILED FROM HIS KINGDOM.

I FOLLOWED HIM, WITH MY BROTHER-IN-
LAW LAKSHMANA, AND WE CAME TO THE
CHITRAKUTA FOREST.

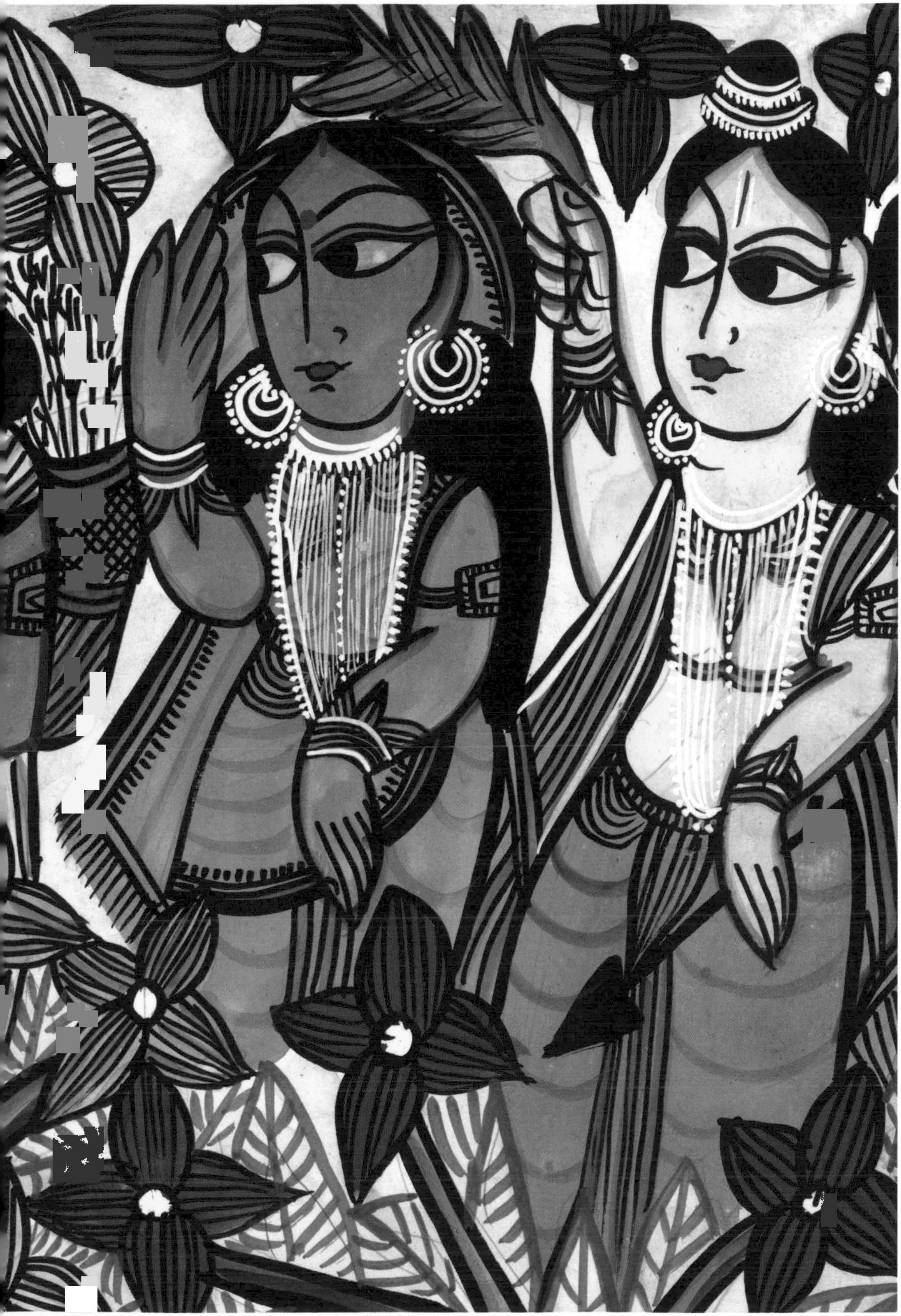

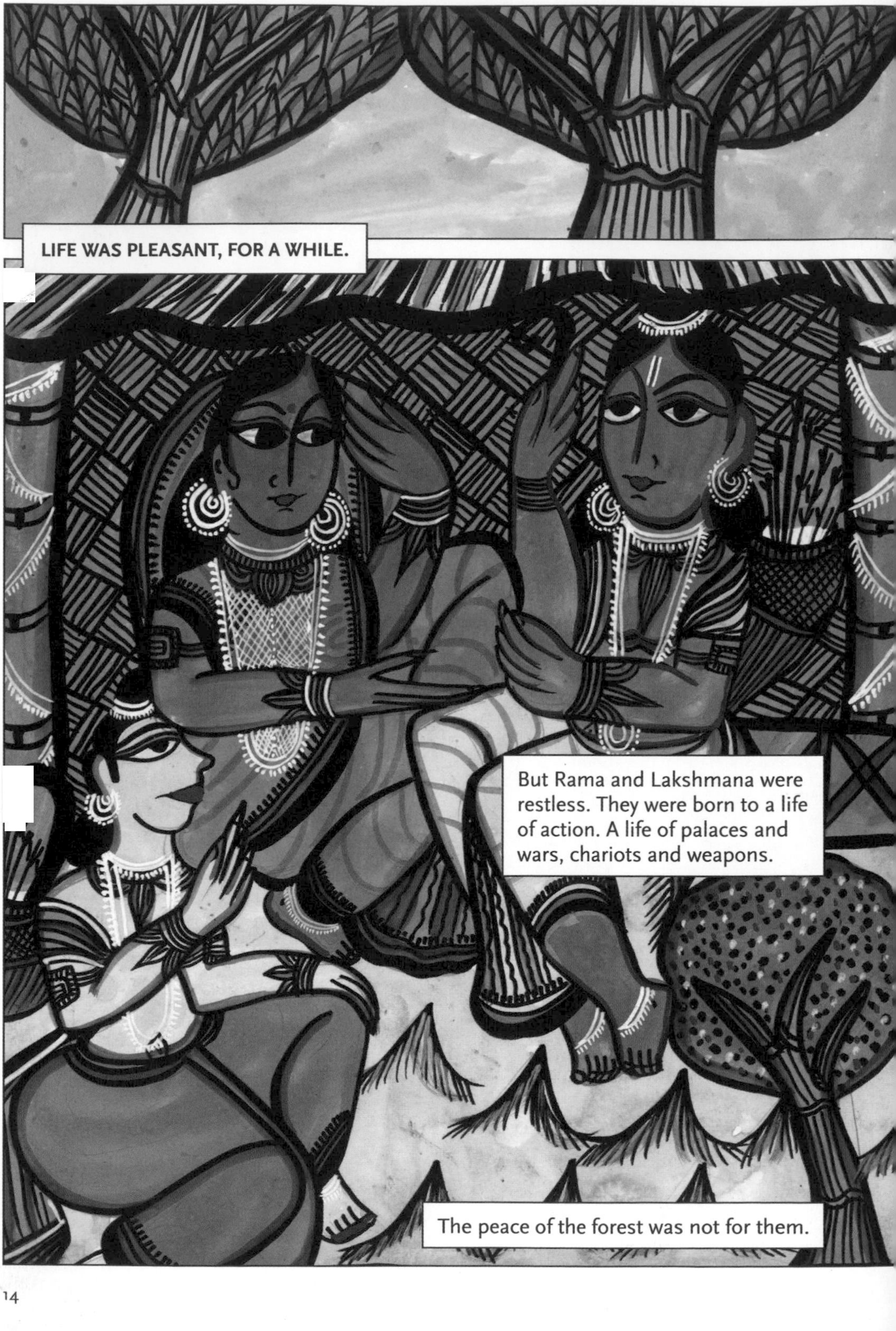
LIFE WAS PLEASANT, FOR A WHILE.
But Rama and Lakshmana were restless. They were born to a life of action. A life of palaces and wars, chariots and weapons.
The peace of the forest was not for them.

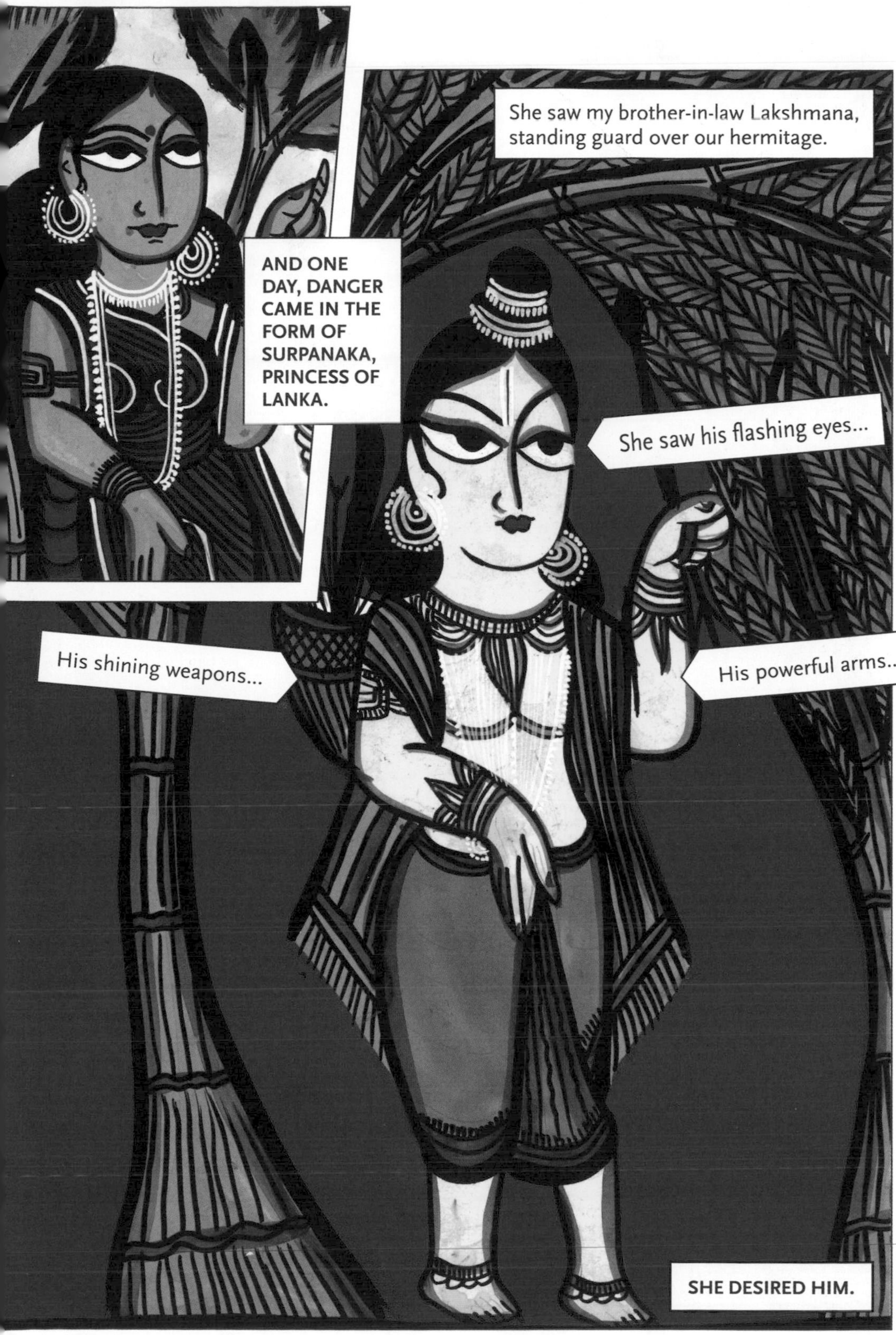
AND ONE DAY, DANGER CAME IN THE FORM OF SURPANAKA, PRINCESS OF LANKA.
She saw my brother-in-law Lakshmana, standing guard over our hermitage.
She saw his flashing eyes...
His shining weapons...
His powerful arms...
SHE DESIRED HIM.

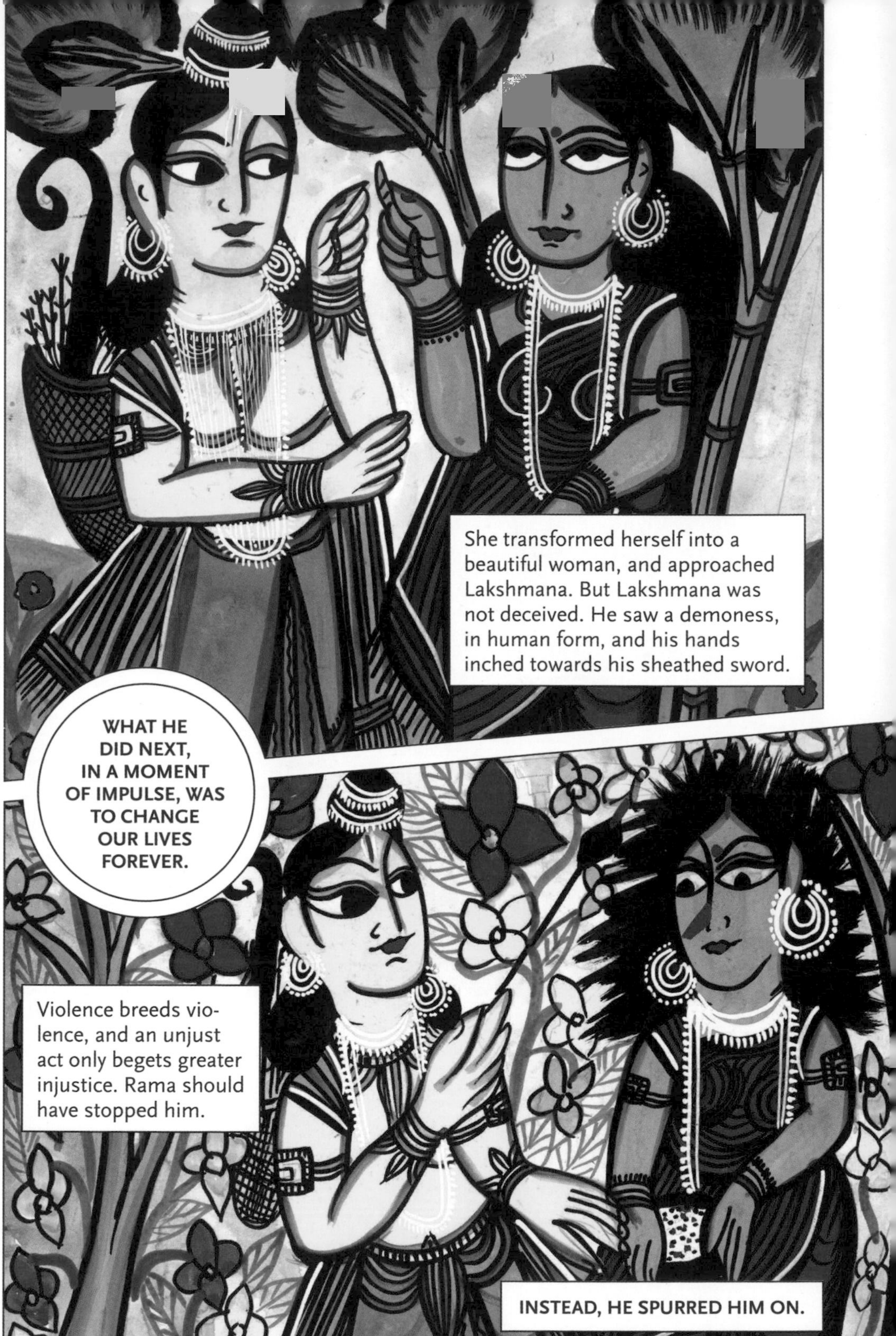
She transformed herself into a beautiful woman, and approached Lakshmana. But Lakshmana was not deceived. He saw a demoness, in human form, and his hands inched towards his sheathed sword.
WHAT HE DID NEXT, IN A MOMENT OF IMPULSE, WAS TO CHANGE OUR LIVES FOREVER.
Violence breeds violence, and an unjust act only begets greater injustice. Rama should have stopped him.
INSTEAD, HE SPURRED HIM ON.

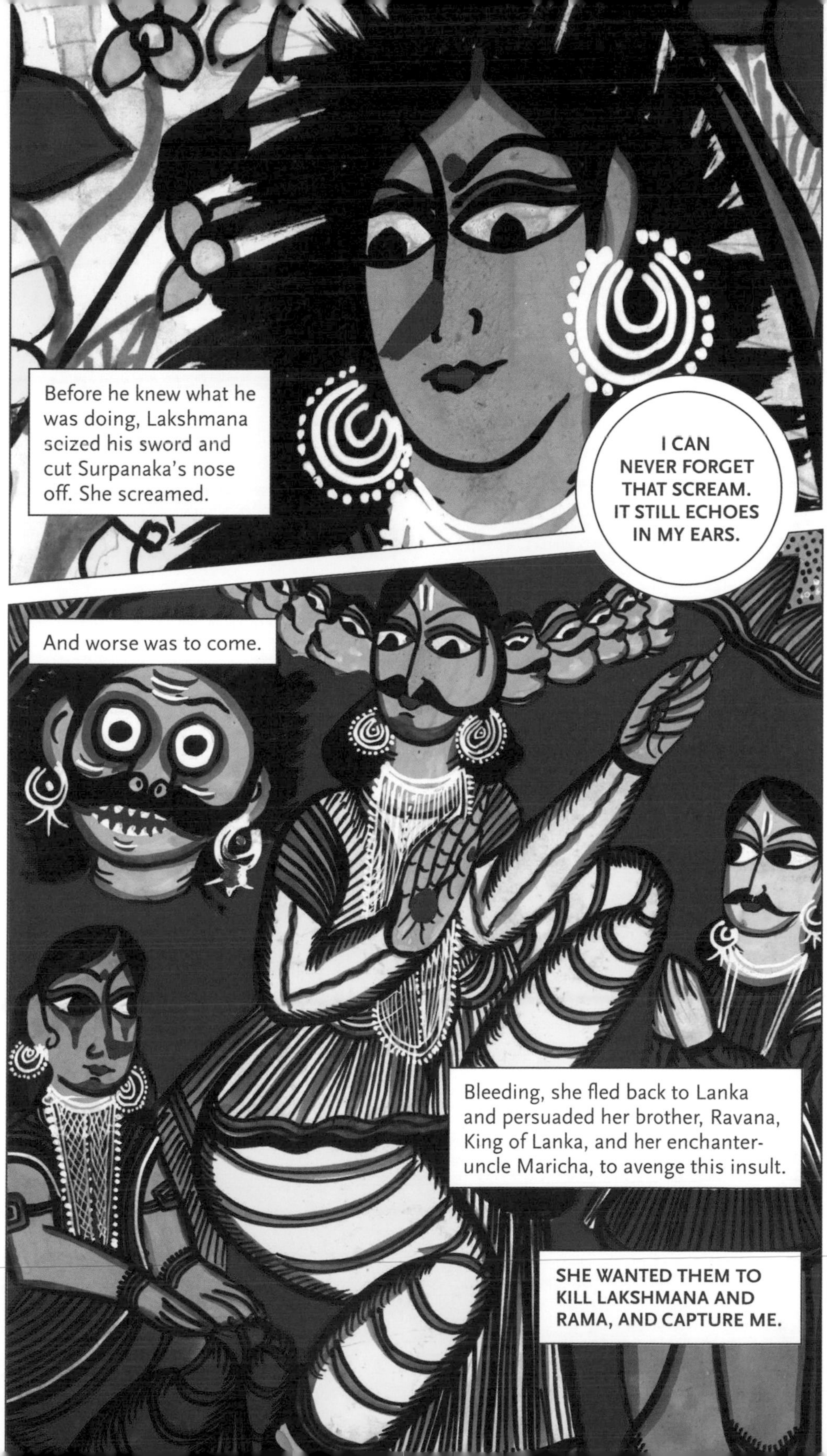
Before he knew what he was doing, Lakshmana seized his sword and cut Surpanaka's nose off. She screamed.
I CAN NEVER FORGET THAT SCREAM. IT STILL ECHOES IN MY EARS.
And worse was to come.
Bleeding, she fled back to Lanka and persuaded her brother, Ravana, King of Lanka, and her enchanter-uncle Maricha, to avenge this insult.
SHE WANTED THEM TO KILL LAKSHMANA AND RAMA, AND CAPTURE ME.

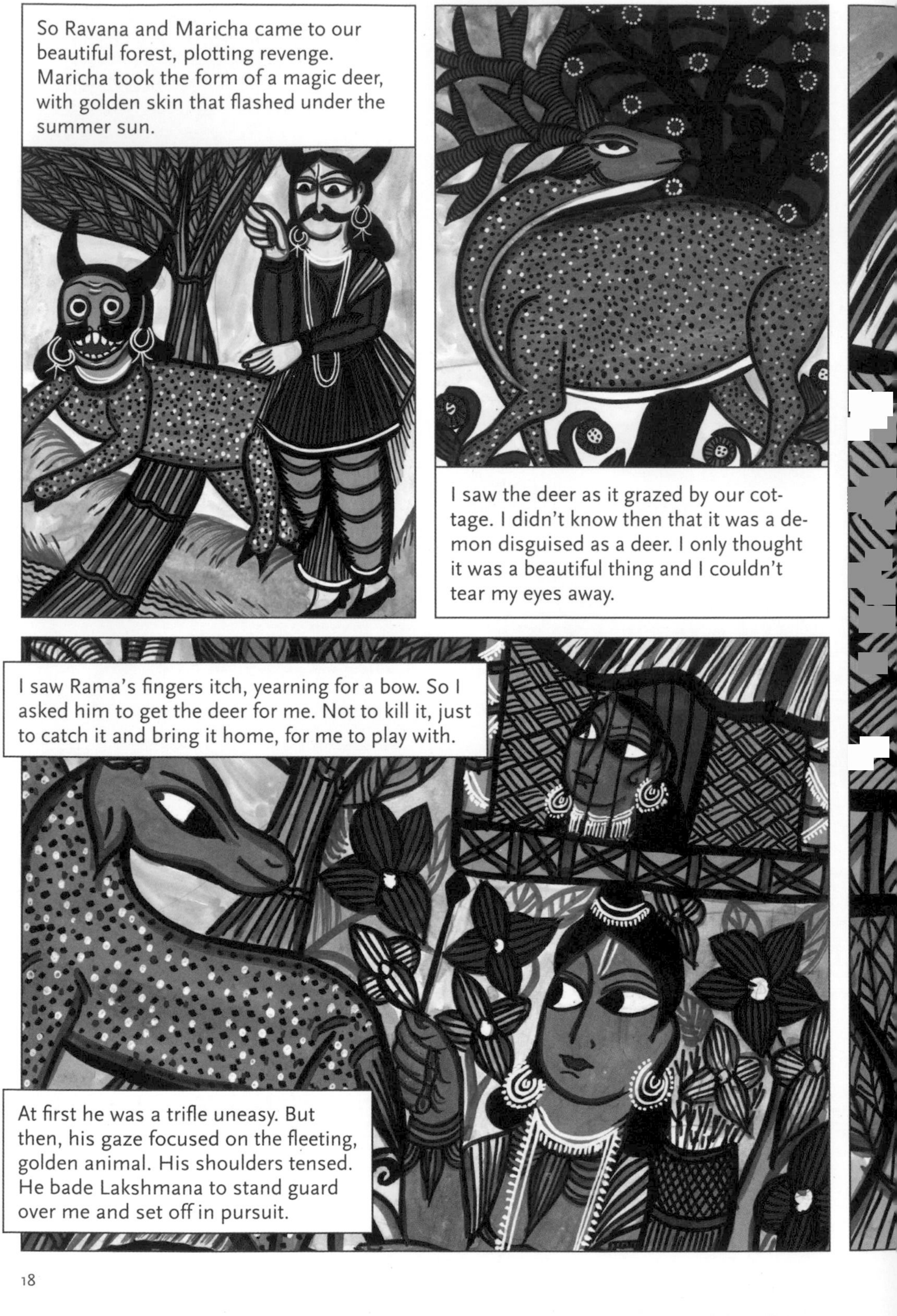
So Ravana and Maricha came to our beautiful forest, plotting revenge. Maricha took the form of a magic deer, with golden skin that flashed under the summer sun.
I saw the deer as it grazed by our cottage. I didn't know then that it was a demon disguised as a deer. I only thought it was a beautiful thing and I couldn't tear my eyes away.
I saw Rama's fingers itch, yearning for a bow. So I asked him to get the deer for me. Not to kill it, just to catch it and bring it home, for me to play with.
At first he was a trifle uneasy. But then, his gaze focused on the fleeting, golden animal. His shoulders tensed. He bade Lakshmana to stand guard over me and set off in pursuit.

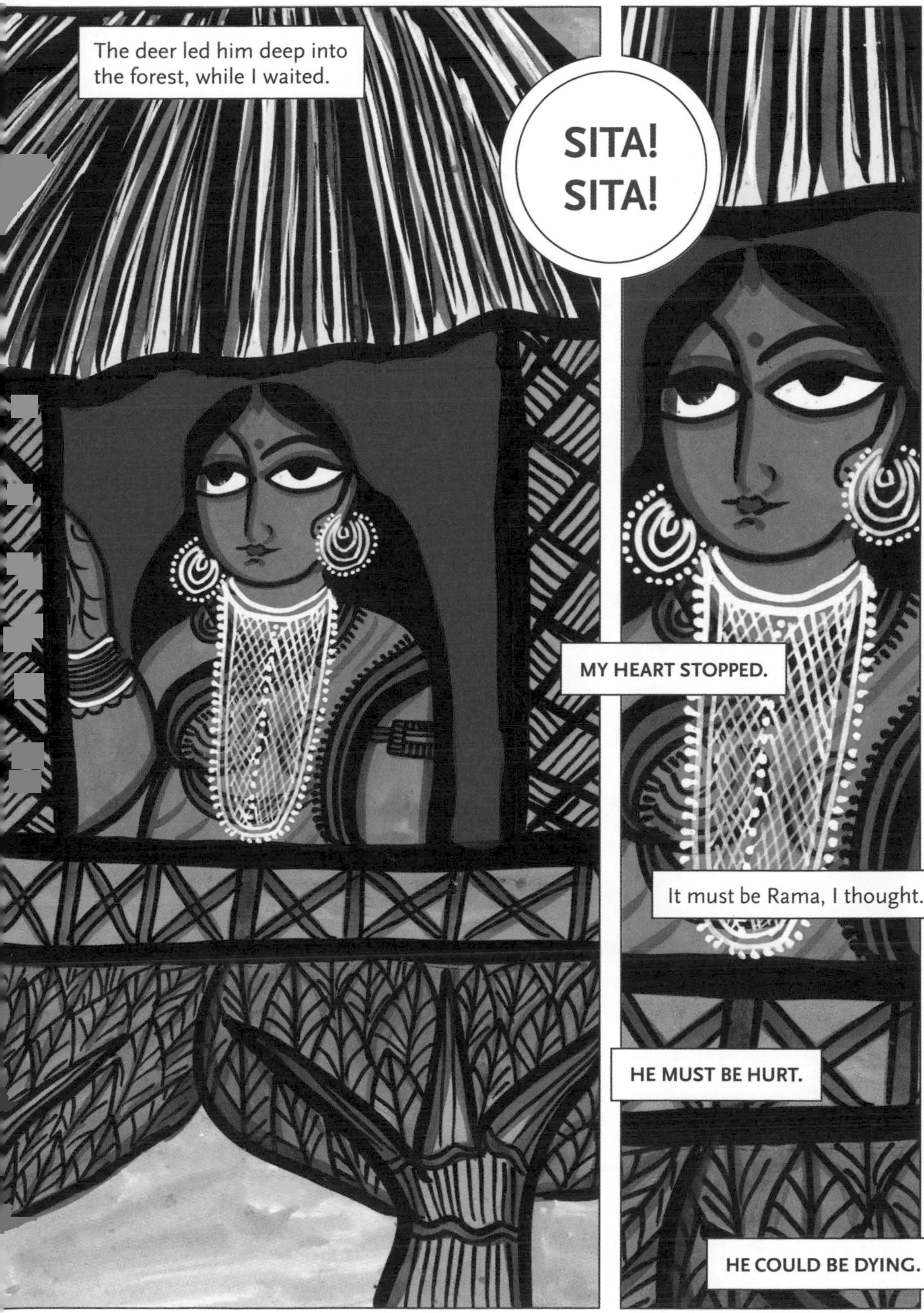
The deer led him deep into the forest, while I waited.
SITA! SITA!
MY HEART STOPPED.
It must be Rama, I thought.
HE MUST BE HURT.
HE COULD BE DYING.

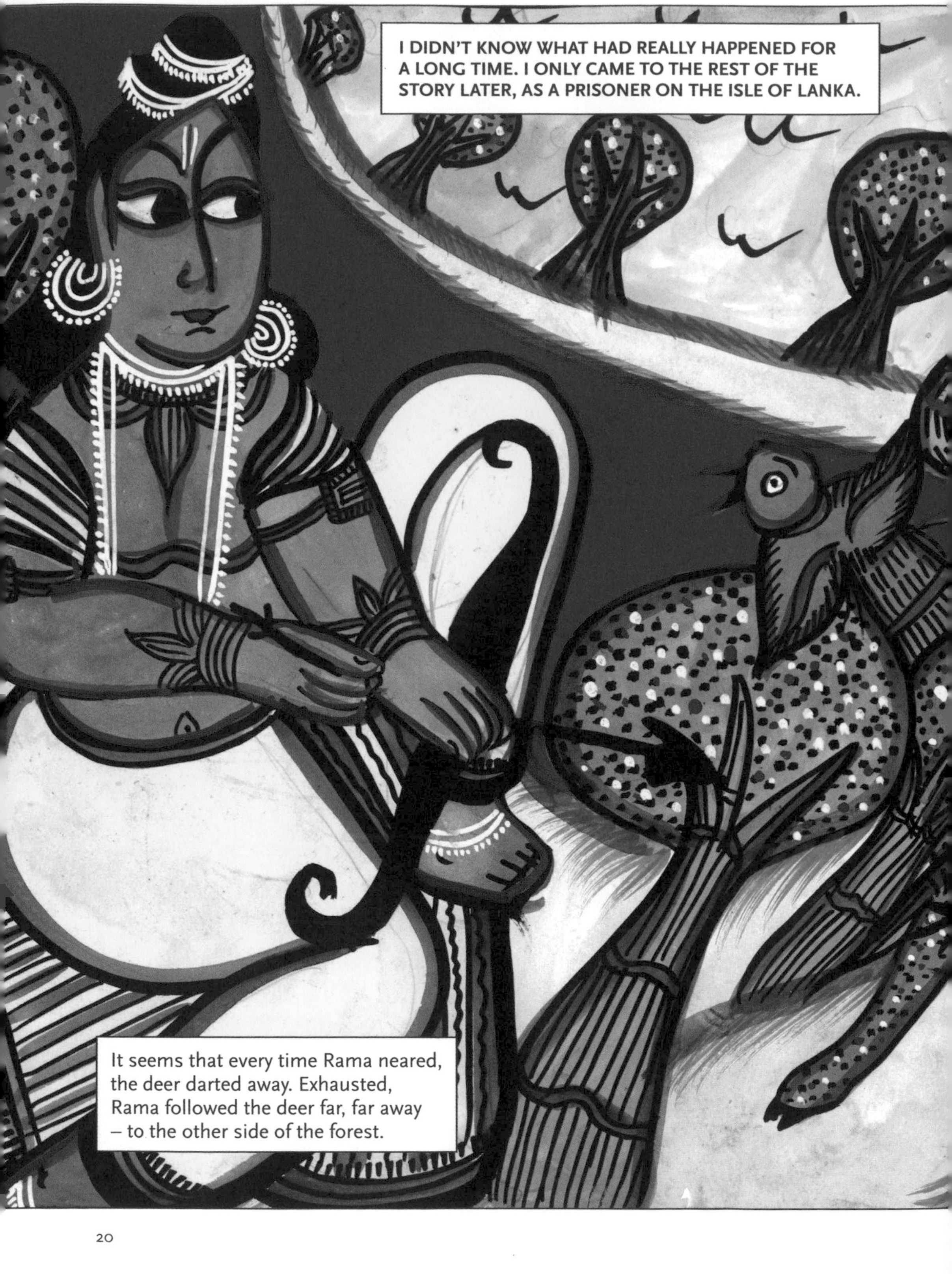

I DIDN'T KNOW WHAT HAD REALLY HAPPENED FOR A LONG TIME. I ONLY CAME TO THE REST OF THE STORY LATER, AS A PRISONER ON THE ISLE OF LANKA.
It seems that every time Rama neared, the deer darted away. Exhausted, Rama followed the deer far, far away – to the other side of the forest.

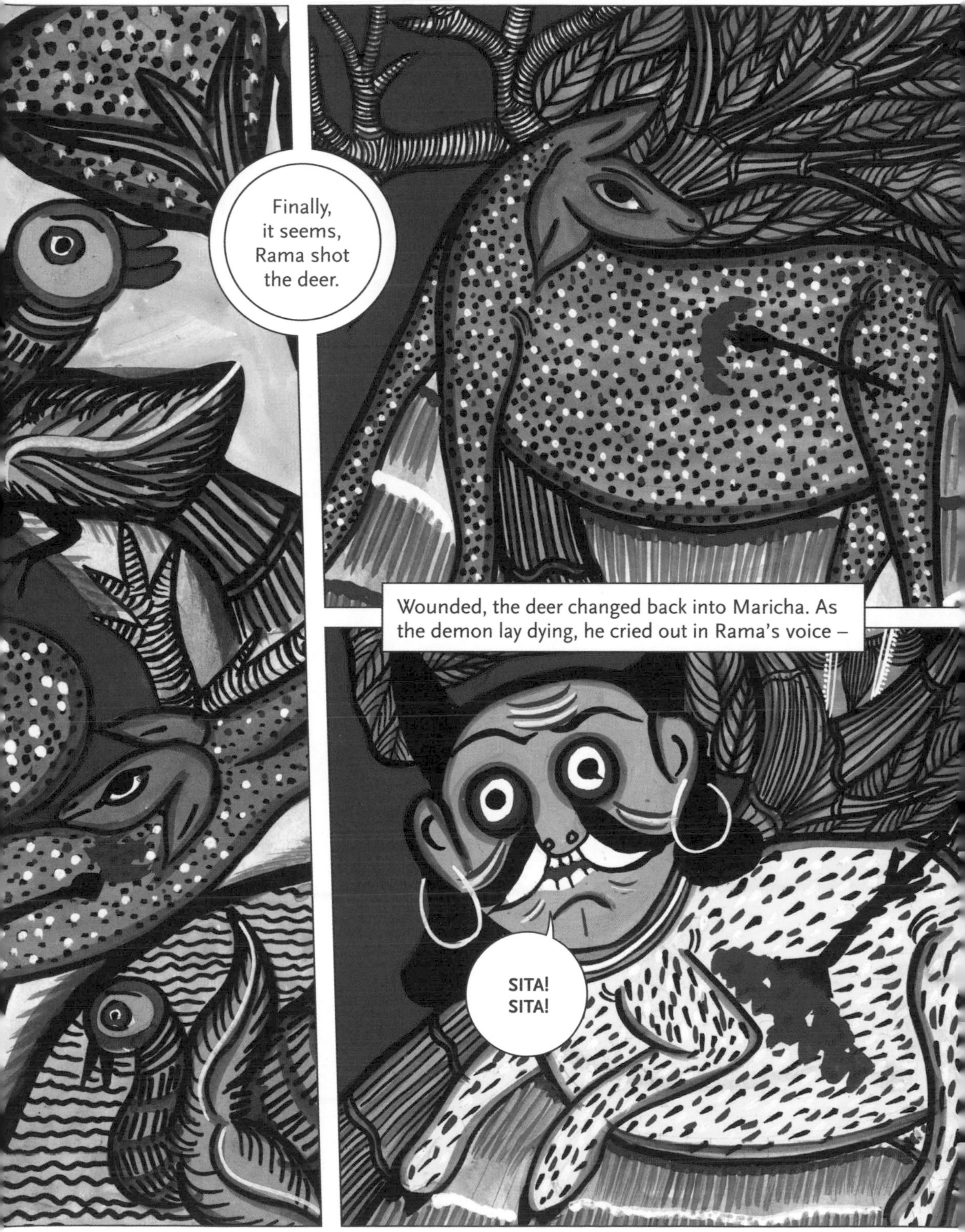
Finally, it seems, Rama shot the deer.
Wounded, the deer changed back into Maricha. As the demon lay dying, he cried out in Rama's voice –
SITA! SITA!

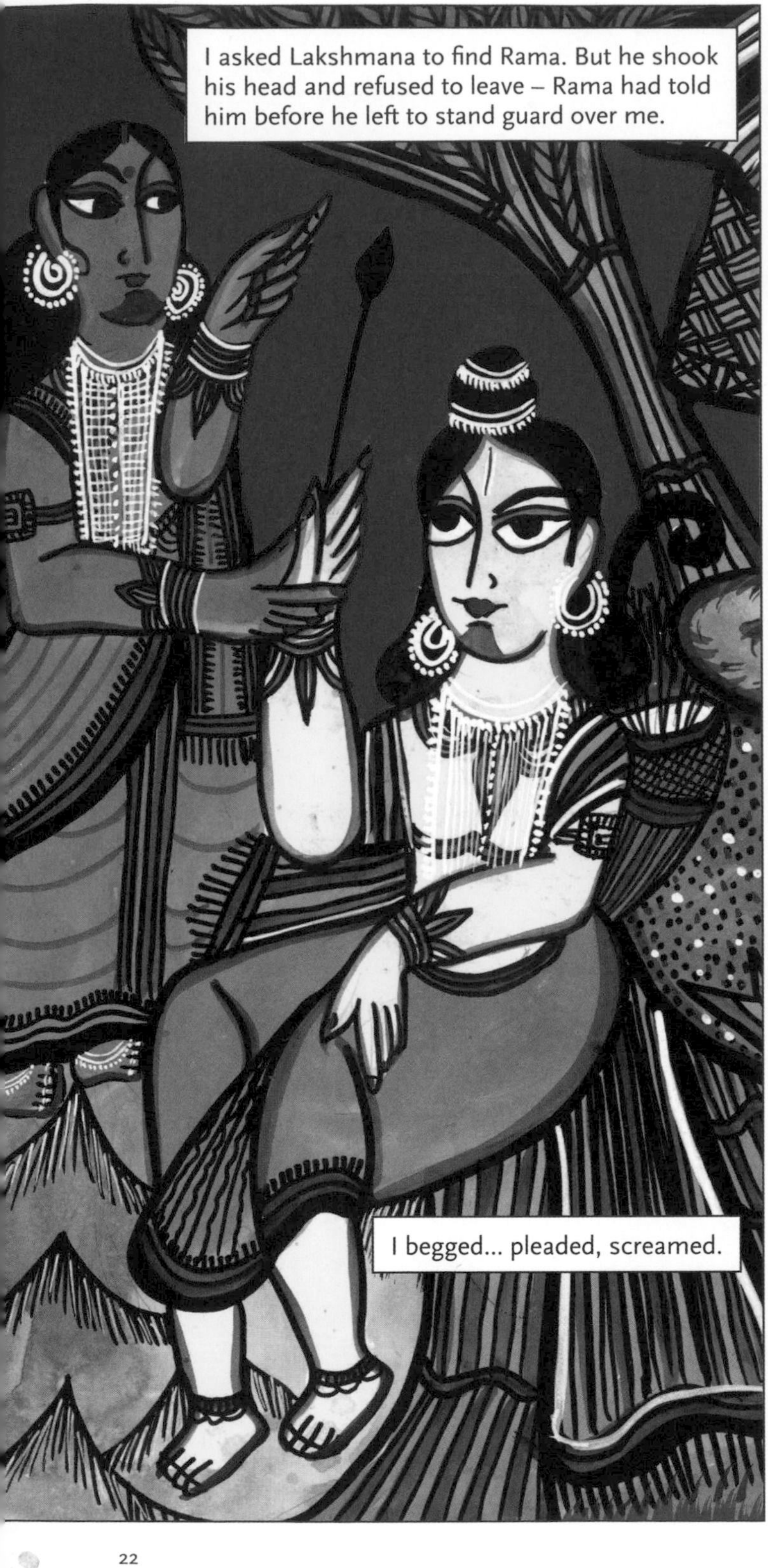
I asked Lakshmana to find Rama. But he shook his head and refused to leave – Rama had told him before he left to stand guard over me.
I begged... pleaded, screamed.

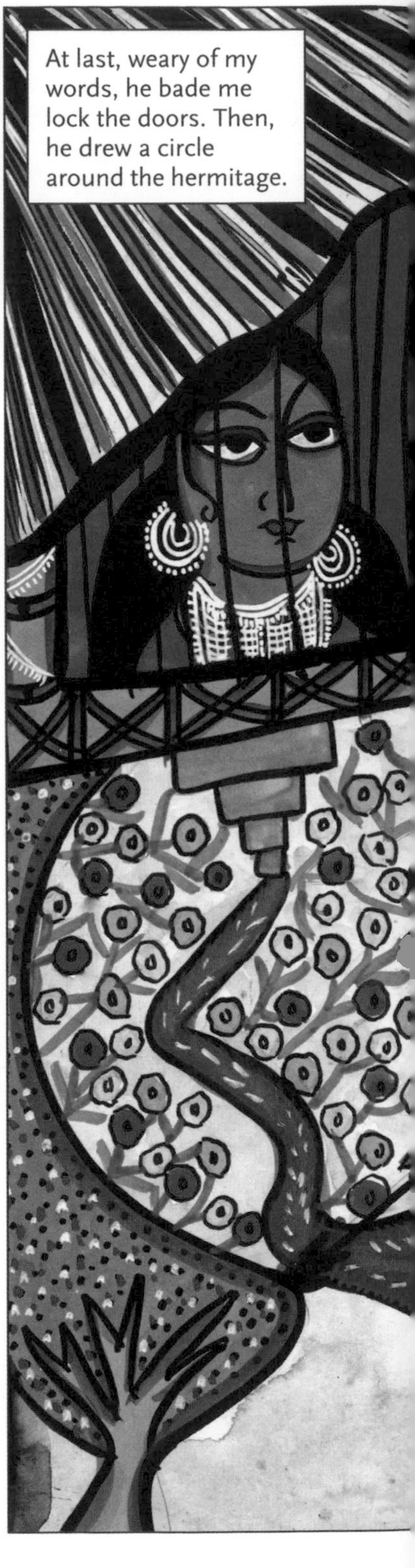
At last, weary of my words, he bade me lock the doors. Then, he drew a circle around the hermitage.

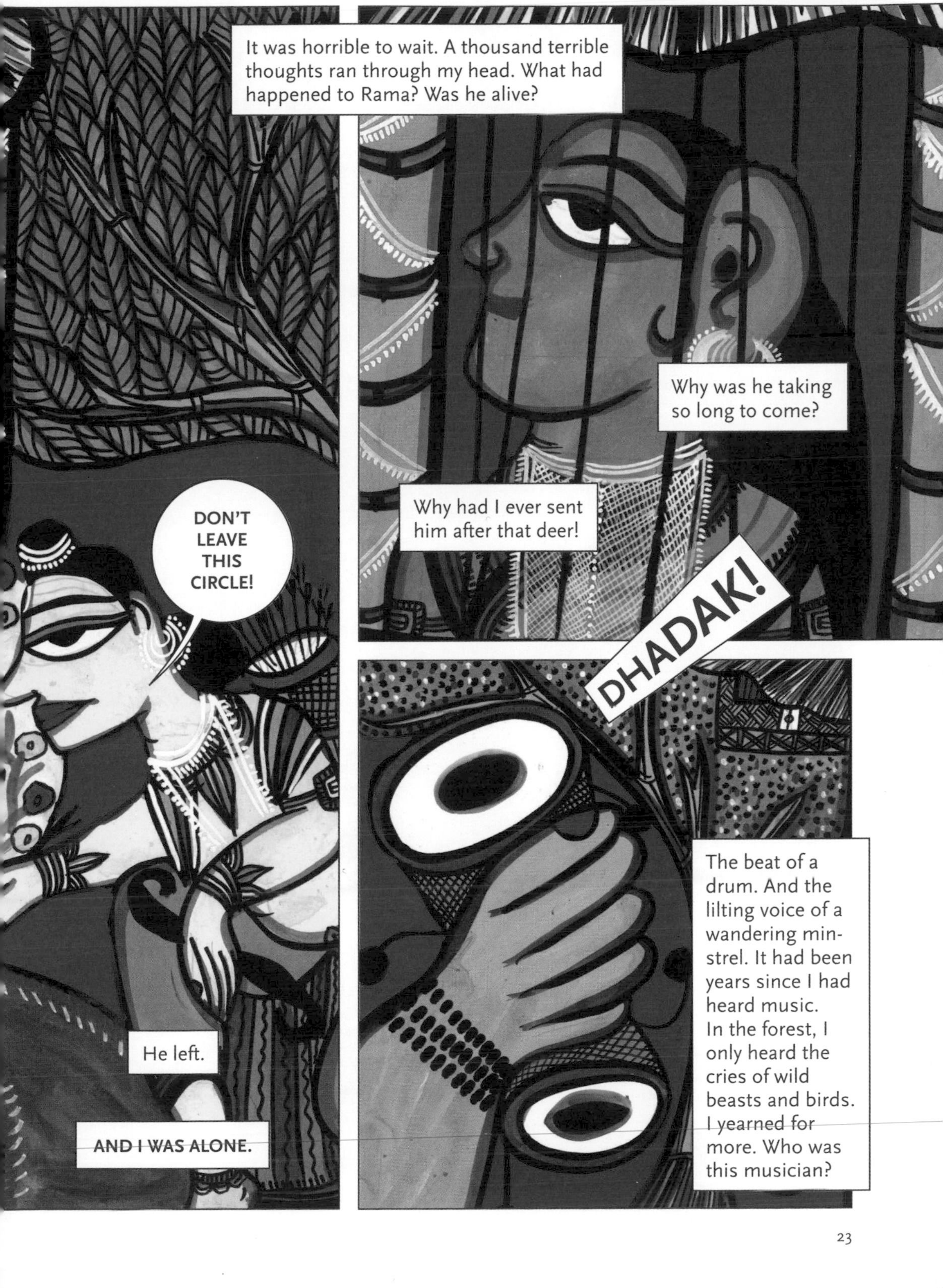
It was horrible to wait. A thousand terrible thoughts ran through my head. What had happened to Rama? Was he alive?
DON'T LEAVE THIS CIRCLE!
Why was he taking so long to come?
Why had I ever sent him after that deer!
He left.
AND I WAS ALONE.
DHADAK!
The beat of a drum. And the lilting voice of a wandering minstrel. It had been years since I had heard music. In the forest, I only heard the cries of wild beasts and birds. I yearned for more. Who was this musician?

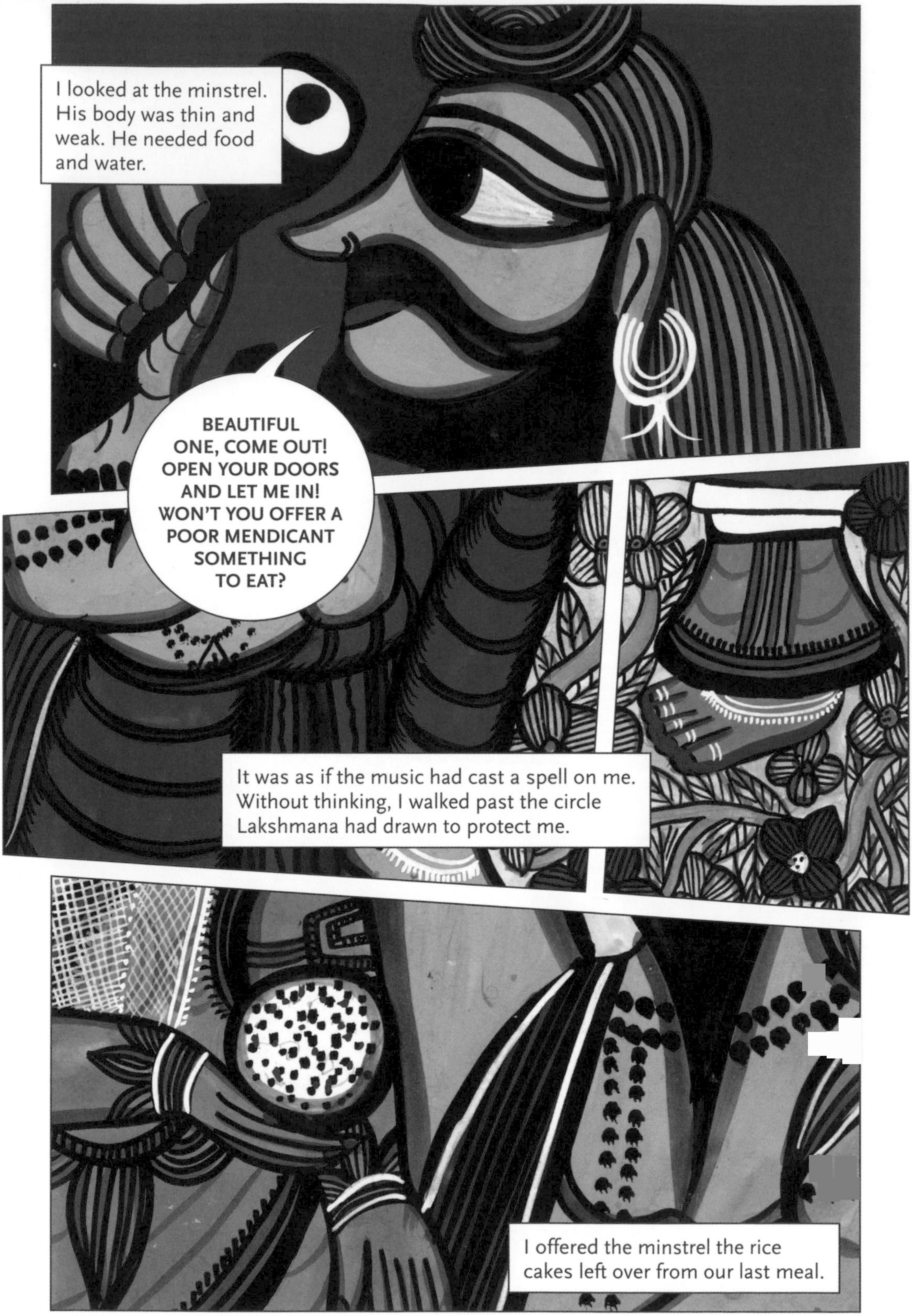
I looked at the minstrel. His body was thin and weak. He needed food and water.
BEAUTIFUL ONE, COME OUT! OPEN YOUR DOORS AND LET ME IN! WON'T YOU OFFER A POOR MENDICANT SOMETHING TO EAT?
It was as if the music had cast a spell on me. Without thinking, I walked past the circle Lakshmana had drawn to protect me.
I offered the minstrel the rice cakes left over from our last meal.

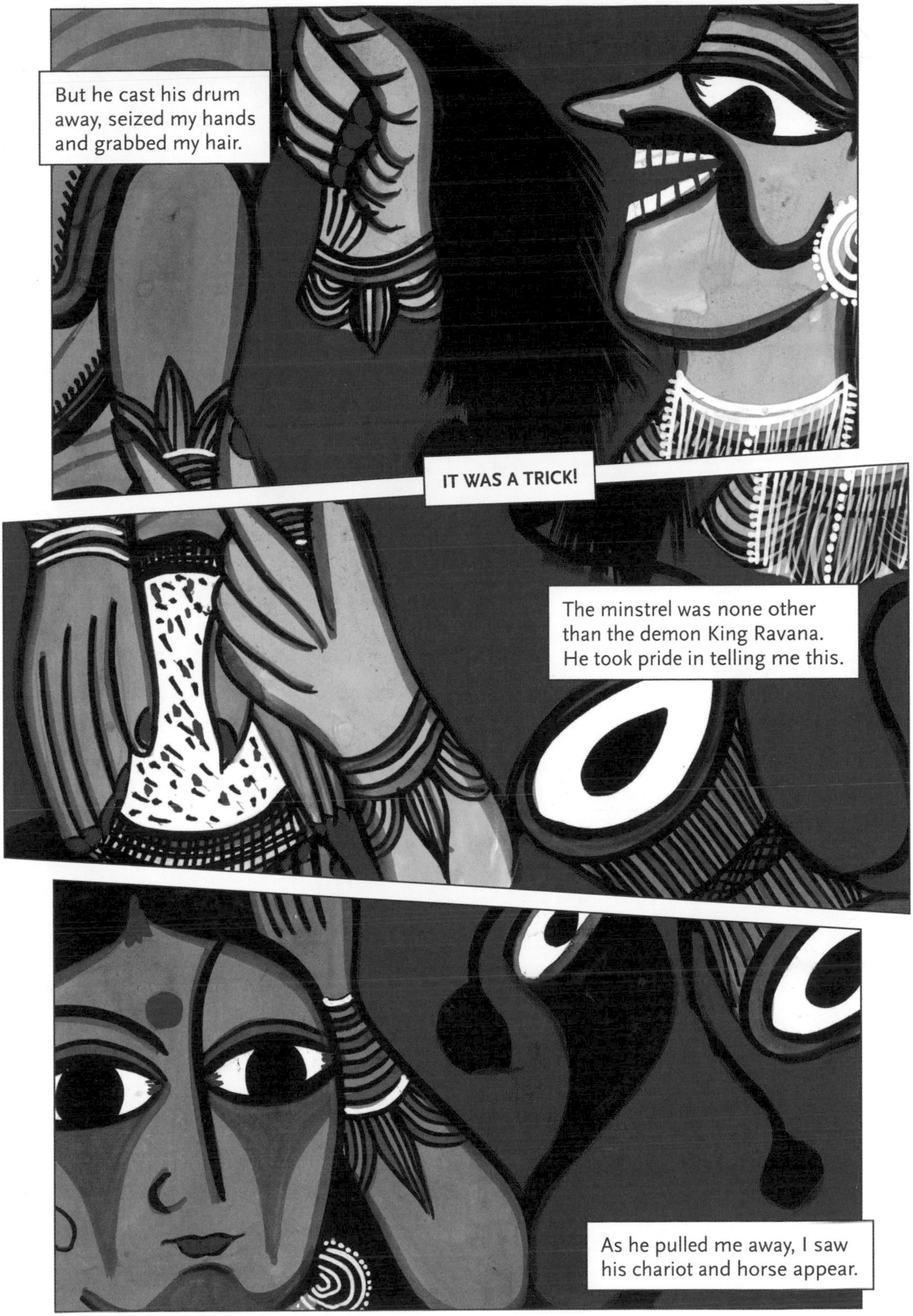

But he cast his drum away, seized my hands and grabbed my hair.
IT WAS A TRICK!
The minstrel was none other than the demon King Ravana. He took pride in telling me this.
As he pulled me away, I saw his chariot and horse appear.

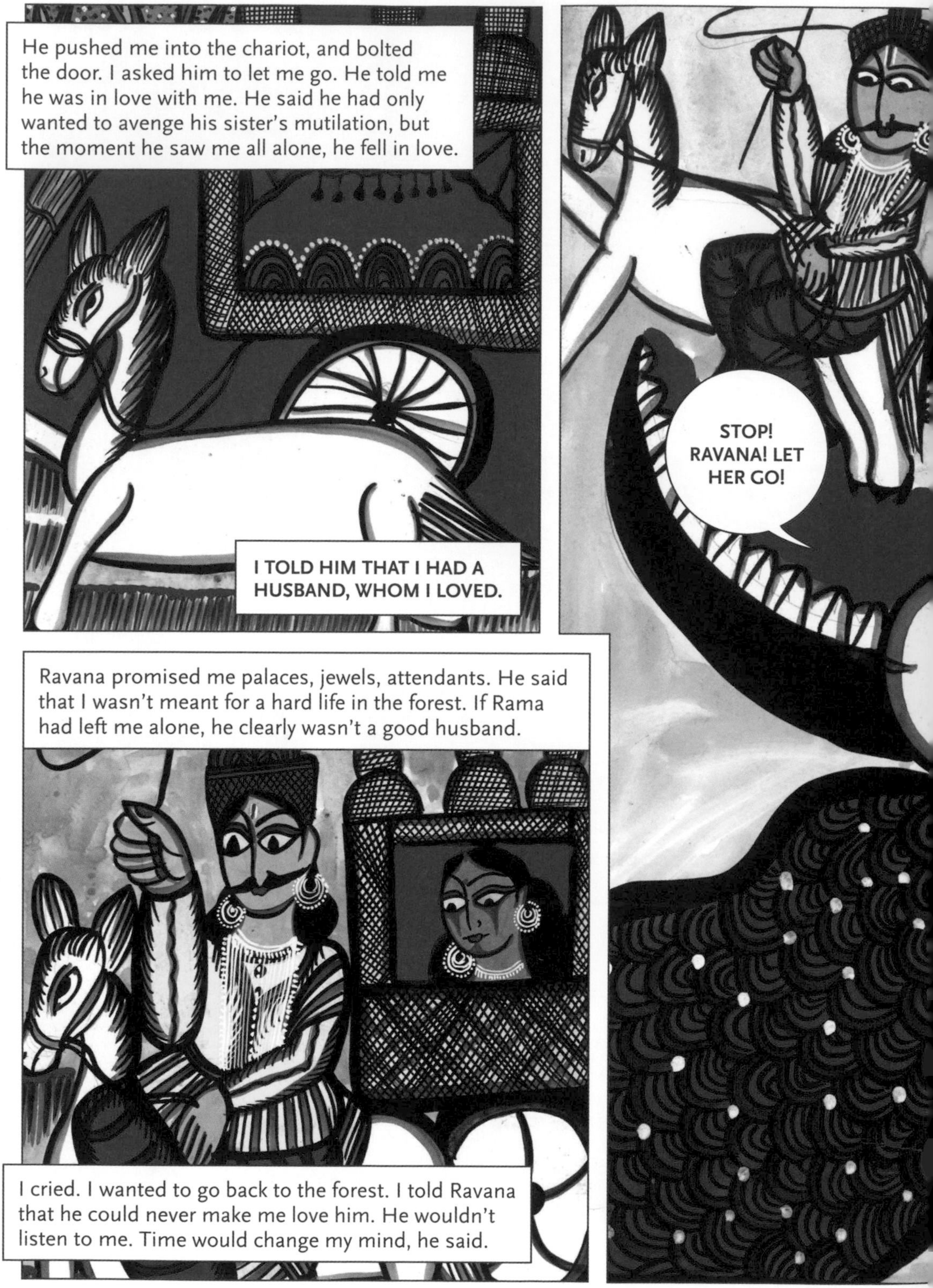
He pushed me into the chariot, and bolted the door. I asked him to let me go. He told me he was in love with me. He said he had only wanted to avenge his sister's mutilation, but the moment he saw me all alone, he fell in love.
I TOLD HIM THAT I HAD A HUSBAND, WHOM I LOVED.
Ravana promised me palaces, jewels, attendants. He said that I wasn't meant for a hard life in the forest. If Rama had left me alone, he clearly wasn't a good husband.
I cried. I wanted to go back to the forest. I told Ravana that he could never make me love him. He wouldn't listen to me. Time would change my mind, he said.
STOP! RAVANA! LET HER GO!

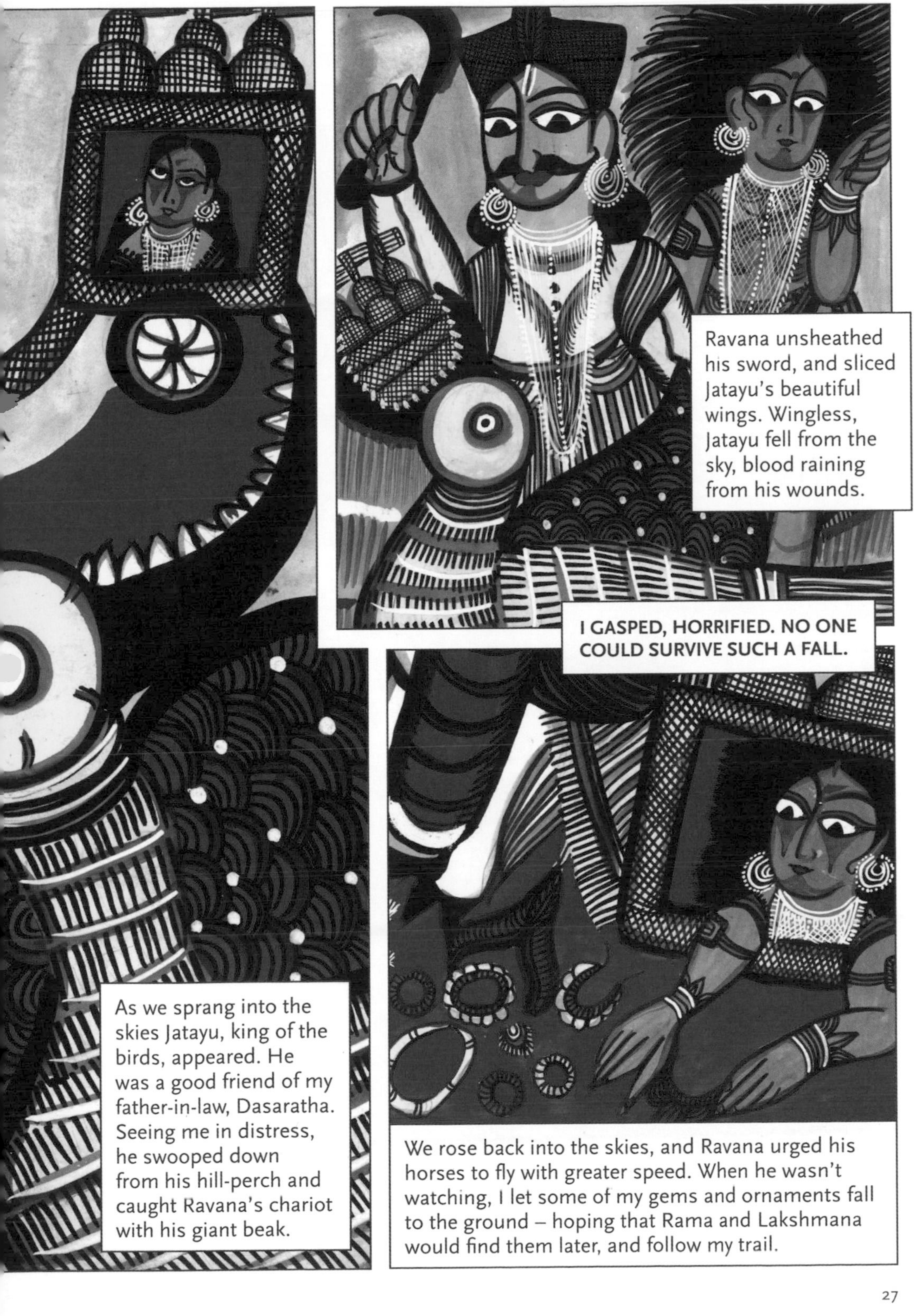
Ravana unsheathed his sword, and sliced Jatayu's beautiful wings. Wingless, Jatayu fell from the sky, blood raining from his wounds.
I GASPED, HORRIFIED. NO ONE COULD SURVIVE SUCH A FALL.
As we sprang into the skies Jatayu, king of the birds, appeared. He was a good friend of my father-in-law, Dasaratha. Seeing me in distress, he swooped down from his hill-perch and caught Ravana's chariot with his giant beak.
We rose back into the skies, and Ravana urged his horses to fly with greater speed. When he wasn't watching, I let some of my gems and ornaments fall to the ground – hoping that Rama and Lakshmana would find them later, and follow my trail.

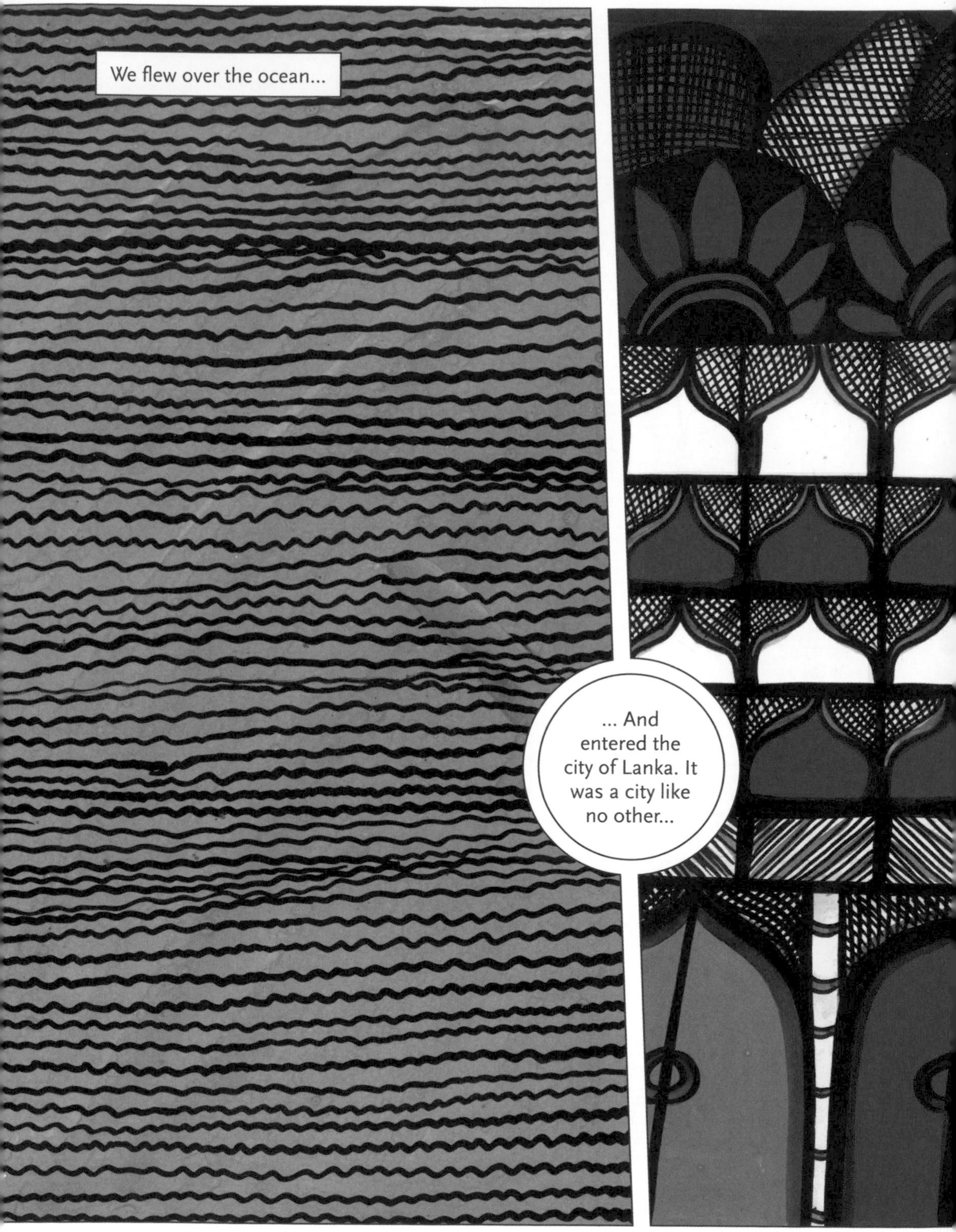
We flew over the ocean...
... And entered the city of Lanka. It was a city like no other...

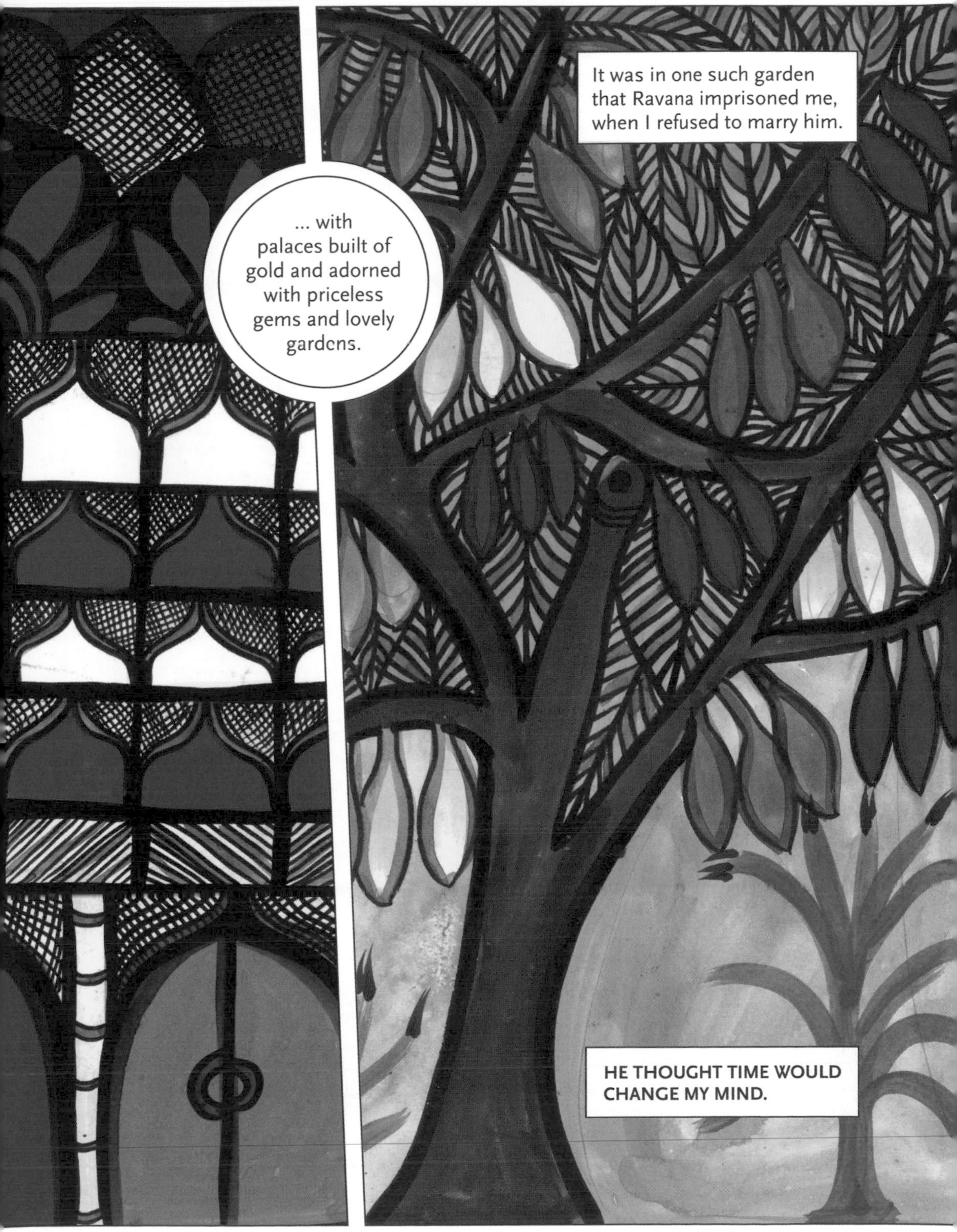
... with palaces built of gold and adorned with priceless gems and lovely gardens.
It was in one such garden that Ravana imprisoned me, when I refused to marry him.
HE THOUGHT TIME WOULD CHANGE MY MIND.

HE POSTED A GUARD OF DEMONS
– RAKSHASAS AND RAKSHASIS –
TO WATCH OVER ME. TO PREVENT
ME FROM ESCAPING.

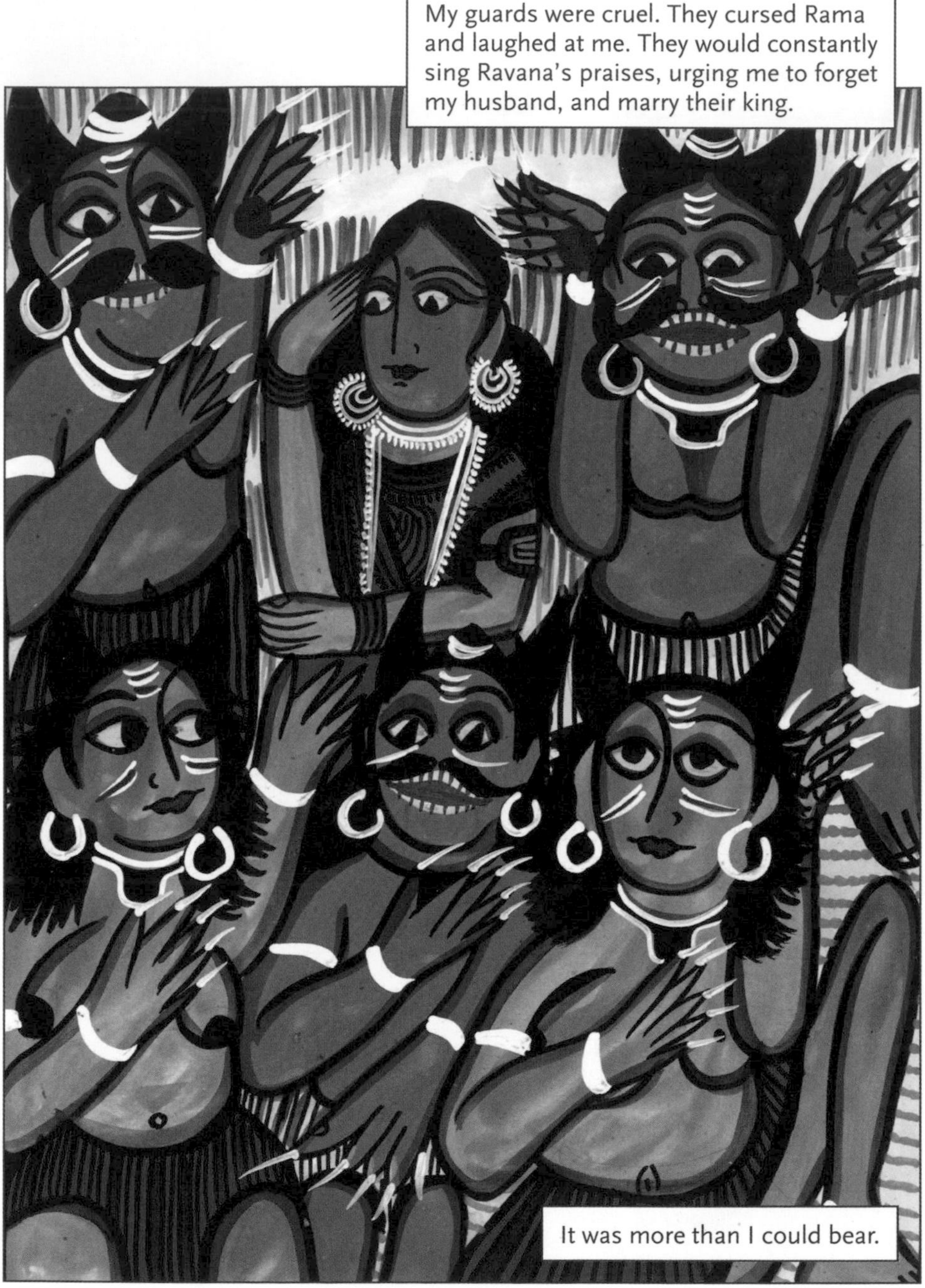
My guards were cruel. They cursed Rama and laughed at me. They would constantly sing Ravana's praises, urging me to forget my husband, and marry their king.
It was more than I could bear.

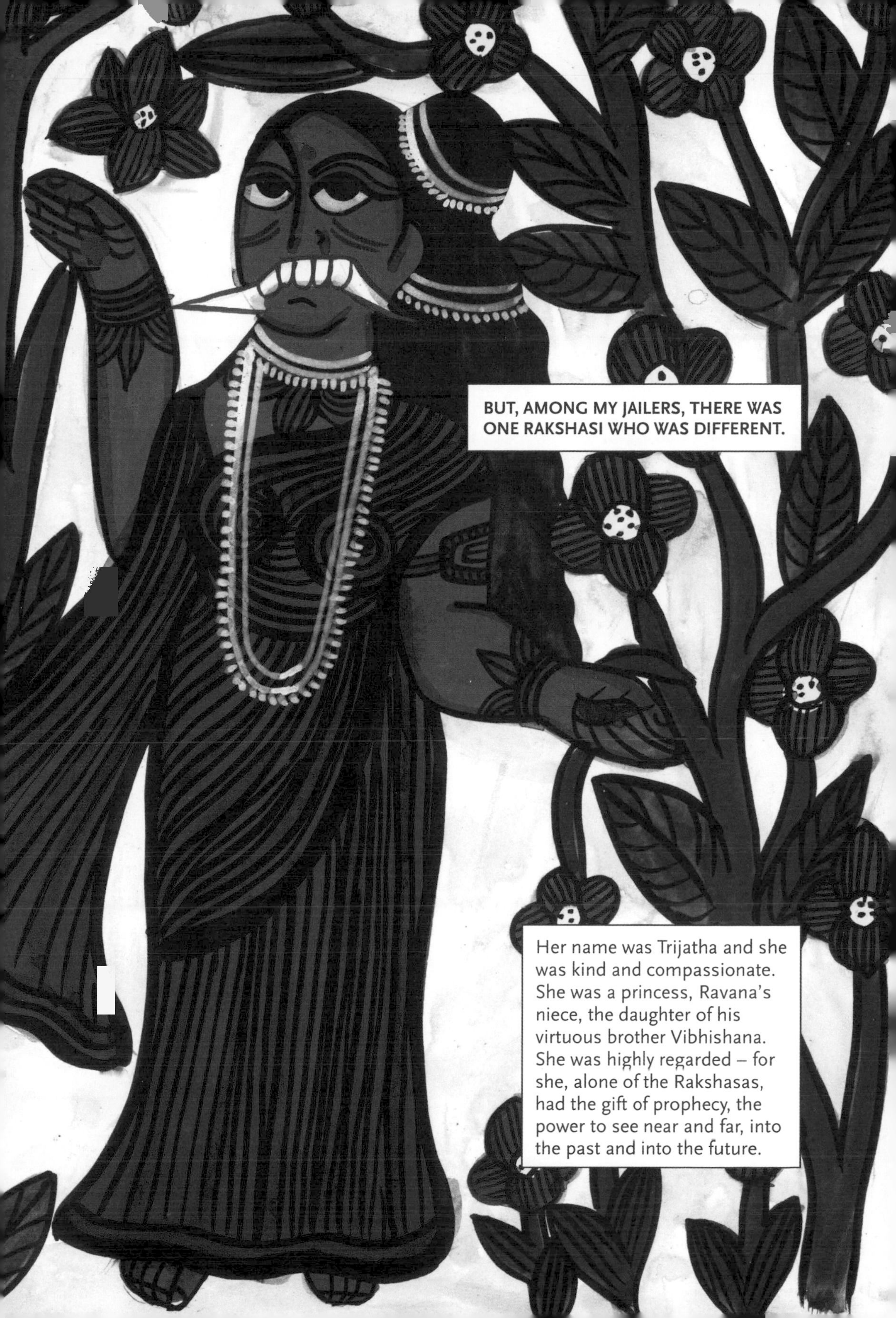
BUT, AMONG MY JAILERS, THERE WAS ONE RAKSHASI WHO WAS DIFFERENT.
Her name was Trijatha and she was kind and compassionate. She was a princess, Ravana's niece, the daughter of his virtuous brother Vibhishana. She was highly regarded – for she, alone of the Rakshasas, had the gift of prophecy, the power to see near and far, into the past and into the future.

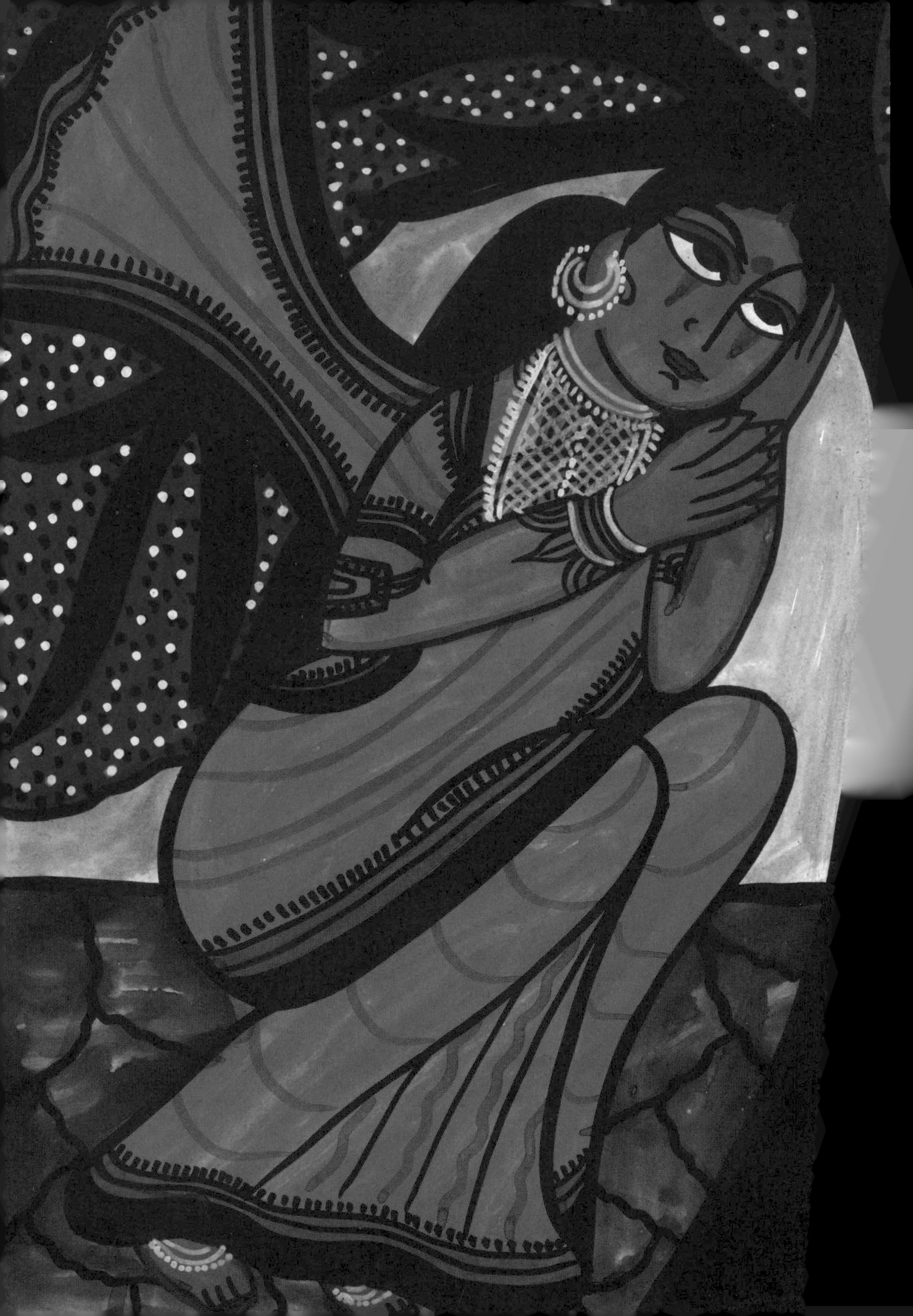

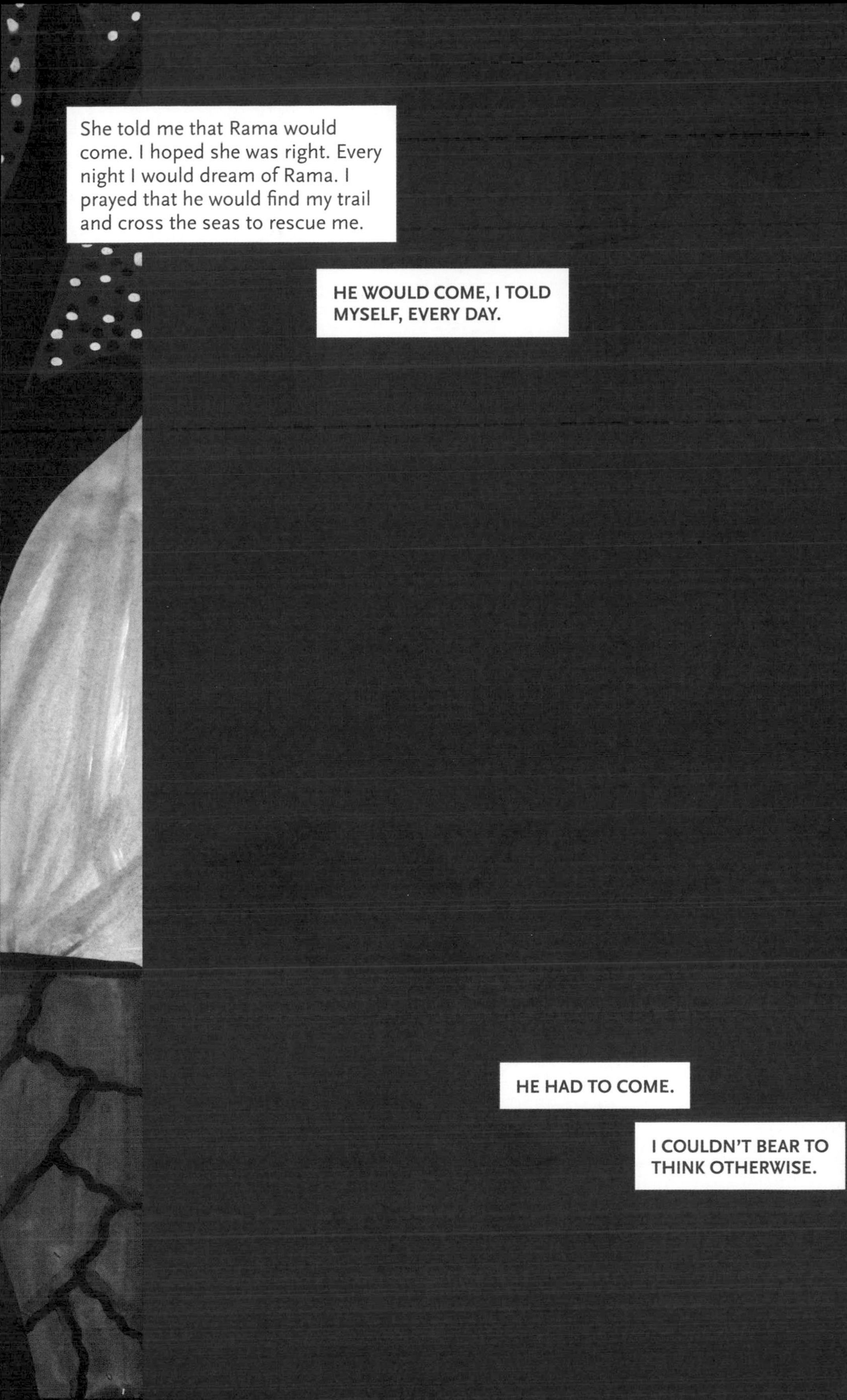
She told me that Rama would come. I hoped she was right. Every night I would dream of Rama. I prayed that he would find my trail and cross the seas to rescue me.
HE WOULD COME, I TOLD MYSELF, EVERY DAY.
HE HAD TO COME.
I COULDN'T BEAR TO THINK OTHERWISE.

ONE DAY, I SAW A CURIOUS CREATURE IN THE GARDEN. IT WAS A MONKEY, HIDDEN HIGH IN THE BRANCHES OF A MANGO TREE, HIS EYES BRIGHT AND CURIOUS. HE WAS WATCHING ME.

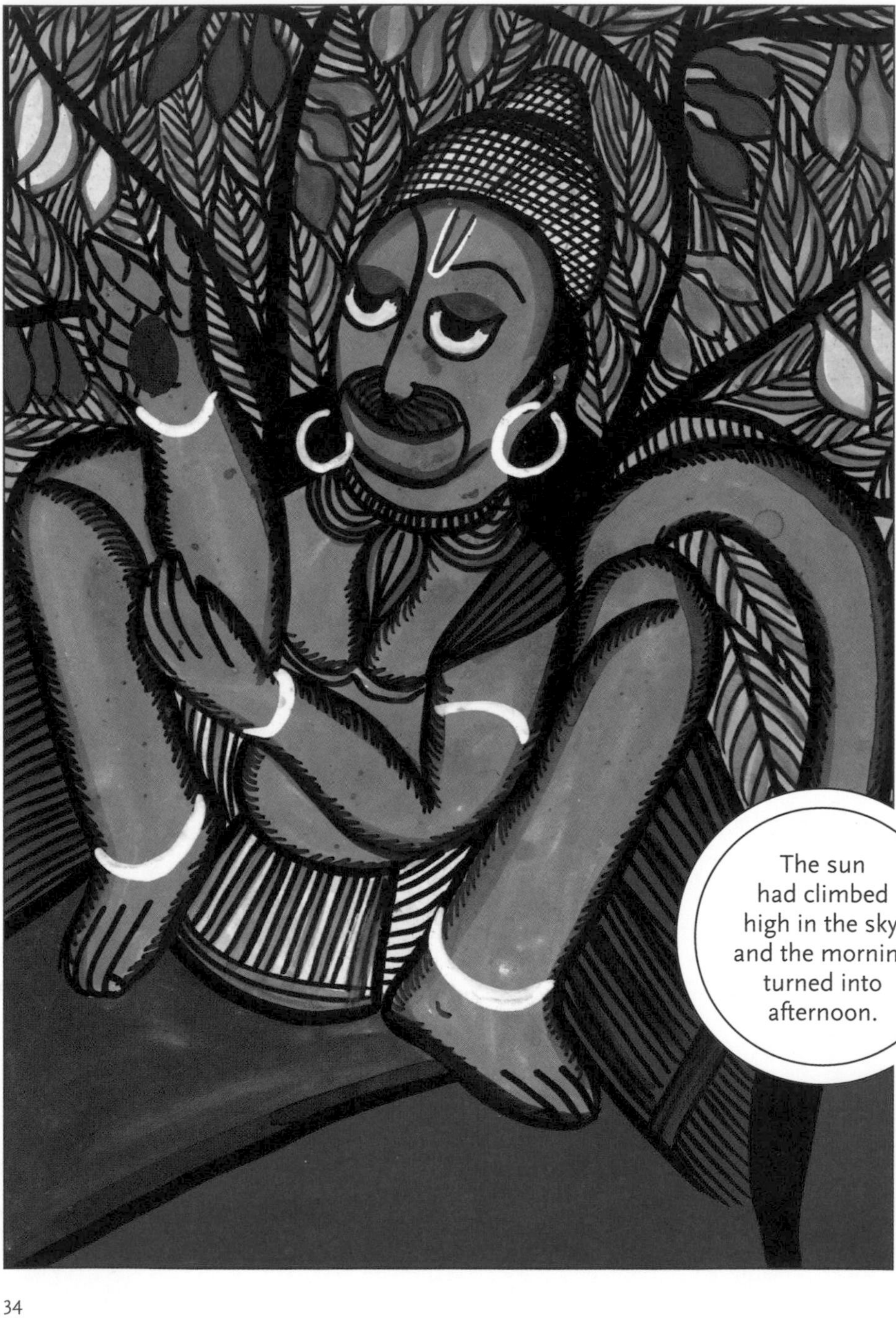
The sun had climbed high in the sky, and the morning turned into afternoon.

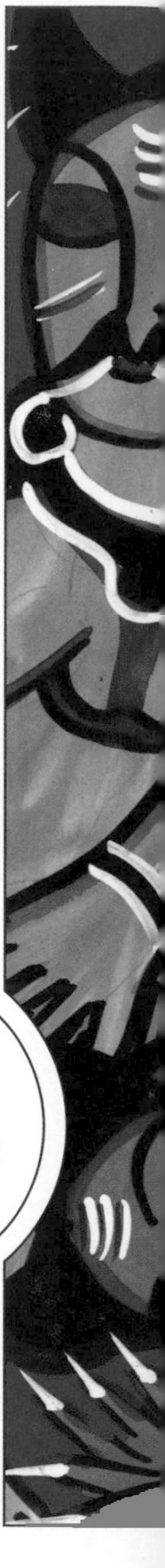

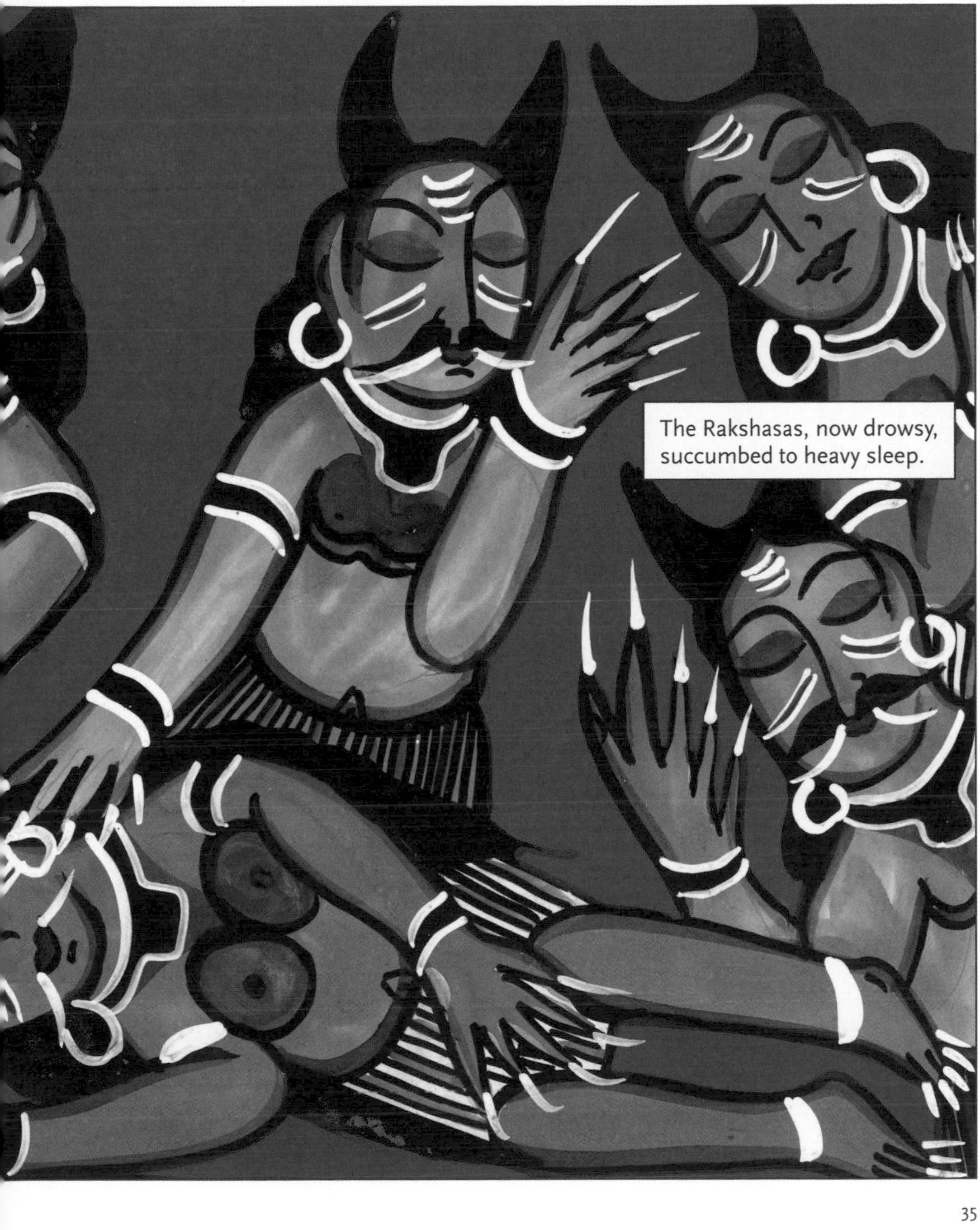
The Rakshasas, now drowsy,
succumbed to heavy sleep.

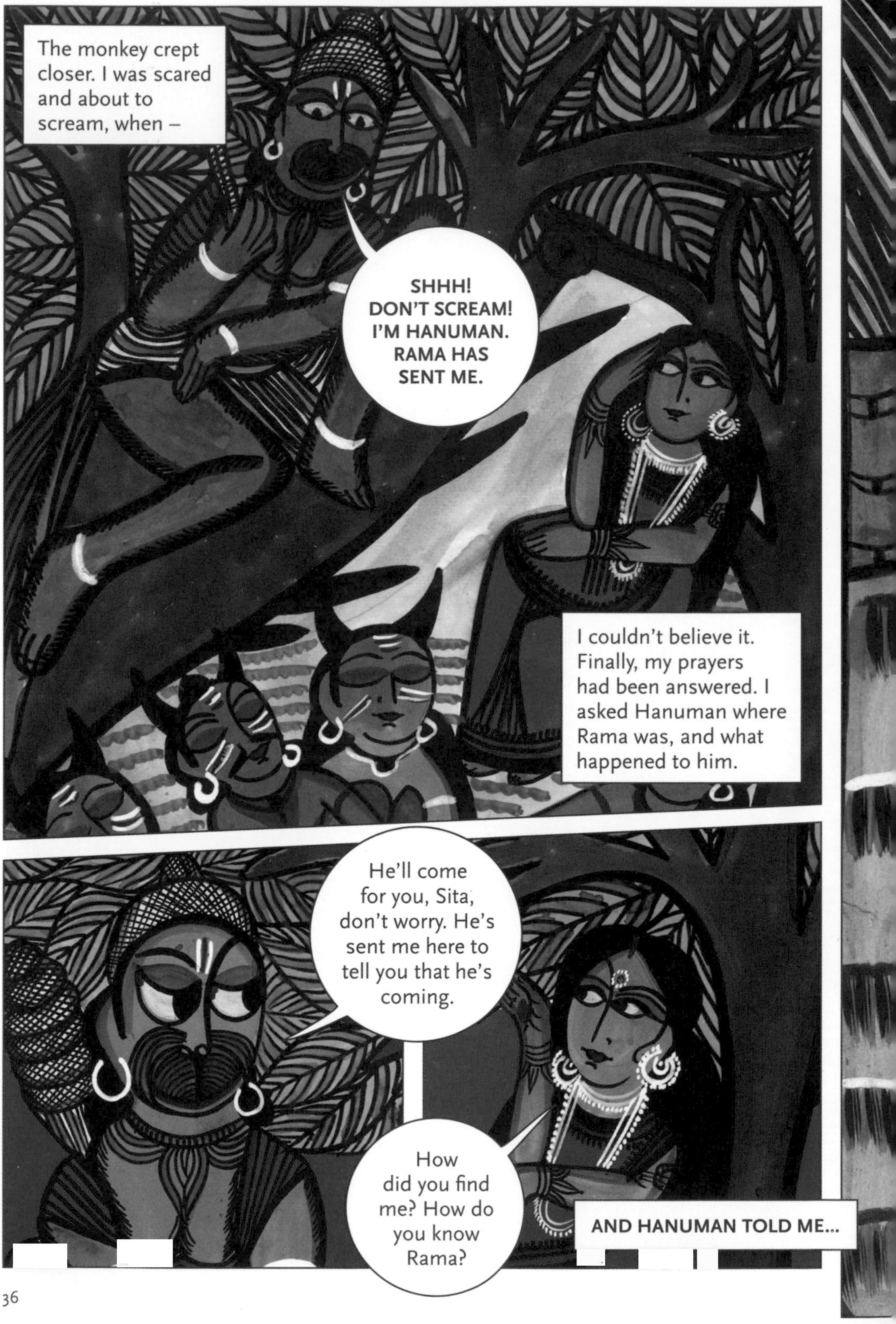
The monkey crept closer. I was scared and about to scream, when –
SHHH! DON'T SCREAM! I'M HANUMAN. RAMA HAS SENT ME.
I couldn't believe it. Finally, my prayers had been answered. I asked Hanuman where Rama was, and what happened to him.
He'll come for you, Sita, don't worry. He's sent me here to tell you that he's coming.
How did you find me? How do you know Rama?
AND HANUMAN TOLD ME...

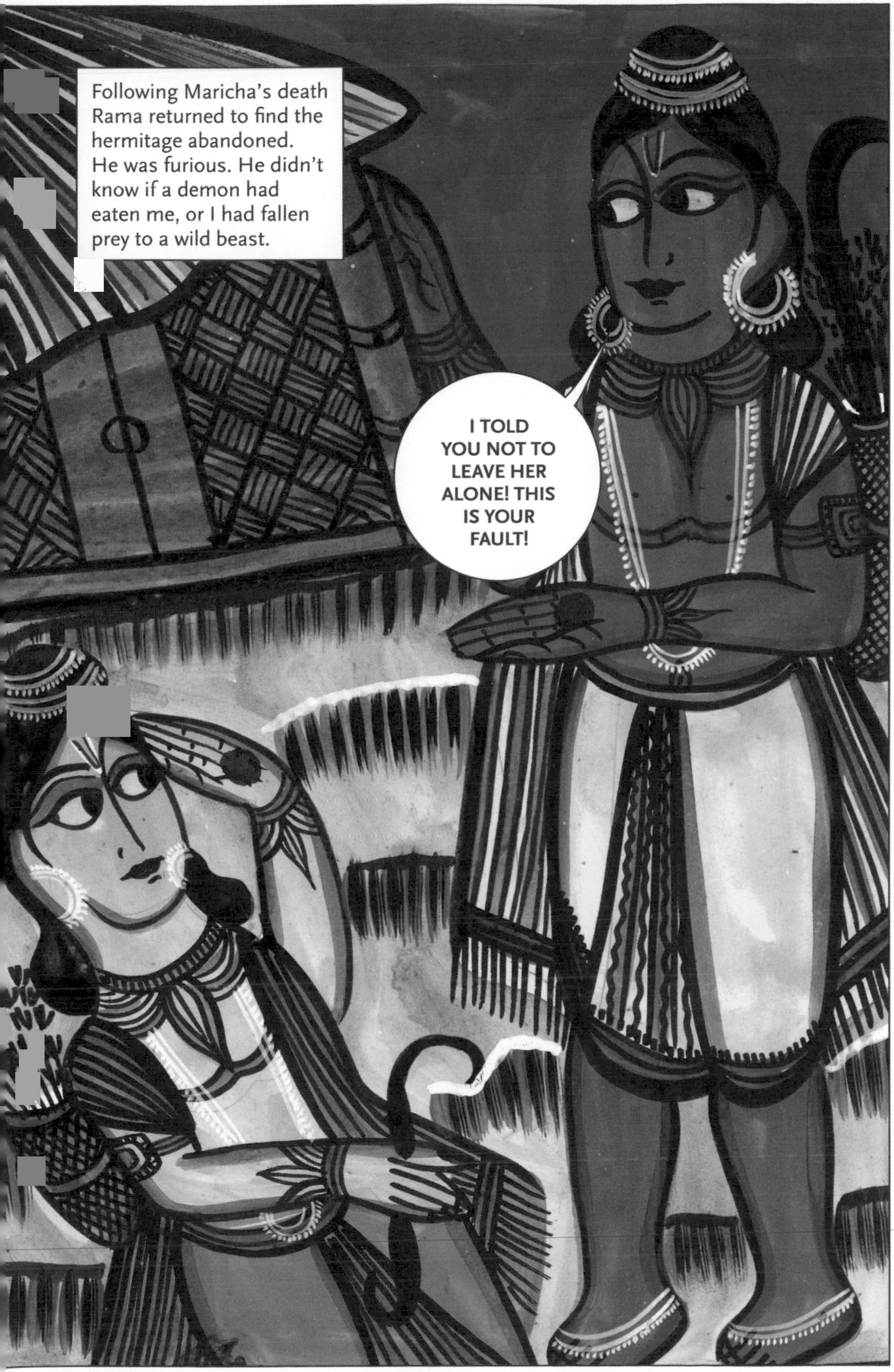
Following Maricha's death Rama returned to find the hermitage abandoned. He was furious. He didn't know if a demon had eaten me, or I had fallen prey to a wild beast.
I TOLD YOU NOT TO LEAVE HER ALONE! THIS IS YOUR FAULT!

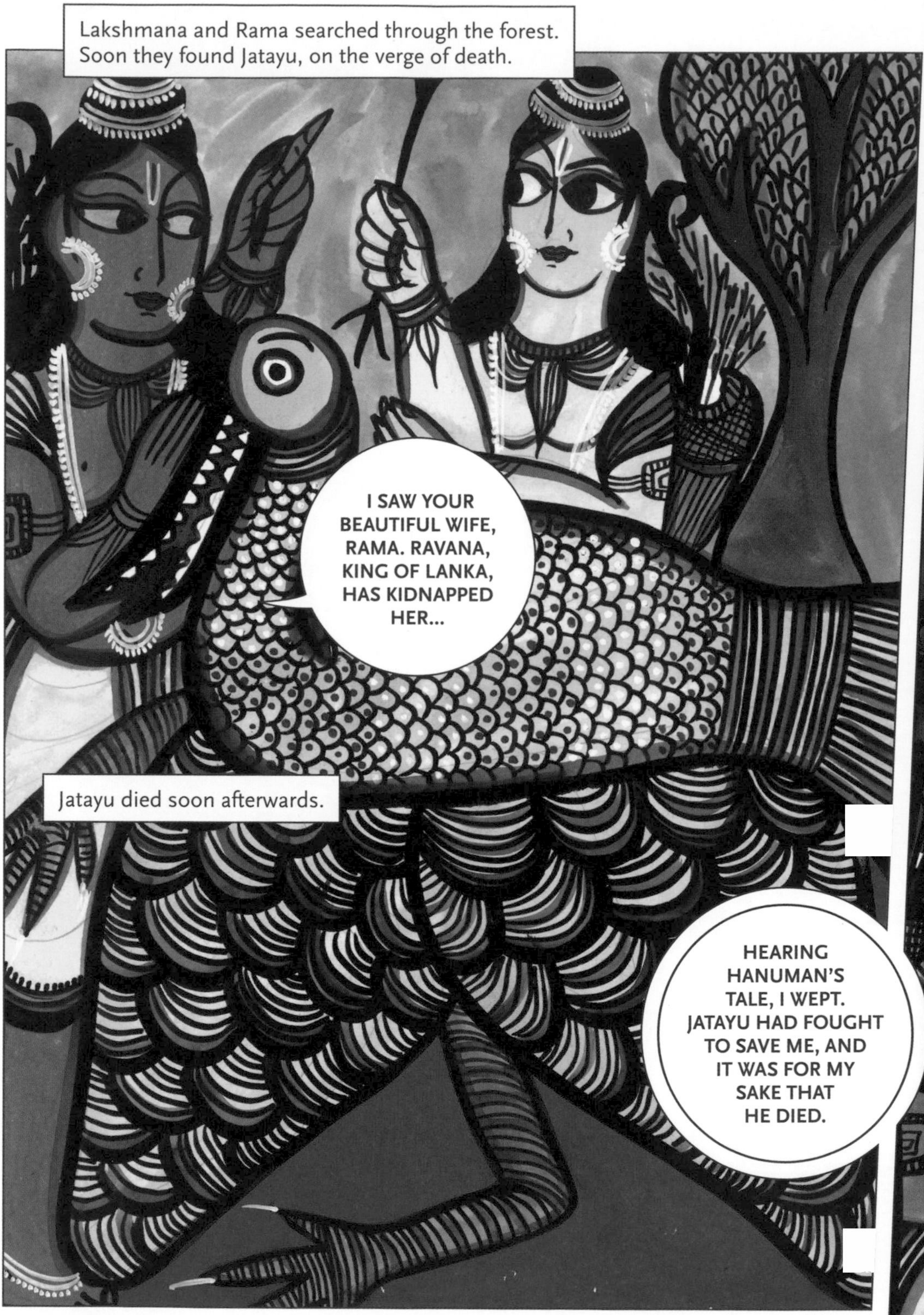
Lakshmana and Rama searched through the forest. Soon they found Jatayu, on the verge of death.
I SAW YOUR BEAUTIFUL WIFE, RAMA. RAVANA, KING OF LANKA, HAS KIDNAPPED HER...
Jatayu died soon afterwards.
HEARING HANUMAN'S TALE, I WEPT. JATAYU HAD FOUGHT TO SAVE ME, AND IT WAS FOR MY SAKE THAT HE DIED.

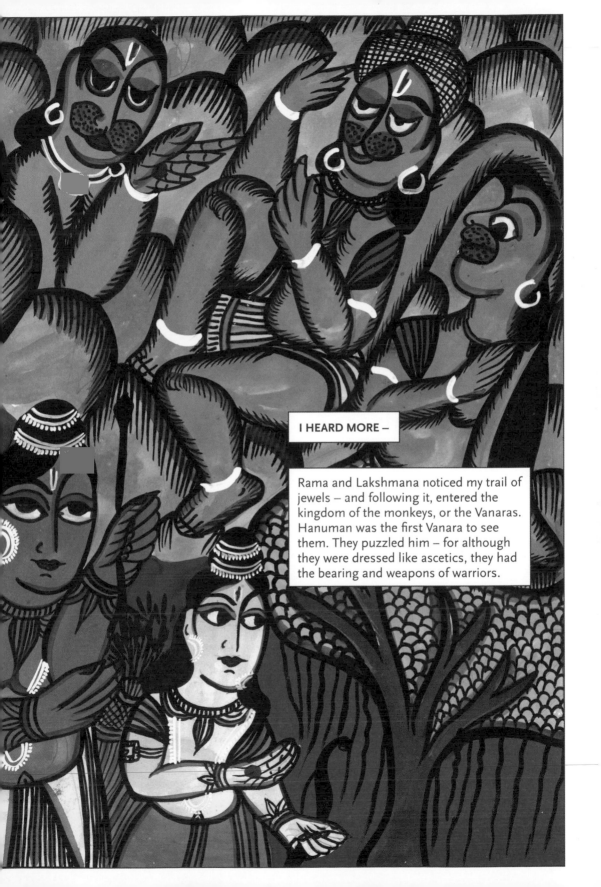

I HEARD MORE –

Rama and Lakshmana noticed my trail of jewels – and following it, entered the kingdom of the monkeys, or the Vanaras. Hanuman was the first Vanara to see them. They puzzled him – for although they were dressed like ascetics, they had the bearing and weapons of warriors.

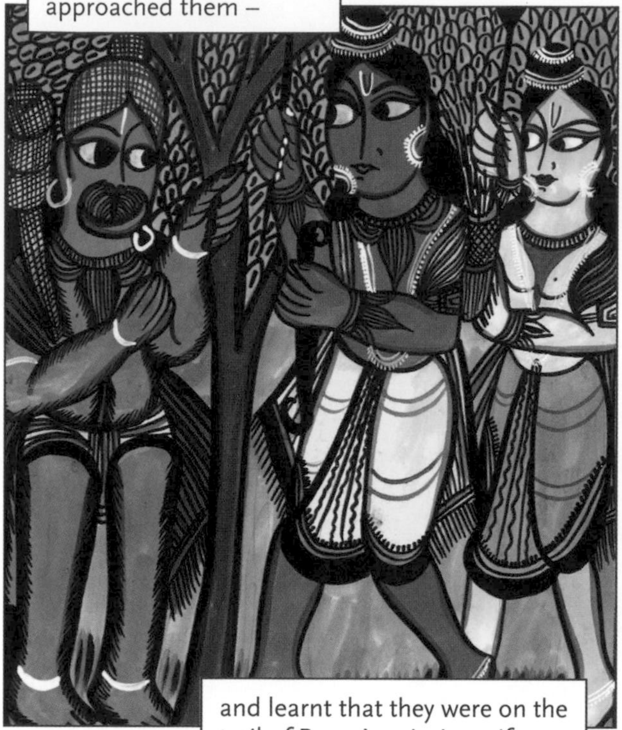
Intrigued, Hanuman had approached them –
and learnt that they were on the trail of Rama's missing wife.

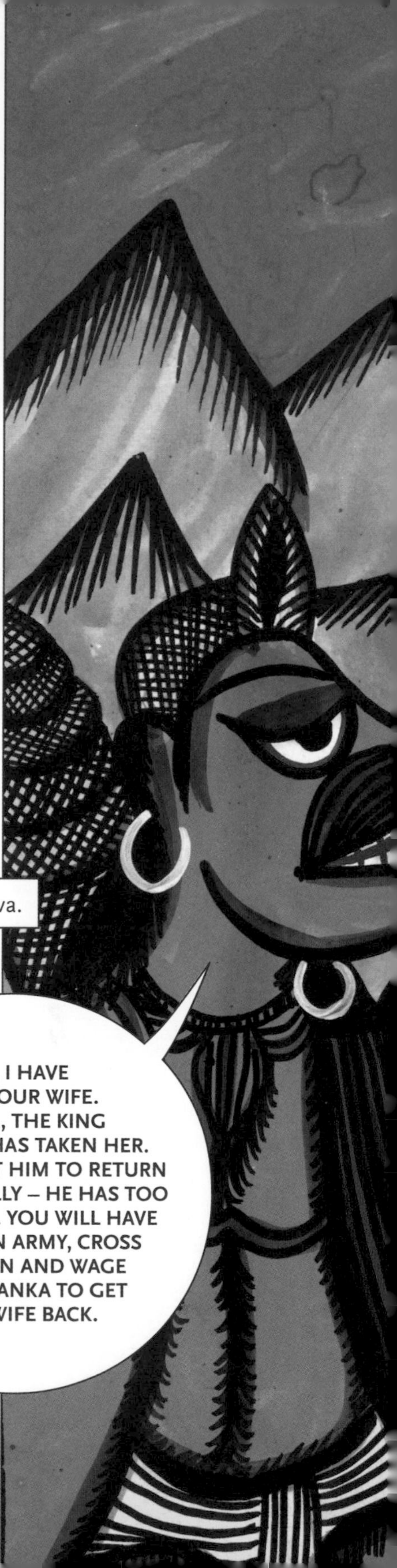
He took them to meet his chief, Sugriva.
YES, I HAVE SEEN YOUR WIFE. RAVANA, THE KING OF LANKA, HAS TAKEN HER. DON'T EXPECT HIM TO RETURN HER PEACEFULLY – HE HAS TOO MUCH PRIDE. YOU WILL HAVE TO RAISE AN ARMY, CROSS THE OCEAN AND WAGE WAR ON LANKA TO GET YOUR WIFE BACK.

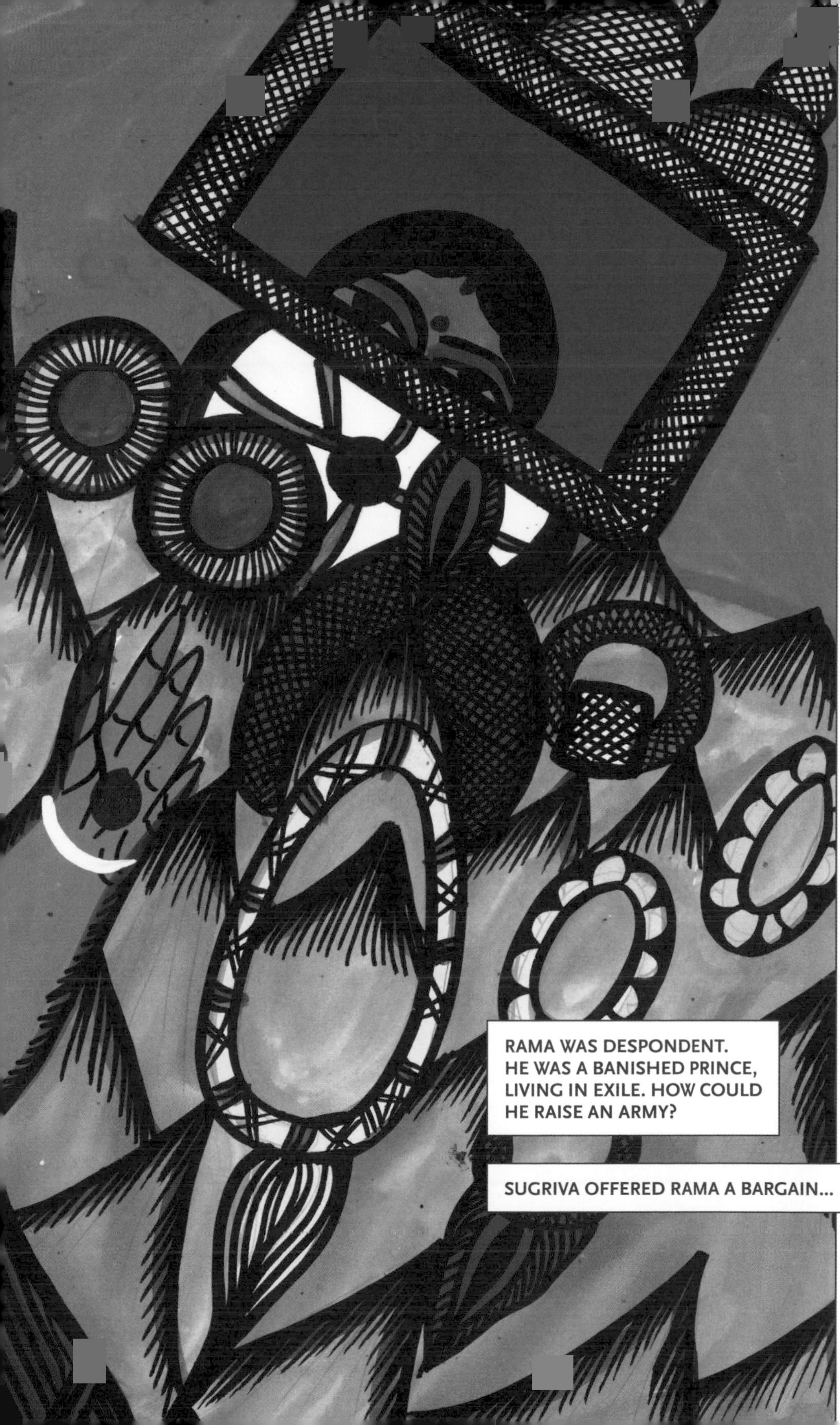
RAMA WAS DESPONDENT.
HE WAS A BANISHED PRINCE,
LIVING IN EXILE. HOW COULD
HE RAISE AN ARMY?
SUGRIVA OFFERED RAMA A BARGAIN...

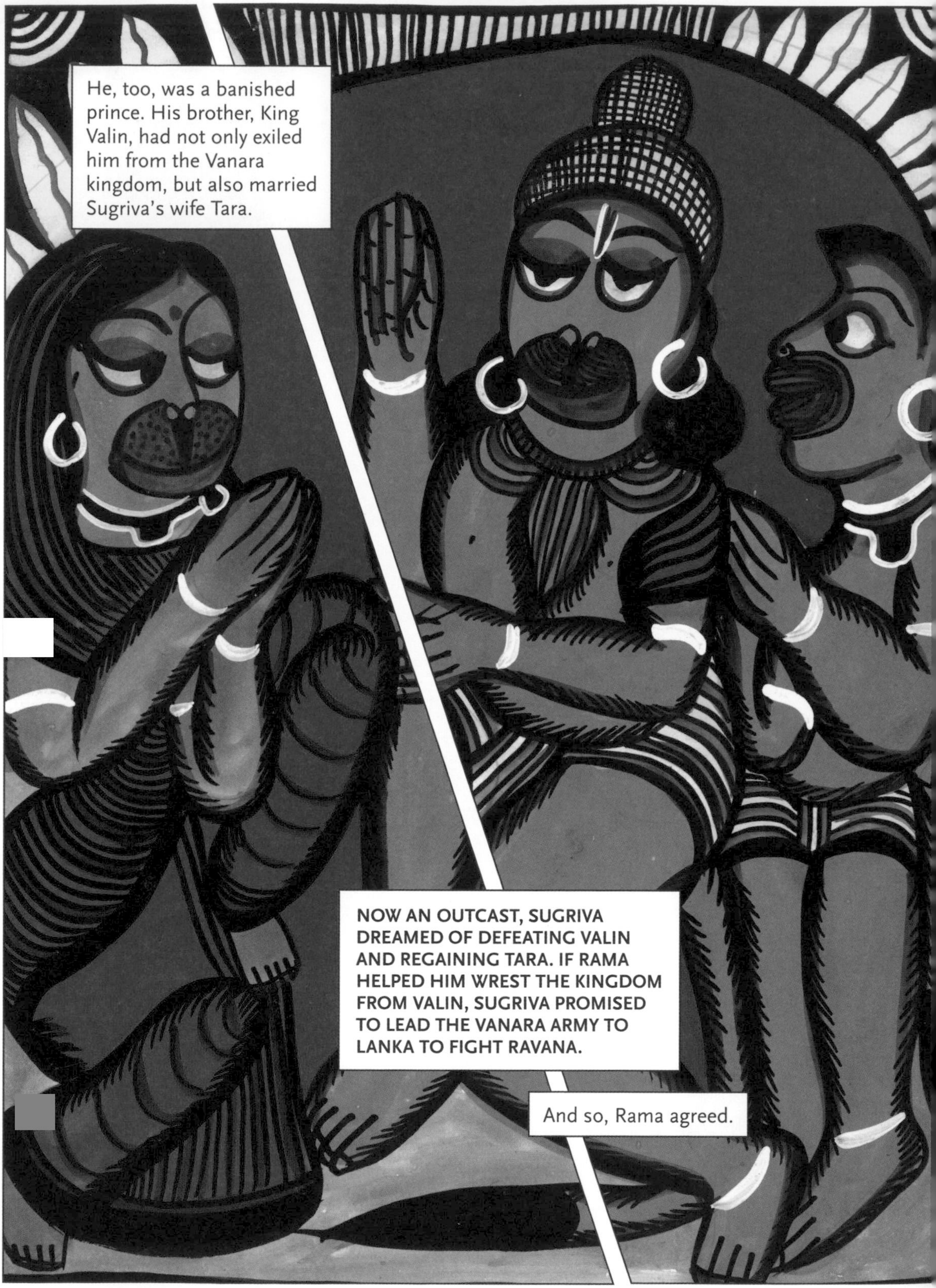
He, too, was a banished prince. His brother, King Valin, had not only exiled him from the Vanara kingdom, but also married Sugriva's wife Tara.
NOW AN OUTCAST, SUGRIVA DREAMED OF DEFEATING VALIN AND REGAINING TARA. IF RAMA HELPED HIM WREST THE KINGDOM FROM VALIN, SUGRIVA PROMISED TO LEAD THE VANARA ARMY TO LANKA TO FIGHT RAVANA.
And so, Rama agreed.

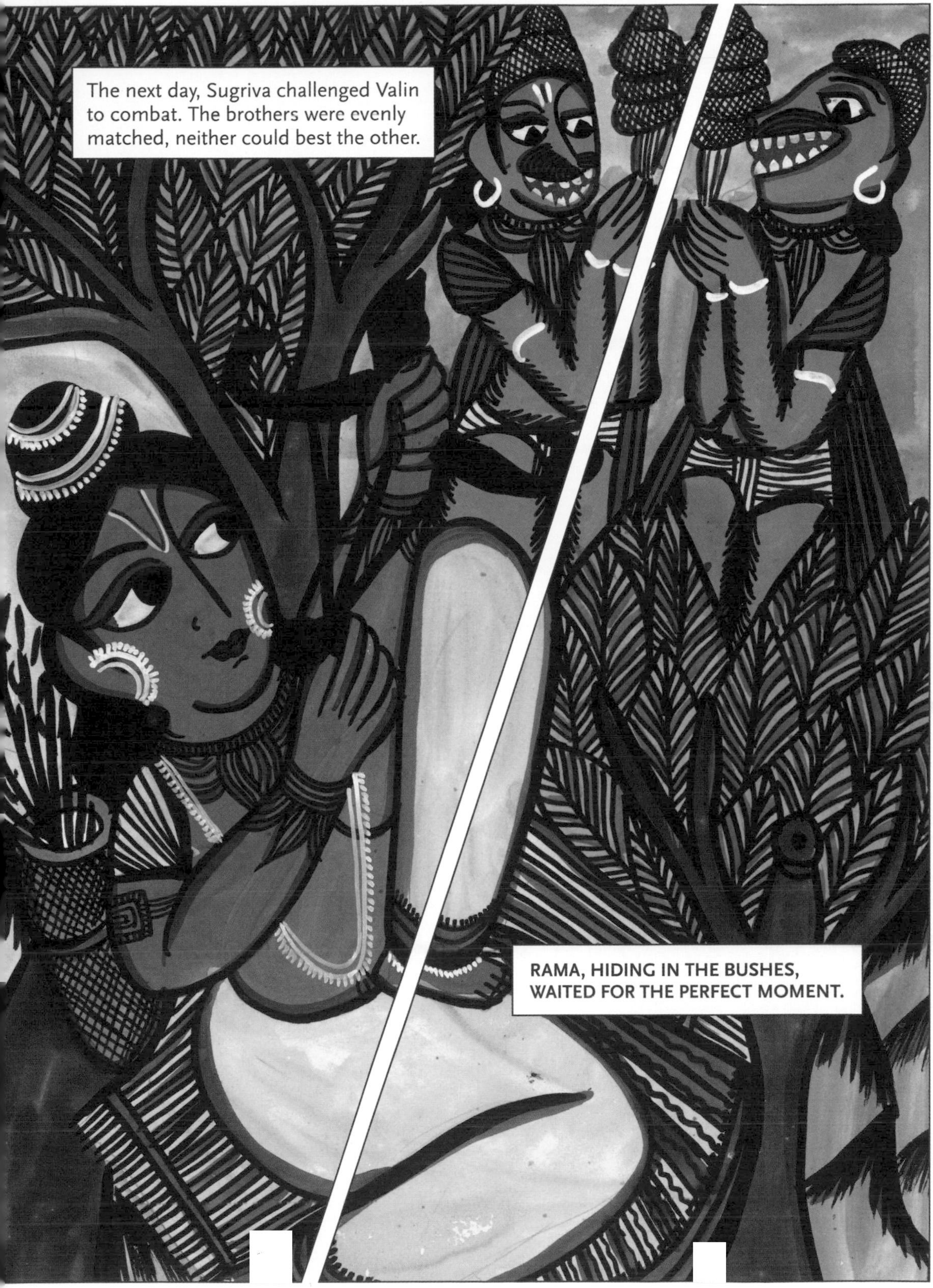
The next day, Sugriva challenged Valin to combat. The brothers were evenly matched, neither could best the other.
RAMA, HIDING IN THE BUSHES, WAITED FOR THE PERFECT MOMENT.

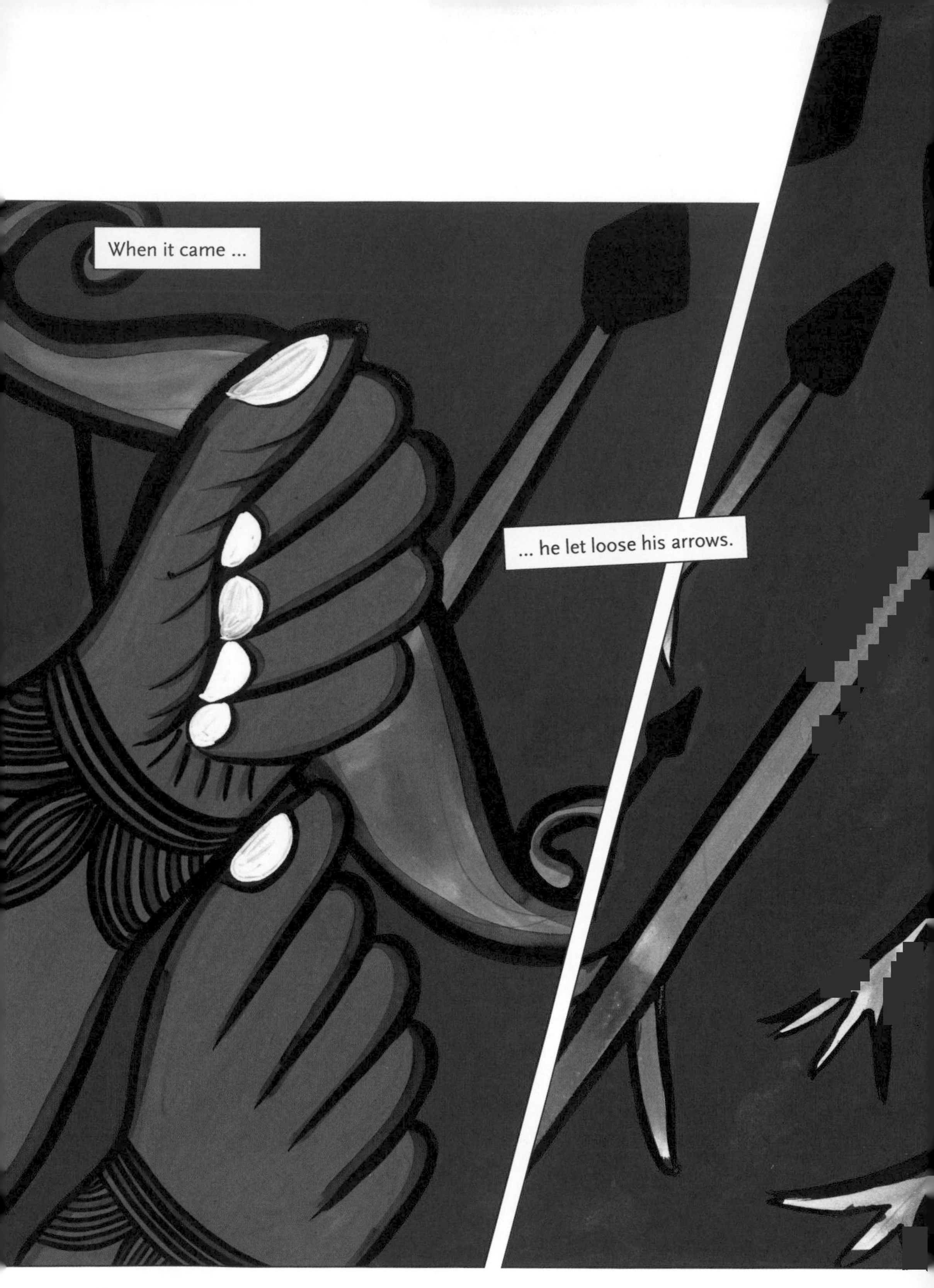
When it came ...
... he let loose his arrows.

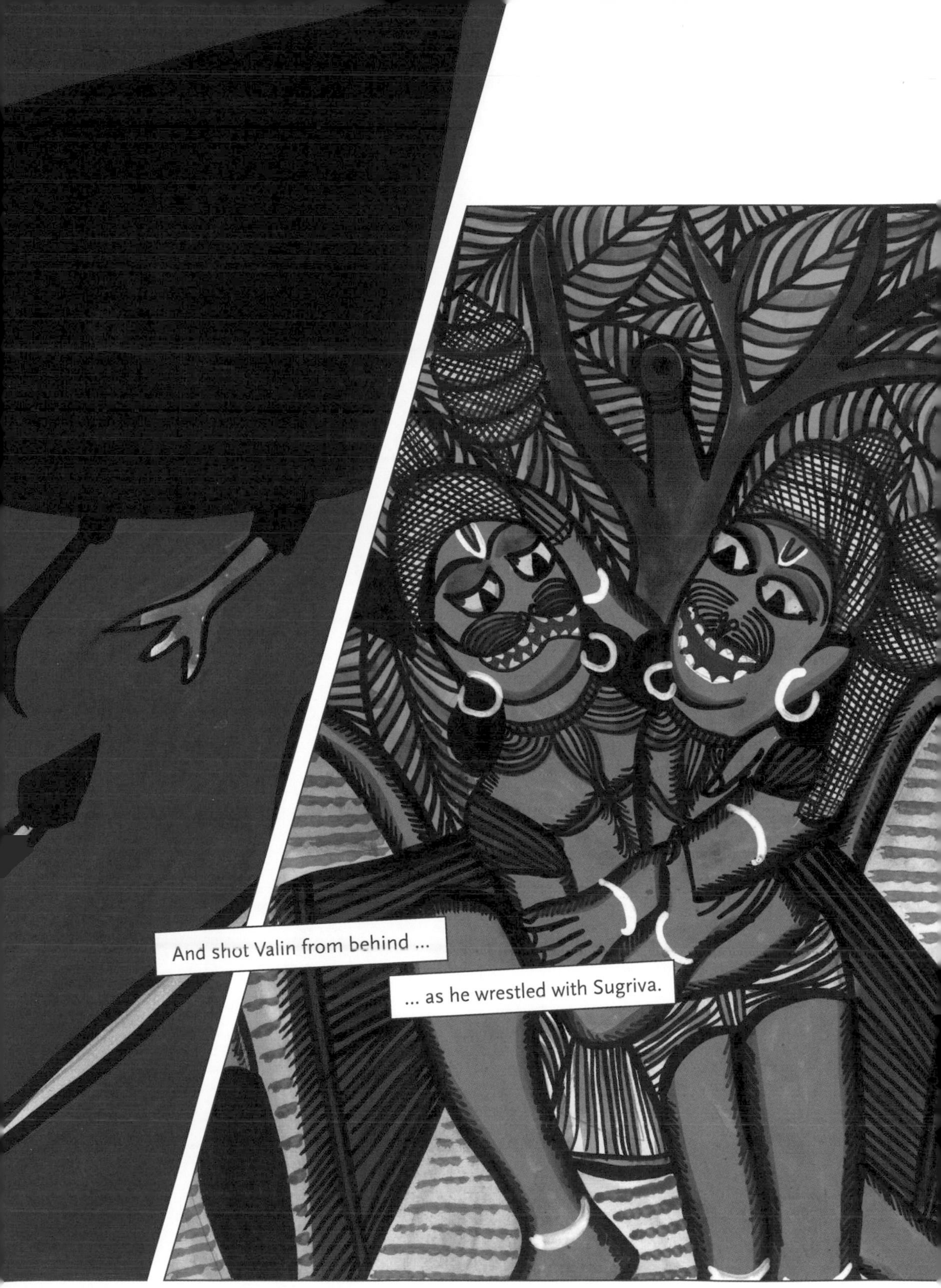
And shot Valin from behind ...
... as he wrestled with Sugriva.

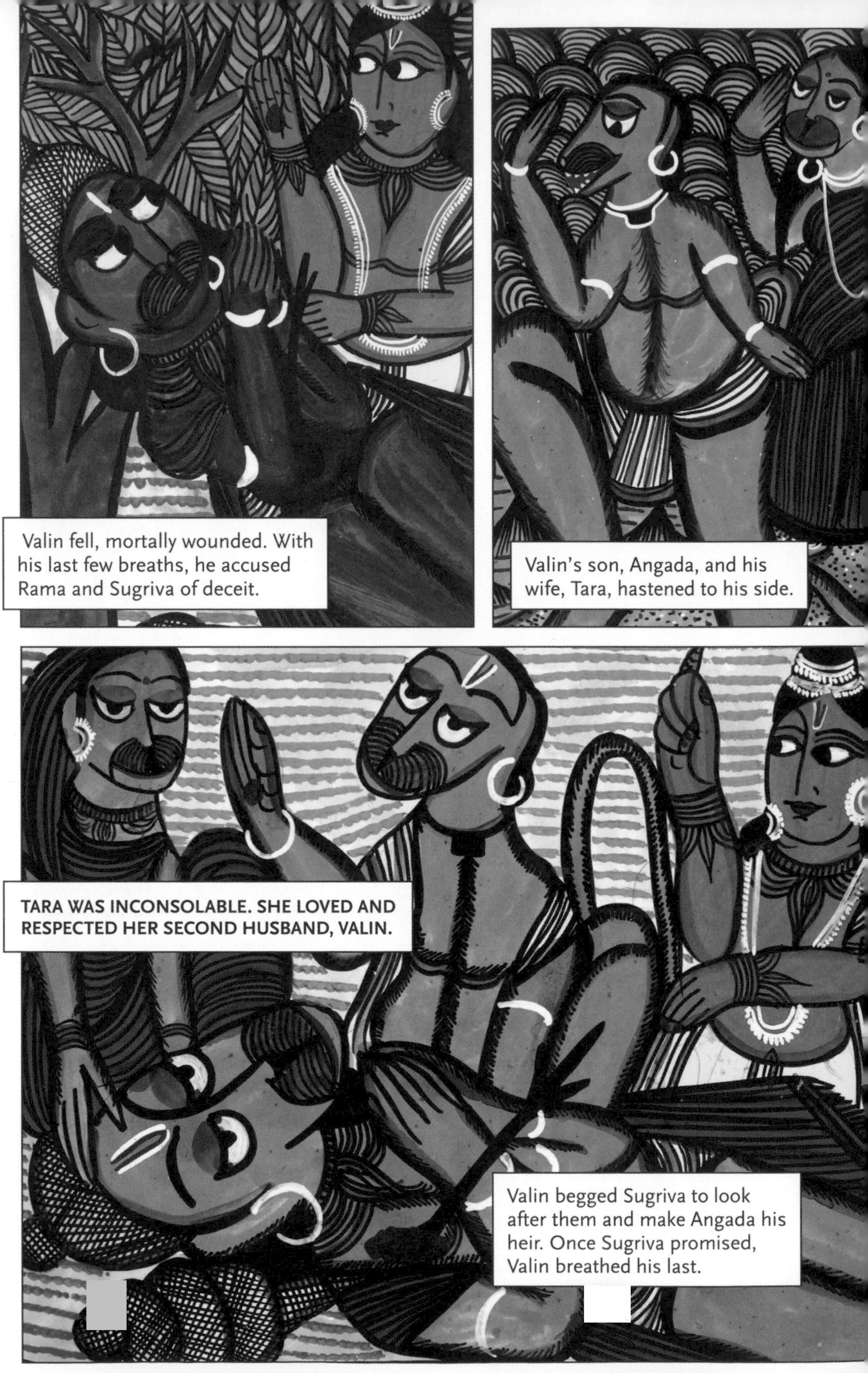
Valin fell, mortally wounded. With his last few breaths, he accused Rama and Sugriva of deceit.
Valin's son, Angada, and his wife, Tara, hastened to his side.
TARA WAS INCONSOLABLE. SHE LOVED AND RESPECTED HER SECOND HUSBAND, VALIN.
Valin begged Sugriva to look after them and make Angada his heir. Once Sugriva promised, Valin breathed his last.

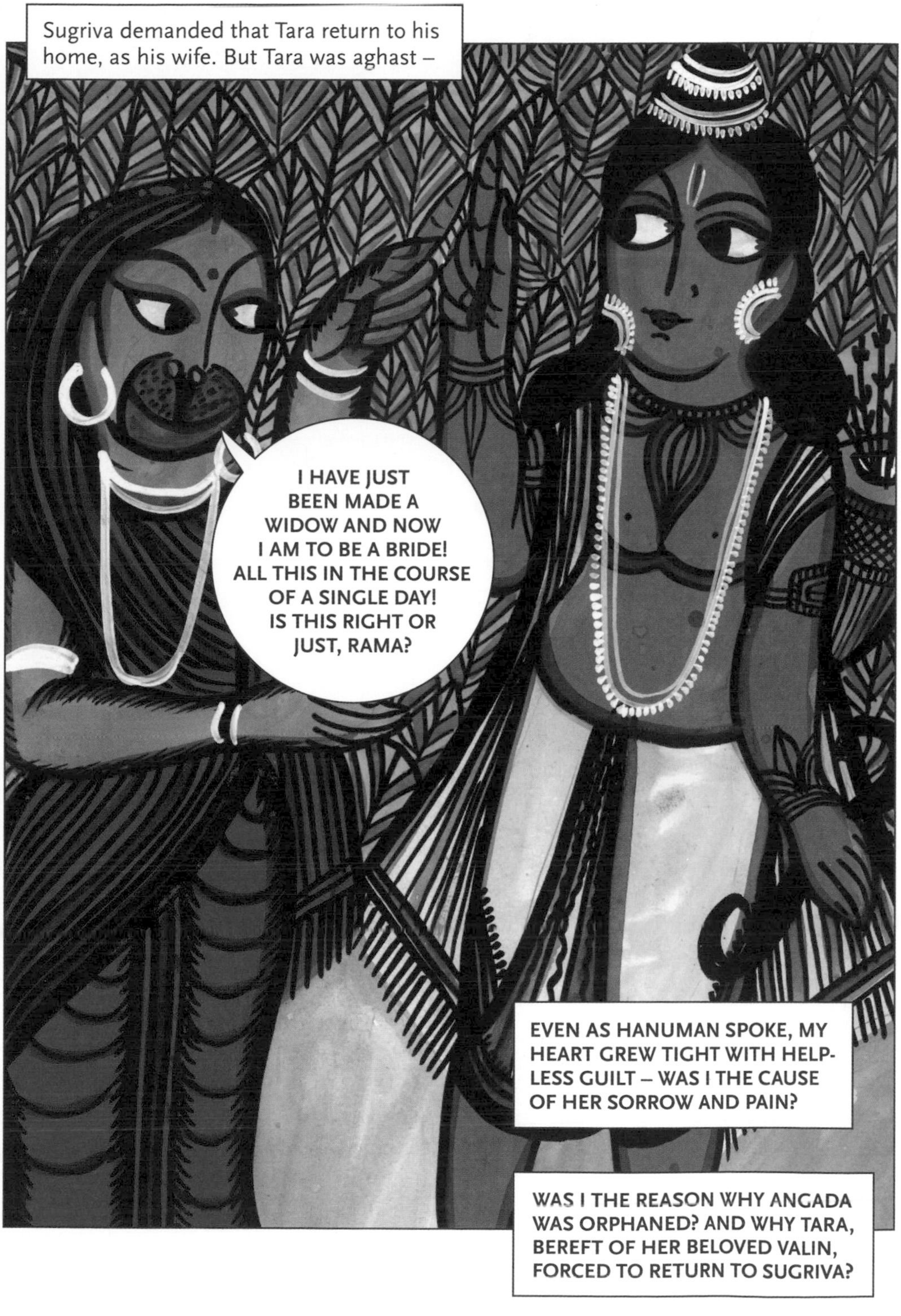
Sugriva demanded that Tara return to his home, as his wife. But Tara was aghast –
I HAVE JUST BEEN MADE A WIDOW AND NOW I AM TO BE A BRIDE! ALL THIS IN THE COURSE OF A SINGLE DAY! IS THIS RIGHT OR JUST, RAMA?
EVEN AS HANUMAN SPOKE, MY HEART GREW TIGHT WITH HELP-LESS GUILT – WAS I THE CAUSE OF HER SORROW AND PAIN?
WAS I THE REASON WHY ANGADA WAS ORPHANED? AND WHY TARA, BEREFT OF HER BELOVED VALIN, FORCED TO RETURN TO SUGRIVA?

Now that Sugriva was king, he ordered Hanuman to leap across the ocean and search for Sita in Lanka.

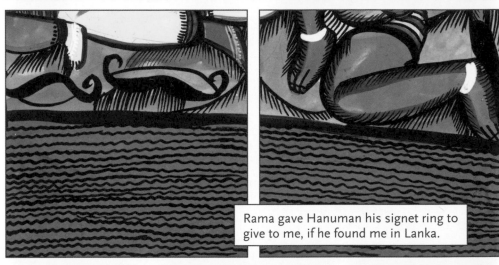

Rama gave Hanuman his signet ring to give to me, if he found me in Lanka.

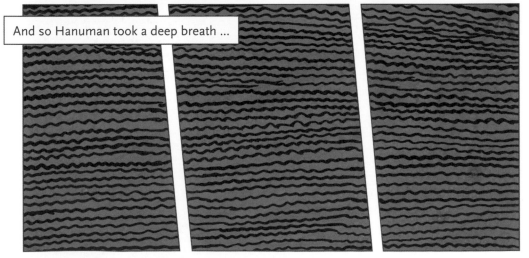

And so Hanuman took a deep breath ...

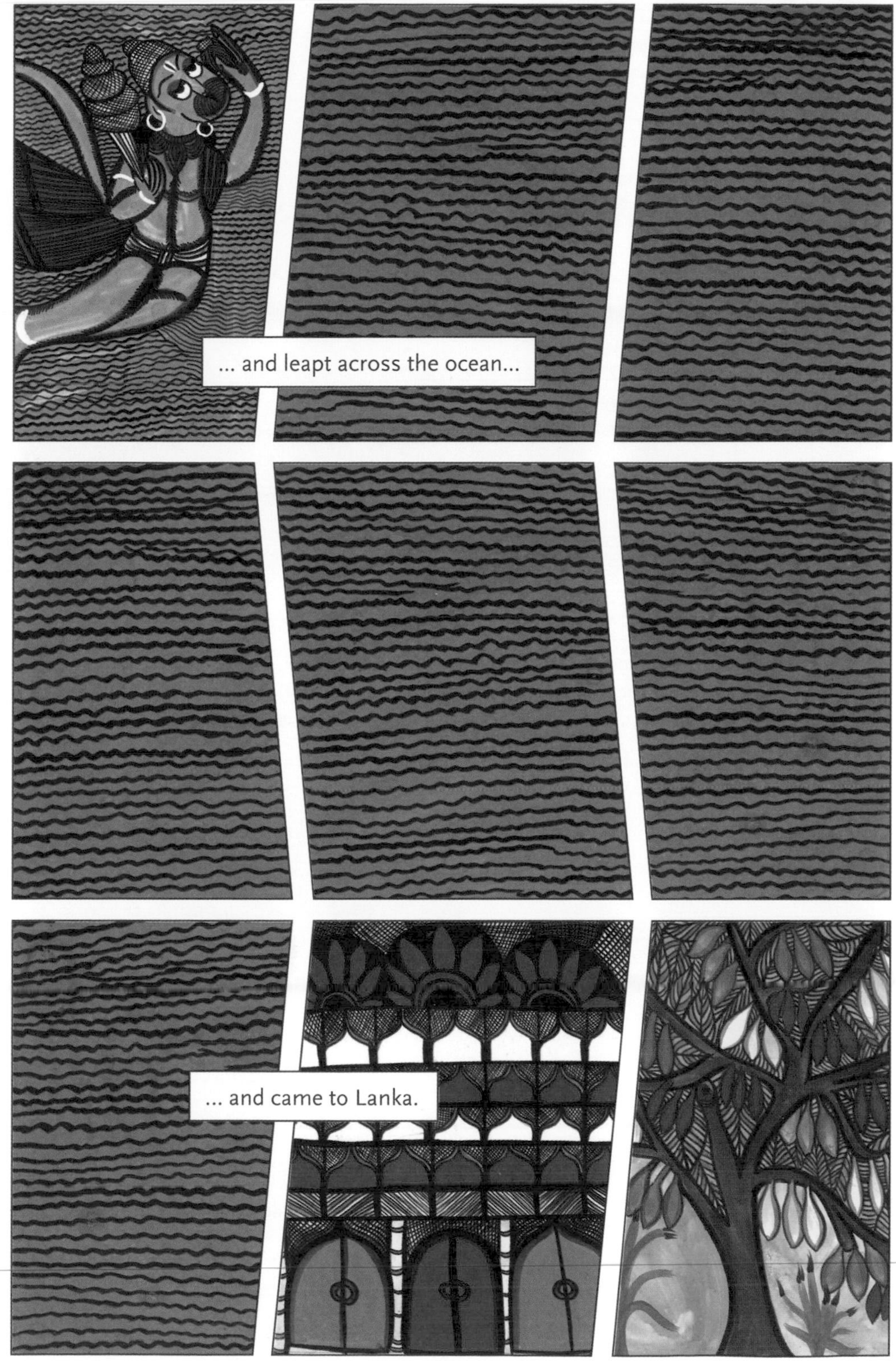
... and leapt across the ocean...
... and came to Lanka.

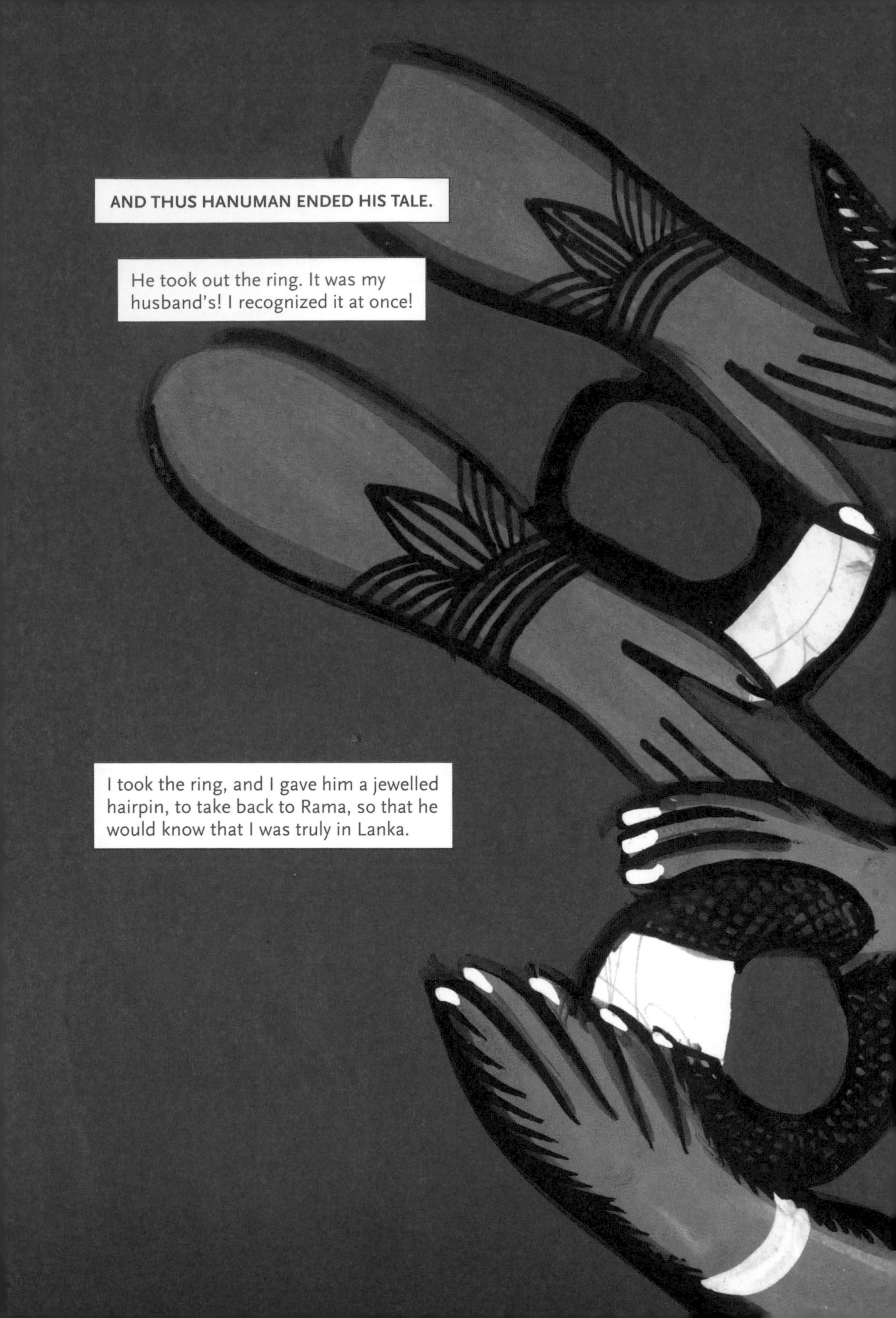
AND THUS HANUMAN ENDED HIS TALE.
He took out the ring. It was my husband's! I recognized it at once!
I took the ring, and I gave him a jewelled hairpin, to take back to Rama, so that he would know that I was truly in Lanka.

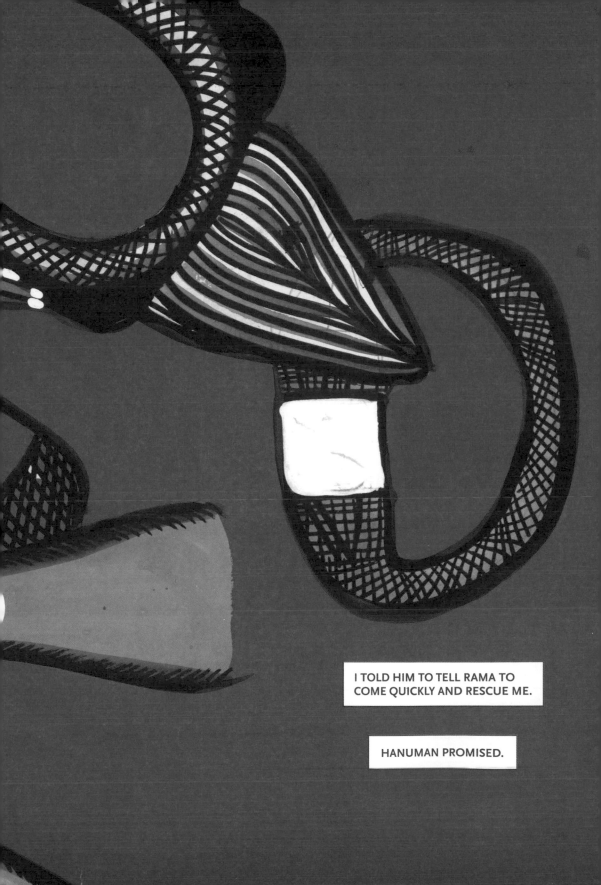

I TOLD HIM TO TELL RAMA TO COME QUICKLY AND RESCUE ME.

HANUMAN PROMISED.

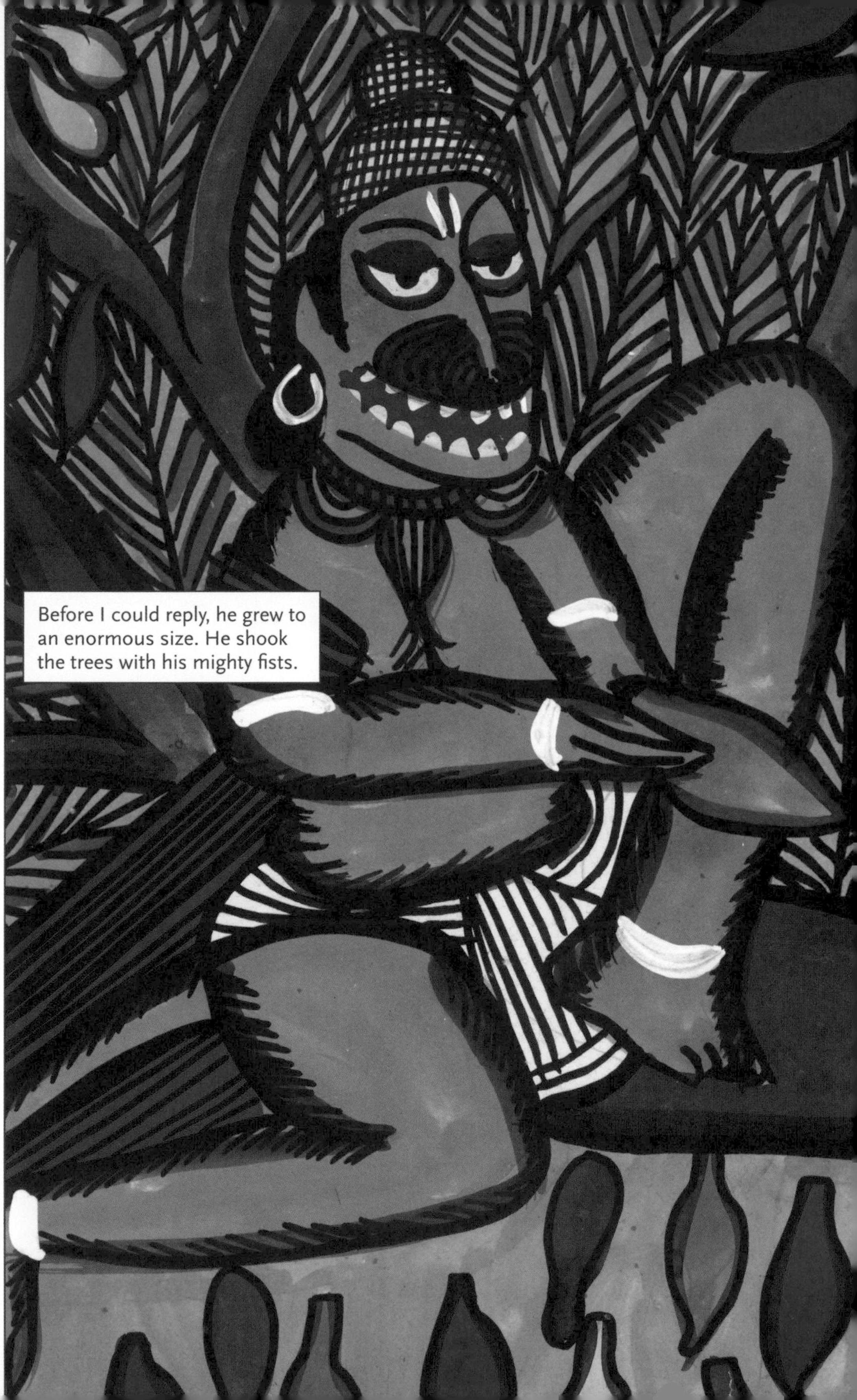
Before I could reply, he grew to an enormous size. He shook the trees with his mighty fists.

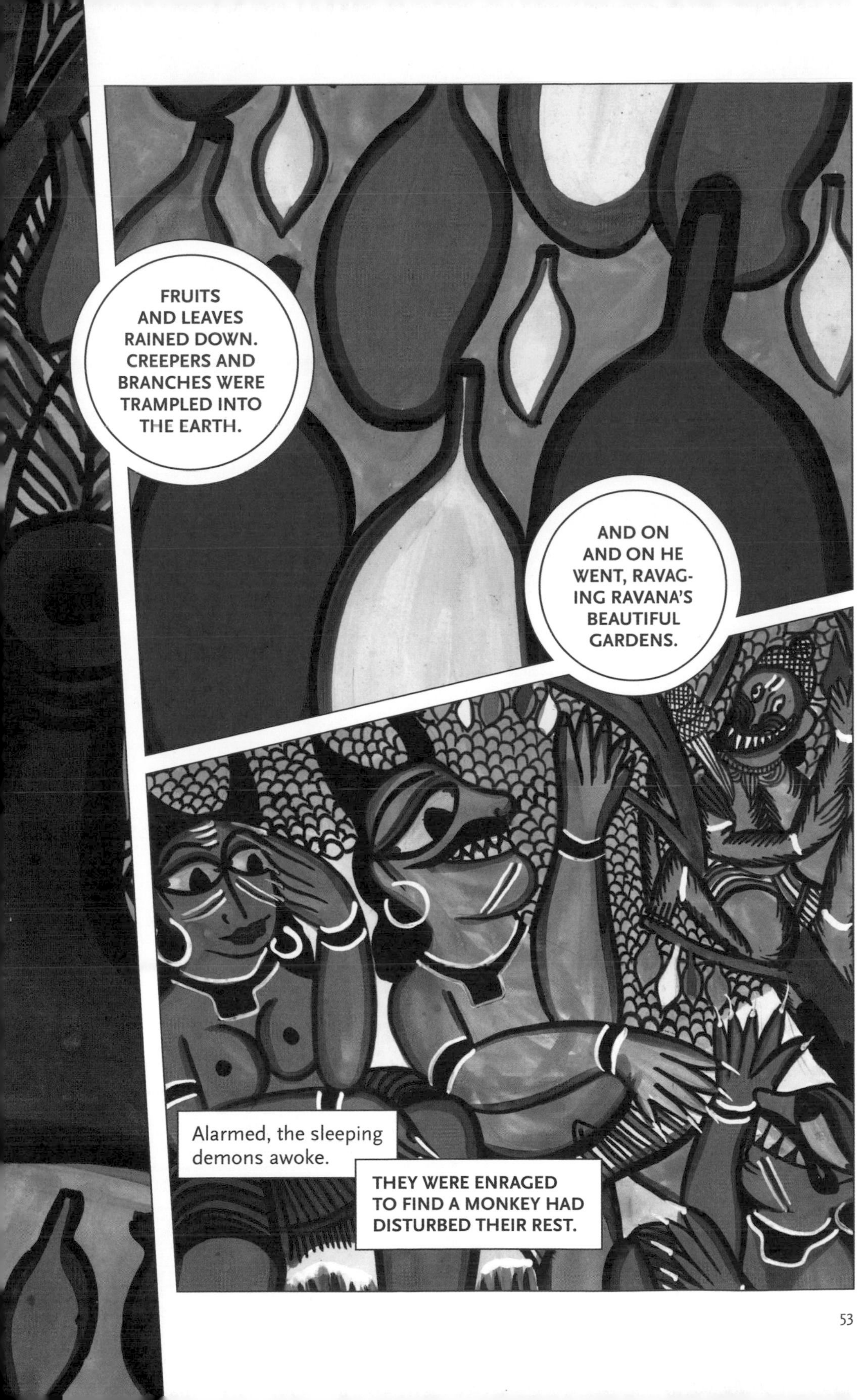
FRUITS AND LEAVES RAINED DOWN. CREEPERS AND BRANCHES WERE TRAMPLED INTO THE EARTH.
AND ON AND ON HE WENT, RAVAGING RAVANA'S BEAUTIFUL GARDENS.
Alarmed, the sleeping demons awoke.
THEY WERE ENRAGED TO FIND A MONKEY HAD DISTURBED THEIR REST.

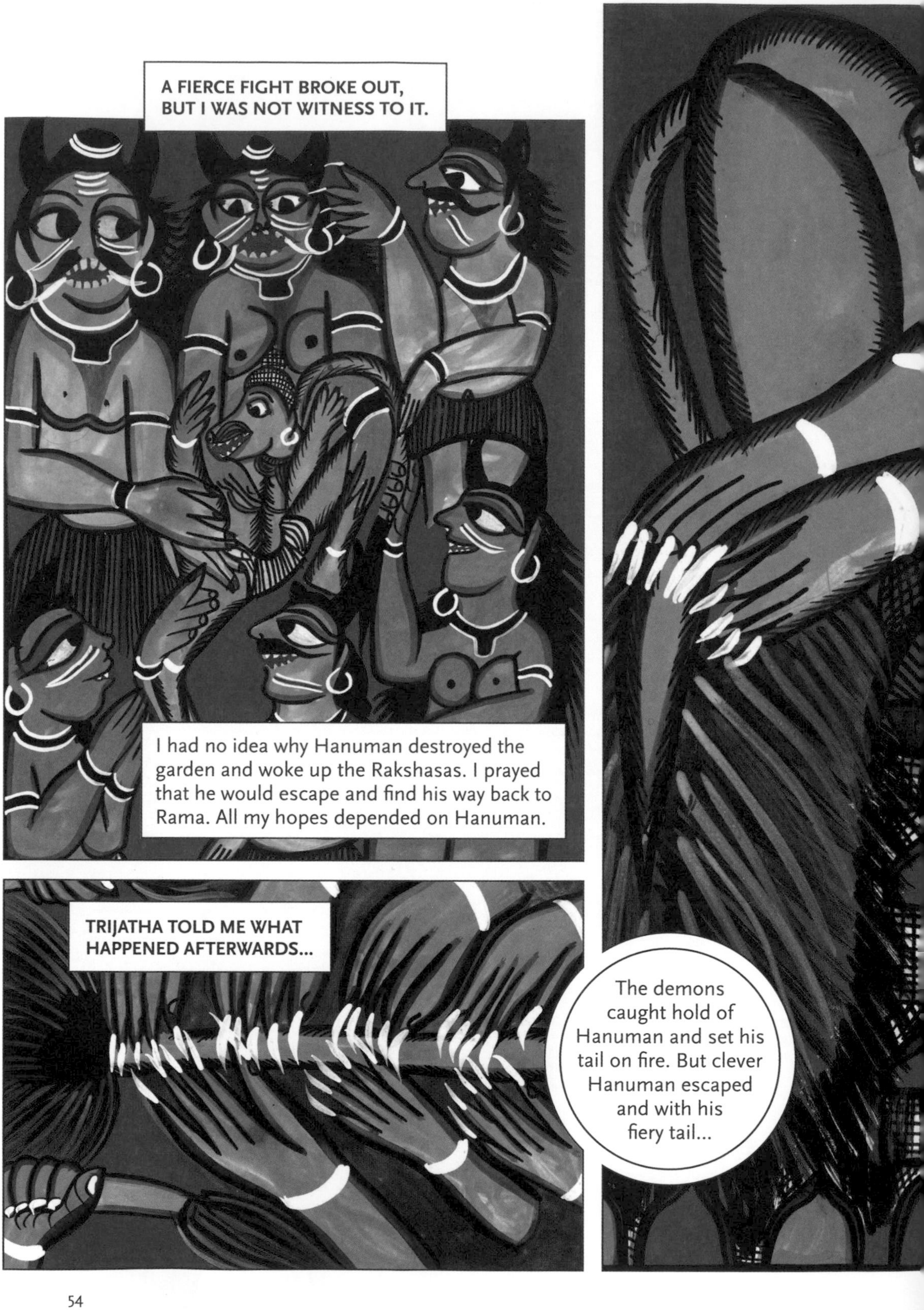
A FIERCE FIGHT BROKE OUT, BUT I WAS NOT WITNESS TO IT.
I had no idea why Hanuman destroyed the garden and woke up the Rakshasas. I prayed that he would escape and find his way back to Rama. All my hopes depended on Hanuman.
TRIJATHA TOLD ME WHAT HAPPENED AFTERWARDS...
The demons caught hold of Hanuman and set his tail on fire. But clever Hanuman escaped and with his fiery tail...

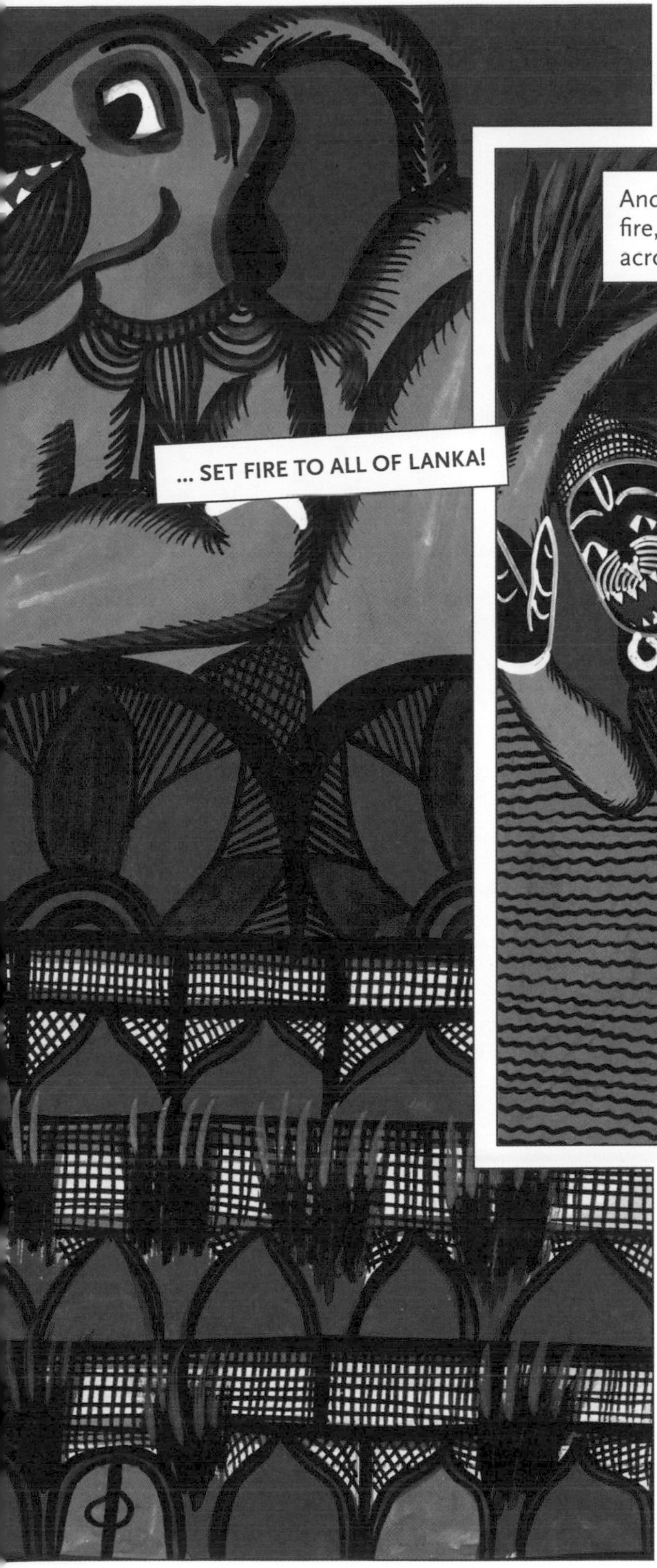
... SET FIRE TO ALL OF LANKA!

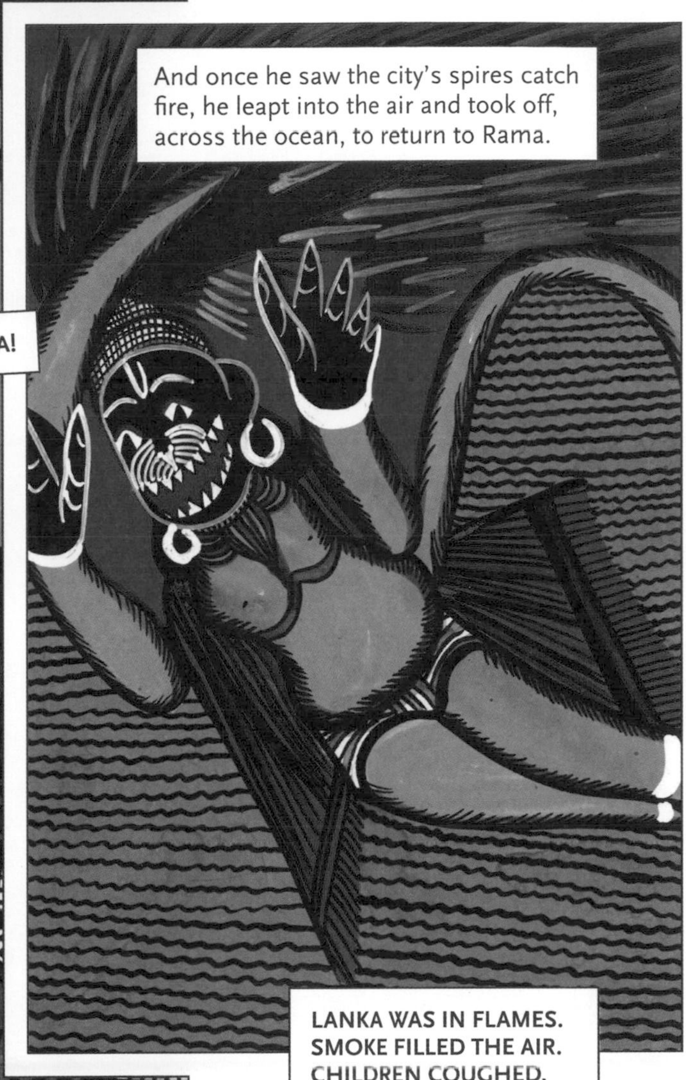
And once he saw the city's spires catch fire, he leapt into the air and took off, across the ocean, to return to Rama.
LANKA WAS IN FLAMES. SMOKE FILLED THE AIR. CHILDREN COUGHED, LUNGS FILLED WITH SOOT AND DUST.

I HEARD THE CRIES OF MY RAKSHASA JAILERS RENT THE AIR, AS THEY WATCHED THEIR HOMES GO UP IN FLAMES.

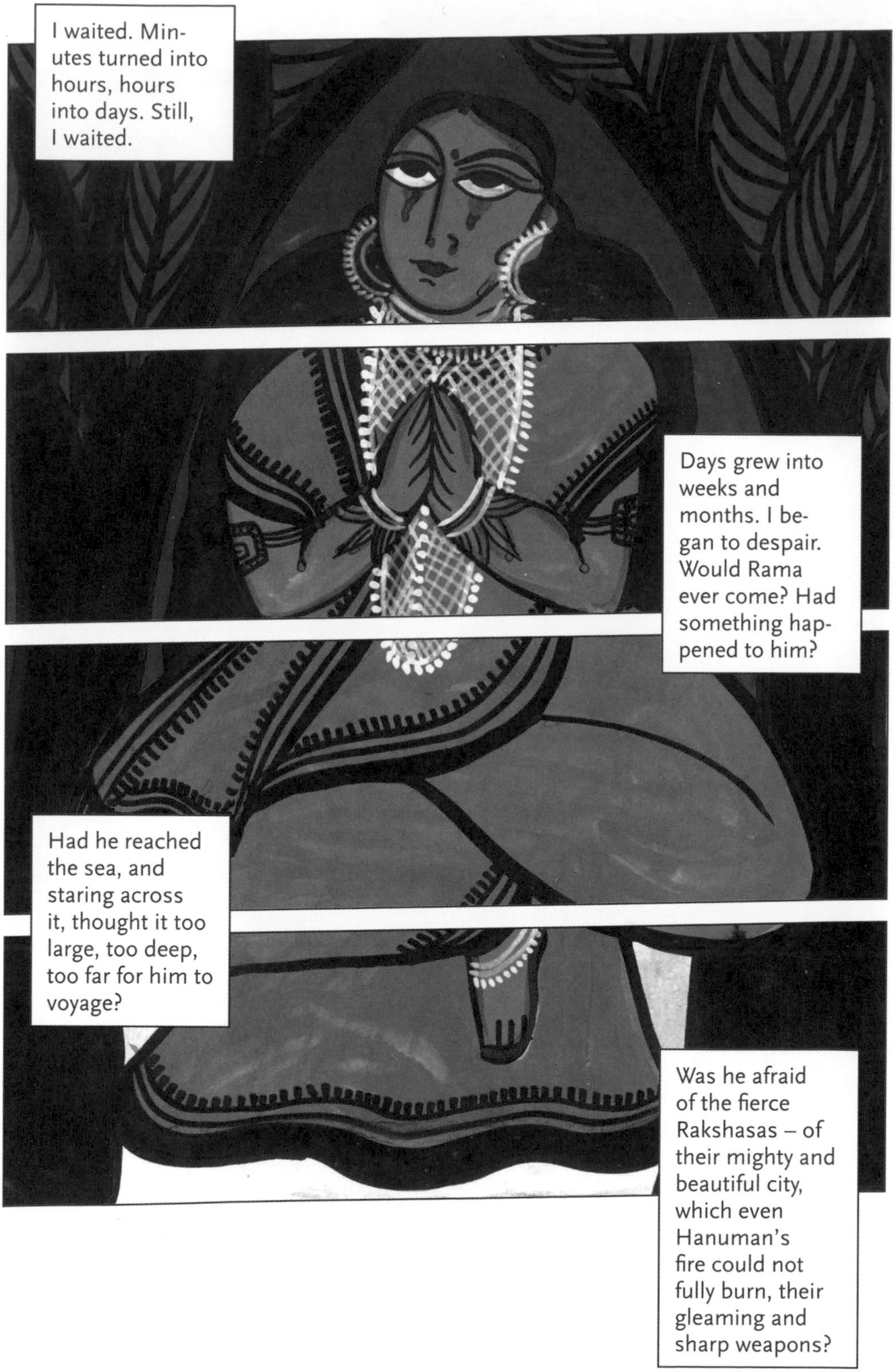
I waited. Minutes turned into hours, hours into days. Still, I waited.
Days grew into weeks and months. I began to despair. Would Rama ever come? Had something happened to him?
Had he reached the sea, and staring across it, thought it too large, too deep, too far for him to voyage?
Was he afraid of the fierce Rakshasas – of their mighty and beautiful city, which even Hanuman's fire could not fully burn, their gleaming and sharp weapons?

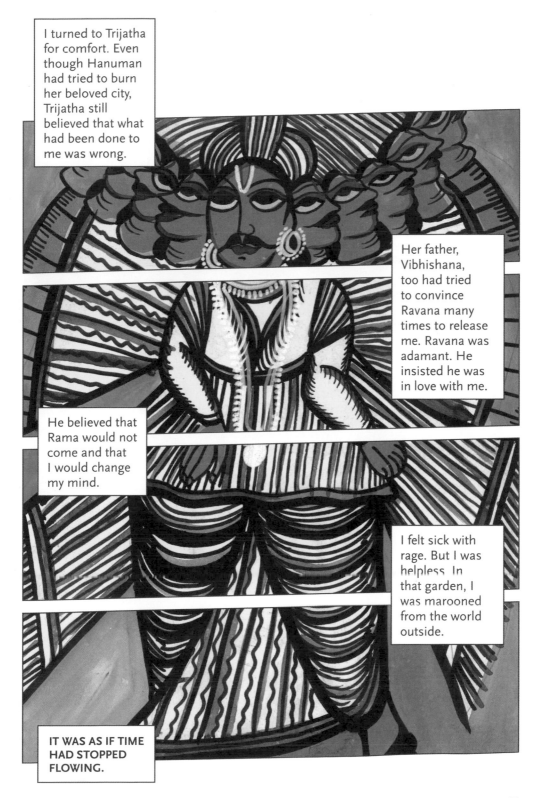

I turned to Trijatha for comfort. Even though Hanuman had tried to burn her beloved city, Trijatha still believed that what had been done to me was wrong.

Her father, Vibhishana, too had tried to convince Ravana many times to release me. Ravana was adamant. He insisted he was in love with me.

He believed that Rama would not come and that I would change my mind.

I felt sick with rage. But I was helpless. In that garden, I was marooned from the world outside.

IT WAS AS IF TIME HAD STOPPED FLOWING.

Until one day Trijatha came to me with a dream:

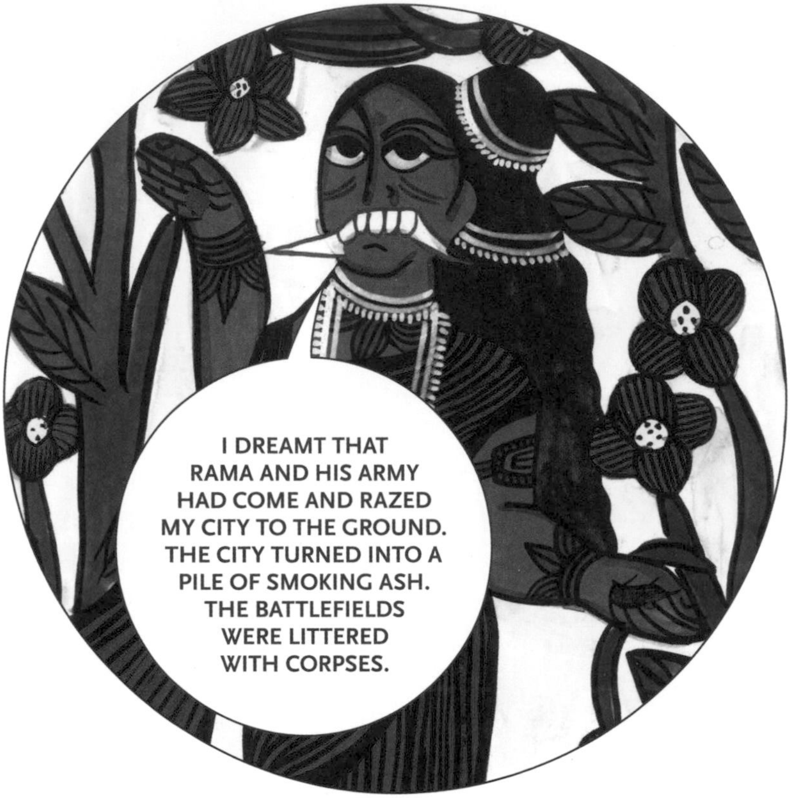
I DREAMT THAT RAMA AND HIS ARMY HAD COME AND RAZED MY CITY TO THE GROUND. THE CITY TURNED INTO A PILE OF SMOKING ASH. THE BATTLEFIELDS WERE LITTERED WITH CORPSES.

TRIJATHA WAS ANGUISHED. HER DREAMS ALWAYS CAME TRUE. SHE HAD TOLD HER FATHER, VIBHISHANA, AND THAT MORNING HE CAME TO THE GARDEN. THERE WAS A LOT WEIGHING ON HIS MIND. HE HAD BEEN FIGHTING WITH RAVANA, ARGUING THAT I SHOULD BE RETURNED TO RAMA. RAVANA REFUSED.

Vibhishana asked me many questions about Rama. I told him –

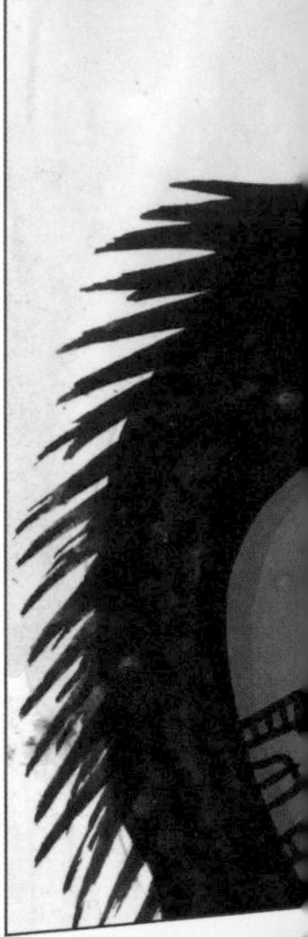

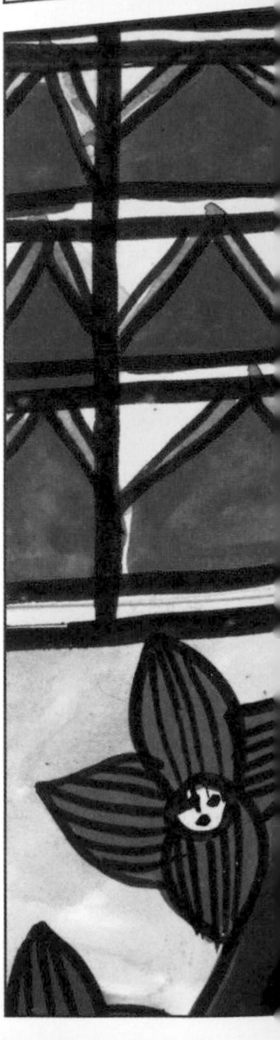

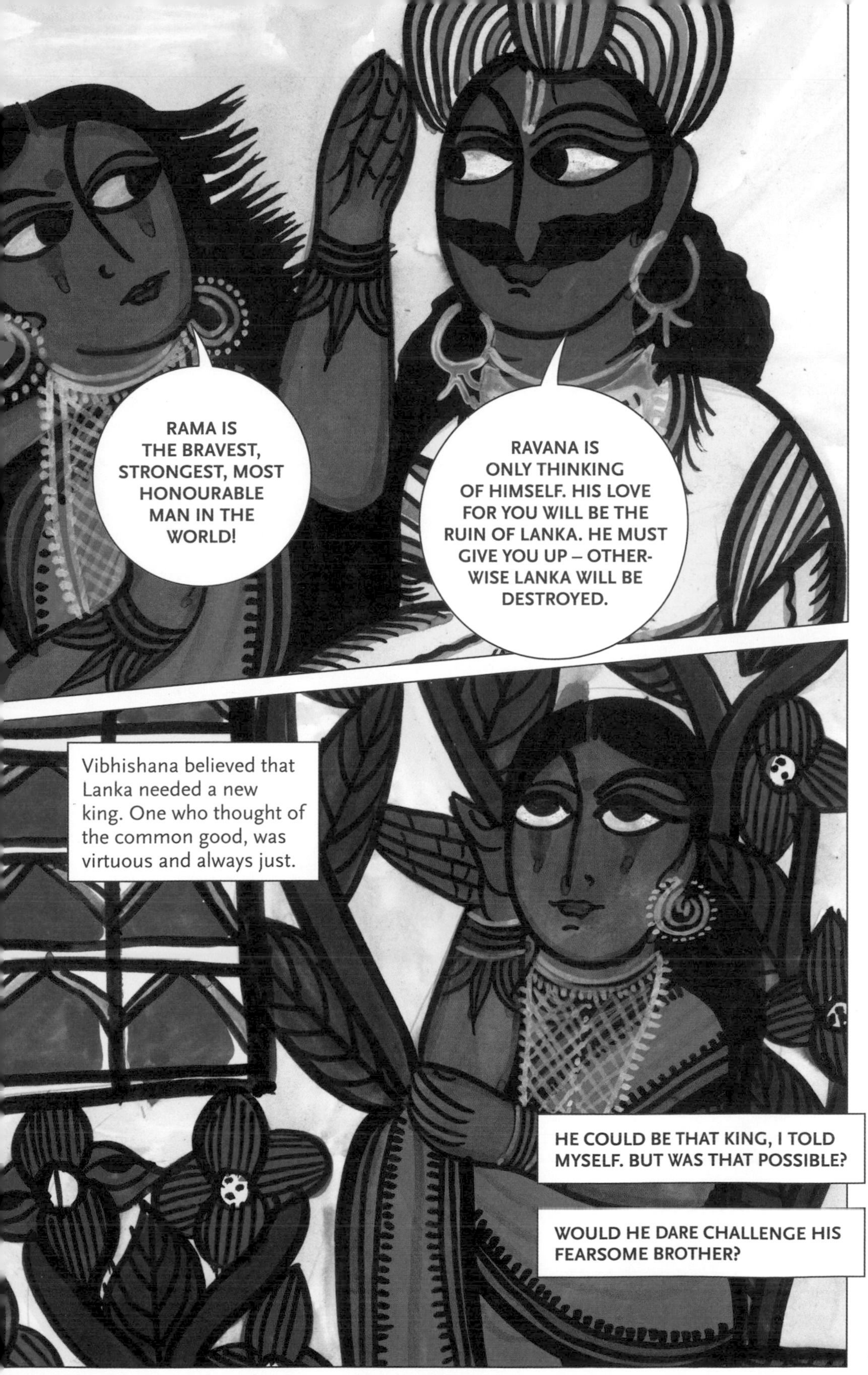
RAMA IS THE BRAVEST, STRONGEST, MOST HONOURABLE MAN IN THE WORLD!
RAVANA IS ONLY THINKING OF HIMSELF. HIS LOVE FOR YOU WILL BE THE RUIN OF LANKA. HE MUST GIVE YOU UP – OTHERWISE LANKA WILL BE DESTROYED.
Vibhishana believed that Lanka needed a new king. One who thought of the common good, was virtuous and always just.
HE COULD BE THAT KING, I TOLD MYSELF. BUT WAS THAT POSSIBLE?
WOULD HE DARE CHALLENGE HIS FEARSOME BROTHER?

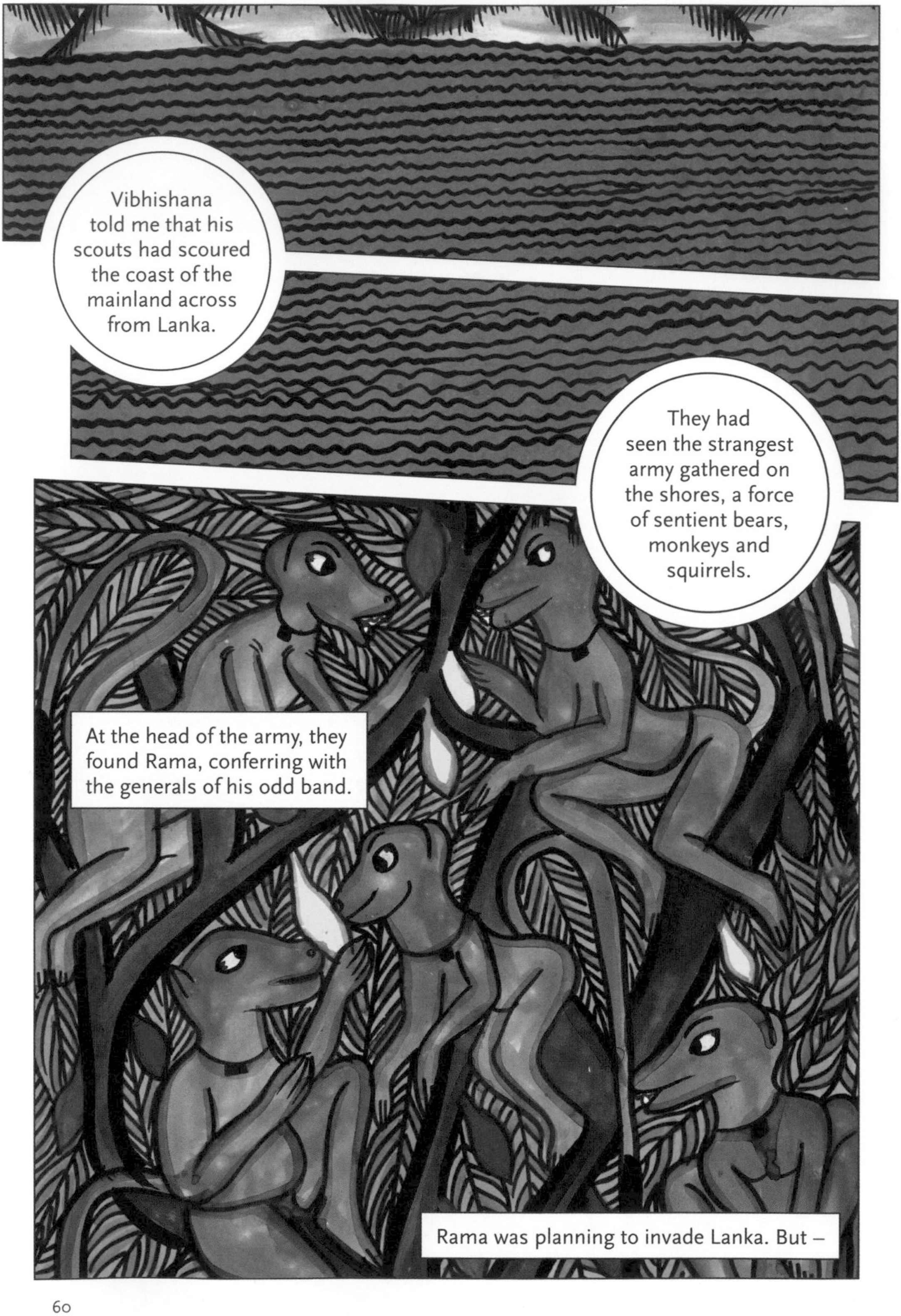
Vibhishana told me that his scouts had scoured the coast of the mainland across from Lanka.
They had seen the strangest army gathered on the shores, a force of sentient bears, monkeys and squirrels.
At the head of the army, they found Rama, conferring with the generals of his odd band.
Rama was planning to invade Lanka. But –

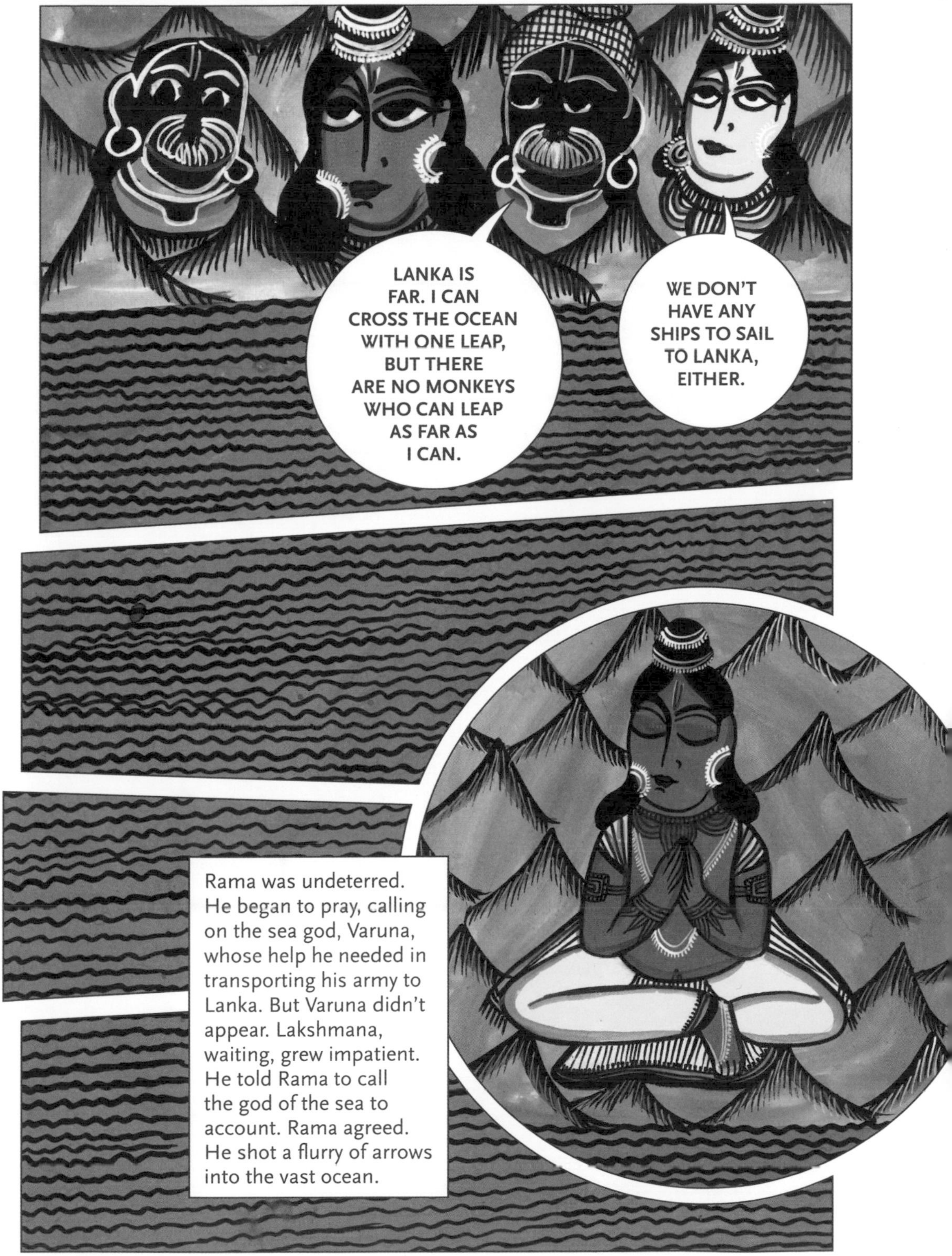
LANKA IS FAR. I CAN CROSS THE OCEAN WITH ONE LEAP, BUT THERE ARE NO MONKEYS WHO CAN LEAP AS FAR AS I CAN.
WE DON'T HAVE ANY SHIPS TO SAIL TO LANKA, EITHER.
Rama was undeterred. He began to pray, calling on the sea god, Varuna, whose help he needed in transporting his army to Lanka. But Varuna didn't appear. Lakshmana, waiting, grew impatient. He told Rama to call the god of the sea to account. Rama agreed. He shot a flurry of arrows into the vast ocean.

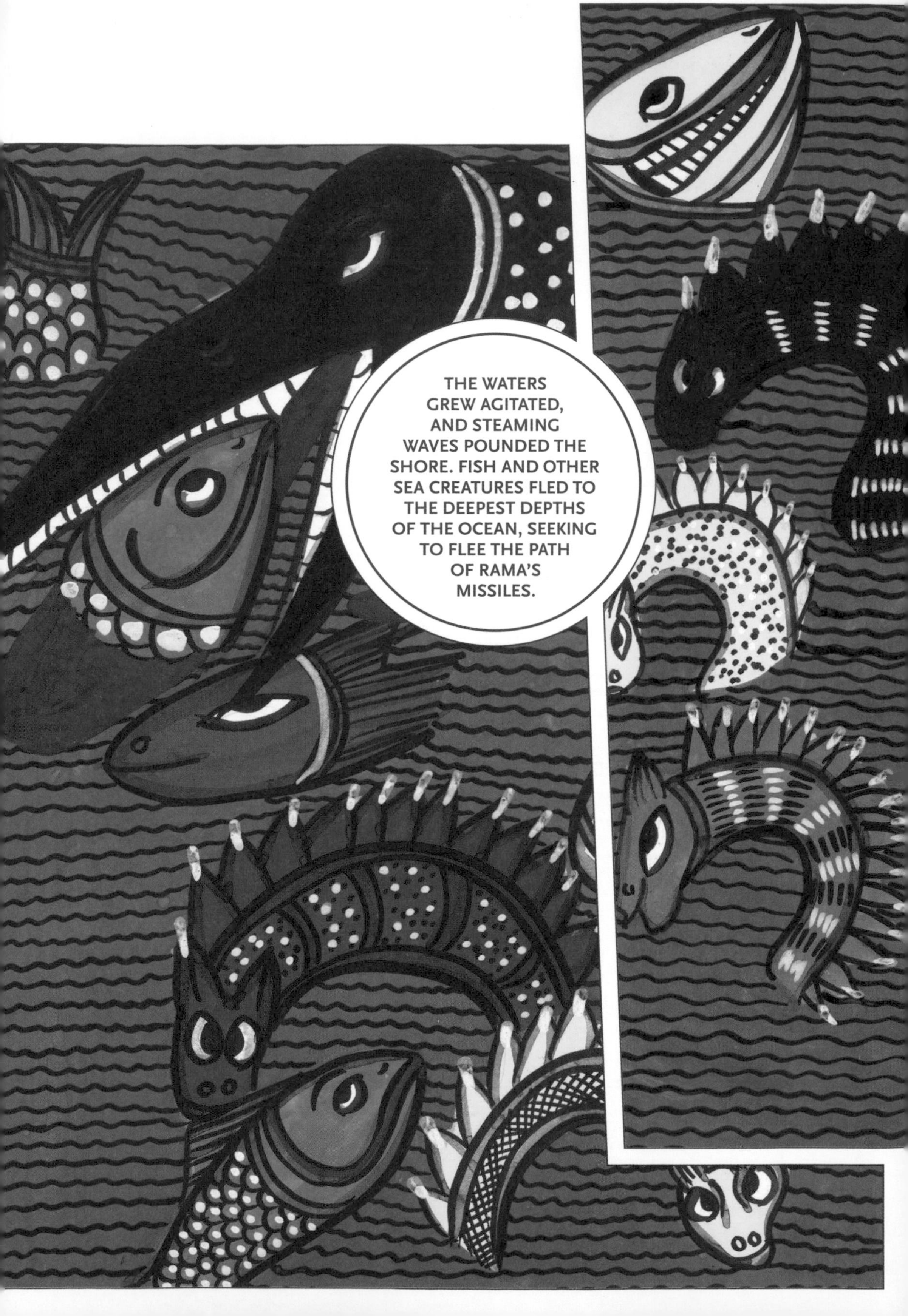
THE WATERS GROW AGITATED, AND STEAMING WAVES POUNDED THE SHORE. FISH AND OTHER SEA CREATURES FLED TO THE DEEPEST DEPTHS OF THE OCEAN, SEEKING TO FLEE THE PATH OF RAMA'S MISSILES.

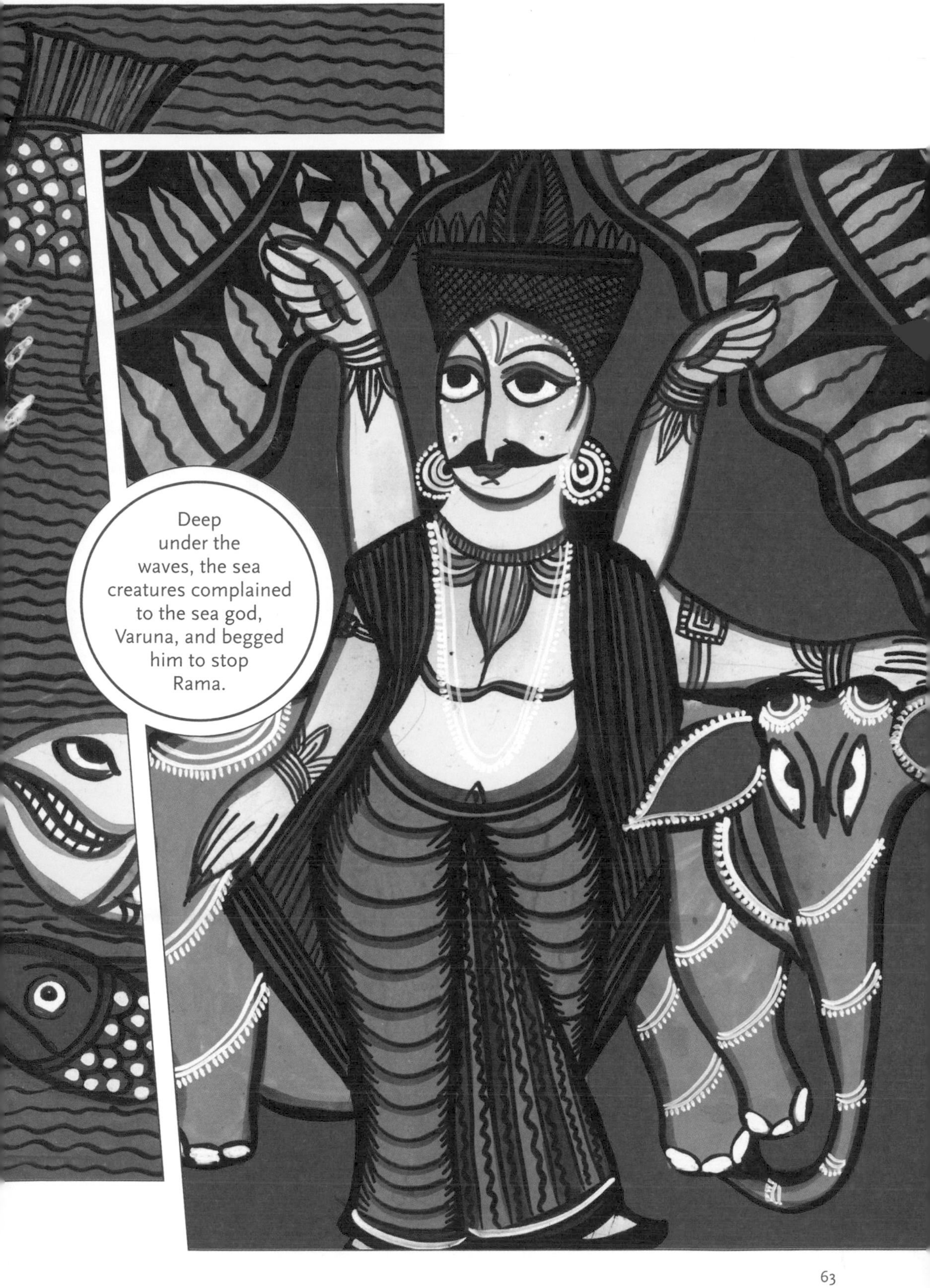
Deep under the waves, the sea creatures complained to the sea god, Varuna, and begged him to stop Rama.

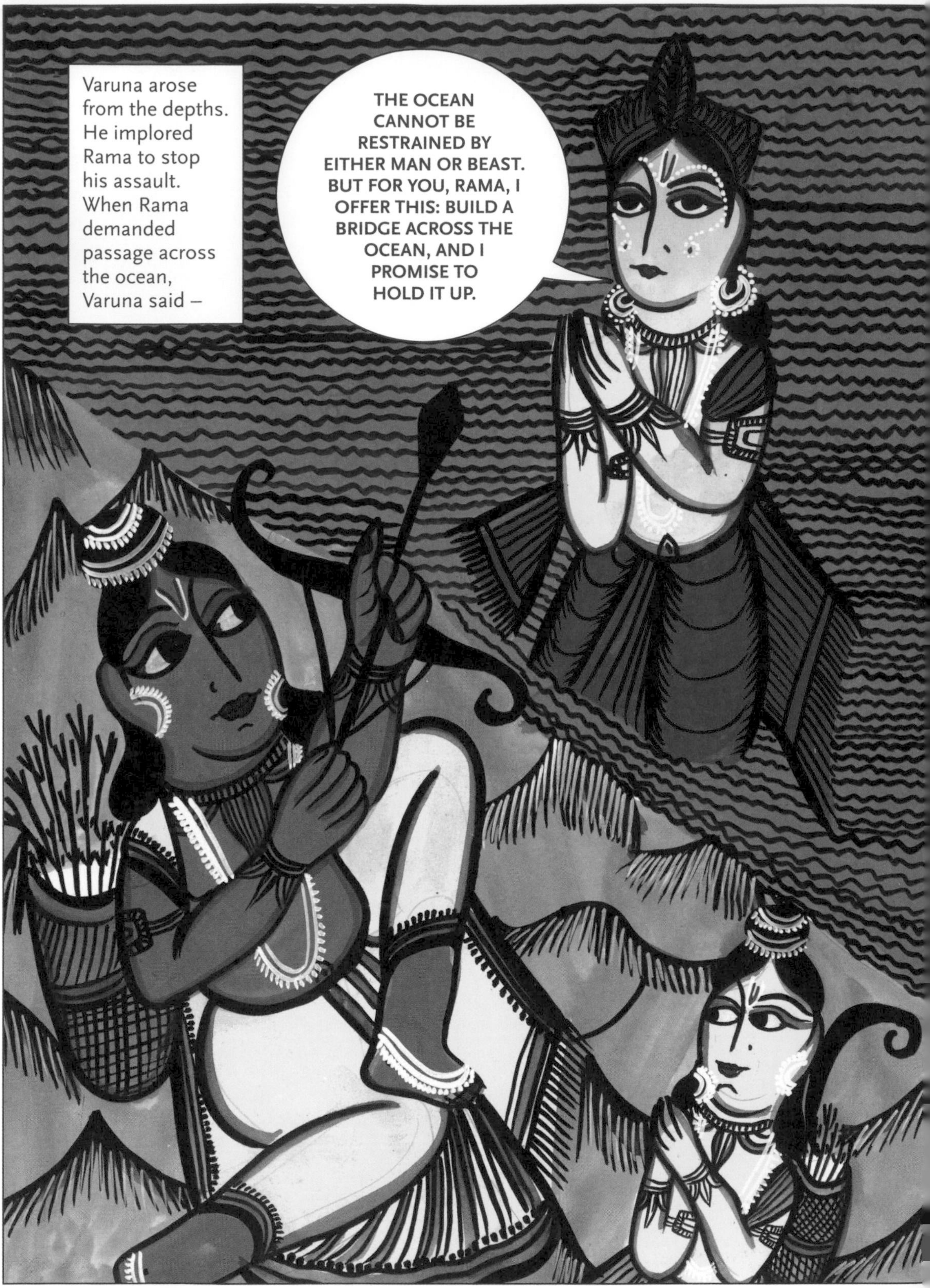
Varuna arose from the depths. He implored Rama to stop his assault. When Rama demanded passage across the ocean, Varuna said –
THE OCEAN CANNOT BE RESTRAINED BY EITHER MAN OR BEAST. BUT FOR YOU, RAMA, I OFFER THIS: BUILD A BRIDGE ACROSS THE OCEAN, AND I PROMISE TO HOLD IT UP.

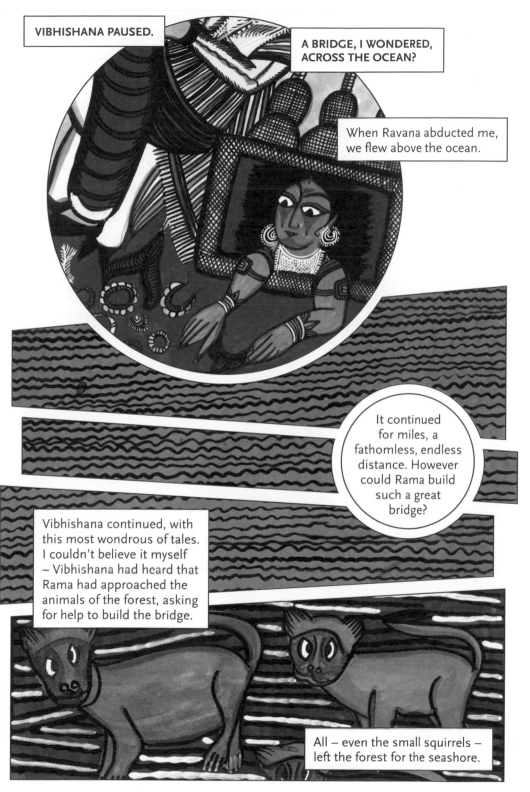

VIBHISHANA PAUSED.

A BRIDGE, I WONDERED, ACROSS THE OCEAN?

When Ravana abducted me, we flew above the ocean.

It continued for miles, a fathomless, endless distance. However could Rama build such a great bridge?

Vibhishana continued, with this most wondrous of tales. I couldn't believe it myself – Vibhishana had heard that Rama had approached the animals of the forest, asking for help to build the bridge.

All – even the small squirrels – left the forest for the seashore.

Under the supervision of the Vanara architect Nala...

... the squirrels, and all the other animals worked together...

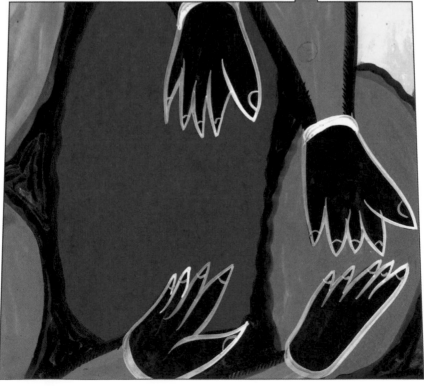

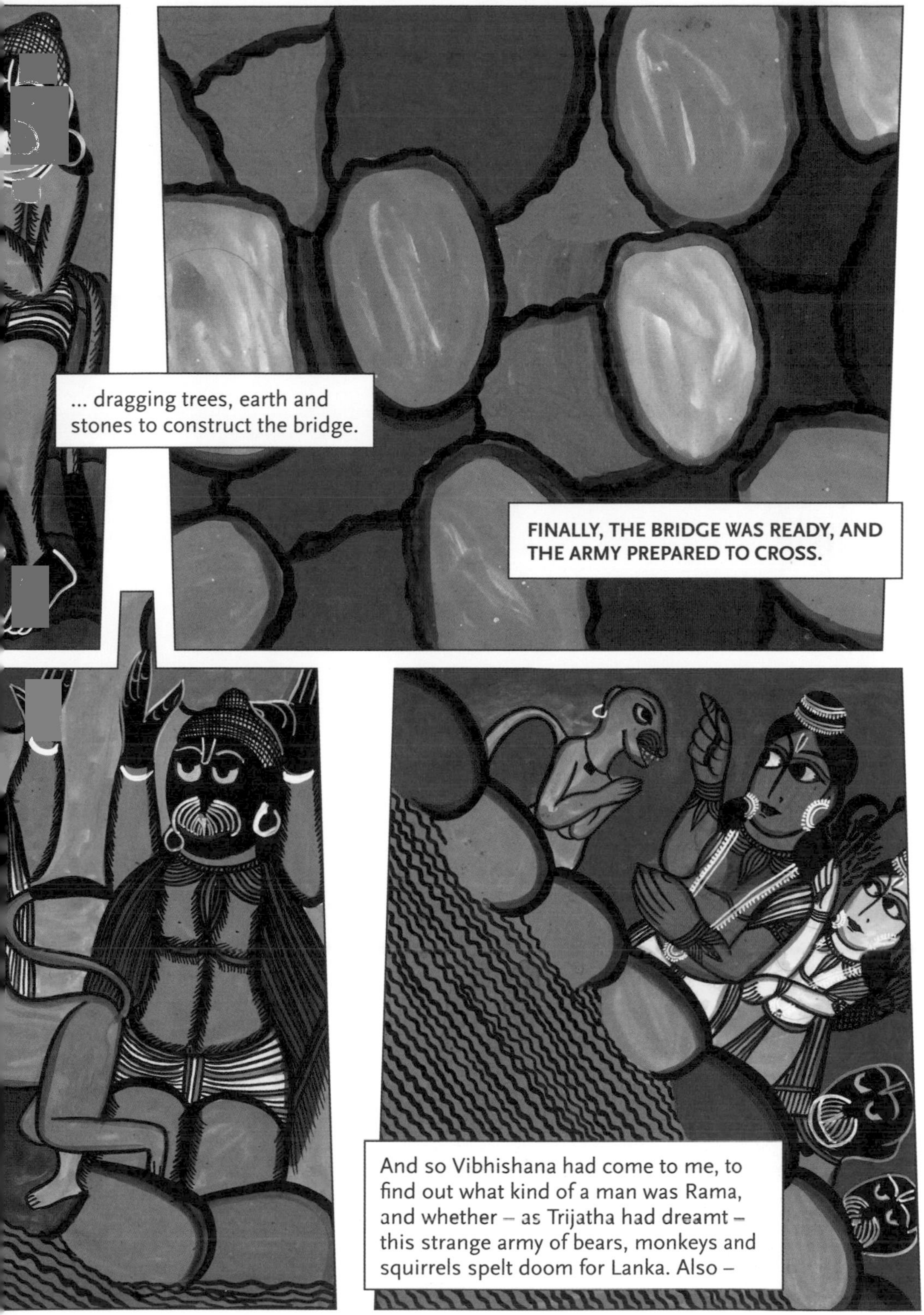
... dragging trees, earth and stones to construct the bridge.
FINALLY, THE BRIDGE WAS READY, AND THE ARMY PREPARED TO CROSS.
And so Vibhishana had come to me, to find out what kind of a man was Rama, and whether – as Trijatha had dreamt – this strange army of bears, monkeys and squirrels spelt doom for Lanka. Also –

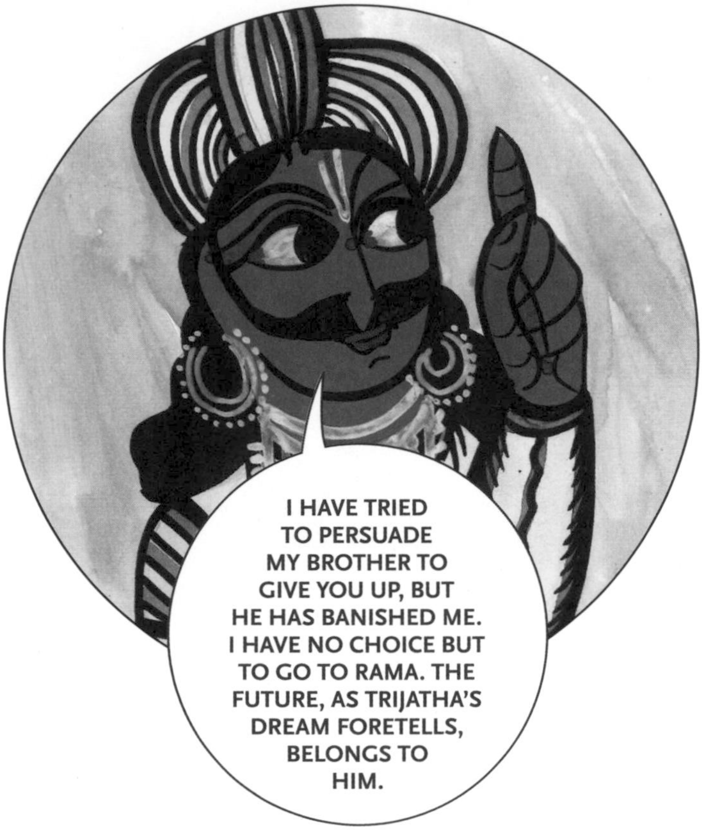
I HAVE TRIED TO PERSUADE MY BROTHER TO GIVE YOU UP, BUT HE HAS BANISHED ME. I HAVE NO CHOICE BUT TO GO TO RAMA. THE FUTURE, AS TRIJATHA'S DREAM FORETELLS, BELONGS TO HIM.

He asked Trijatha to go with him. But my friend was loyal to both me and Lanka. She couldn't leave her people, even knowing that the future held only destruction for Lanka. Knowing the future had not altered her course of action in the past, nor would it lead her away from Lanka in the present.

She would remain in Lanka, to tell me the truth, to be my friend and console me in those moments when I succumbed to despair.

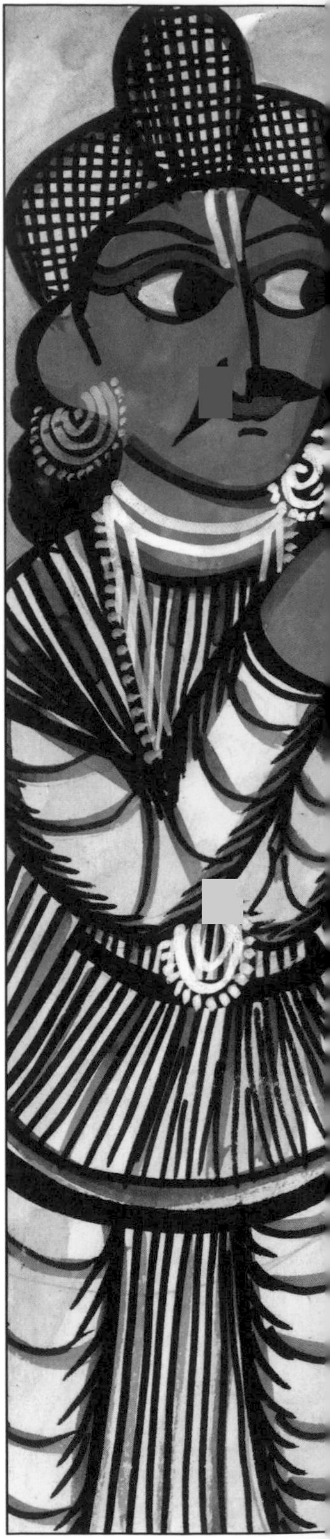

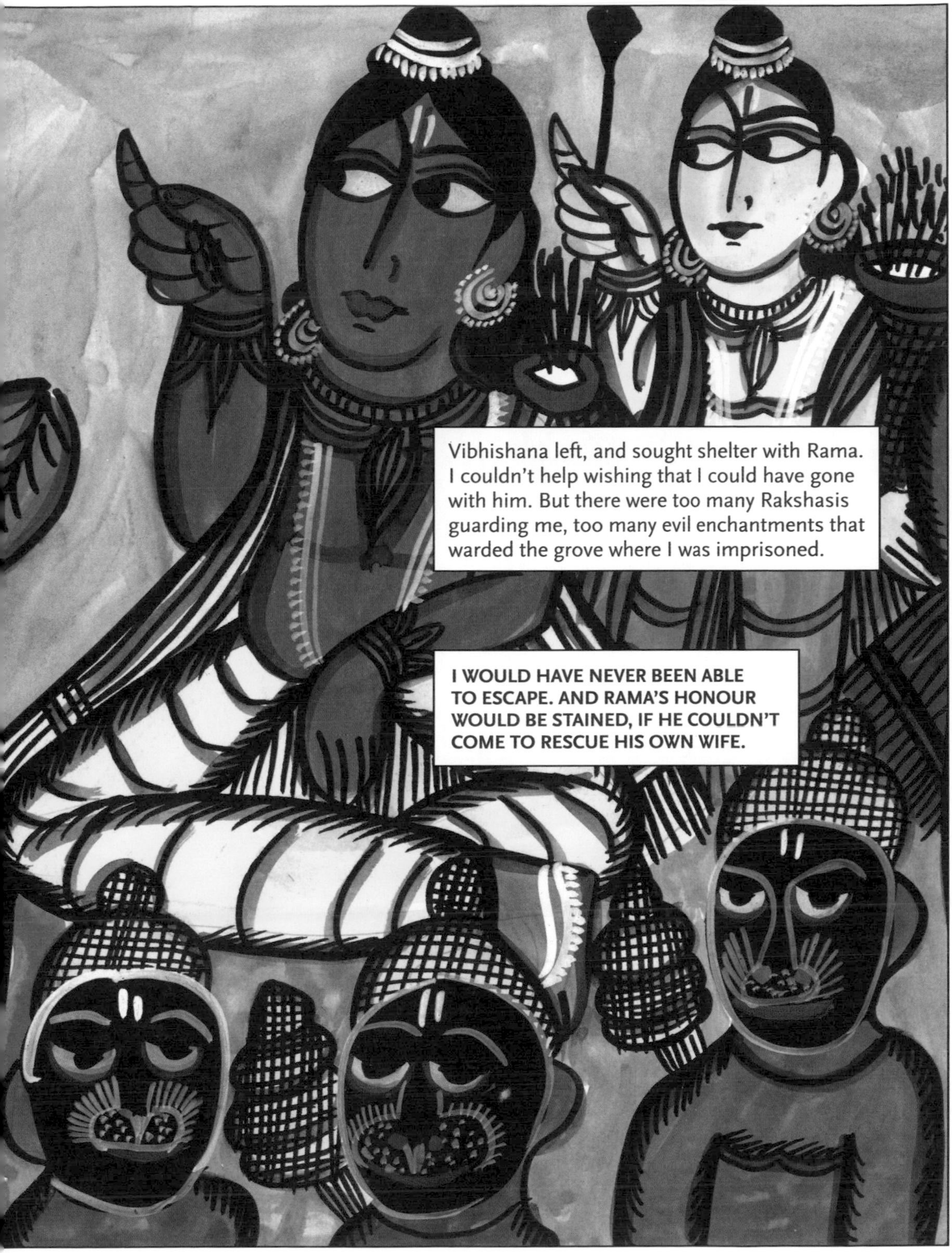
Vibhishana left, and sought shelter with Rama. I couldn't help wishing that I could have gone with him. But there were too many Rakshasis guarding me, too many evil enchantments that warded the grove where I was imprisoned.
I WOULD HAVE NEVER BEEN ABLE TO ESCAPE. AND RAMA'S HONOUR WOULD BE STAINED, IF HE COULDN'T COME TO RESCUE HIS OWN WIFE.

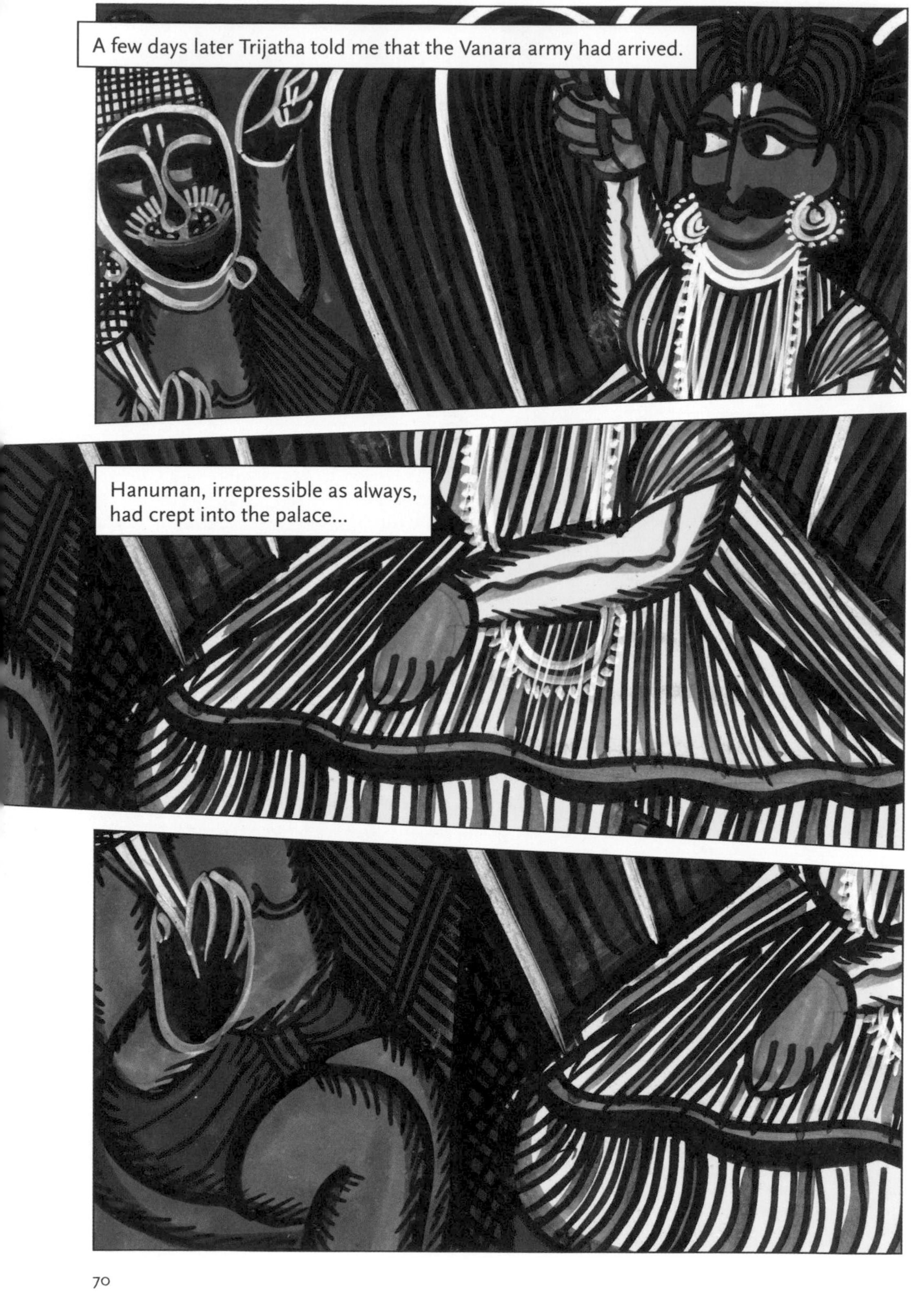
A few days later Trijatha told me that the Vanara army had arrived.
Hanuman, irrepressible as always, had crept into the palace...

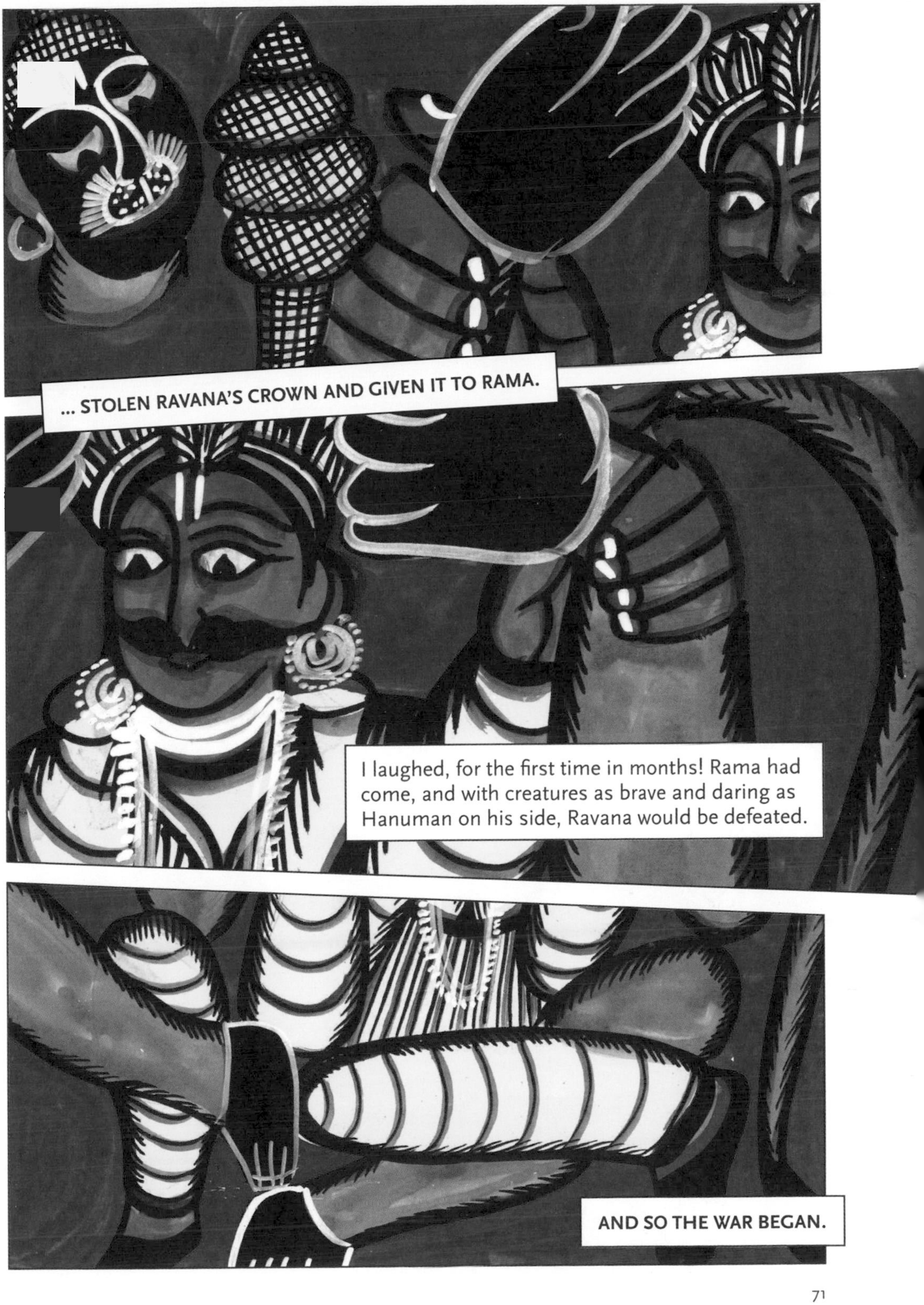
... STOLEN RAVANA'S CROWN AND GIVEN IT TO RAMA.
I laughed, for the first time in months! Rama had come, and with creatures as brave and daring as Hanuman on his side, Ravana would be defeated.
AND SO THE WAR BEGAN.

I WAS NOT WITNESS TO THE WAR.

HOW COULD I BE, TRAPPED AS I WAS IN MY PRISON?

BUT TRIJATHA PROMISED TO BE MY EARS AND EYES. EVERY DAY SHE BROUGHT ME NEWS OF WHAT HAD HAPPENED ON THE BATTLEFIELD.

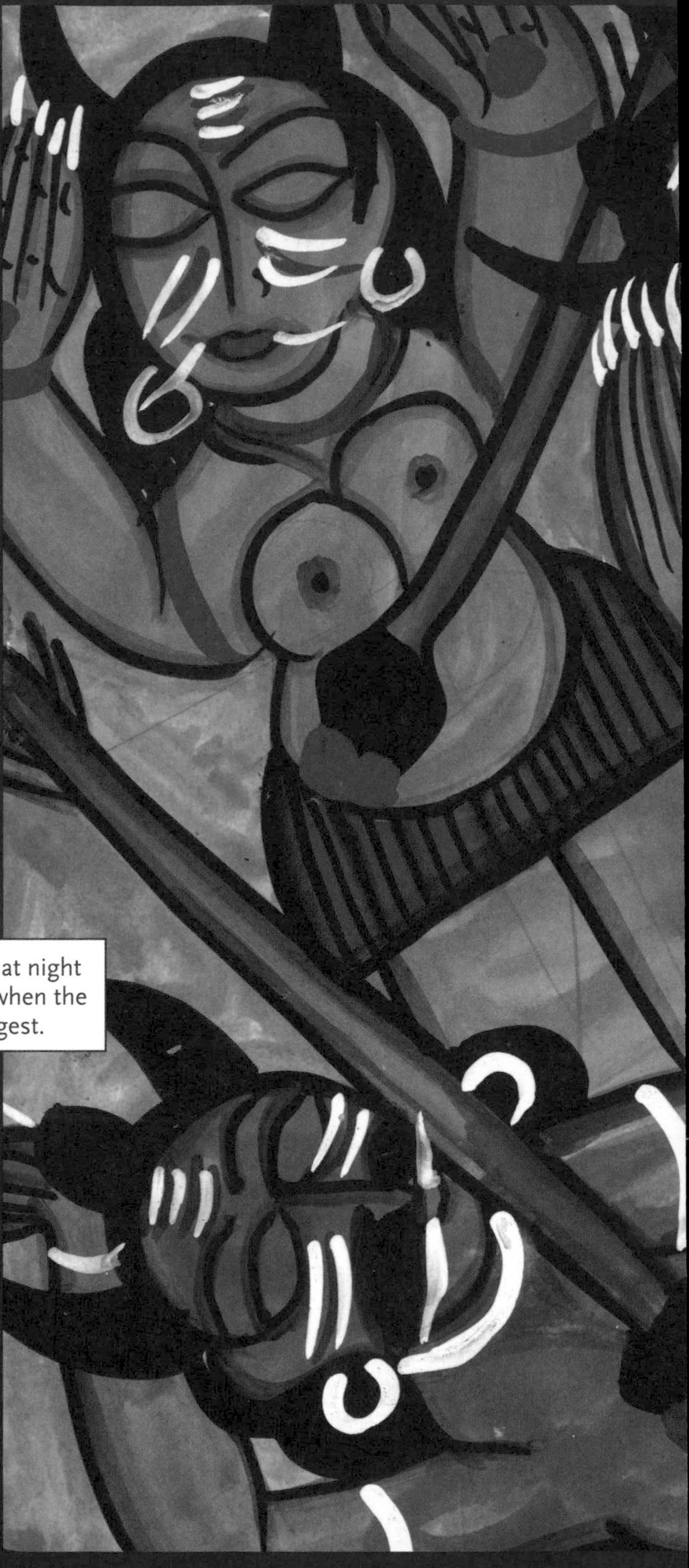

The battles happened at night for that was the time when the Rakshasas were strongest.

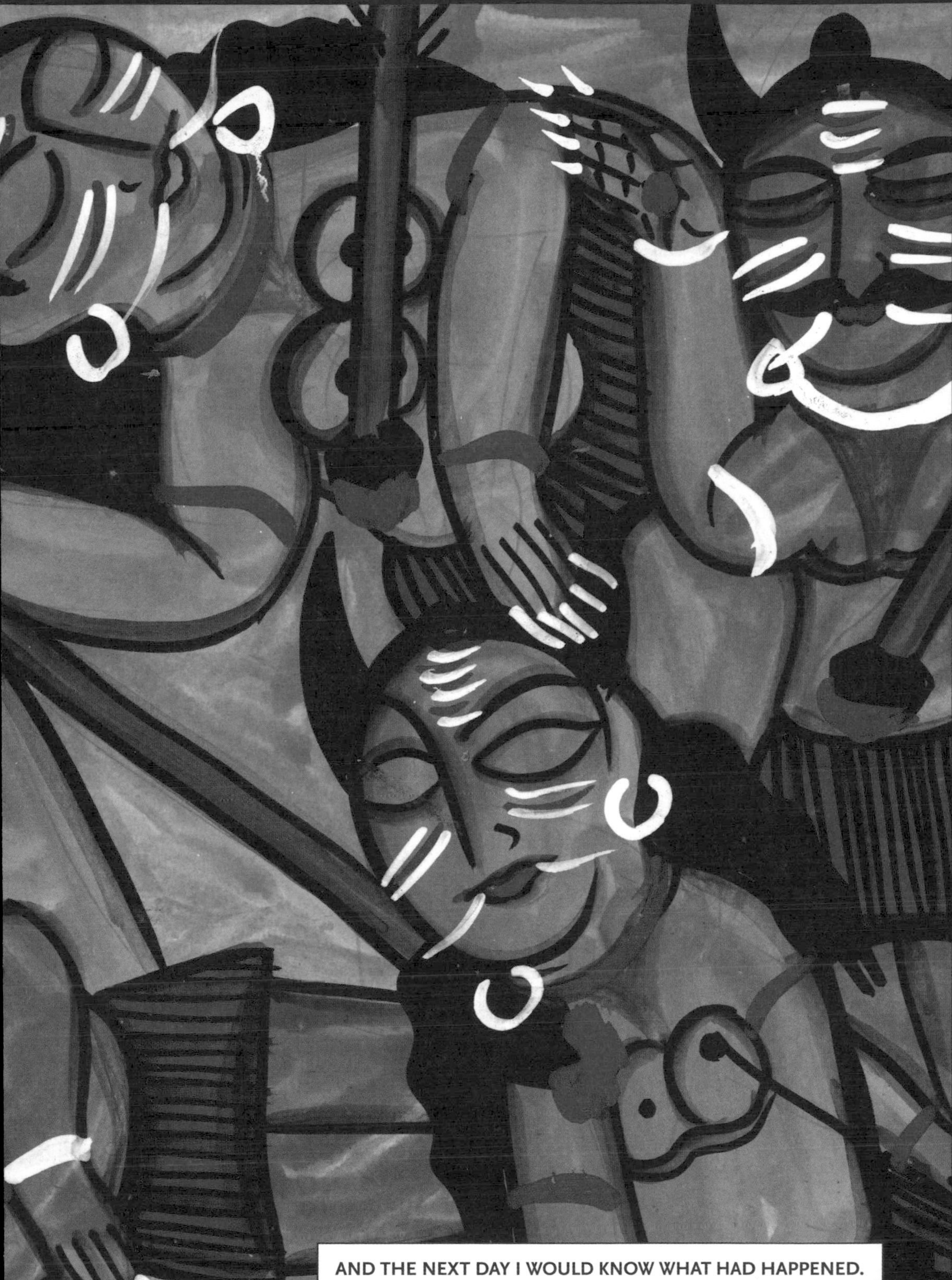
AND THE NEXT DAY I WOULD KNOW WHAT HAD HAPPENED.

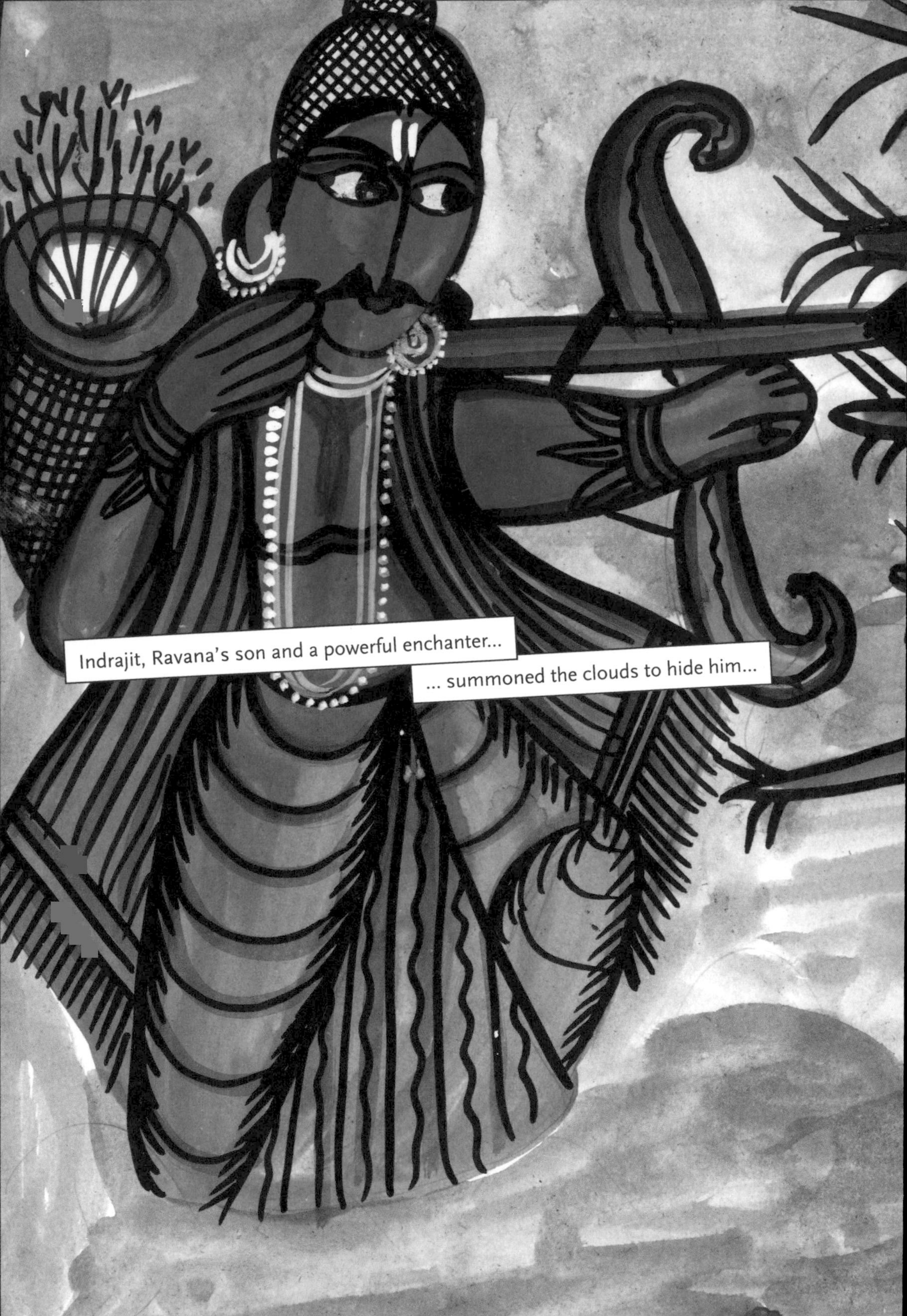
Indrajit, Ravana's son and a powerful enchanter...
... summoned the clouds to hide him...

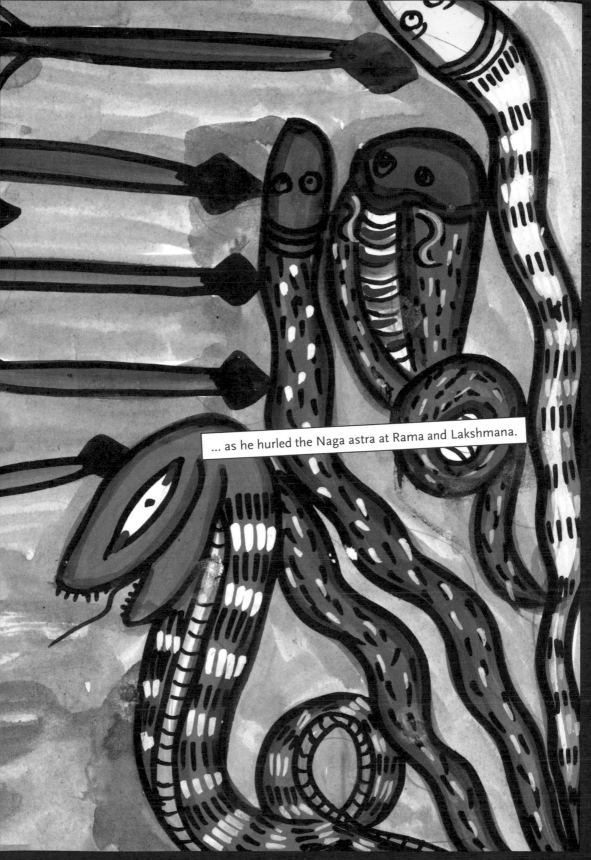

... as he hurled the Naga astra at Rama and Lakshmana.

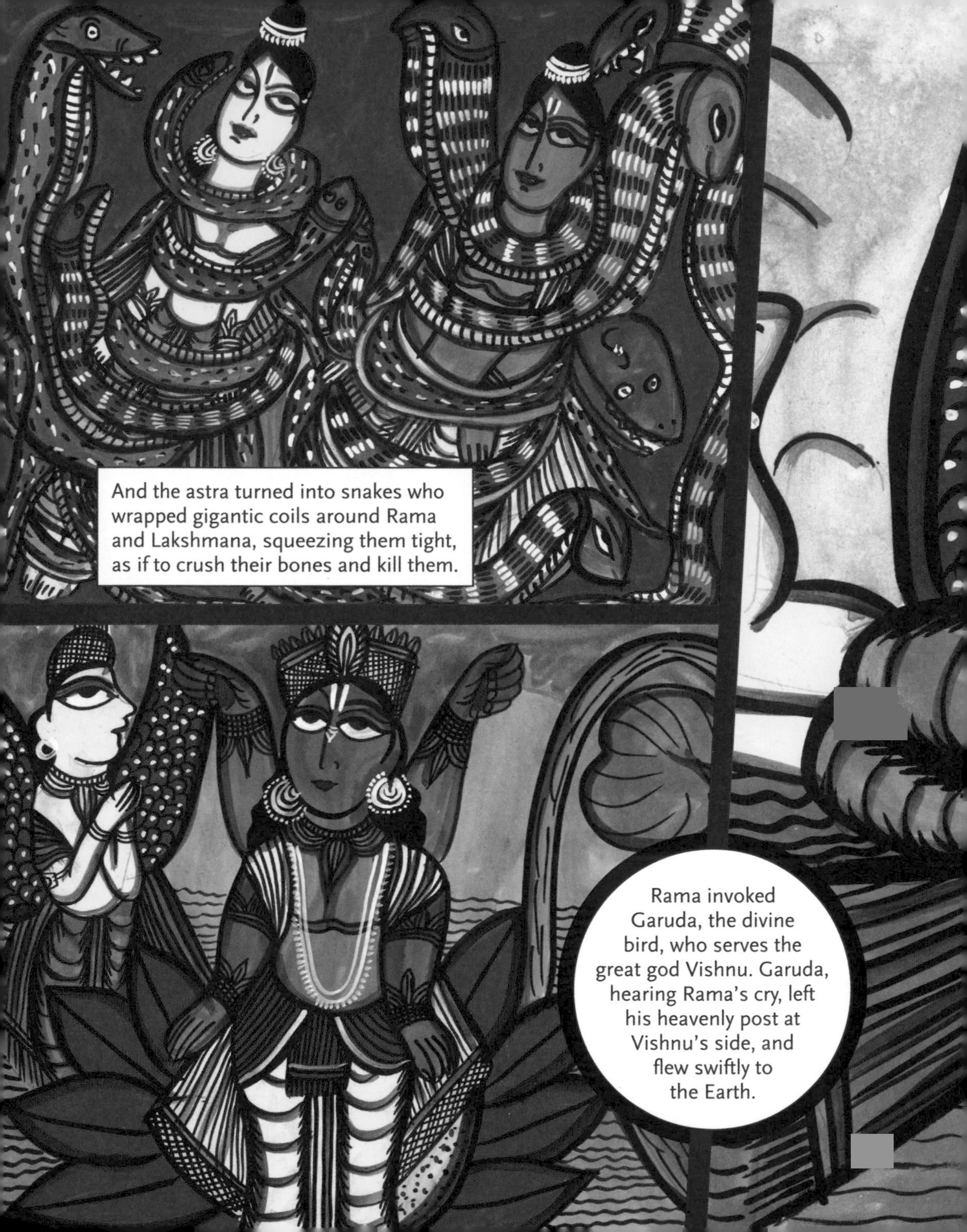
And the astra turned into snakes who wrapped gigantic coils around Rama and Lakshmana, squeezing them tight, as if to crush their bones and kill them.
Rama invoked Garuda, the divine bird, who serves the great god Vishnu. Garuda, hearing Rama's cry, left his heavenly post at Vishnu's side, and flew swiftly to the Earth.

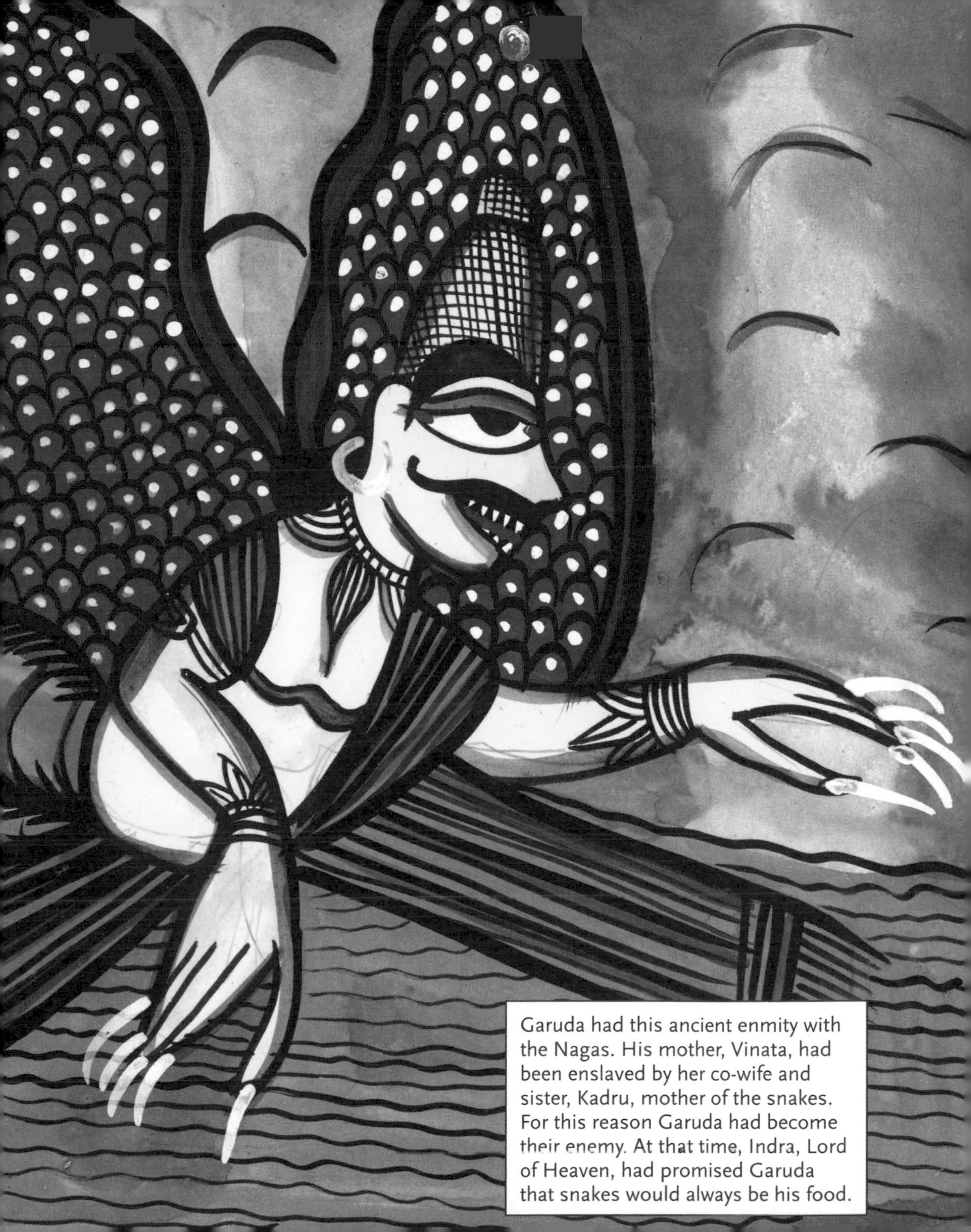

Garuda had this ancient enmity with the Nagas. His mother, Vinata, had been enslaved by her co-wife and sister, Kadru, mother of the snakes. For this reason Garuda had become their enemy. At that time, Indra, Lord of Heaven, had promised Garuda that snakes would always be his food.

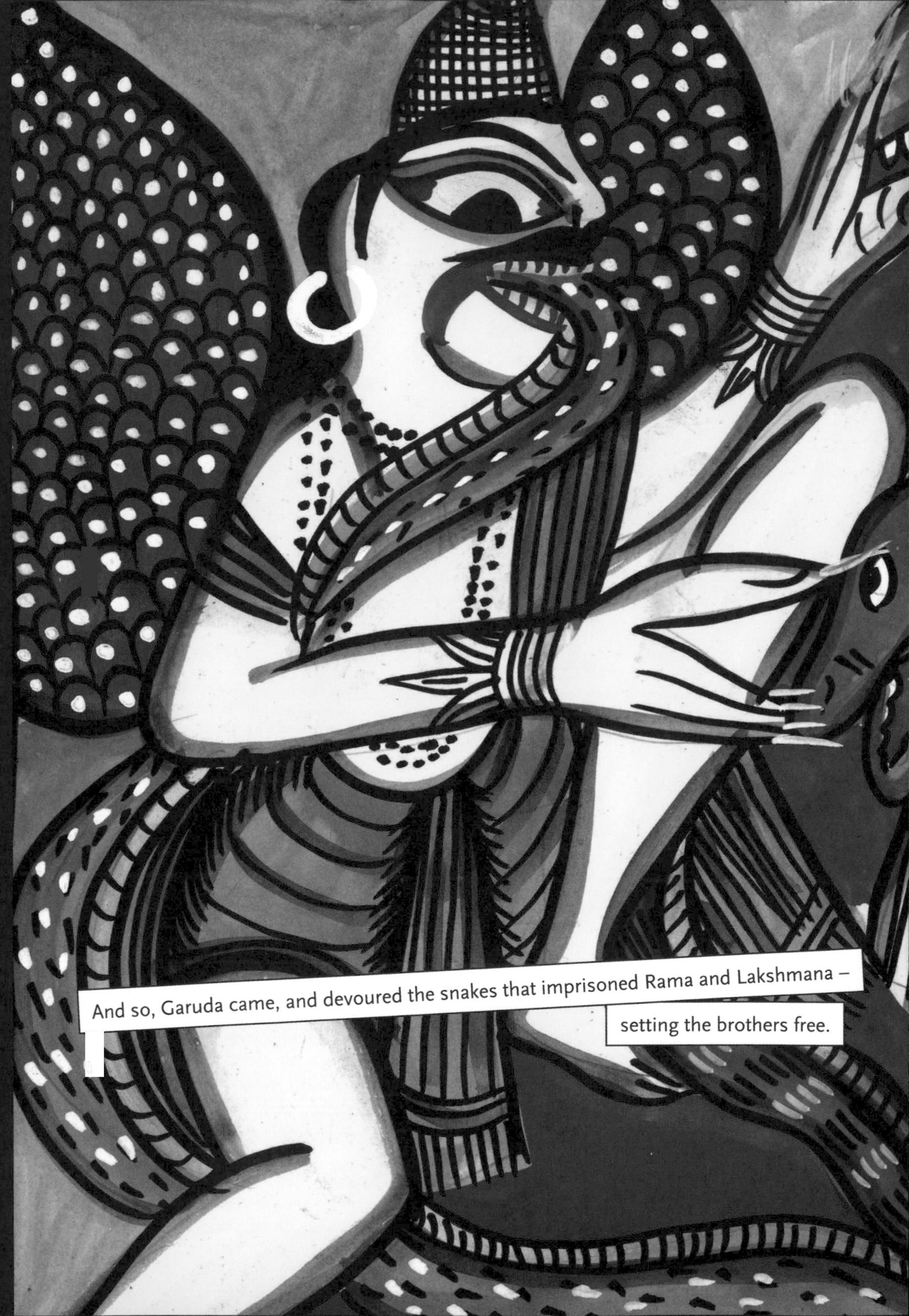
And so, Garuda came, and devoured the snakes that imprisoned Rama and Lakshmana –
setting the brothers free.

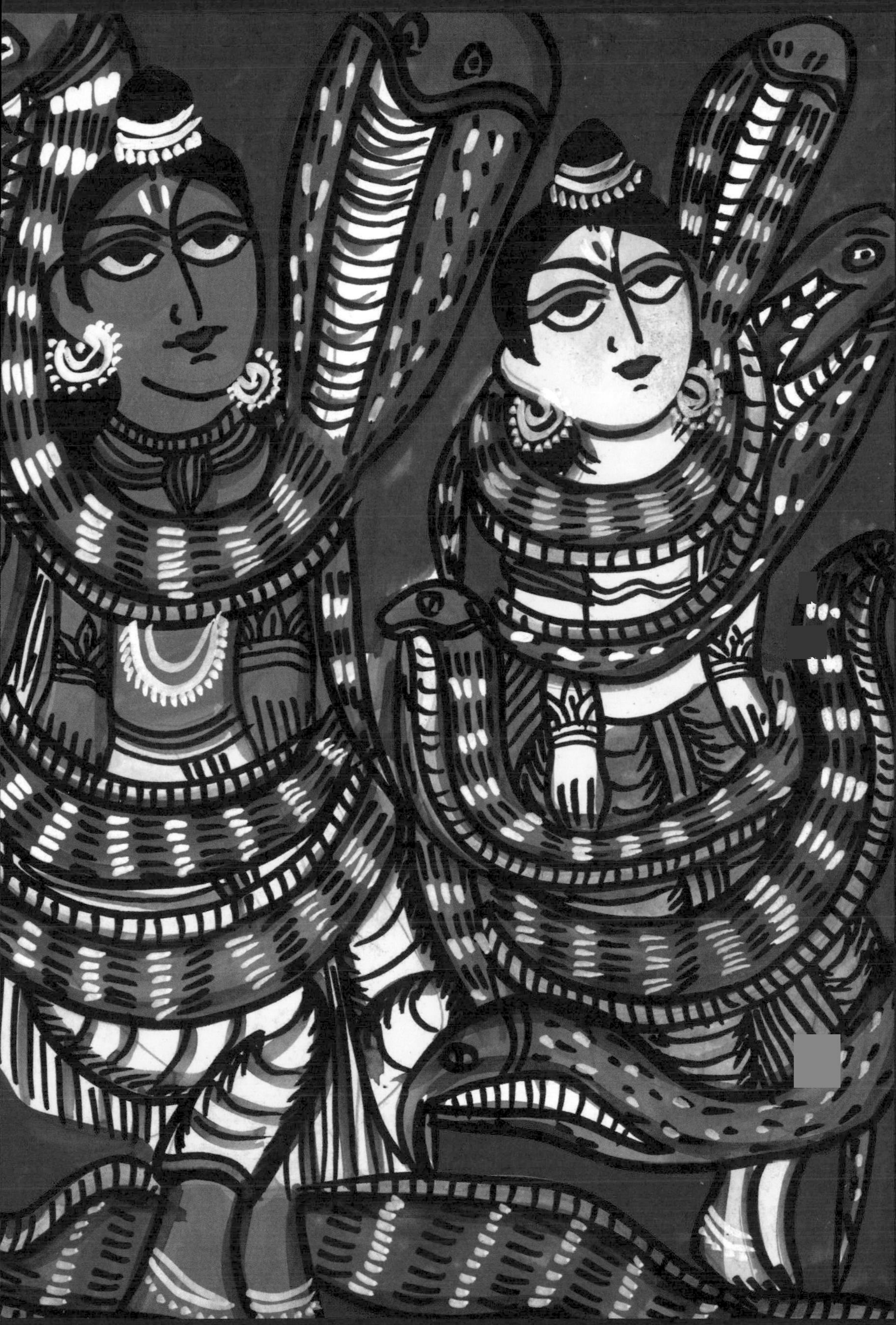

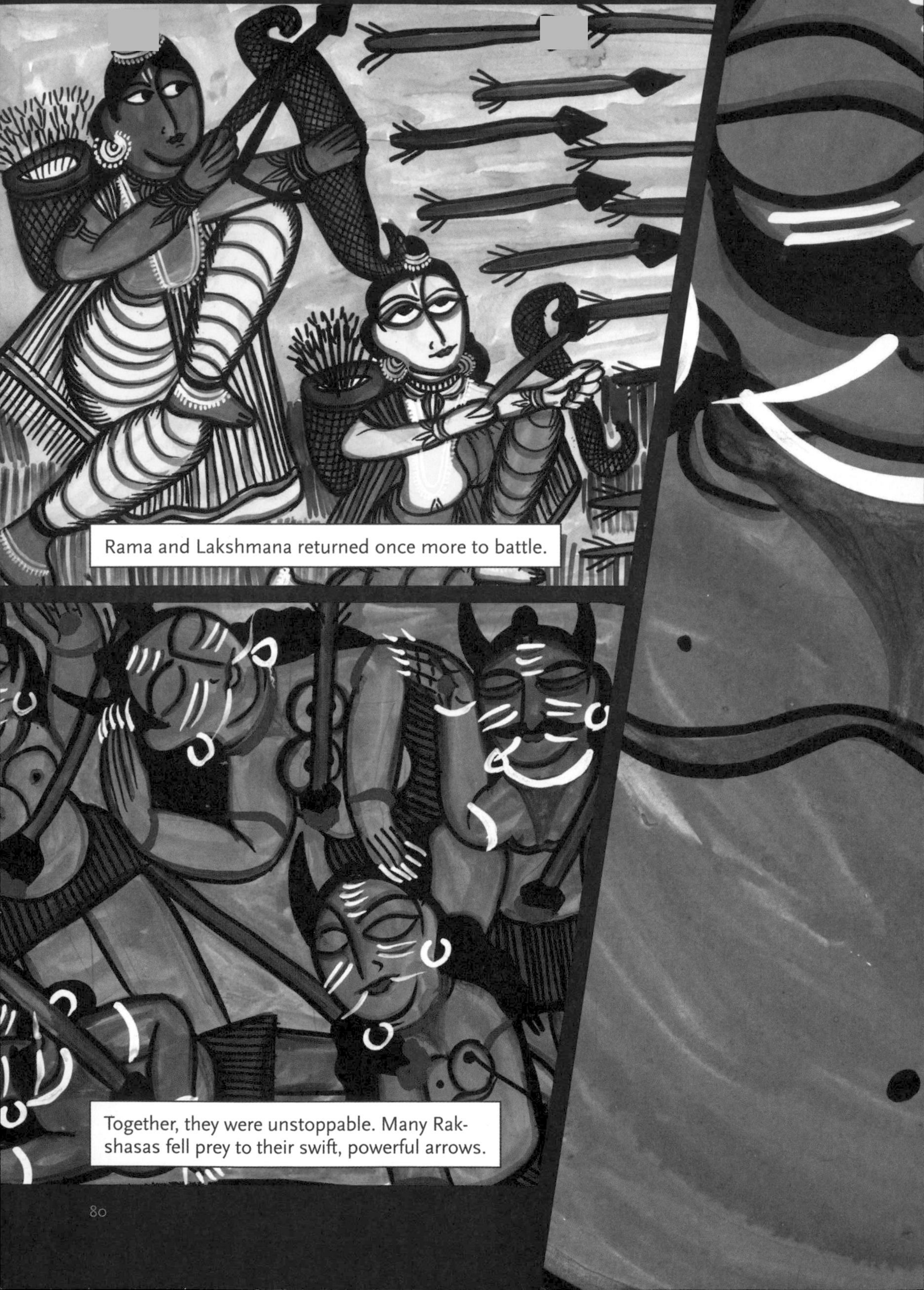
Rama and Lakshmana returned once more to battle.
Together, they were unstoppable. Many Rakshasas fell prey to their swift, powerful arrows.

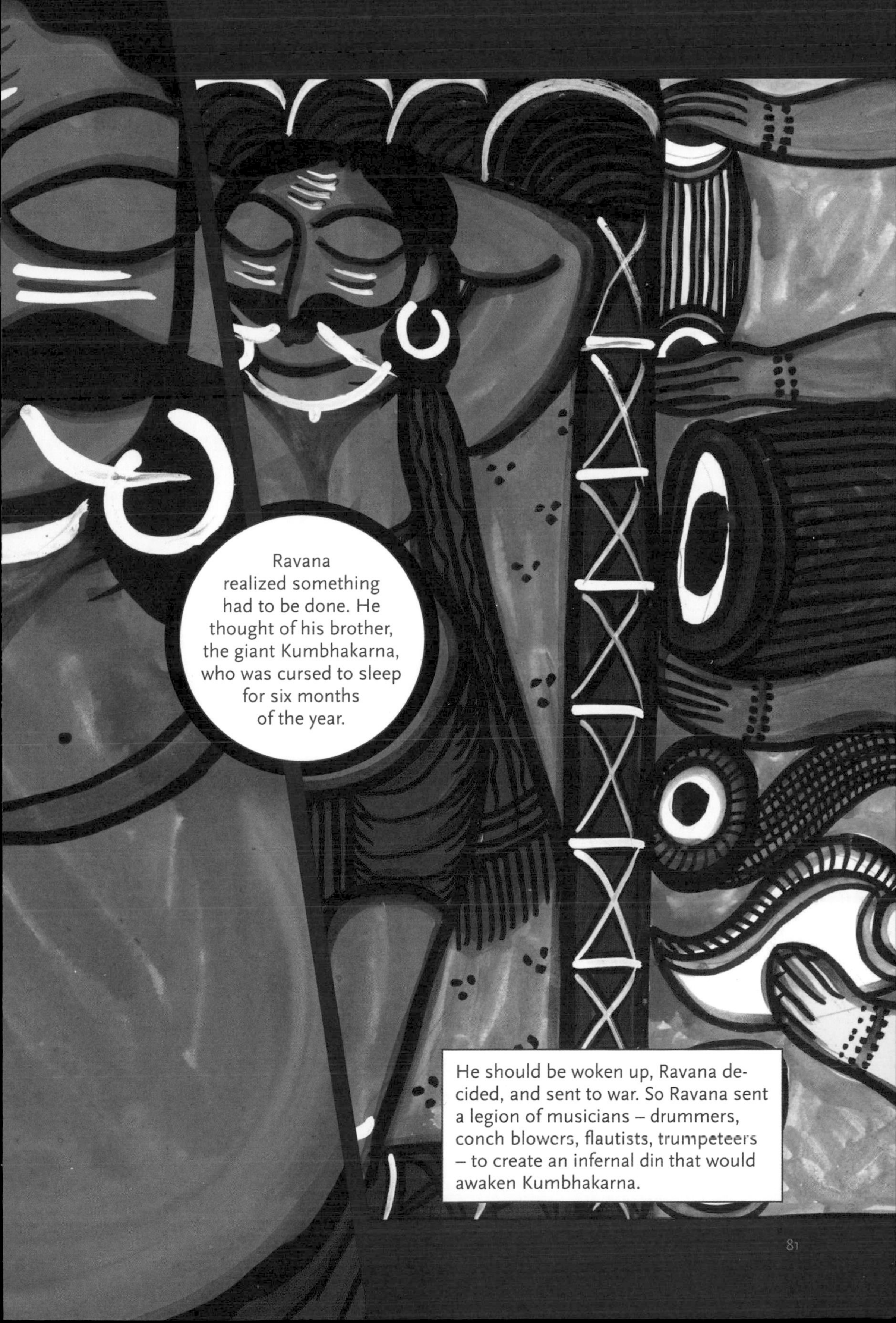
Ravana realized something had to be done. He thought of his brother, the giant Kumbhakarna, who was cursed to sleep for six months of the year.
He should be woken up, Ravana decided, and sent to war. So Ravana sent a legion of musicians – drummers, conch blowers, flautists, trumpeteers – to create an infernal din that would awaken Kumbhakarna.

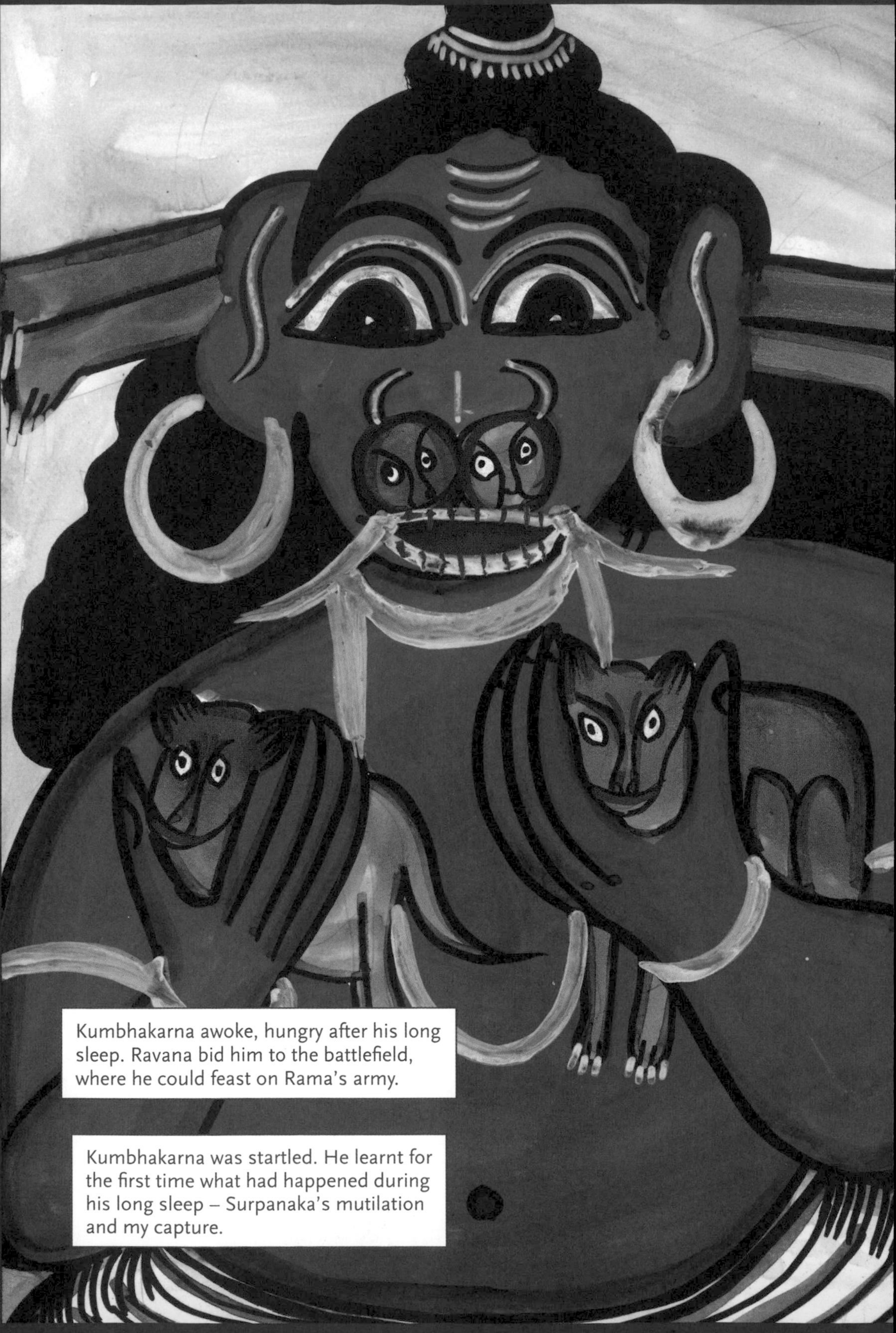
Kumbhakarna awoke, hungry after his long sleep. Ravana bid him to the battlefield, where he could feast on Rama's army.
Kumbhakarna was startled. He learnt for the first time what had happened during his long sleep – Surpanaka's mutilation and my capture.

BUT HE FELT THAT RAVANA WAS IN THE WRONG.

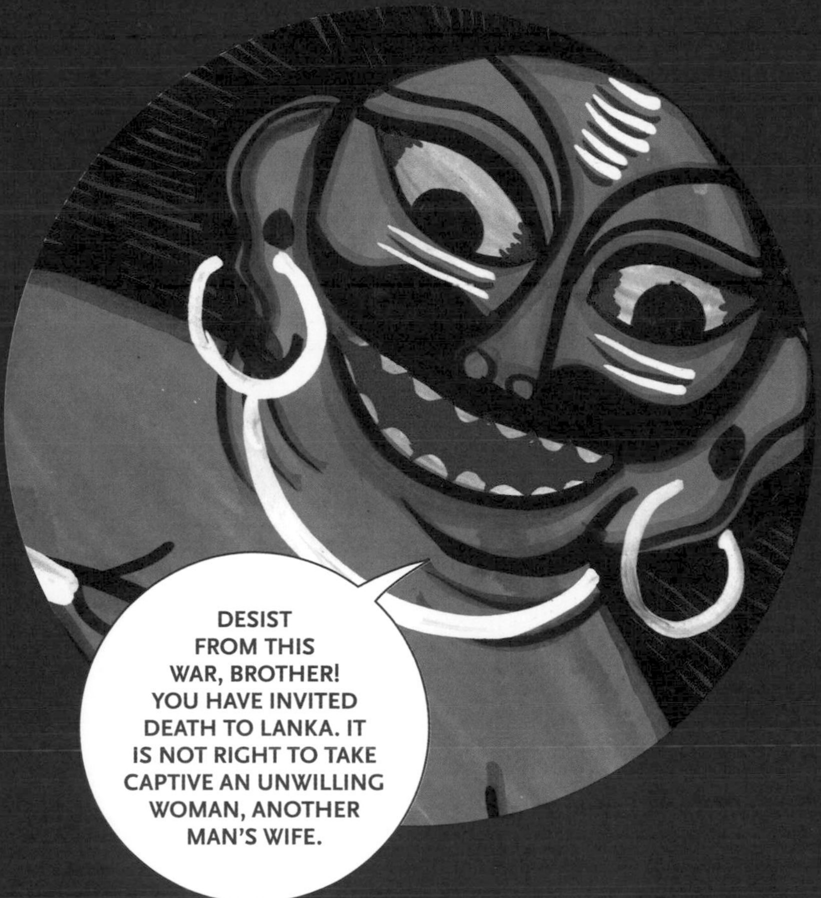
DESIST FROM THIS WAR, BROTHER! YOU HAVE INVITED DEATH TO LANKA. IT IS NOT RIGHT TO TAKE CAPTIVE AN UNWILLING WOMAN, ANOTHER MAN'S WIFE.

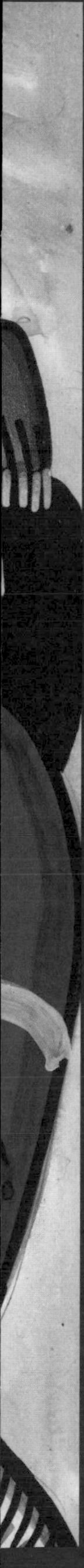

But Ravana would not listen to his brother. Sorrowing, Kumbhakarna prepared for battle. Even though the end of the day might bring death and defeat, he could not abandon his elder brother.

And so he entered the battle, devouring every Vanara that came within the reach of his long arms. Many died that day.

SOMETHING HAD TO BE DONE TO STOP KUMBHAKARNA. NUMEROUS VANARA SOLDIERS TRIED TO CONFRONT HIM, BUT WERE CRUSHED TO DEATH.

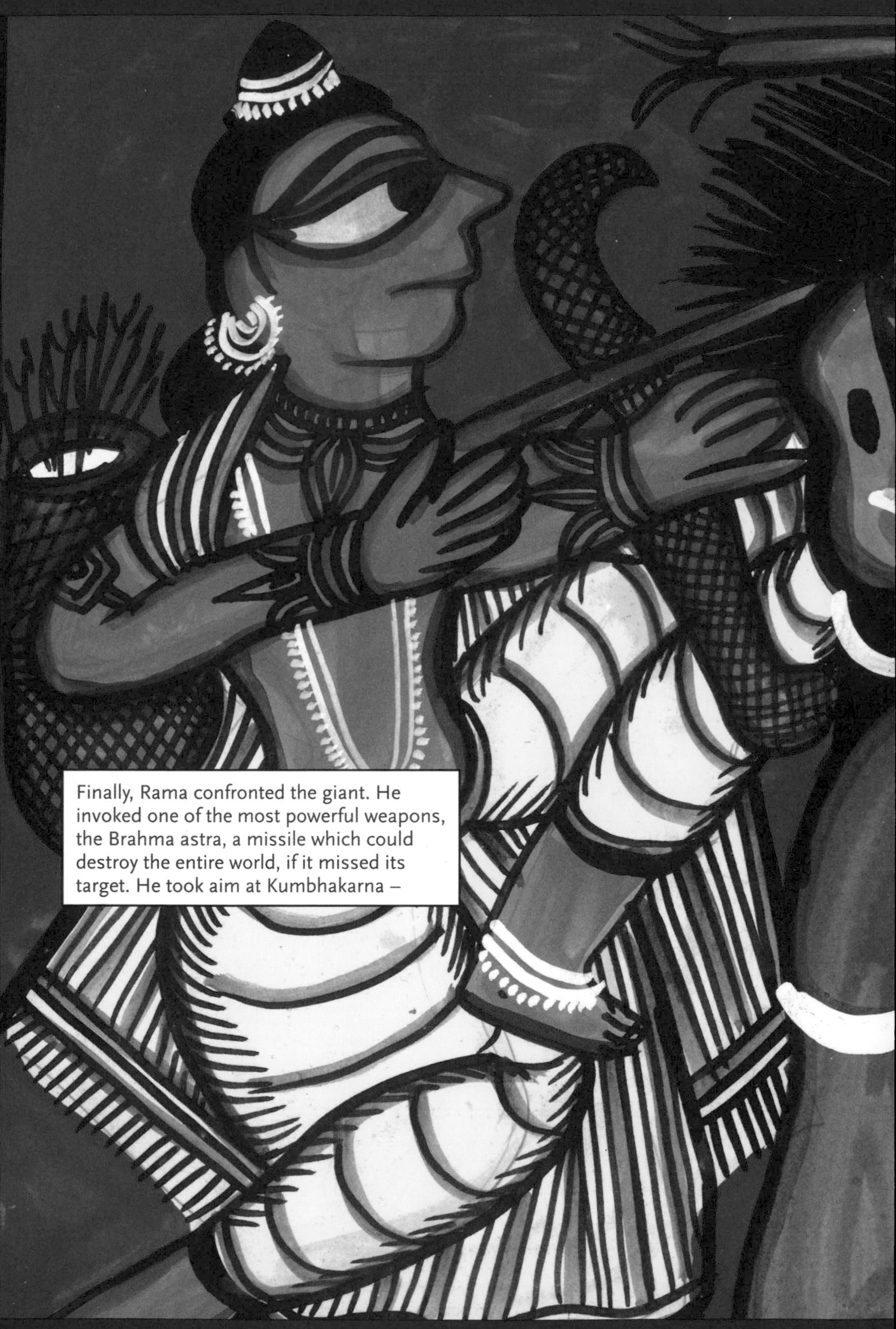
Finally, Rama confronted the giant. He invoked one of the most powerful weapons, the Brahma astra, a missile which could destroy the entire world, if it missed its target. He took aim at Kumbhakarna –

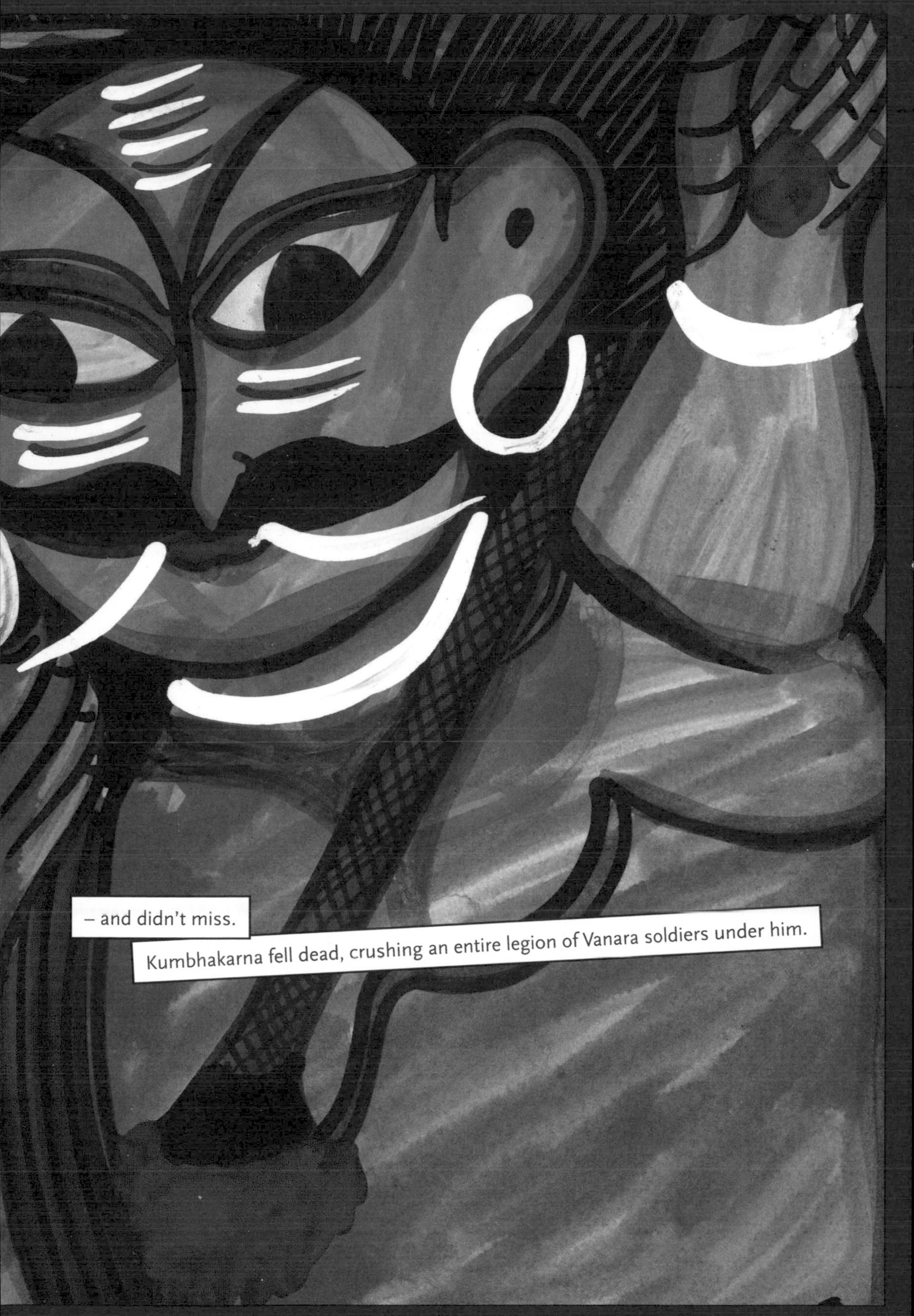
– and didn't miss.
Kumbhakarna fell dead, crushing an entire legion of Vanara soldiers under him.

THE CRIES OF THE WOMEN OF LANKA LAMENTING KUMBHAKARNA'S FALL FILLED MY EARS. EVEN THOUGH HE FOUGHT ON THE SIDE OF MY ENEMY, I COULD NOT HELP BUT FEEL HIS DEATH WAS TRAGIC. FOR HE HAD ADVISED RAVANA WISELY, AND GONE, KNOWINGLY, TO MEET HIS DEATH.

Ravana wept. He vowed to kill Rama and Lakshmana, determined to avenge the death of his brother. He beckoned the powerful sorcerer, Mahiravana to come to him.

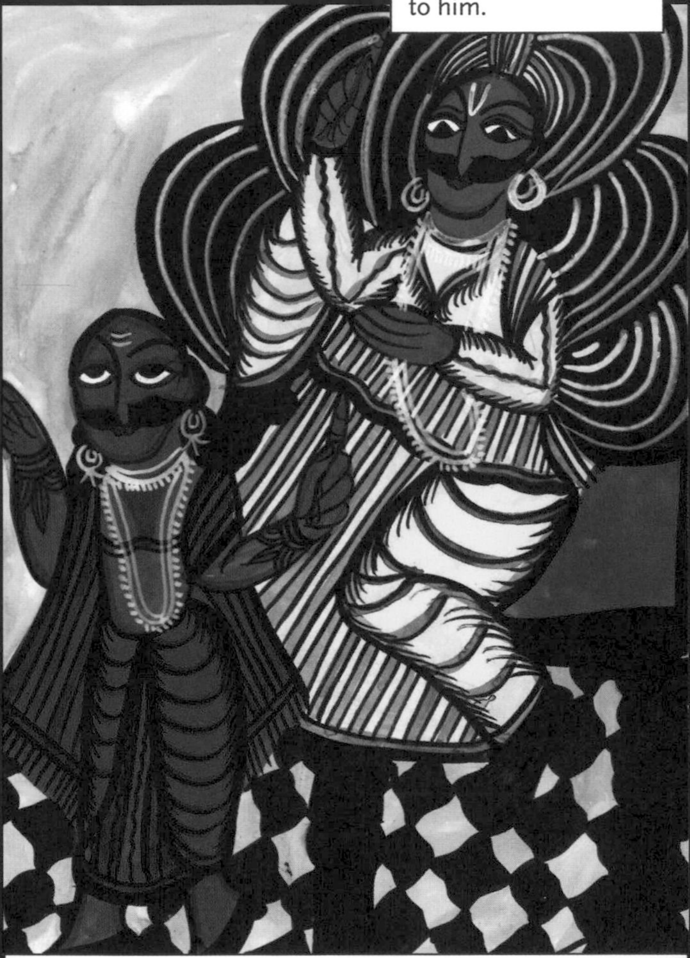

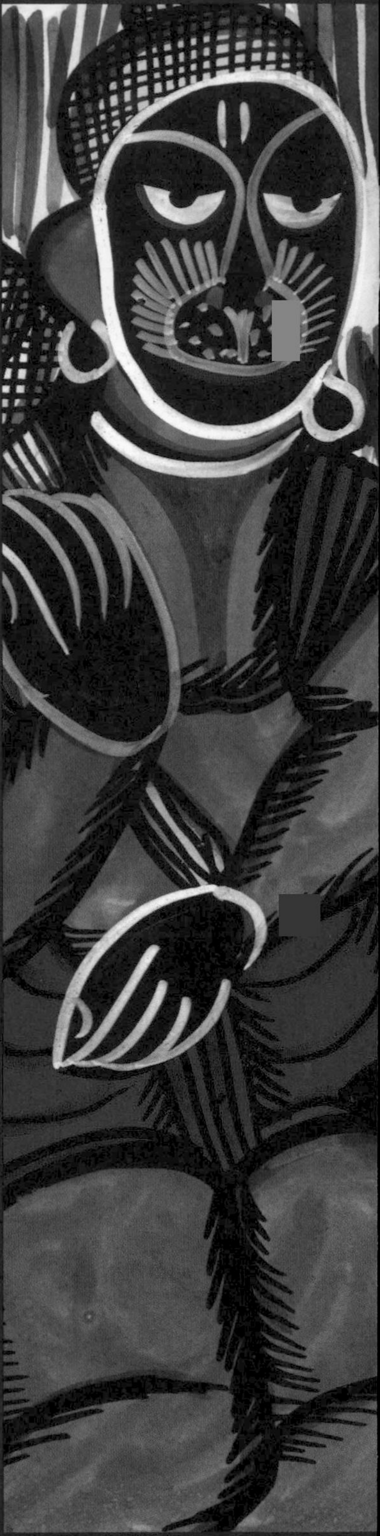

The sorcerer's magic, Ravana was sure, would kill Rama and Lakshmana. Mahiravana agreed to work his magic and announced that he would spirit Rama and Lakshmana away to the nether-world and sacrifice them to the goddess Chandi Devi. Her grace had made him strong, and this sacrifice would render him invincible.

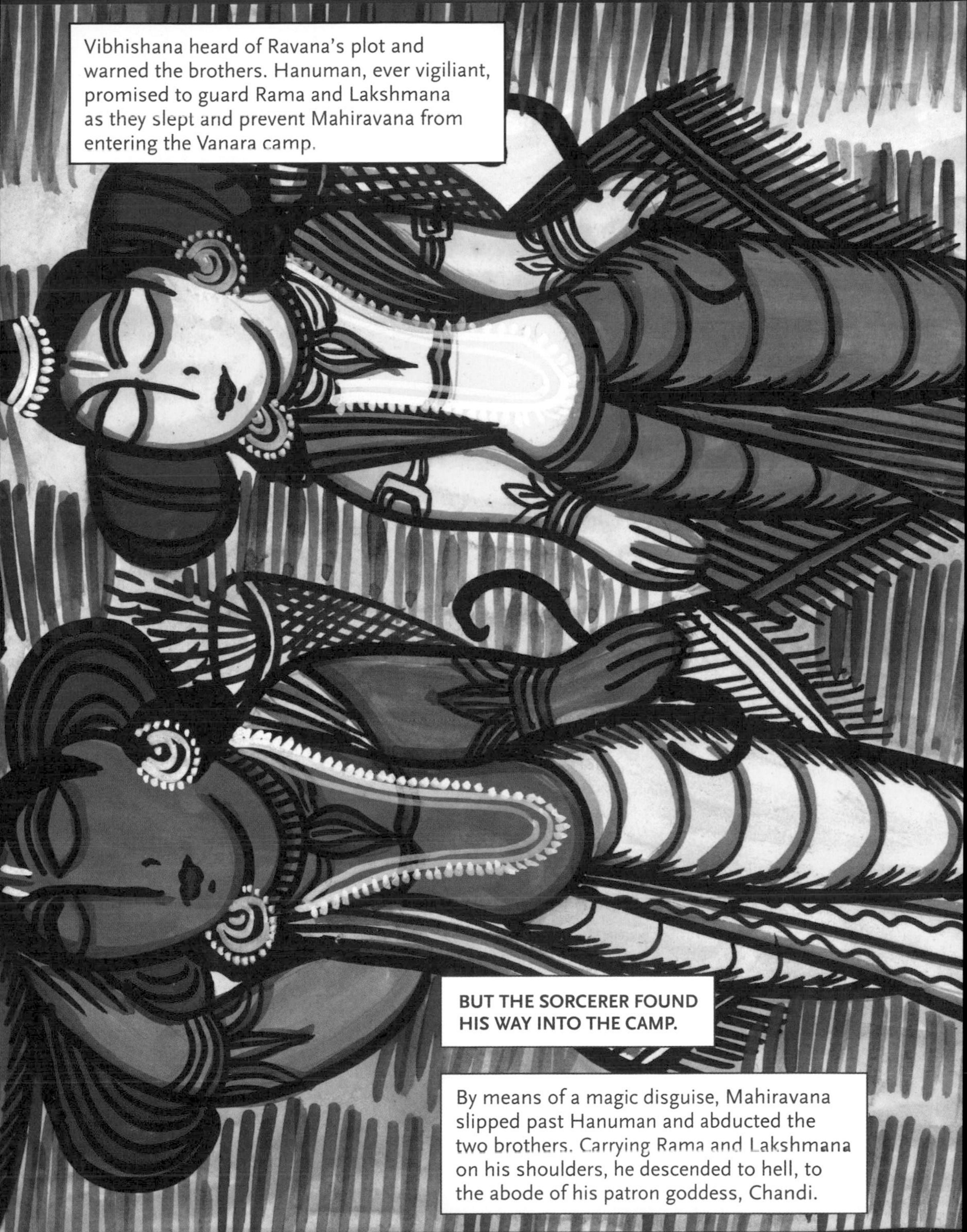
Vibhishana heard of Ravana's plot and warned the brothers. Hanuman, ever vigiliant, promised to guard Rama and Lakshmana as they slept and prevent Mahiravana from entering the Vanara camp.
BUT THE SORCERER FOUND HIS WAY INTO THE CAMP.
By means of a magic disguise, Mahiravana slipped past Hanuman and abducted the two brothers. Carrying Rama and Lakshmana on his shoulders, he descended to hell, to the abode of his patron goddess, Chandi.

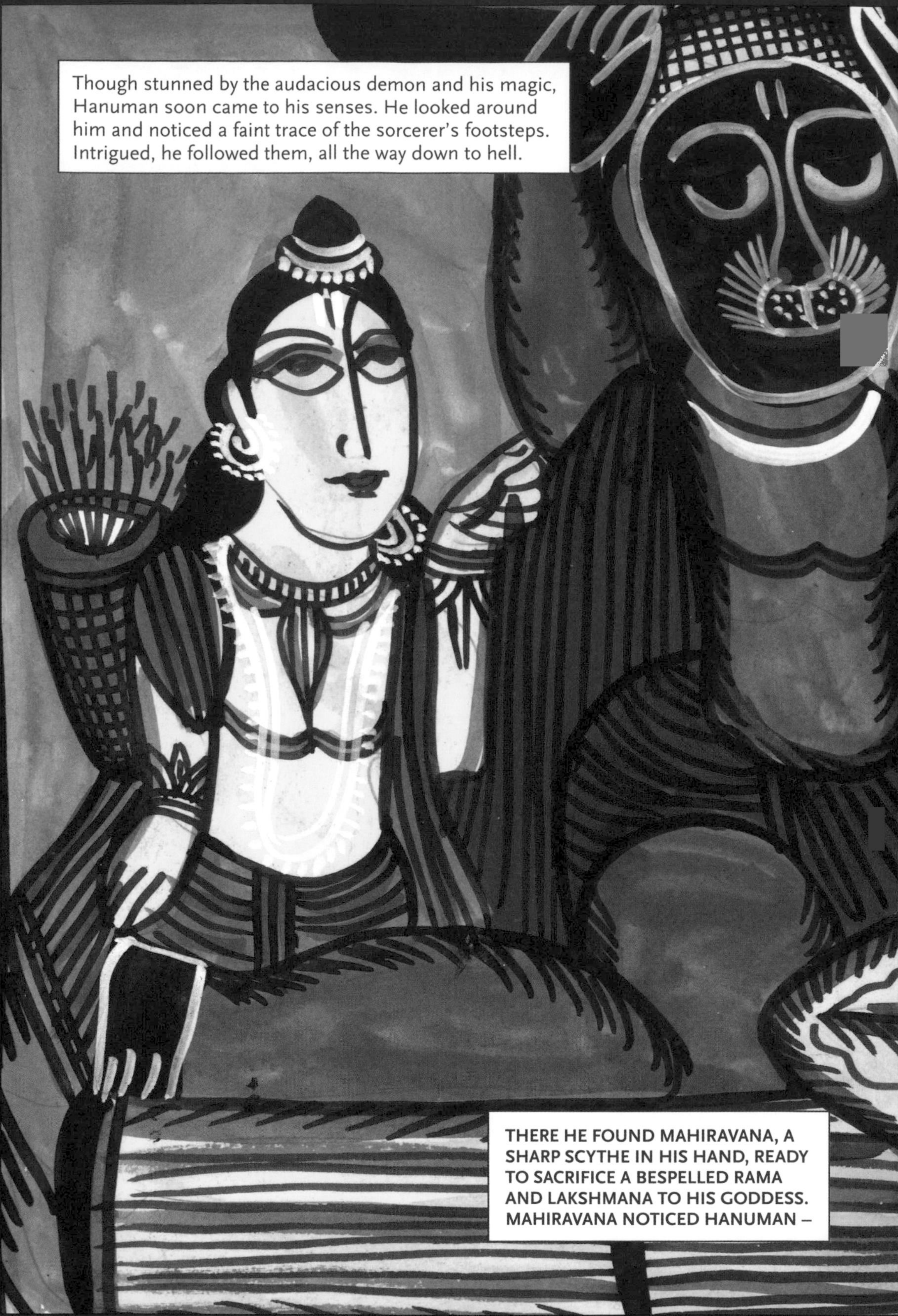
Though stunned by the audacious demon and his magic, Hanuman soon came to his senses. He looked around him and noticed a faint trace of the sorcerer's footsteps. Intrigued, he followed them, all the way down to hell.
THERE HE FOUND MAHIRAVANA, A SHARP SCYTHE IN HIS HAND, READY TO SACRIFICE A BESPELLED RAMA AND LAKSHMANA TO HIS GODDESS. MAHIRAVANA NOTICED HANUMAN –

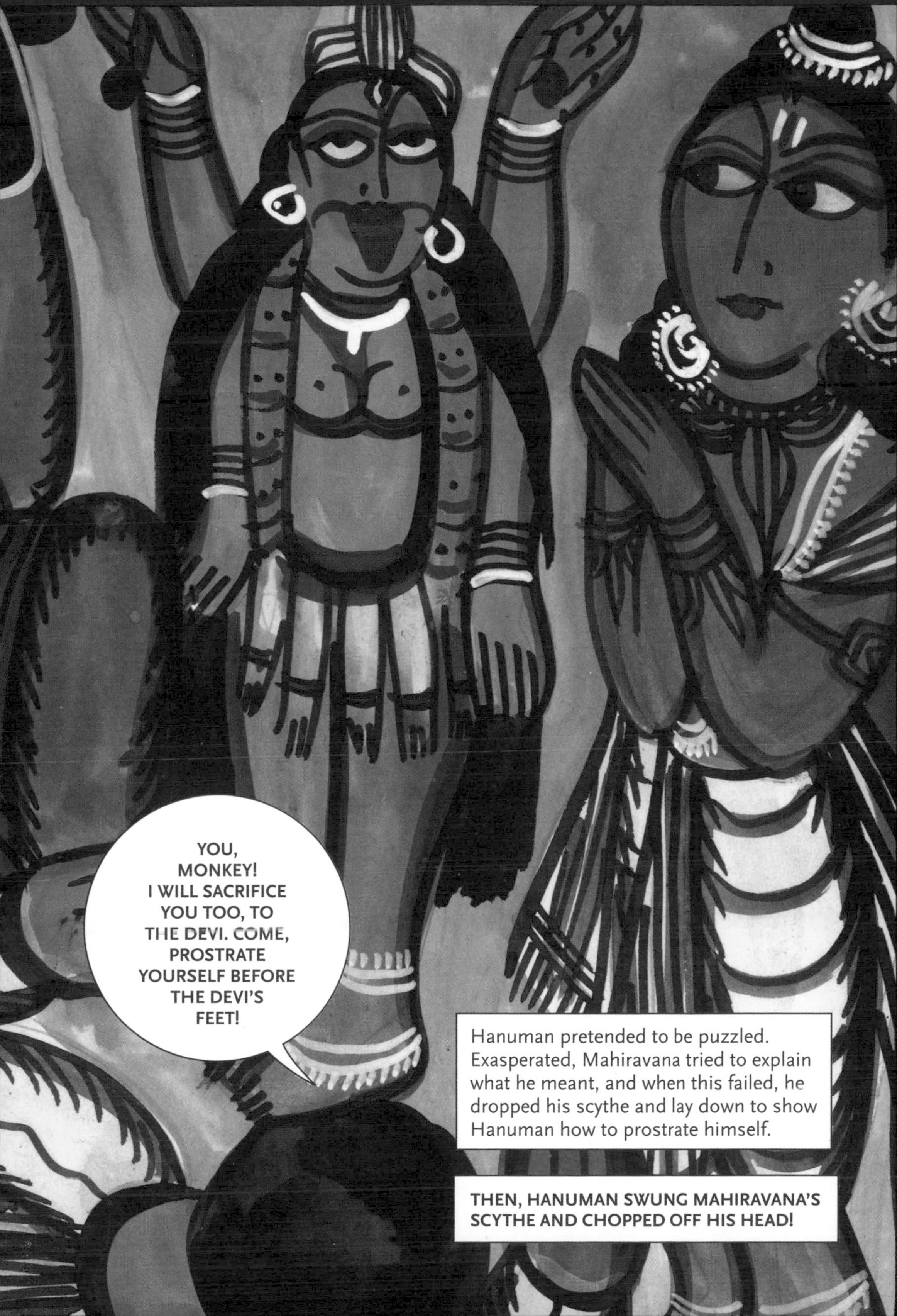
YOU, MONKEY! I WILL SACRIFICE YOU TOO, TO THE DEVI. COME, PROSTRATE YOURSELF BEFORE THE DEVI'S FEET!
Hanuman pretended to be puzzled. Exasperated, Mahiravana tried to explain what he meant, and when this failed, he dropped his scythe and lay down to show Hanuman how to prostrate himself.
THEN, HANUMAN SWUNG MAHIRAVANA'S SCYTHE AND CHOPPED OFF HIS HEAD!

AND RAMA A
LAKSHMANA RETURNED ONCE MORE TO BATTLE.

DETERMINED TO DEFEAT RAMA AND AVENGE THE DEATHS OF ALL THE LANKANS WHO HAD DIED, INDRAJIT HAD DECIDED TO PERFORM A YAGNA, A SACRIFICE TO ENHANCE HIS MAGICAL POWERS.

VIBHISHANA, HEARING OF THE YAGNA, WARNED RAMA –

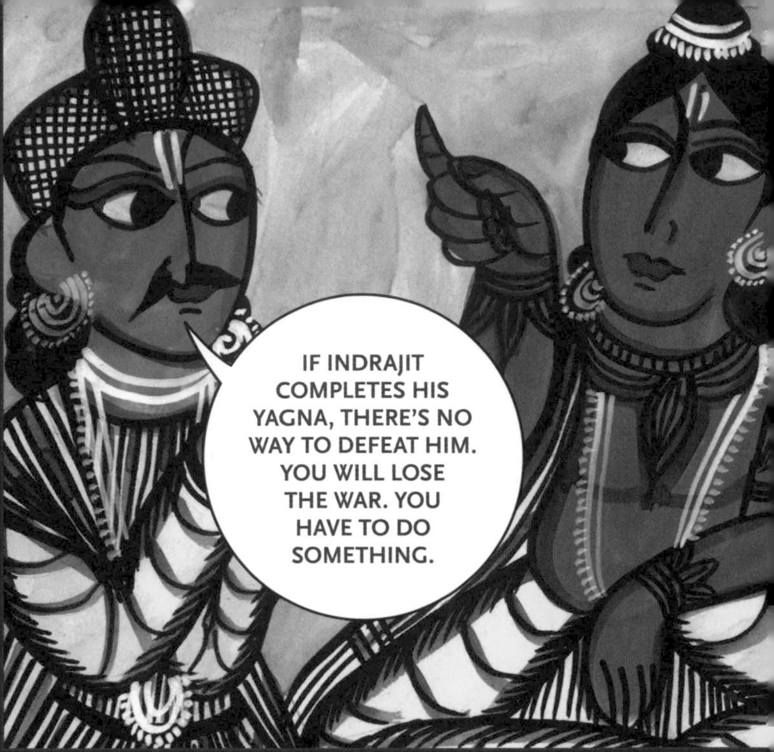
IF INDRAJIT COMPLETES HIS YAGNA, THERE'S NO WAY TO DEFEAT HIM. YOU WILL LOSE THE WAR. YOU HAVE TO DO SOMETHING.

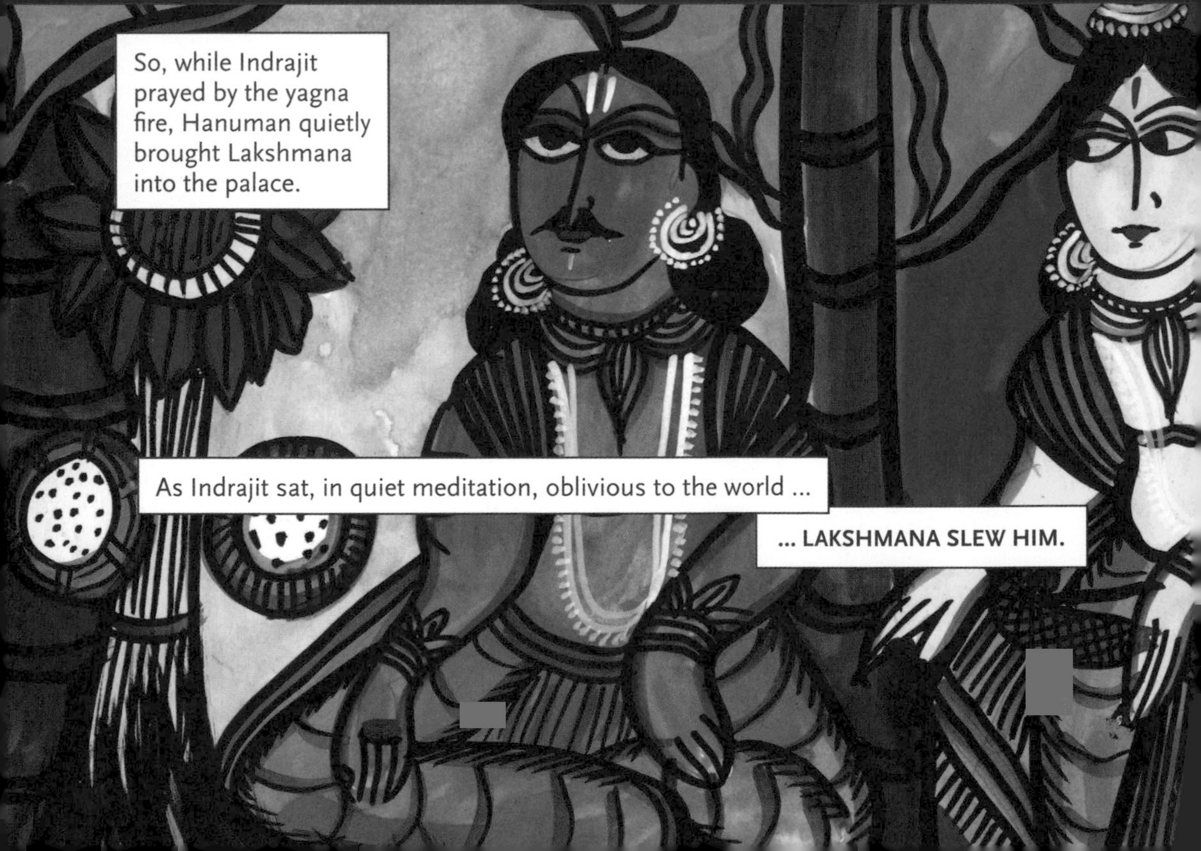
So, while Indrajit prayed by the yagna fire, Hanuman quietly brought Lakshmana into the palace.
As Indrajit sat, in quiet meditation, oblivious to the world ...
... LAKSHMANA SLEW HIM.

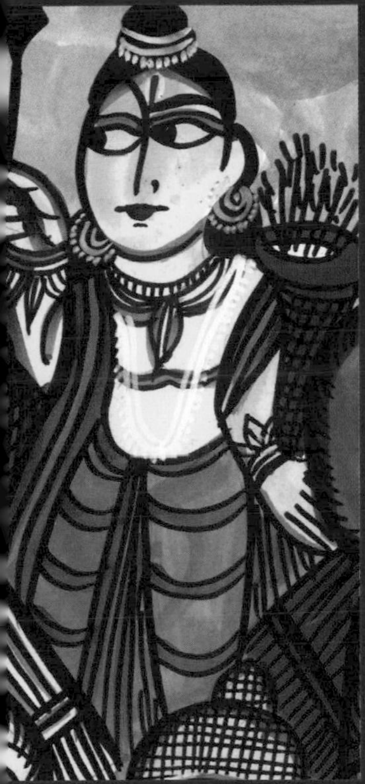

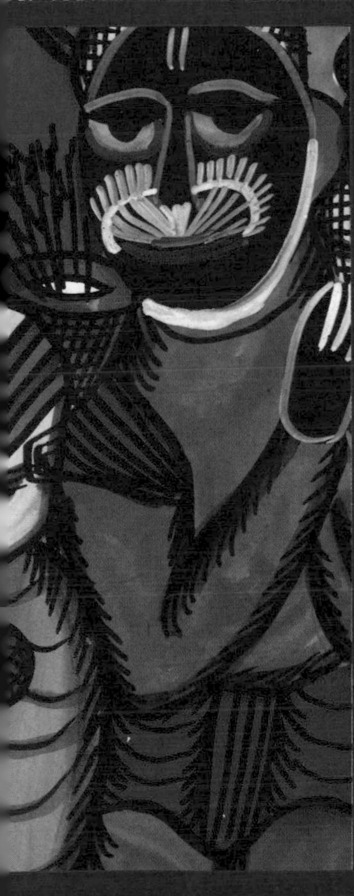

A grieving Trijatha gave me this news.

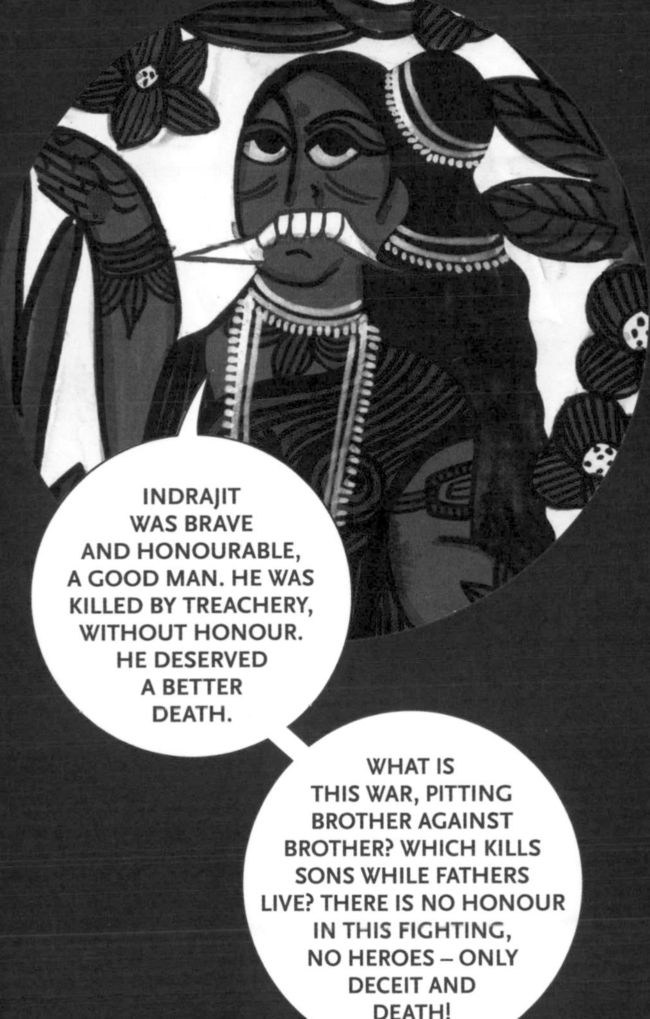
INDRAJIT WAS BRAVE AND HONOURABLE, A GOOD MAN. HE WAS KILLED BY TREACHERY, WITHOUT HONOUR. HE DESERVED A BETTER DEATH.
WHAT IS THIS WAR, PITTING BROTHER AGAINST BROTHER? WHICH KILLS SONS WHILE FATHERS LIVE? THERE IS NO HONOUR IN THIS FIGHTING, NO HEROES – ONLY DECEIT AND DEATH!

I felt Trijatha's anguish. So much death, so much destruction. But I could not grieve – for injustice breeds injustice, and this war was the inevitable result of Ravana's unlawful desire and my unjust imprisonment.

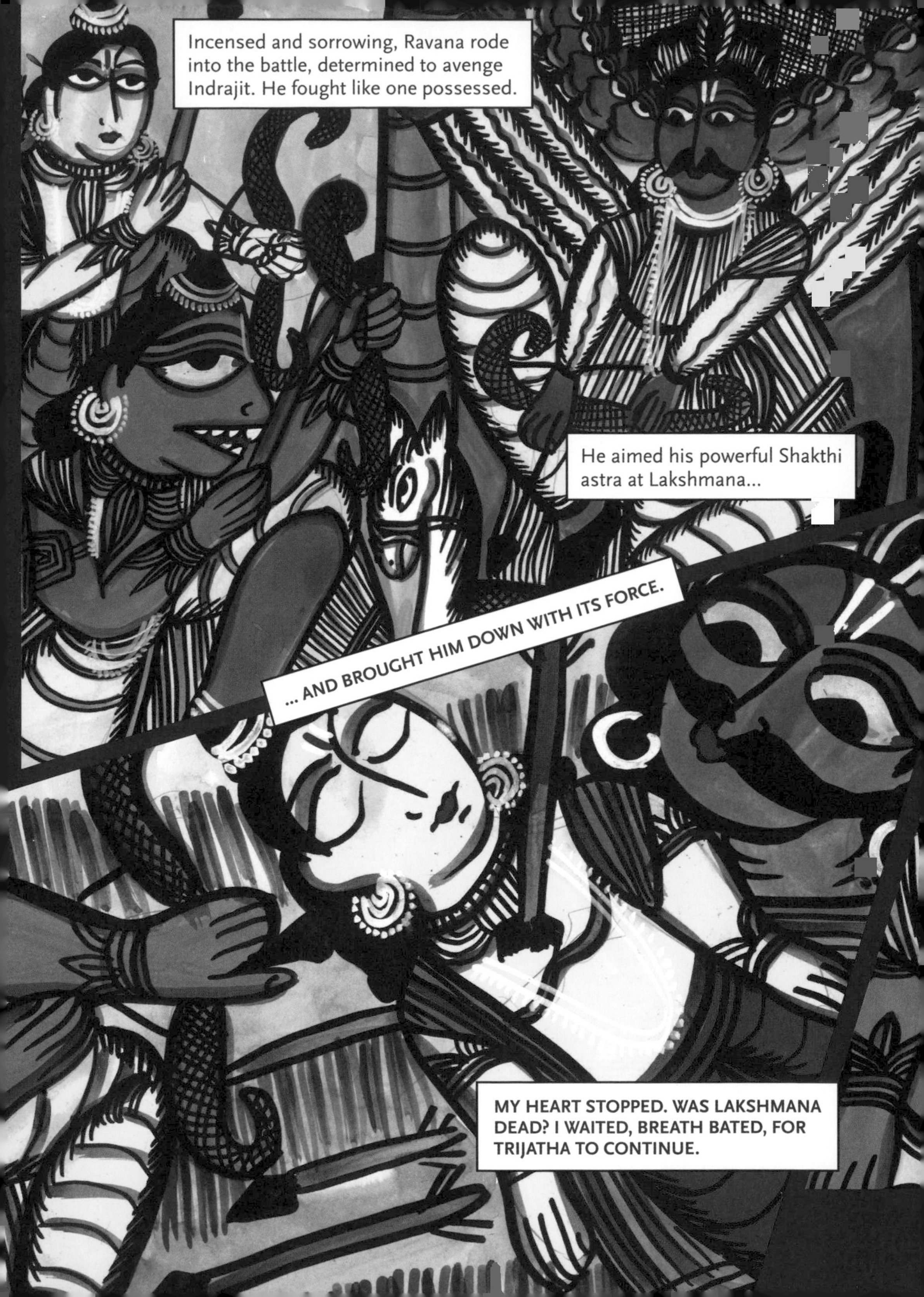
Incensed and sorrowing, Ravana rode into the battle, determined to avenge Indrajit. He fought like one possessed.
He aimed his powerful Shakthi astra at Lakshmana...
... AND BROUGHT HIM DOWN WITH ITS FORCE.
MY HEART STOPPED. WAS LAKSHMANA DEAD? I WAITED, BREATH BATED, FOR TRIJATHA TO CONTINUE.

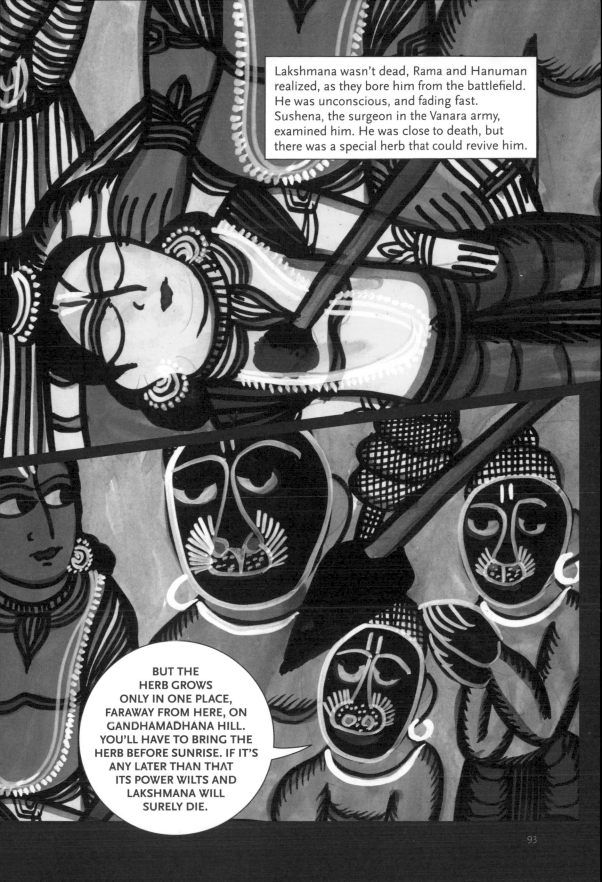

Lakshmana wasn't dead, Rama and Hanuman realized, as they bore him from the battlefield. He was unconscious, and fading fast. Sushena, the surgeon in the Vanara army, examined him. He was close to death, but there was a special herb that could revive him.

BUT THE HERB GROWS ONLY IN ONE PLACE, FARAWAY FROM HERE, ON GANDHAMADHANA HILL. YOU'LL HAVE TO BRING THE HERB BEFORE SUNRISE. IF IT'S ANY LATER THAN THAT ITS POWER WILTS AND LAKSHMANA WILL SURELY DIE.

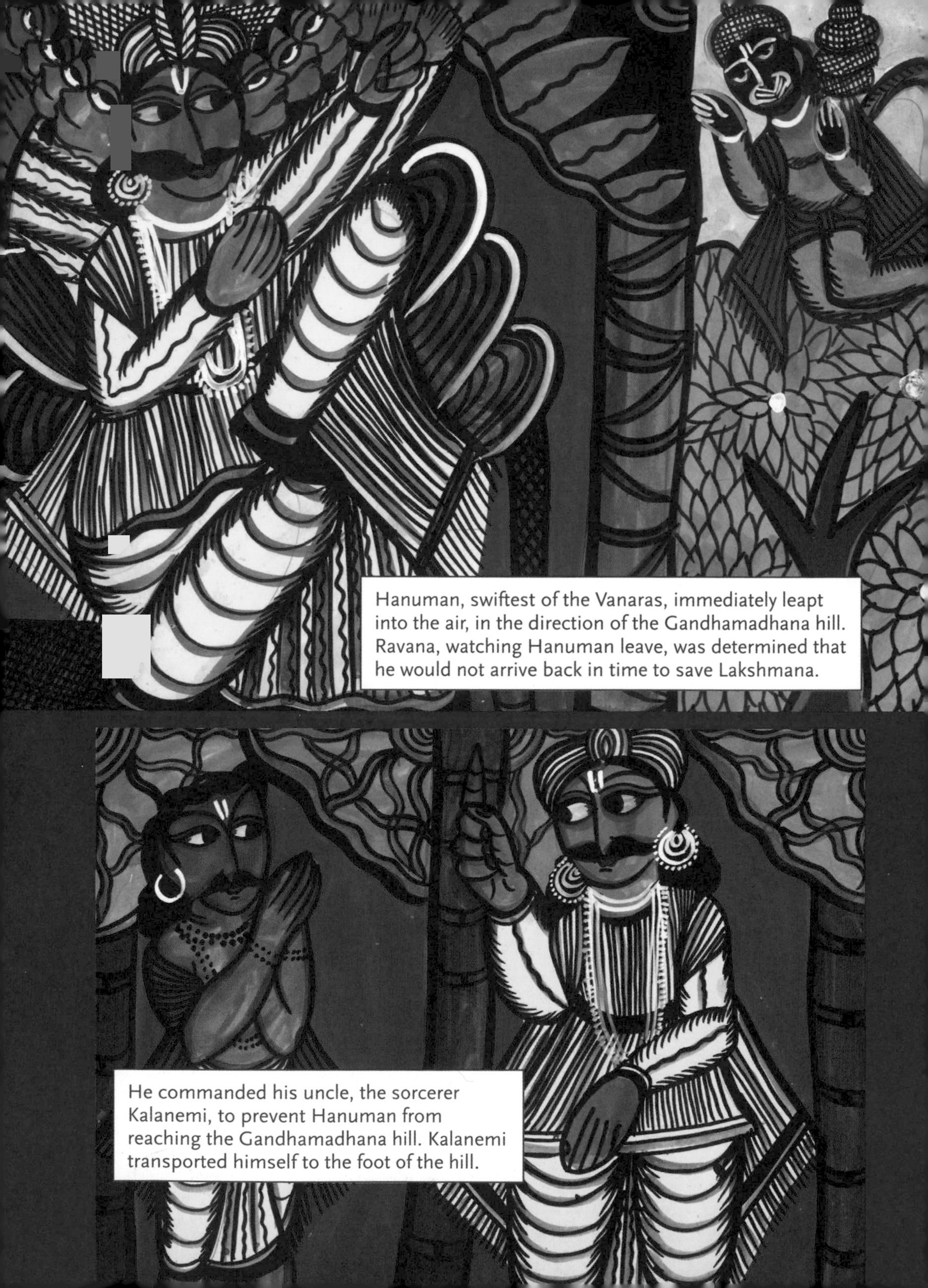
Hanuman, swiftest of the Vanaras, immediately leapt into the air, in the direction of the Gandhamadhana hill. Ravana, watching Hanuman leave, was determined that he would not arrive back in time to save Lakshmana.
He commanded his uncle, the sorcerer Kalanemi, to prevent Hanuman from reaching the Gandhamadhana hill. Kalanemi transported himself to the foot of the hill.

There, he changed form, became a beautiful ascetic youth and waited for Hanuman to pass his way. By his feet he placed an urn full of poisoned water. Kalanemi was counting on the fact that after traveling many hot, dusty miles, Hanuman would be weary and want to quench his thirst. Soon, Hanuman passed by. The ascetic hailed him –

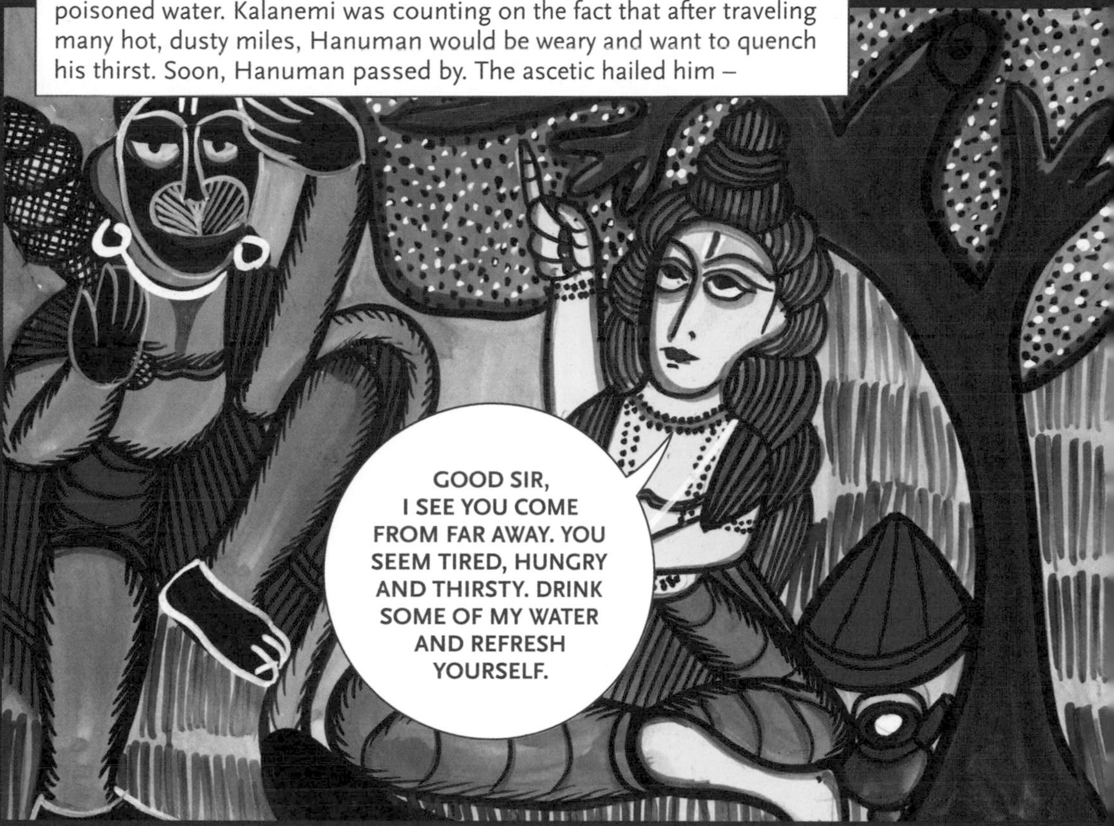
GOOD SIR, I SEE YOU COME FROM FAR AWAY. YOU SEEM TIRED, HUNGRY AND THIRSTY. DRINK SOME OF MY WATER AND REFRESH YOURSELF.

Hanuman drank all the water and wanted more. Kalanemi was amazed. The water had poison in it, and yet it seemed to have no effect on Hanuman. Quickly, he thought of another plan. He told Hanuman –

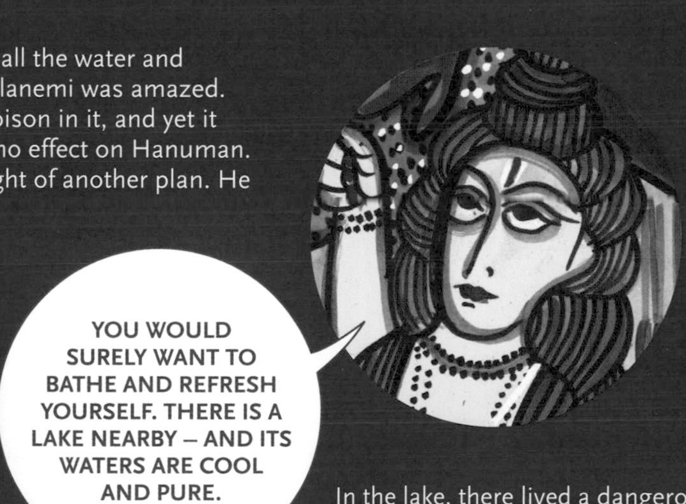
YOU WOULD SURELY WANT TO BATHE AND REFRESH YOURSELF. THERE IS A LAKE NEARBY – AND ITS WATERS ARE COOL AND PURE.

In the lake, there lived a dangerous crocodile. It preyed on all the beasts which came to drink from the lake. If Hanuman went there, the crocodile was sure to devour him.

As Hanuman entered the waters, the crocodile swam close, and pulled him under water. Hanuman gave the crocodile a powerful kick and, immediately, the beast transformed into a beautiful apsara! She told him that she had been under a curse that forced her to remain in the form of a crocodile, and thanked Hanuman for freeing her.

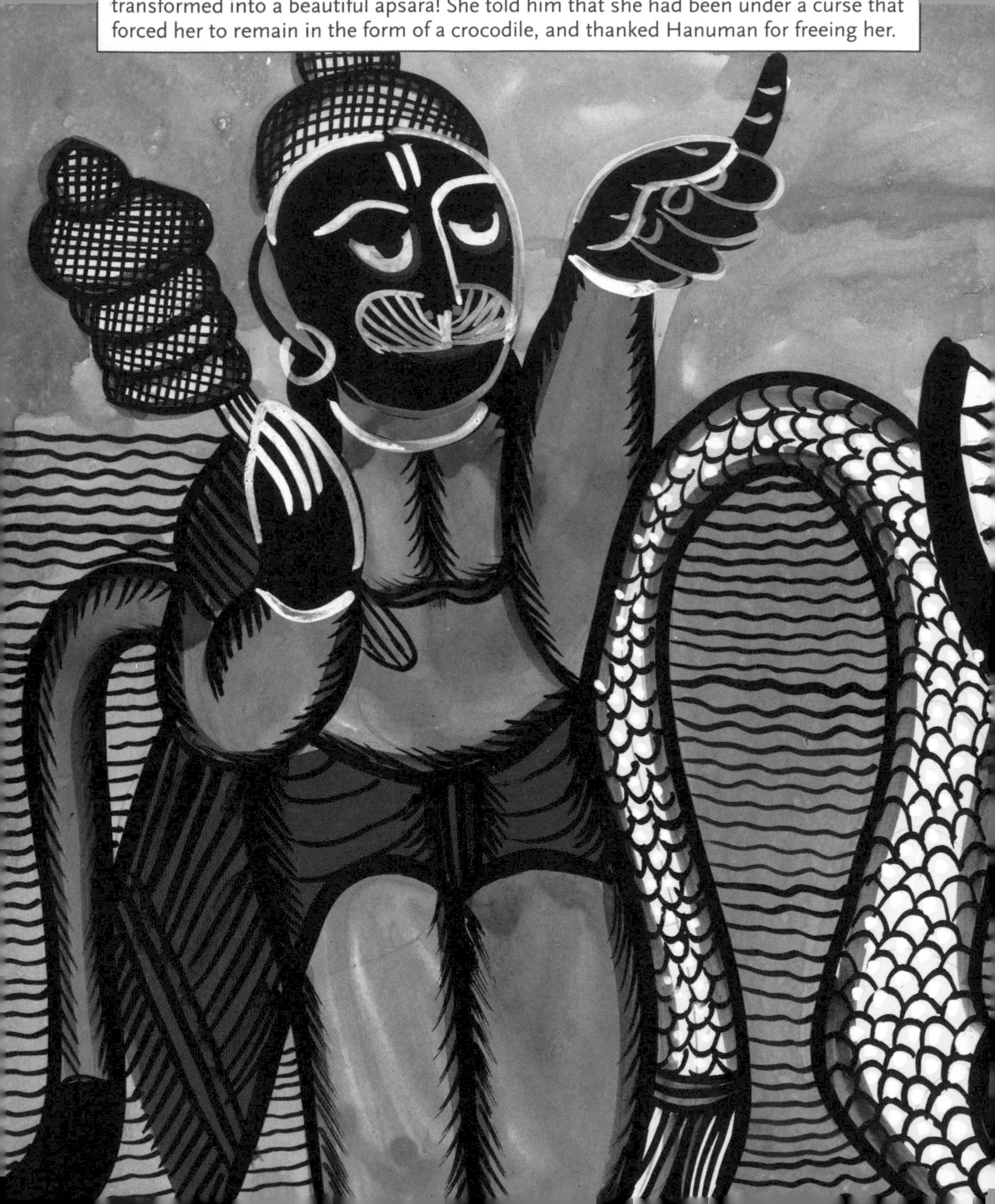

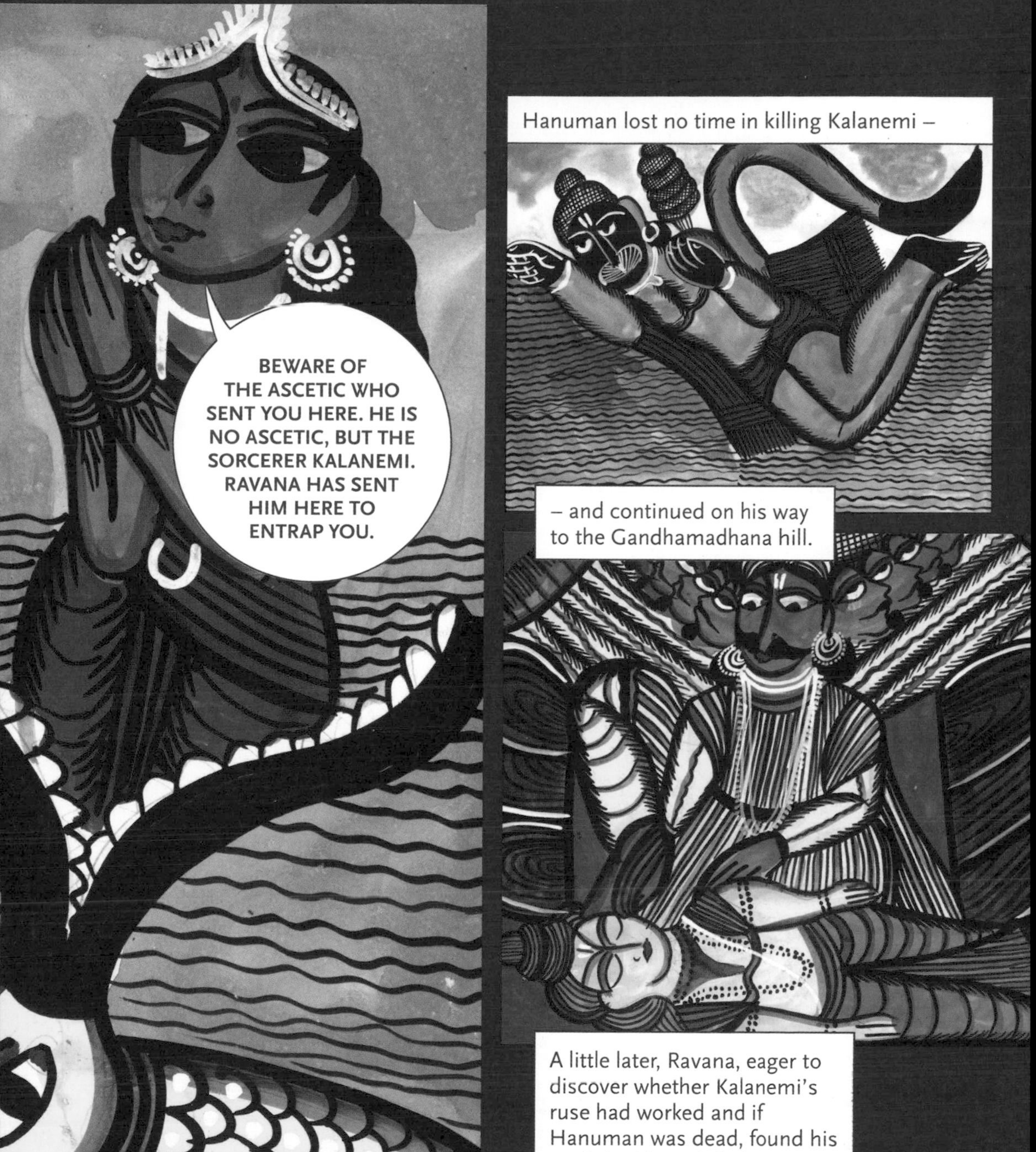
BEWARE OF THE ASCETIC WHO SENT YOU HERE. HE IS NO ASCETIC, BUT THE SORCERER KALANEMI. RAVANA HAS SENT HIM HERE TO ENTRAP YOU.
Hanuman lost no time in killing Kalanemi –
– and continued on his way to the Gandhamadhana hill.
A little later, Ravana, eager to discover whether Kalanemi's ruse had worked and if Hanuman was dead, found his uncle had been killed instead.

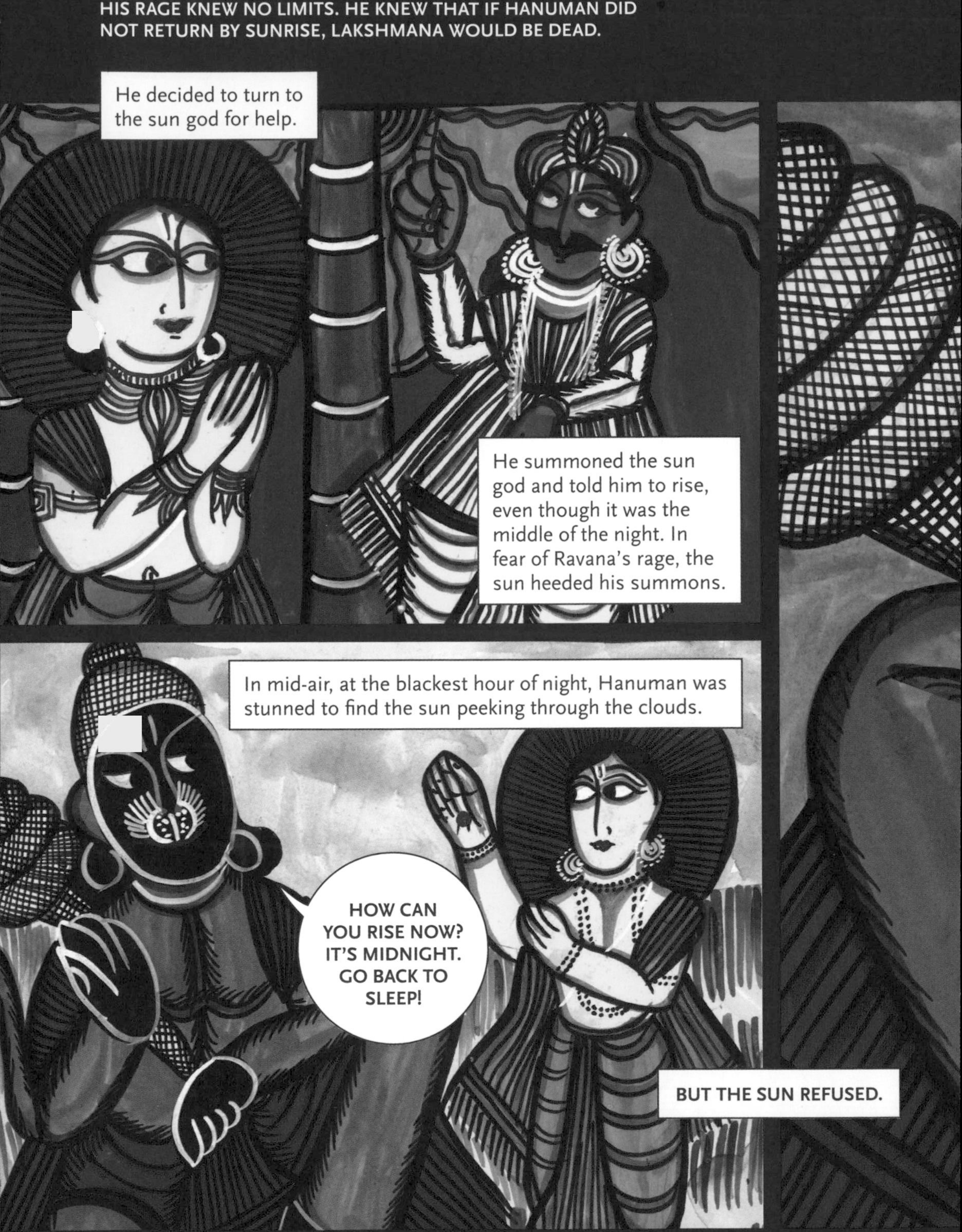
HIS RAGE KNEW NO LIMITS. HE KNEW THAT IF HANUMAN DID NOT RETURN BY SUNRISE, LAKSHMANA WOULD BE DEAD.
He decided to turn to the sun god for help.
He summoned the sun god and told him to rise, even though it was the middle of the night. In fear of Ravana's rage, the sun heeded his summons.
In mid-air, at the blackest hour of night, Hanuman was stunned to find the sun peeking through the clouds.
HOW CAN YOU RISE NOW? IT'S MIDNIGHT. GO BACK TO SLEEP!
BUT THE SUN REFUSED.

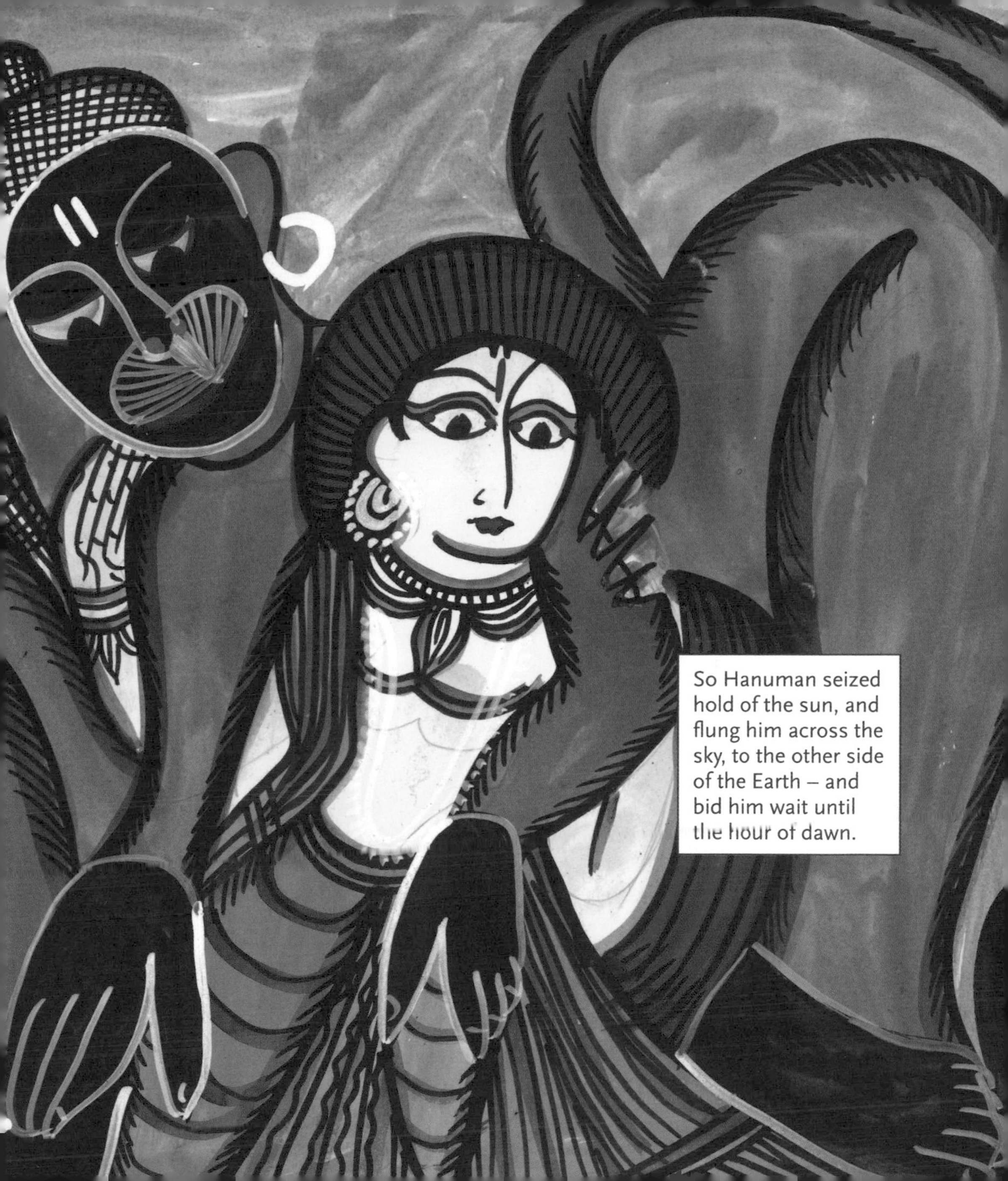

So Hanuman seized hold of the sun, and flung him across the sky, to the other side of the Earth – and bid him wait until the hour of dawn.

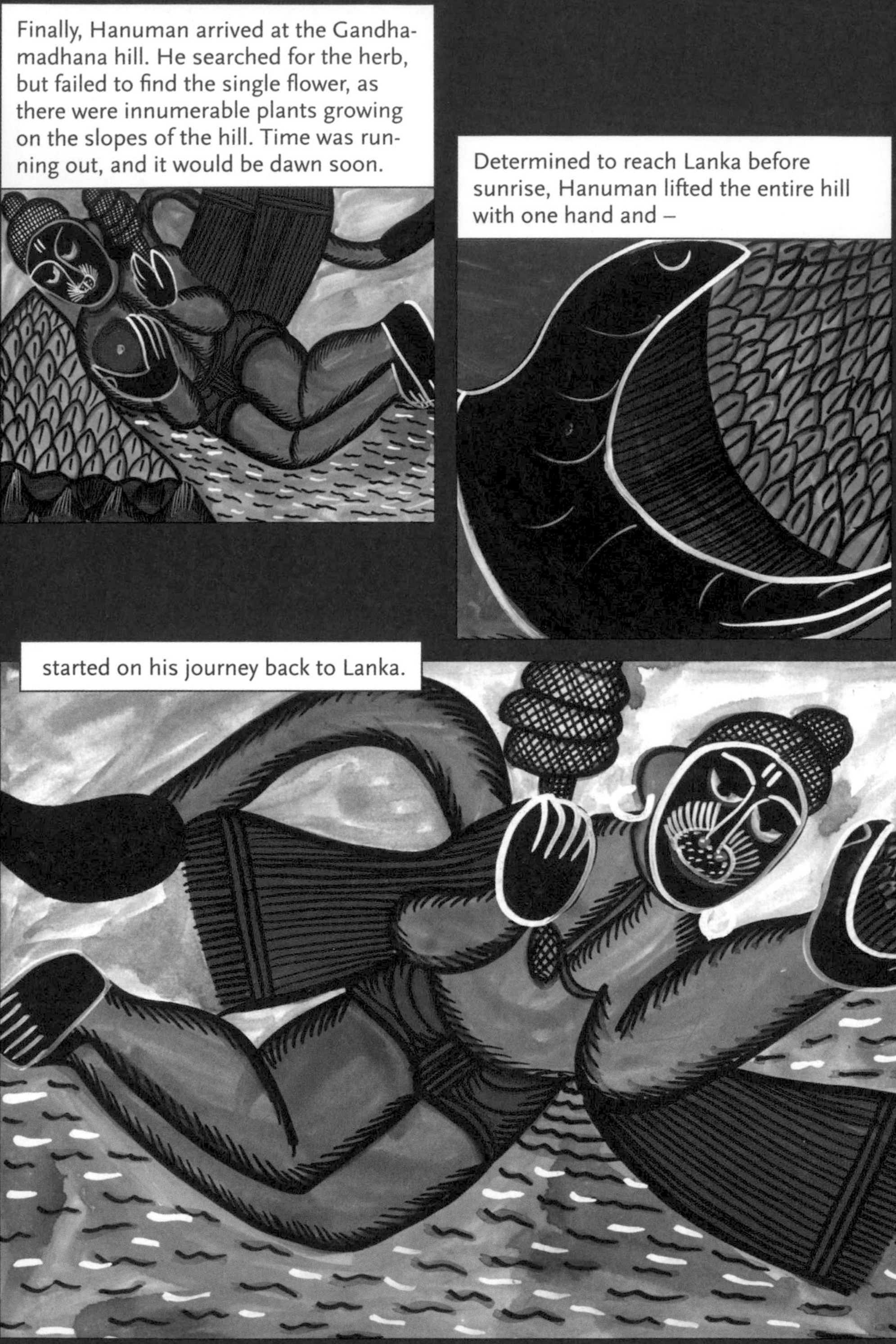
Finally, Hanuman arrived at the Gandhamadhana hill. He searched for the herb, but failed to find the single flower, as there were innumerable plants growing on the slopes of the hill. Time was running out, and it would be dawn soon.
Determined to reach Lanka before sunrise, Hanuman lifted the entire hill with one hand and –
started on his journey back to Lanka.

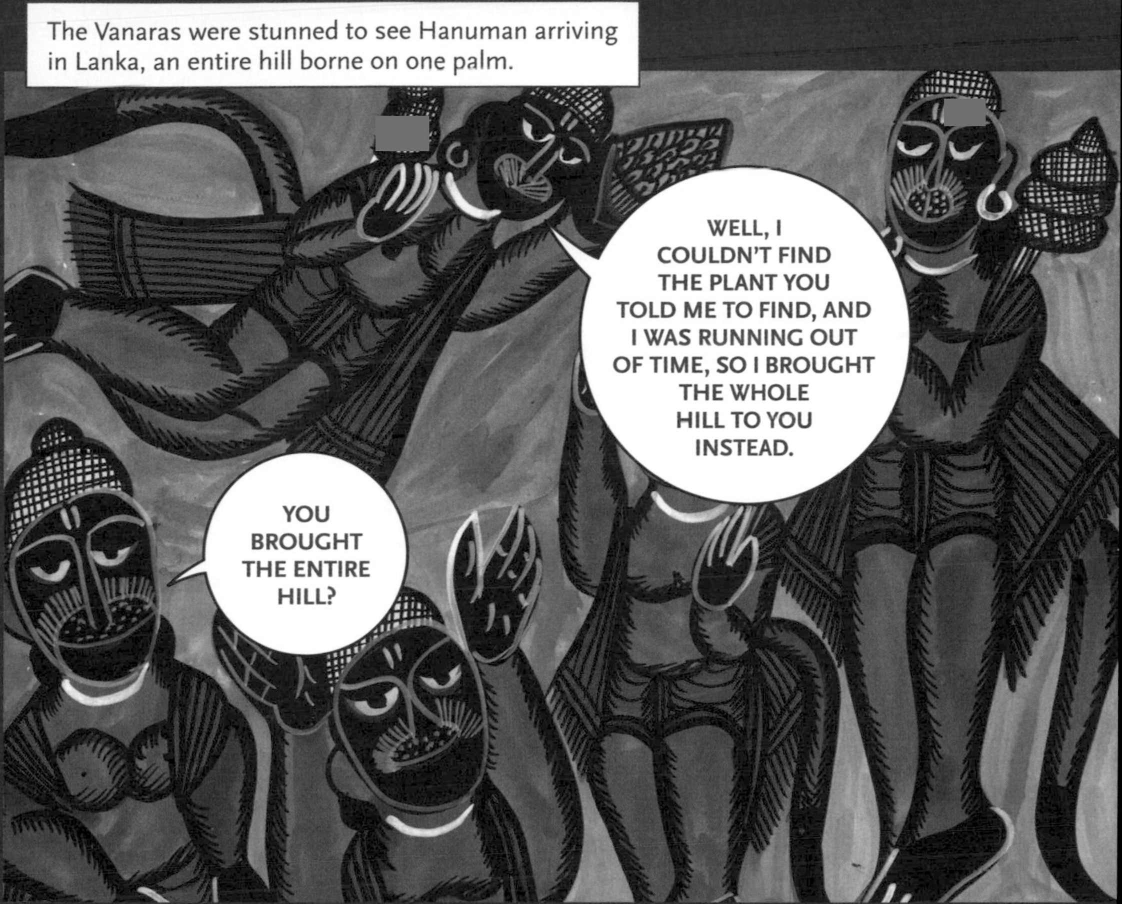
The Vanaras were stunned to see Hanuman arriving in Lanka, an entire hill borne on one palm.
WELL, I COULDN'T FIND THE PLANT YOU TOLD ME TO FIND, AND I WAS RUNNING OUT OF TIME, SO I BROUGHT THE WHOLE HILL TO YOU INSTEAD.
YOU BROUGHT THE ENTIRE HILL?

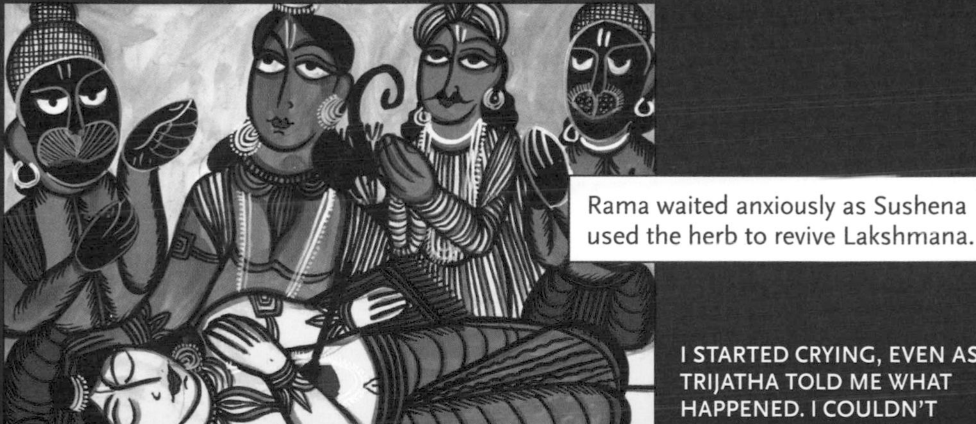
Rama waited anxiously as Sushena used the herb to revive Lakshmana.

I STARTED CRYING, EVEN AS TRIJATHA TOLD ME WHAT HAPPENED. I COULDN'T HELP IT. I COULDN'T IMAGINE LAKSHMANA DEAD. BUT I FELT WONDER TOO – FOR BRAVE HANUMAN, WHO BATTLED ENCHANTERS

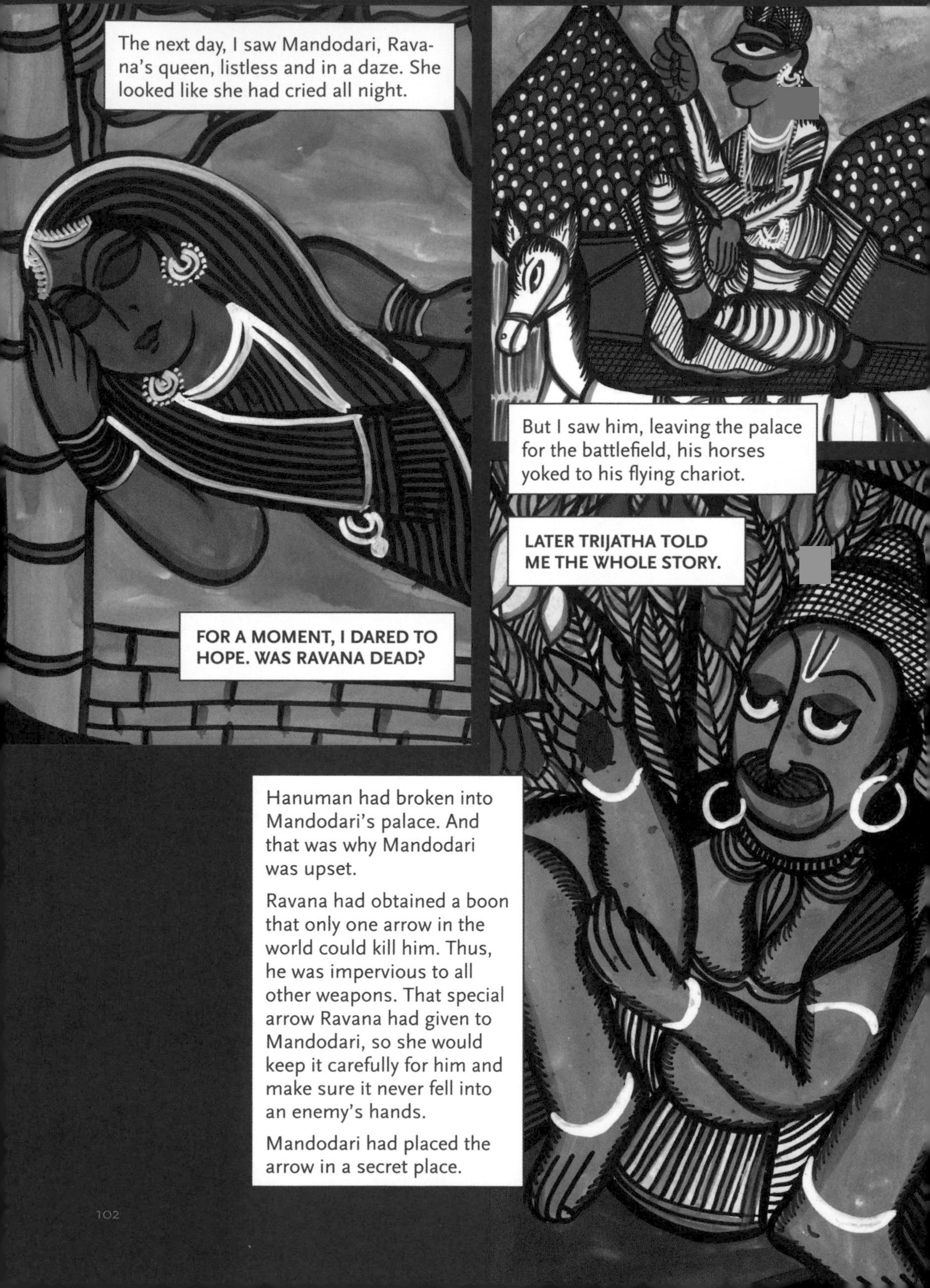
The next day, I saw Mandodari, Ravana's queen, listless and in a daze. She looked like she had cried all night.
FOR A MOMENT, I DARED TO HOPE. WAS RAVANA DEAD?
But I saw him, leaving the palace for the battlefield, his horses yoked to his flying chariot.
LATER TRIJATHA TOLD ME THE WHOLE STORY.
Hanuman had broken into Mandodari's palace. And that was why Mandodari was upset.
Ravana had obtained a boon that only one arrow in the world could kill him. Thus, he was impervious to all other weapons. That special arrow Ravana had given to Mandodari, so she would keep it carefully for him and make sure it never fell into an enemy's hands.
Mandodari had placed the arrow in a secret place.

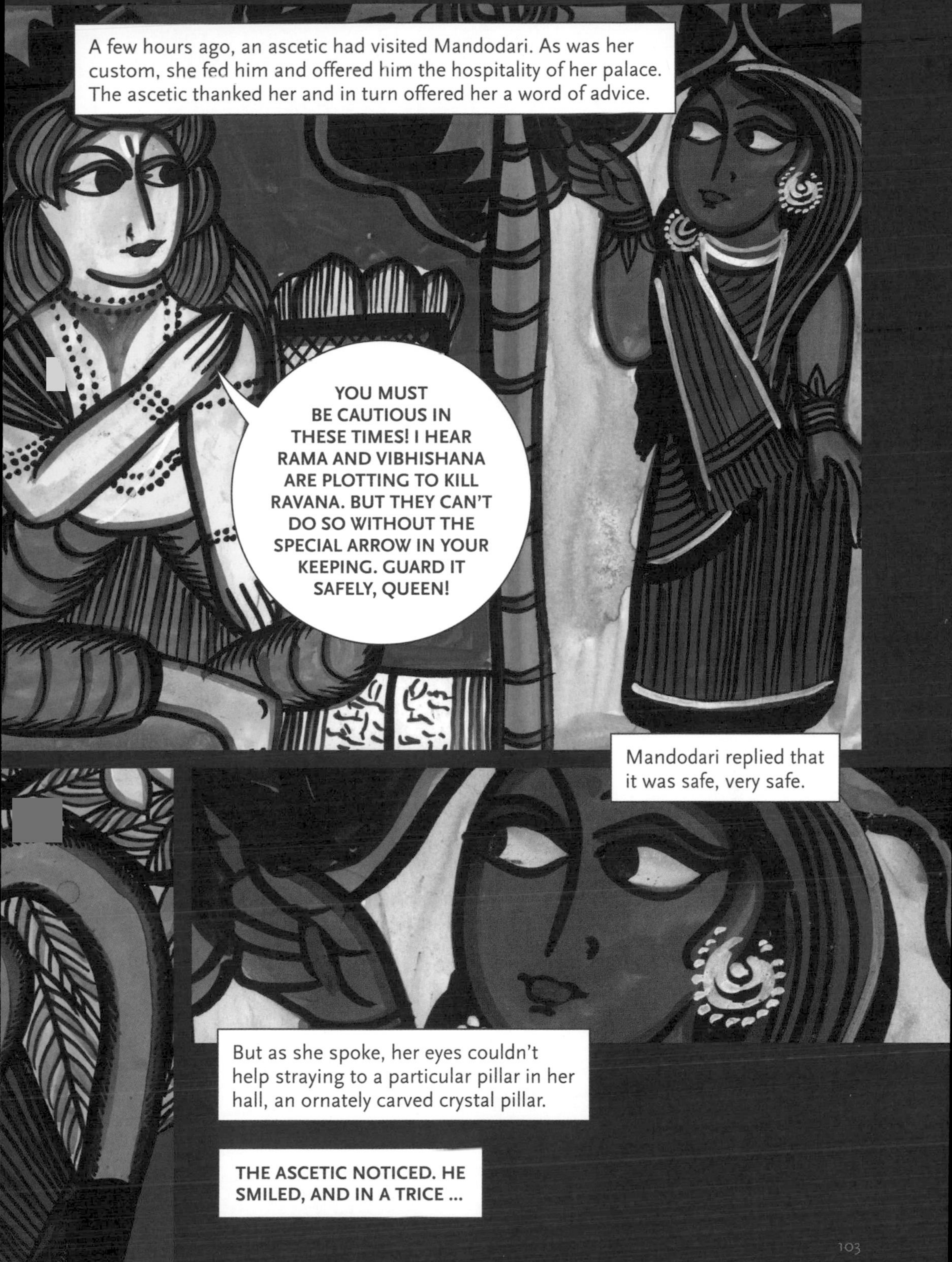
A few hours ago, an ascetic had visited Mandodari. As was her custom, she fed him and offered him the hospitality of her palace. The ascetic thanked her and in turn offered her a word of advice.
YOU MUST BE CAUTIOUS IN THESE TIMES! I HEAR RAMA AND VIBHISHANA ARE PLOTTING TO KILL RAVANA. BUT THEY CAN'T DO SO WITHOUT THE SPECIAL ARROW IN YOUR KEEPING. GUARD IT SAFELY, QUEEN!
Mandodari replied that it was safe, very safe.
But as she spoke, her eyes couldn't help straying to a particular pillar in her hall, an ornately carved crystal pillar.
THE ASCETIC NOTICED. HE SMILED, AND IN A TRICE ...

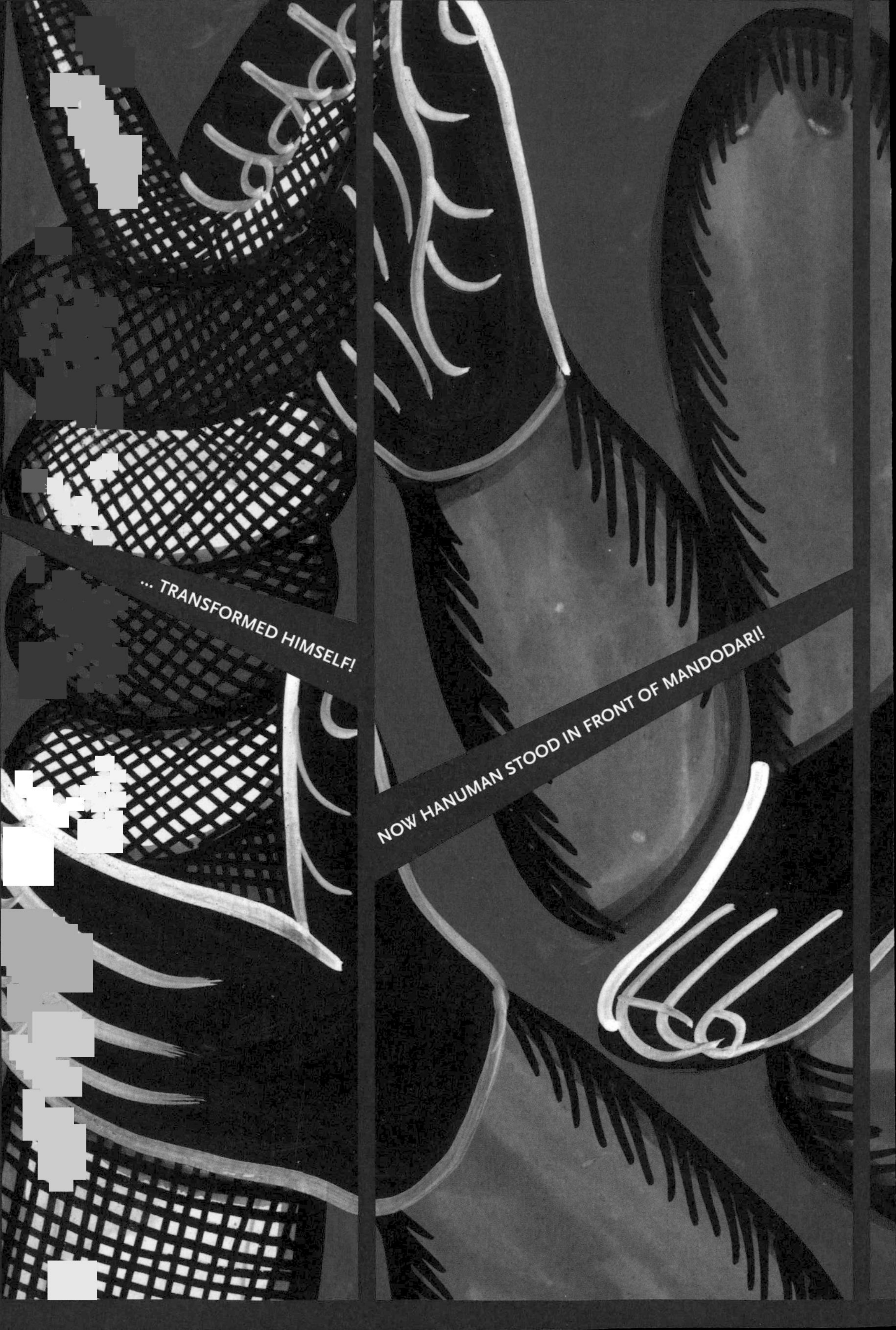
... TRANSFORMED HIMSELF!
NOW HANUMAN STOOD IN FRONT OF MANDODARI!

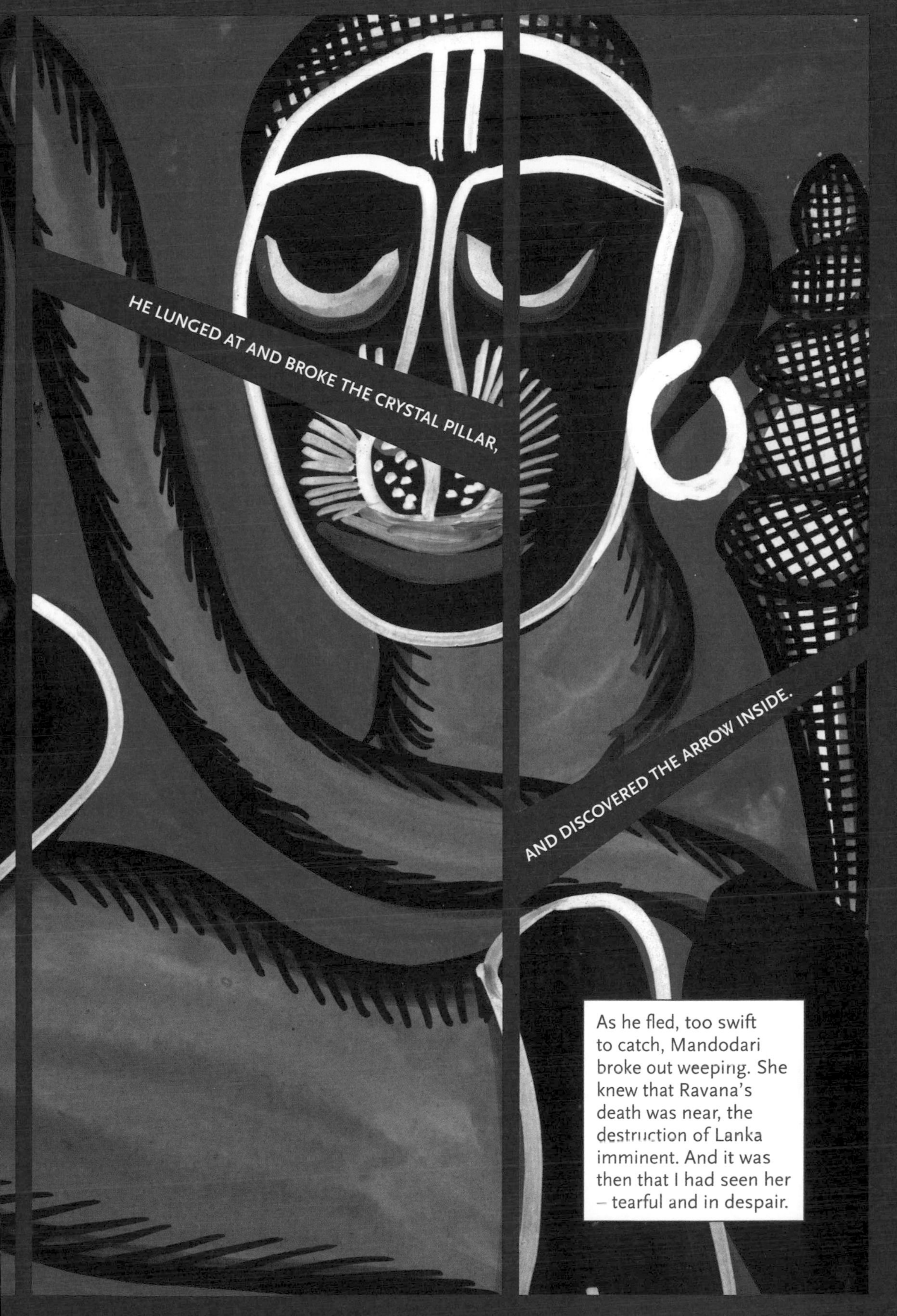
HE LUNGED AT AND BROKE THE CRYSTAL PILLAR,
AND DISCOVERED THE ARROW INSIDE.
As he fled, too swift to catch, Mandodari broke out weeping. She knew that Ravana's death was near, the destruction of Lanka imminent. And it was then that I had seen her – tearful and in despair.

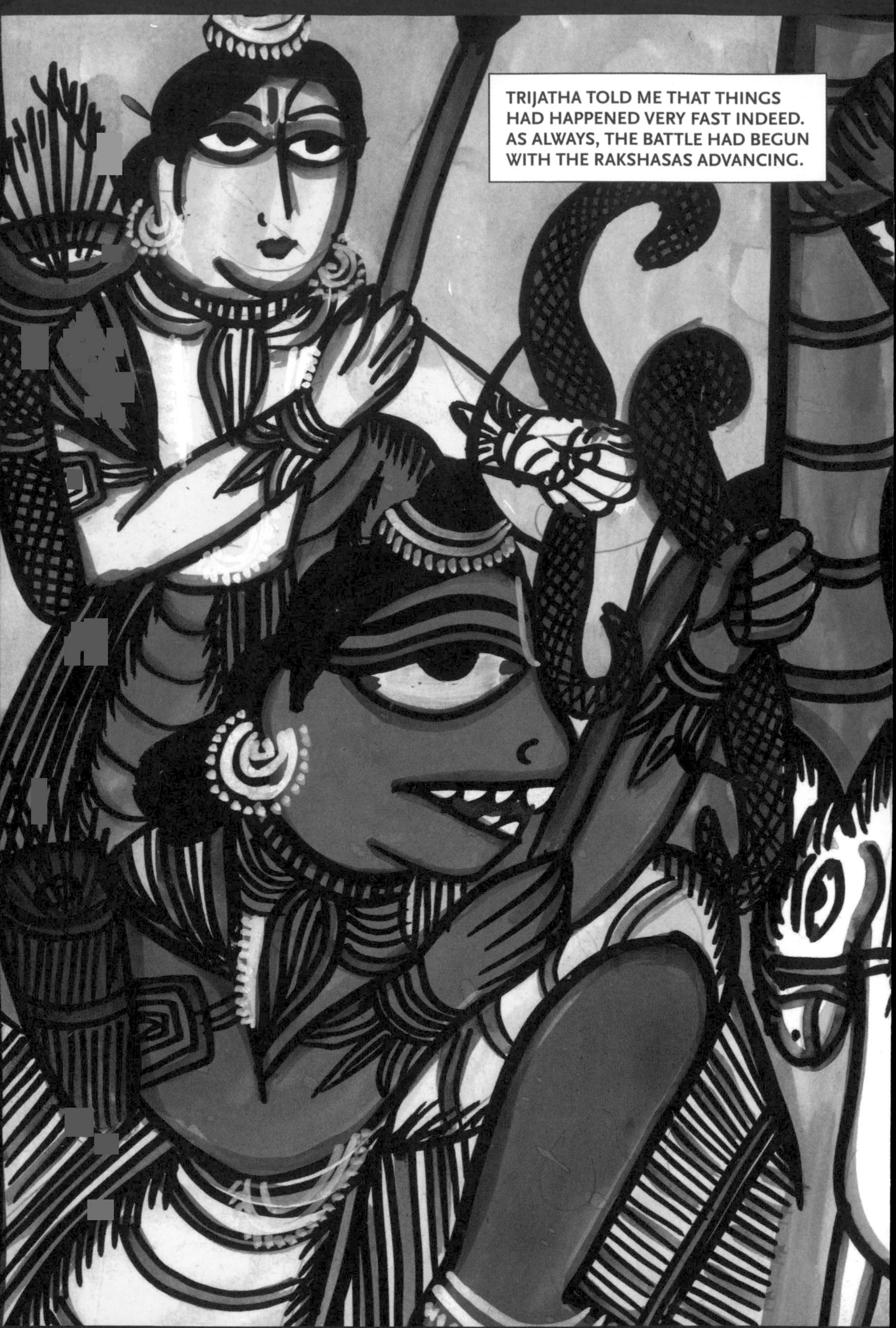
TRIJATHA TOLD ME THAT THINGS HAD HAPPENED VERY FAST INDEED. AS ALWAYS, THE BATTLE HAD BEGUN WITH THE RAKSHASAS ADVANCING.

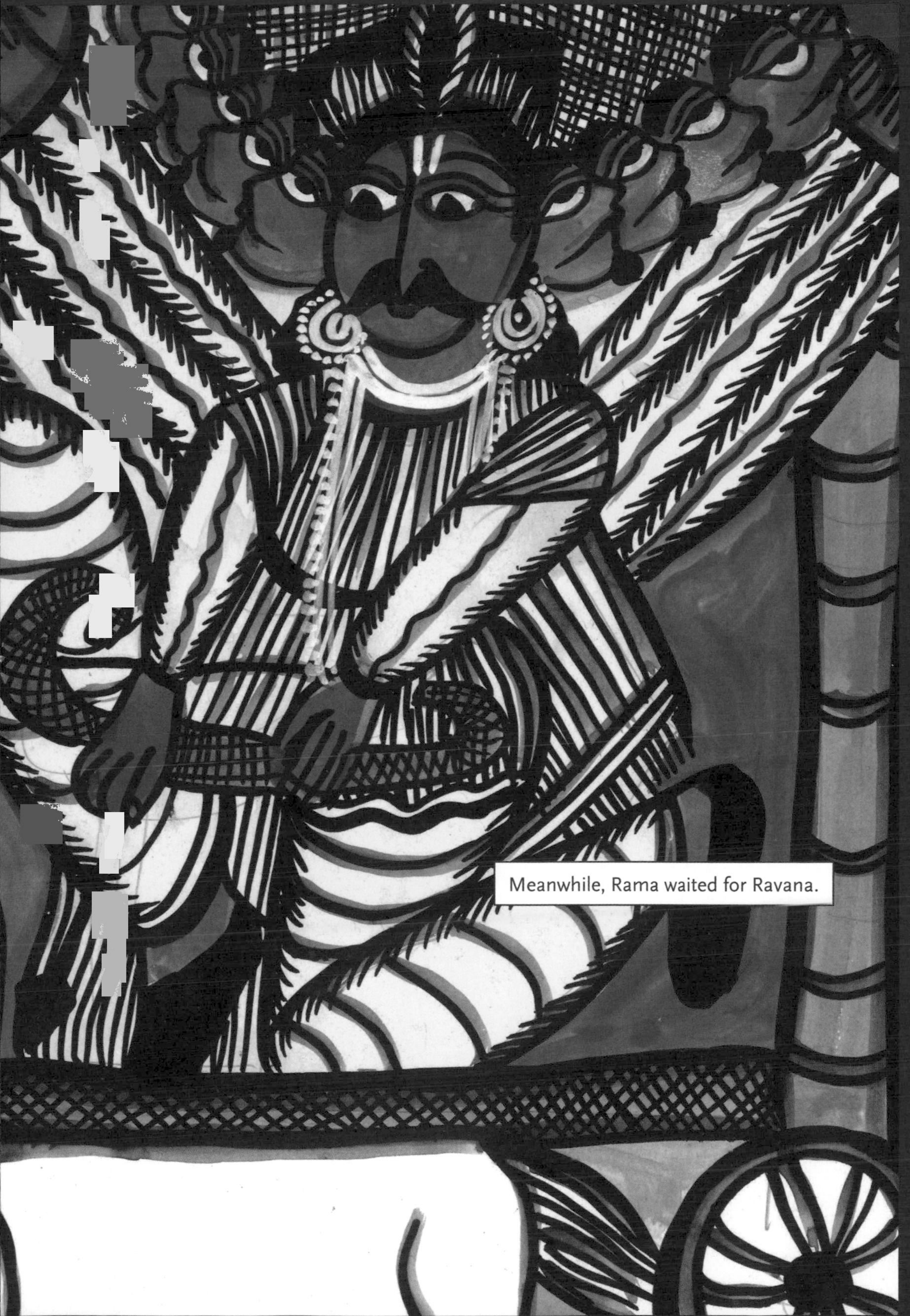
Meanwhile, Rama waited for Ravana.

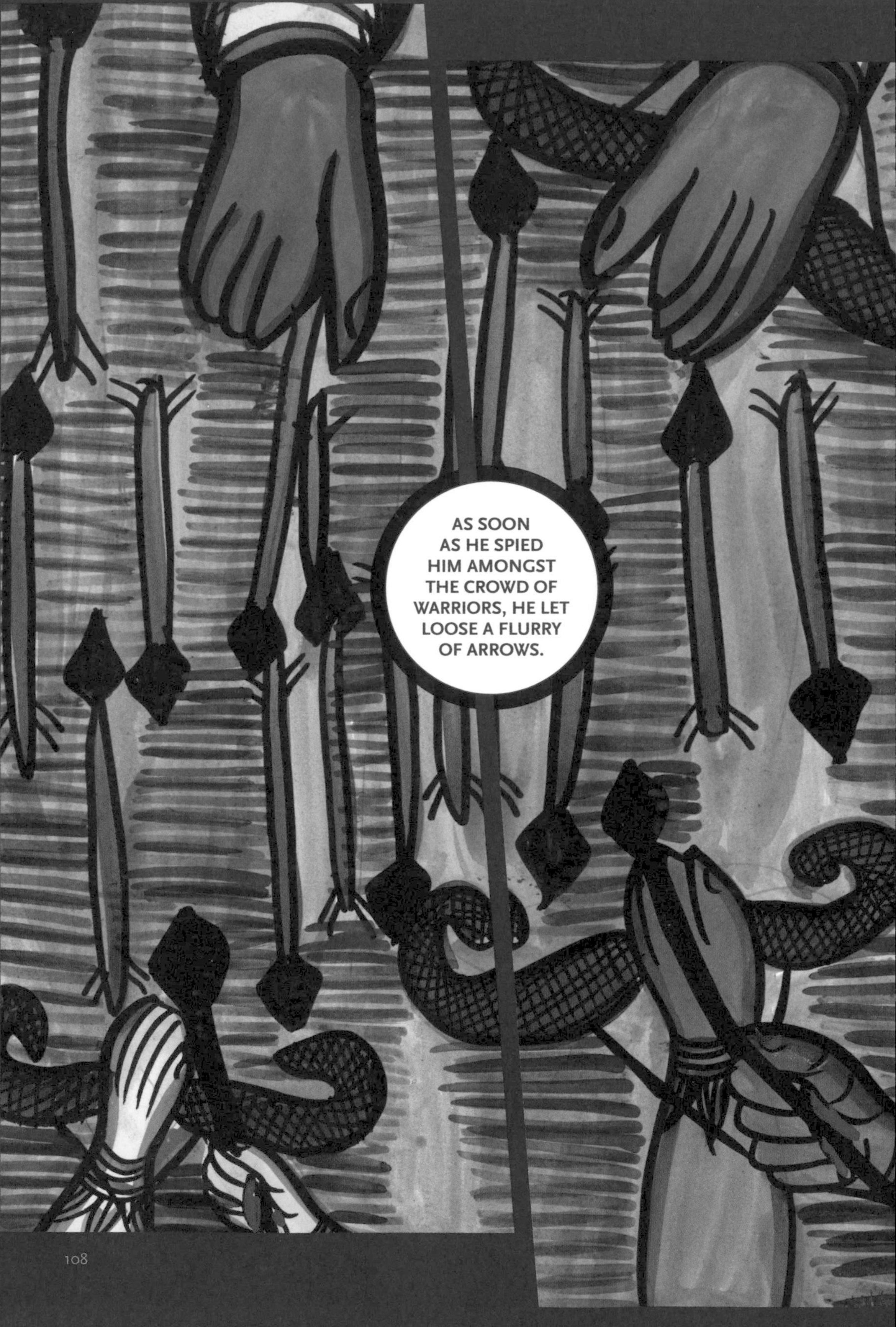
AS SOON AS HE SPIED HIM AMONGST THE CROWD OF WARRIORS, HE LET LOOSE A FLURRY OF ARROWS.

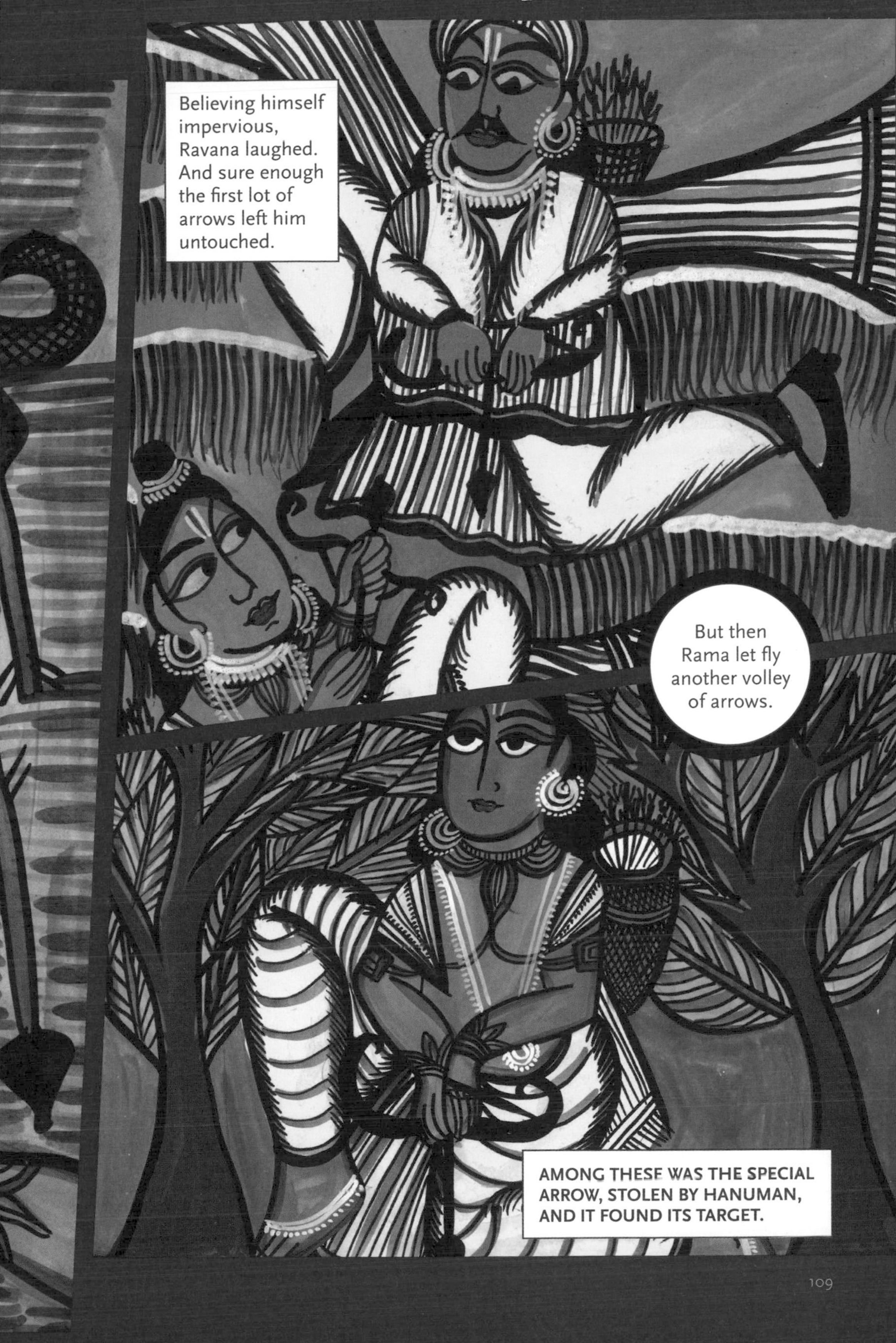
Believing himself impervious, Ravana laughed. And sure enough the first lot of arrows left him untouched.
But then Rama let fly another volley of arrows.
AMONG THESE WAS THE SPECIAL ARROW, STOLEN BY HANUMAN, AND IT FOUND ITS TARGET.

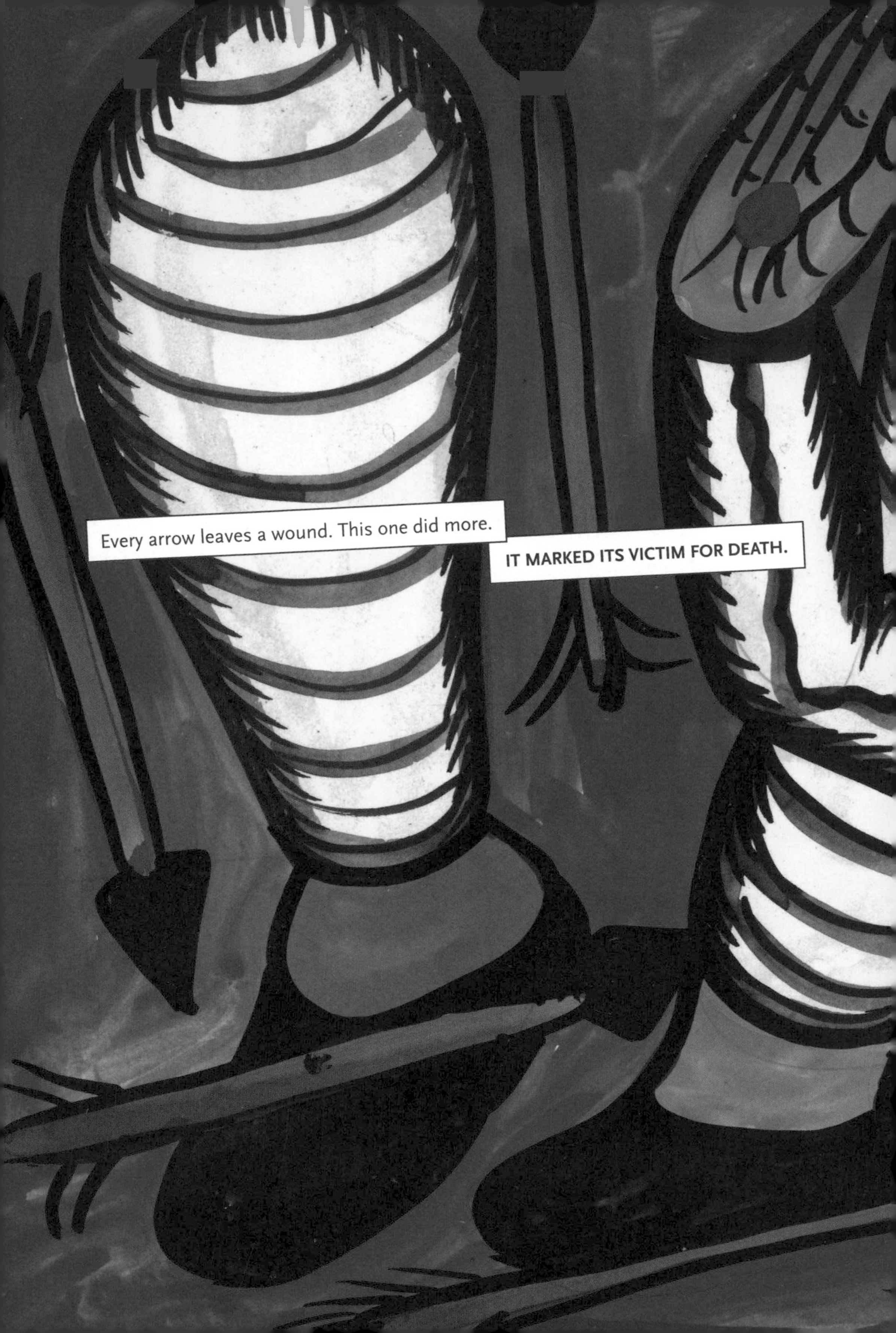
Every arrow leaves a wound. This one did more.
IT MARKED ITS VICTIM FOR DEATH.

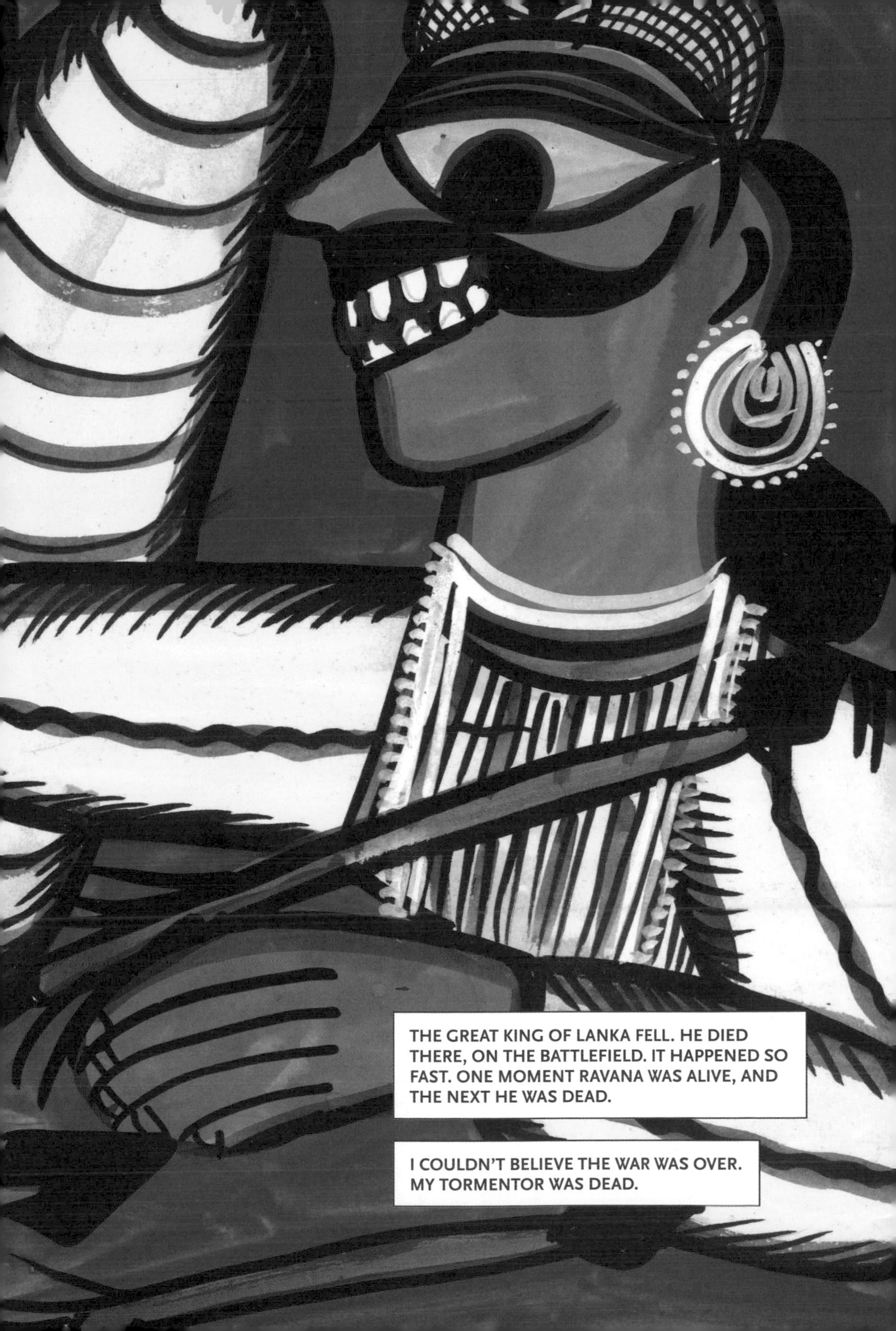
THE GREAT KING OF LANKA FELL. HE DIED THERE, ON THE BATTLEFIELD. IT HAPPENED SO FAST. ONE MOMENT RAVANA WAS ALIVE, AND THE NEXT HE WAS DEAD.
I COULDN'T BELIEVE THE WAR WAS OVER. MY TORMENTOR WAS DEAD.

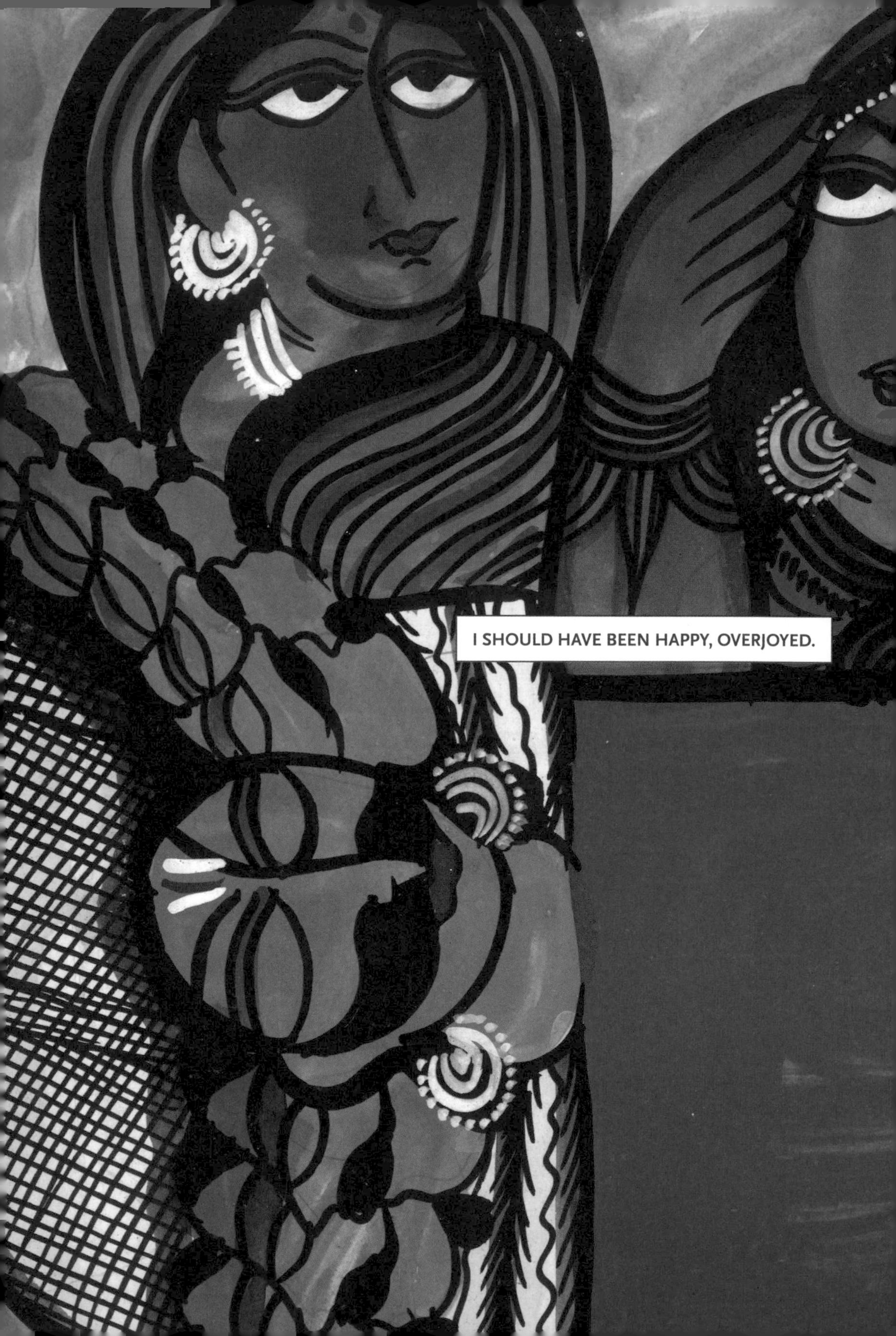
I SHOULD HAVE BEEN HAPPY, OVERJOYED.

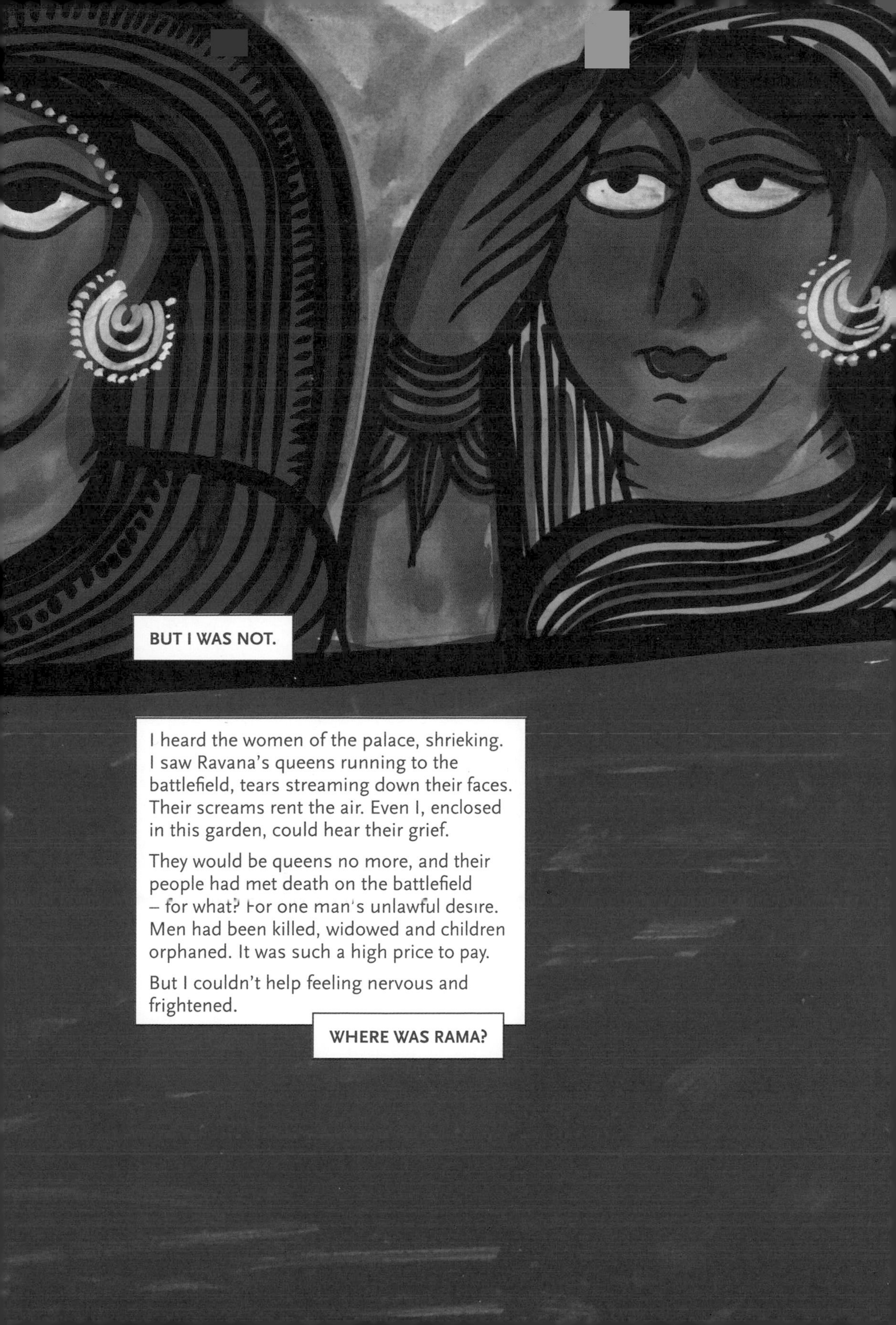
BUT I WAS NOT.
I heard the women of the palace, shrieking. I saw Ravana's queens running to the battlefield, tears streaming down their faces. Their screams rent the air. Even I, enclosed in this garden, could hear their grief.
They would be queens no more, and their people had met death on the battlefield – for what? For one man's unlawful desire. Men had been killed, widowed and children orphaned. It was such a high price to pay.
But I couldn't help feeling nervous and frightened.
WHERE WAS RAMA?

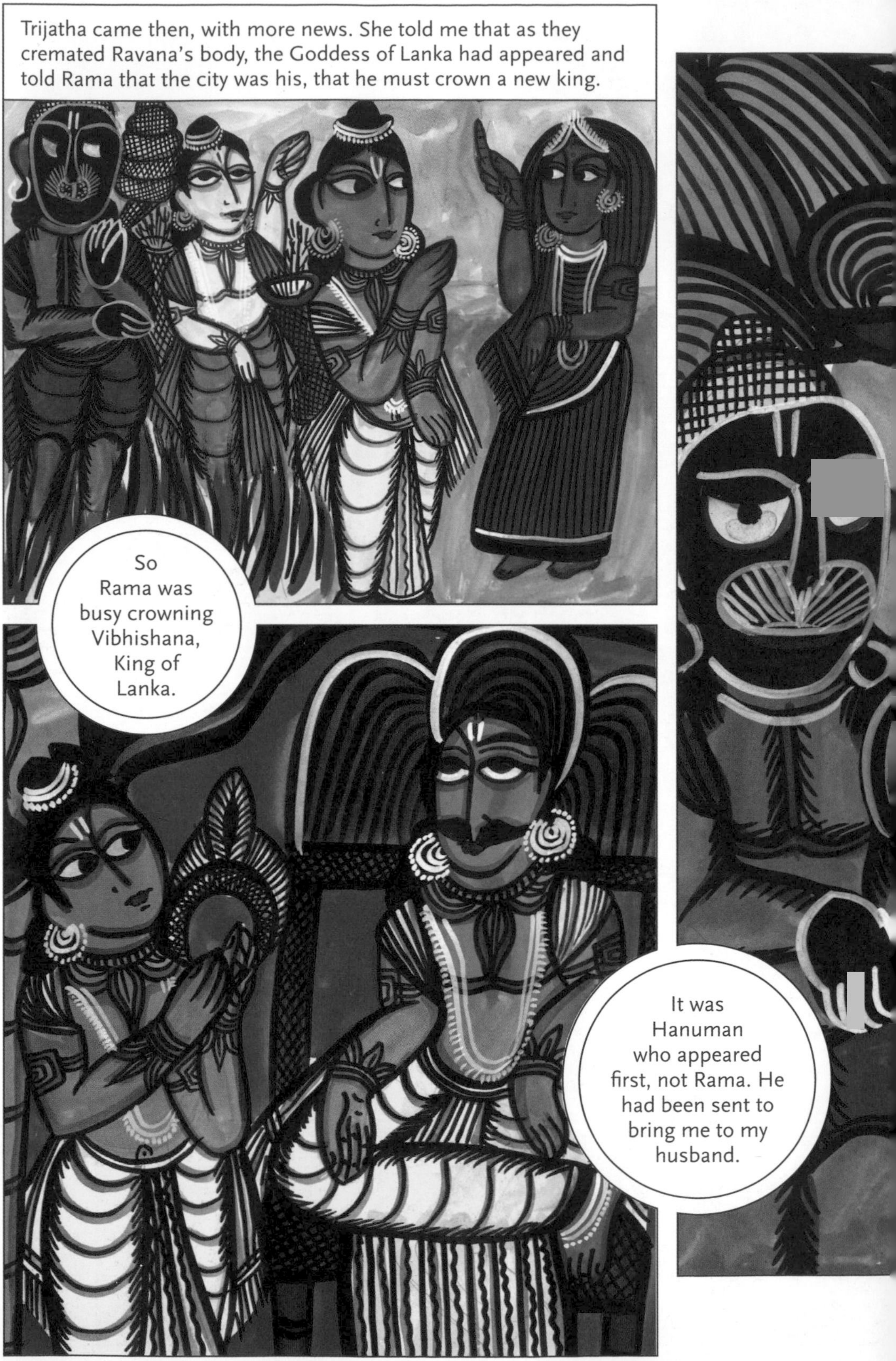
Trijatha came then, with more news. She told me that as they cremated Ravana's body, the Goddess of Lanka had appeared and told Rama that the city was his, that he must crown a new king.
So Rama was busy crowning Vibhishana, King of Lanka.
It was Hanuman who appeared first, not Rama. He had been sent to bring me to my husband.

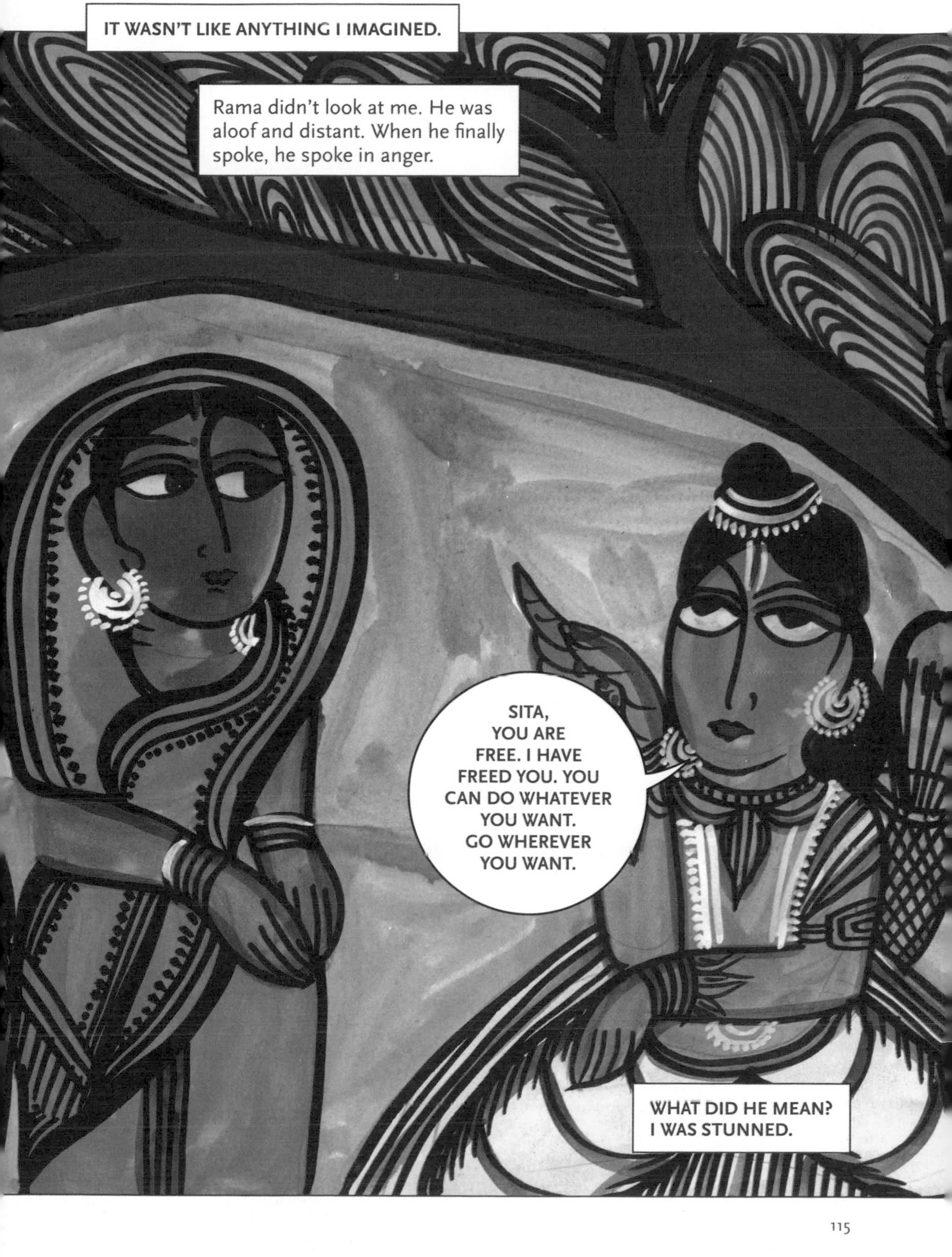
IT WASN'T LIKE ANYTHING I IMAGINED.
Rama didn't look at me. He was aloof and distant. When he finally spoke, he spoke in anger.
SITA, YOU ARE FREE. I HAVE FREED YOU. YOU CAN DO WHATEVER YOU WANT. GO WHEREVER YOU WANT.
WHAT DID HE MEAN? I WAS STUNNED.

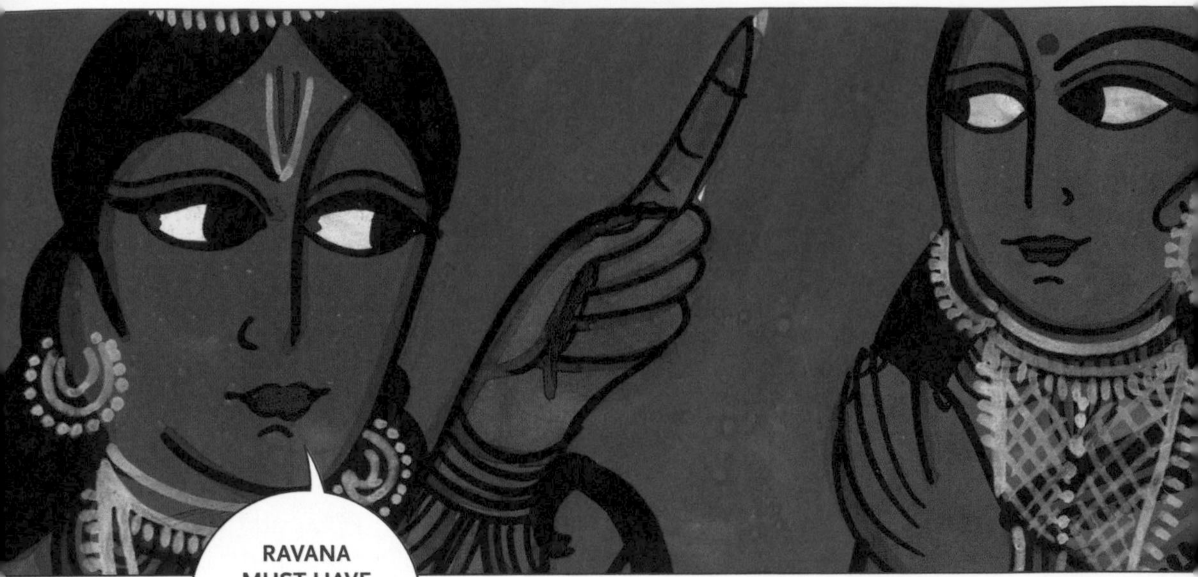
RAVANA MUST HAVE TOUCHED YOU. I CAN'T TAKE YOU BACK.

I couldn't believe what I was hearing. I told Rama that I was pure. That Ravana had never touched me. That – and I was forced to say this – he was honourable.

But Rama didn't speak to me.

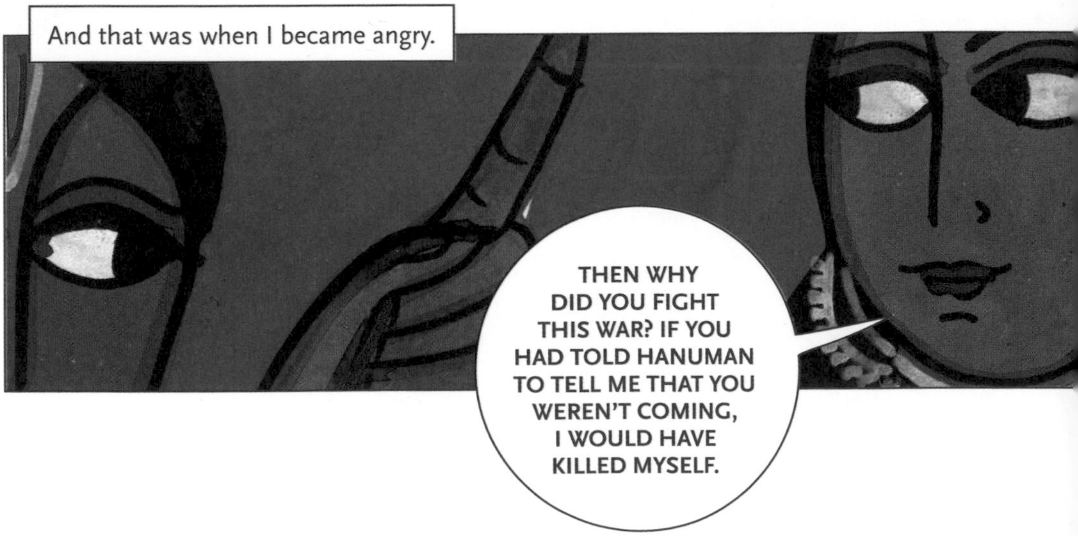
And that was when I became angry.
THEN WHY DID YOU FIGHT THIS WAR? IF YOU HAD TOLD HANUMAN TO TELL ME THAT YOU WEREN'T COMING, I WOULD HAVE KILLED MYSELF.

He then told me he hadn't fought the war for me. He had fought it to redeem his honour.

HIS HONOUR HAD EXACTED A BLOODY PRICE.

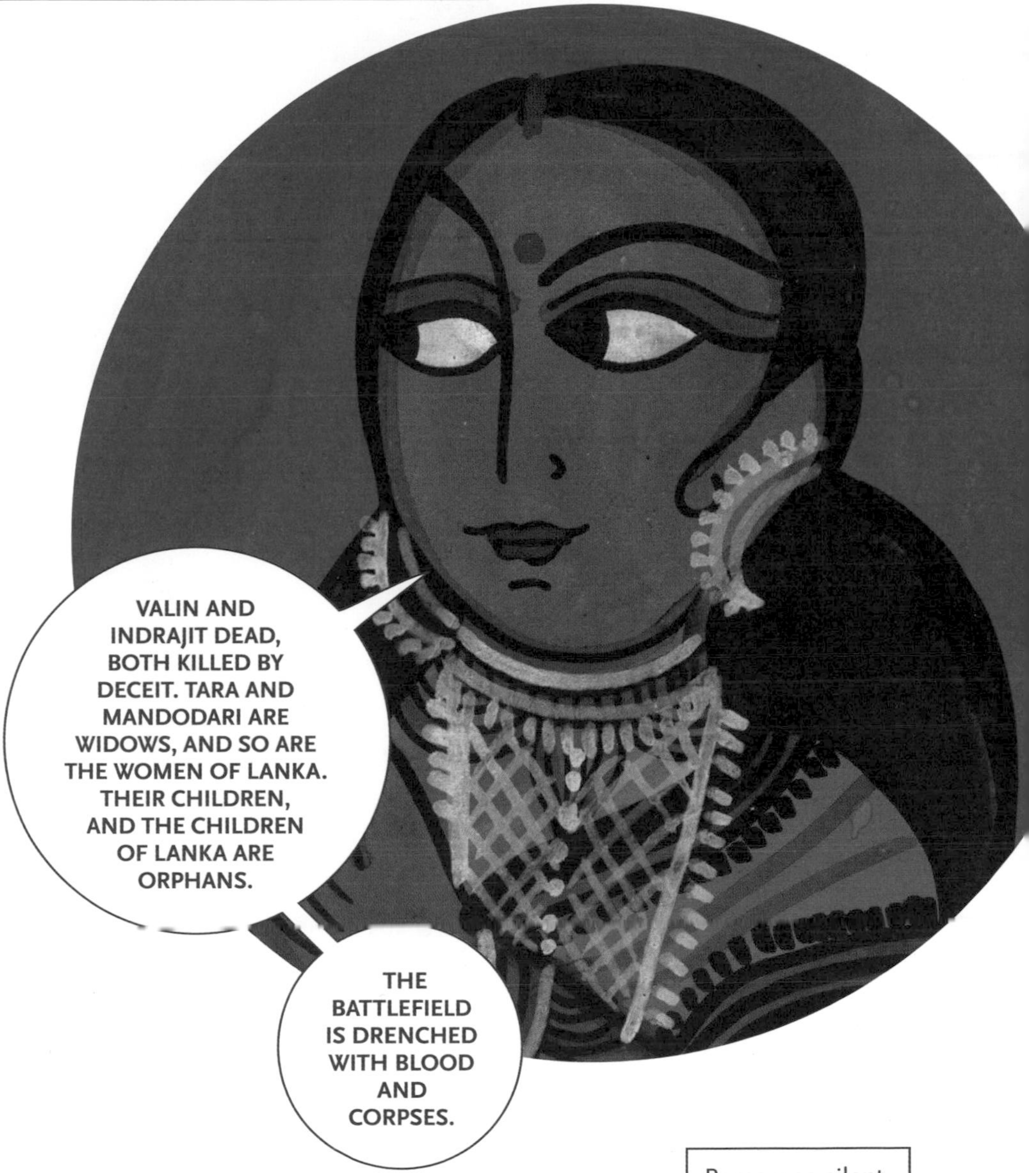
VALIN AND INDRAJIT DEAD, BOTH KILLED BY DECEIT. TARA AND MANDODARI ARE WIDOWS, AND SO ARE THE WOMEN OF LANKA. THEIR CHILDREN, AND THE CHILDREN OF LANKA ARE ORPHANS.
THE BATTLEFIELD IS DRENCHED WITH BLOOD AND CORPSES.

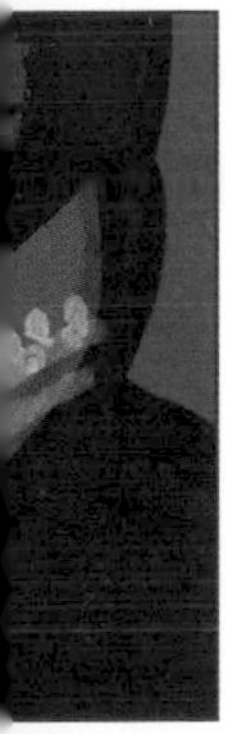

Rama was silent.

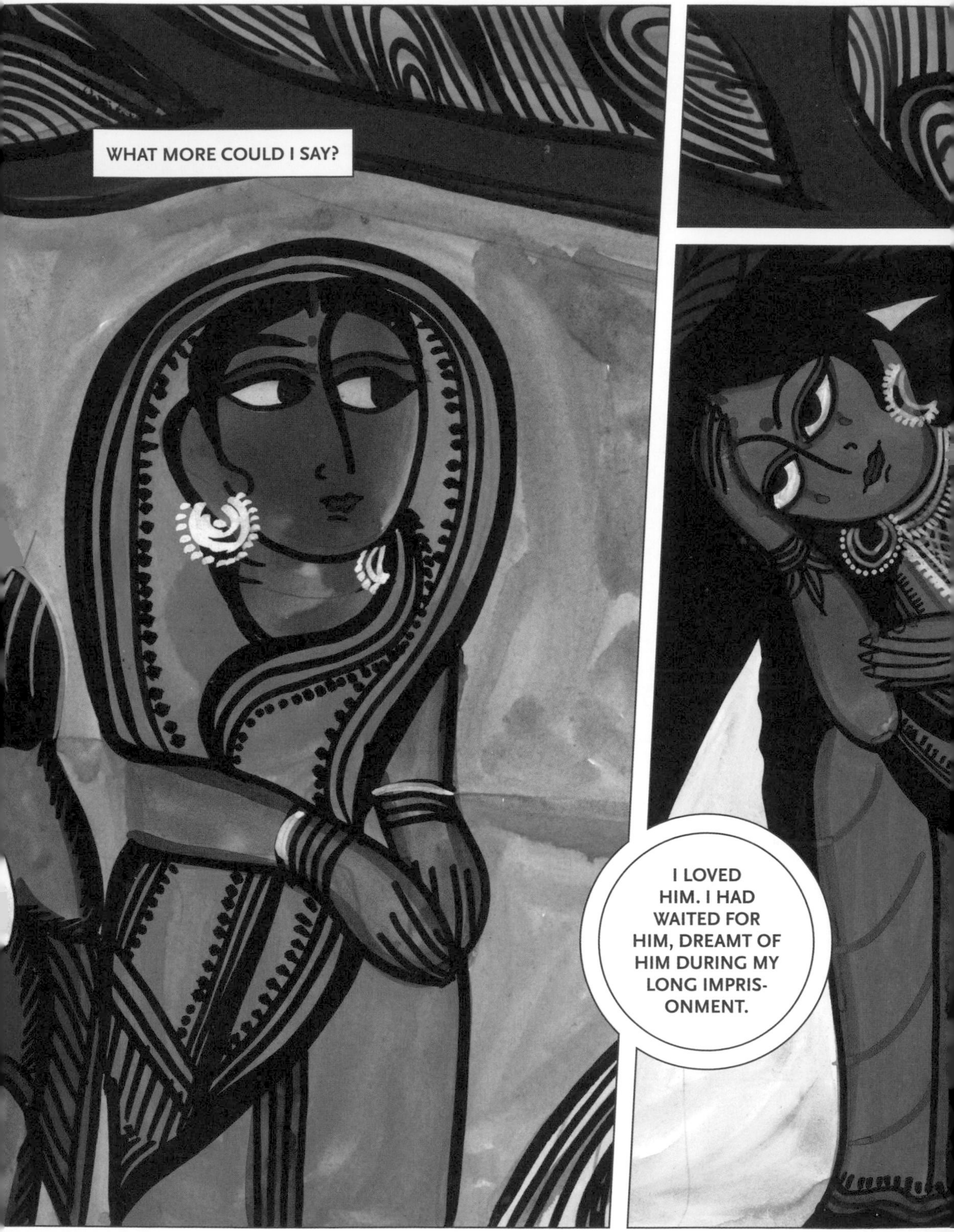
WHAT MORE COULD I SAY?
I LOVED HIM. I HAD WAITED FOR HIM, DREAMT OF HIM DURING MY LONG IMPRIS-ONMENT.

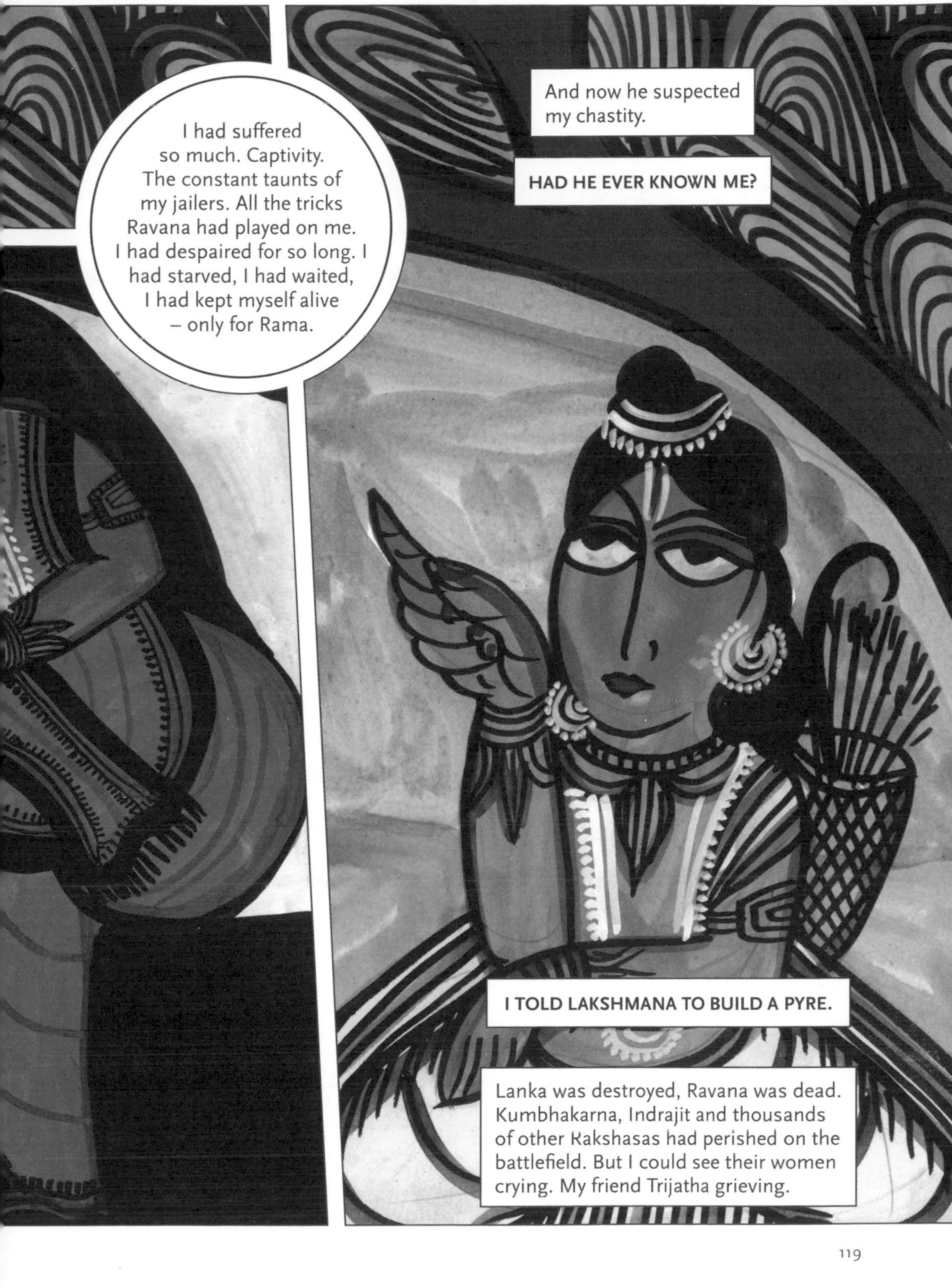
I had suffered so much. Captivity. The constant taunts of my jailers. All the tricks Ravana had played on me. I had despaired for so long. I had starved, I had waited, I had kept myself alive – only for Rama.
And now he suspected my chastity.
HAD HE EVER KNOWN ME?
I TOLD LAKSHMANA TO BUILD A PYRE.
Lanka was destroyed, Ravana was dead. Kumbhakarna, Indrajit and thousands of other Rakshasas had perished on the battlefield. But I could see their women crying. My friend Trijatha grieving.

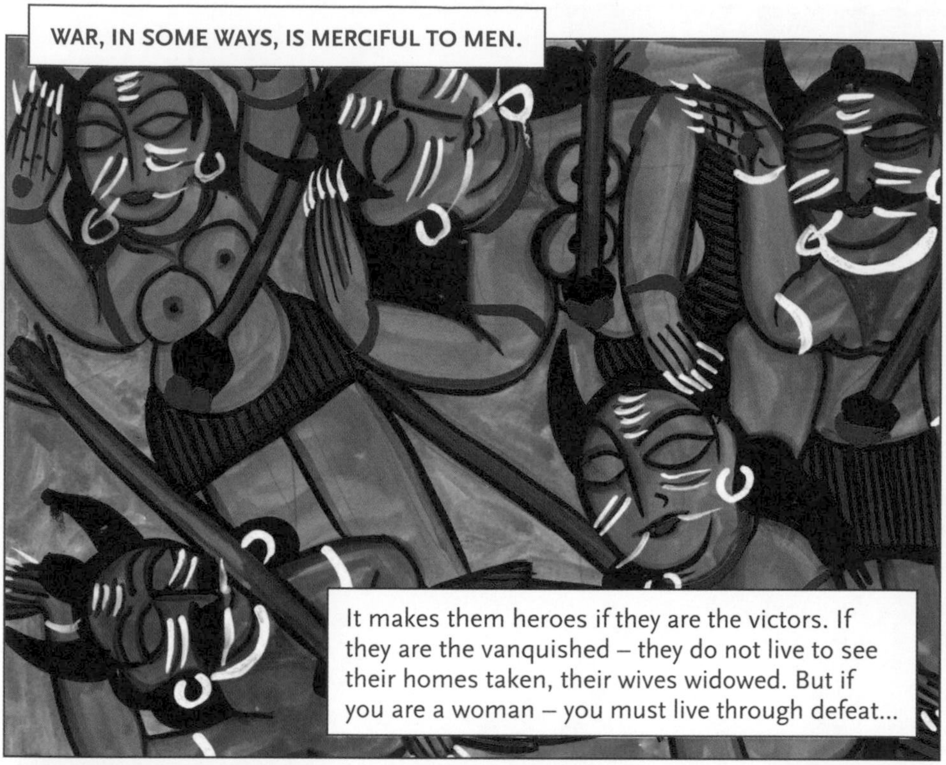
WAR, IN SOME WAYS, IS MERCIFUL TO MEN.
It makes them heroes if they are the victors. If they are the vanquished – they do not live to see their homes taken, their wives widowed. But if you are a woman – you must live through defeat...

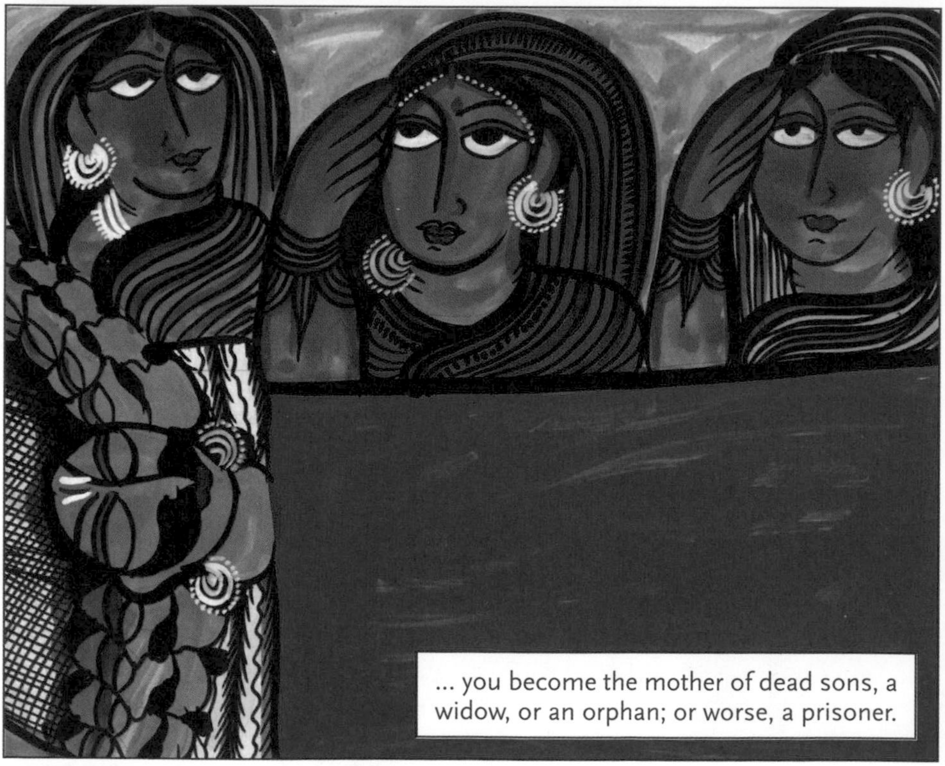
... you become the mother of dead sons, a widow, or an orphan; or worse, a prisoner.

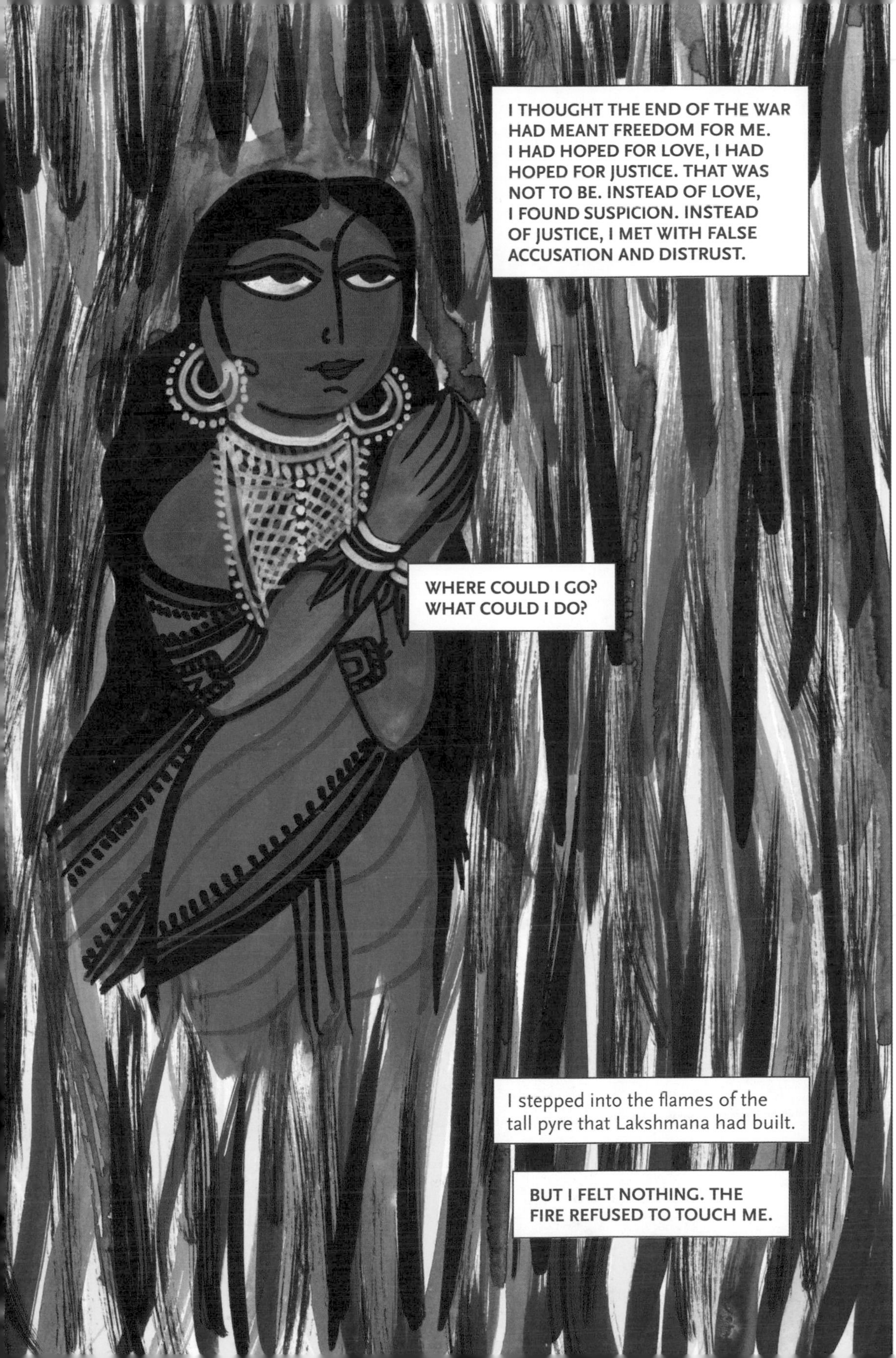
I THOUGHT THE END OF THE WAR HAD MEANT FREEDOM FOR ME. I HAD HOPED FOR LOVE, I HAD HOPED FOR JUSTICE. THAT WAS NOT TO BE. INSTEAD OF LOVE, I FOUND SUSPICION. INSTEAD OF JUSTICE, I MET WITH FALSE ACCUSATION AND DISTRUST.
WHERE COULD I GO? WHAT COULD I DO?
I stepped into the flames of the tall pyre that Lakshmana had built.
BUT I FELT NOTHING. THE FIRE REFUSED TO TOUCH ME.

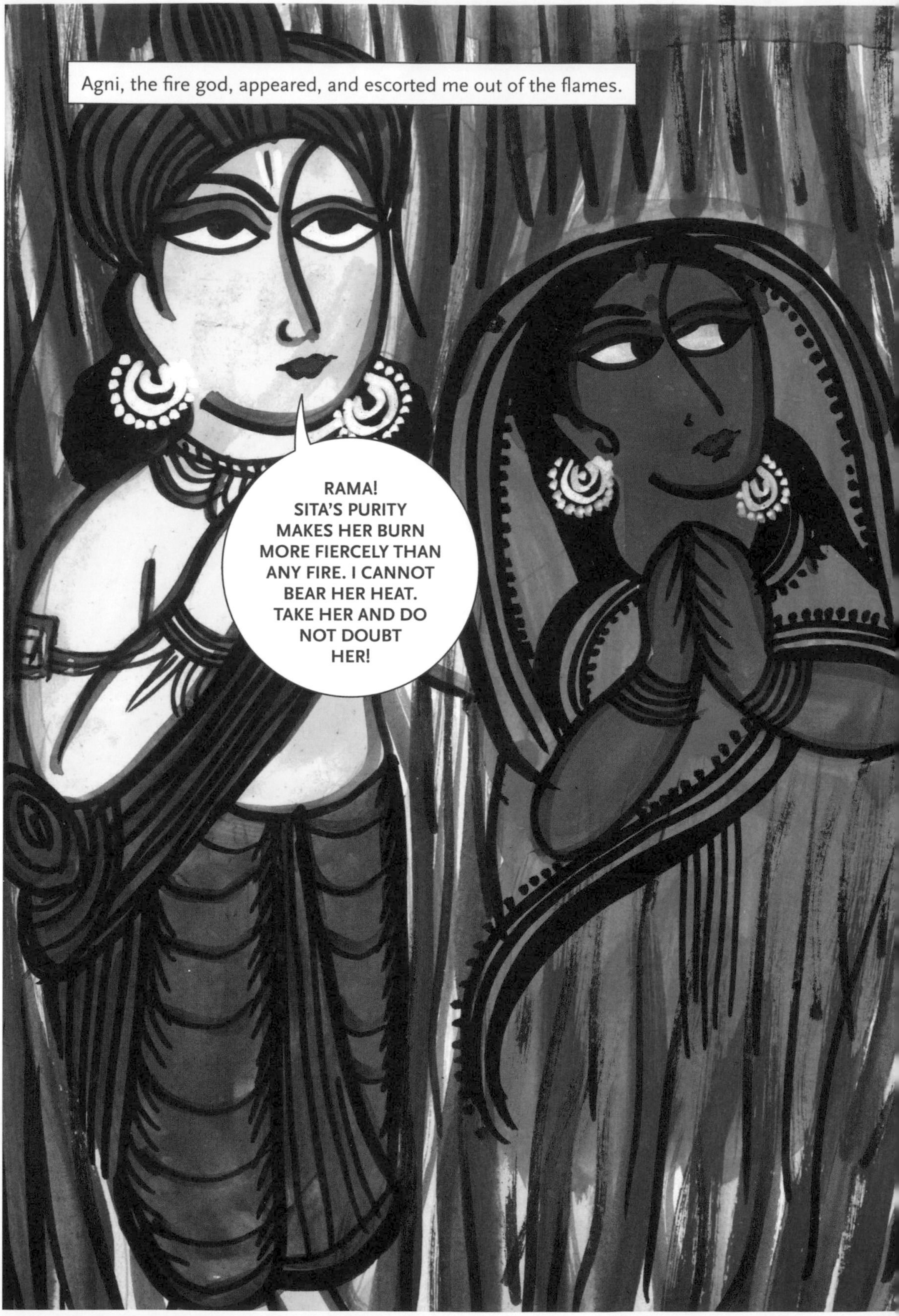
Agni, the fire god, appeared, and escorted me out of the flames.
RAMA! SITA'S PURITY MAKES HER BURN MORE FIERCELY THAN ANY FIRE. I CANNOT BEAR HER HEAT. TAKE HER AND DO NOT DOUBT HER!

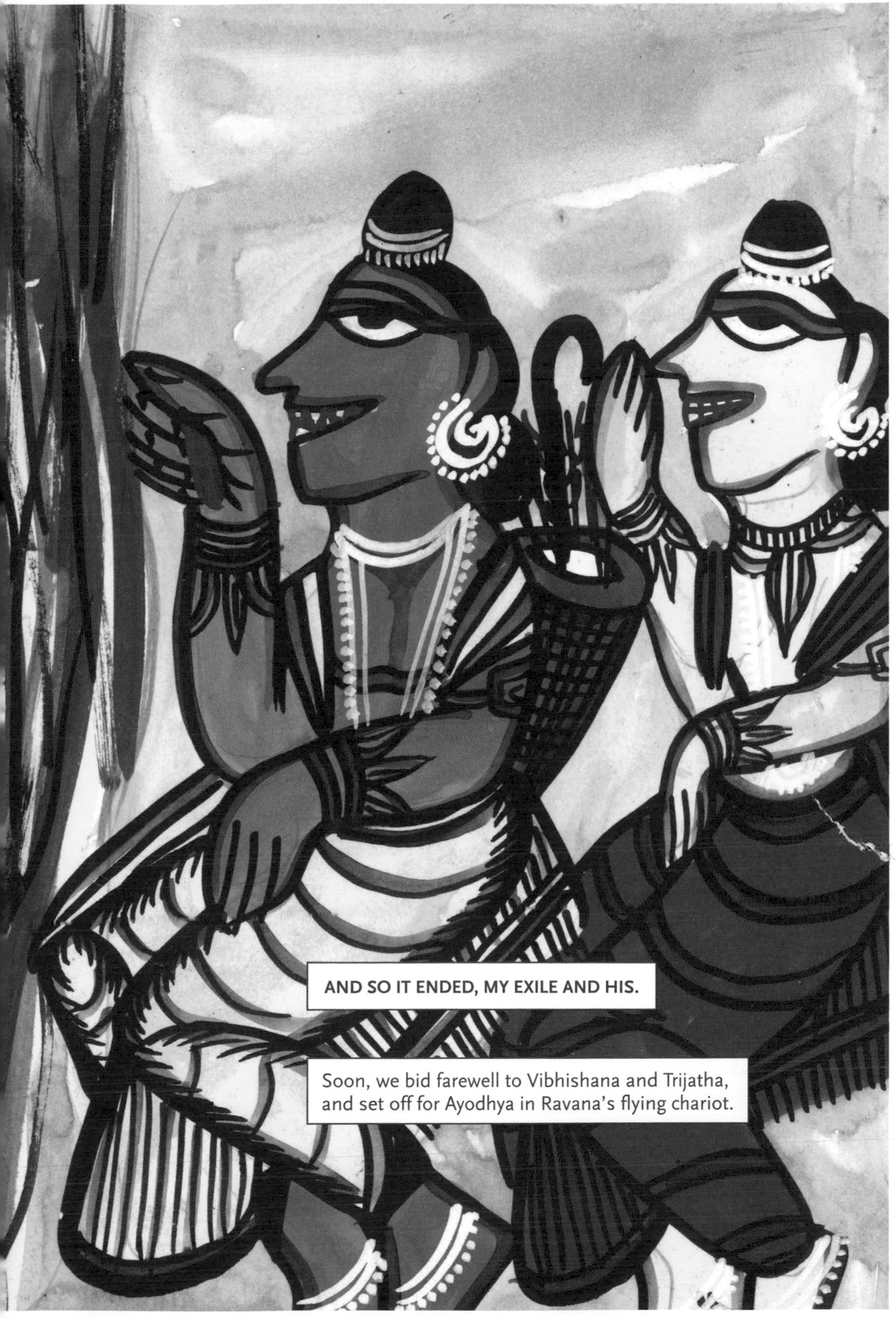
AND SO IT ENDED, MY EXILE AND HIS.
Soon, we bid farewell to Vibhishana and Trijatha, and set off for Ayodhya in Ravana's flying chariot.

RAMA WAS CROWNED KING OF AYODHYA
AND I BECAME HIS QUEEN.

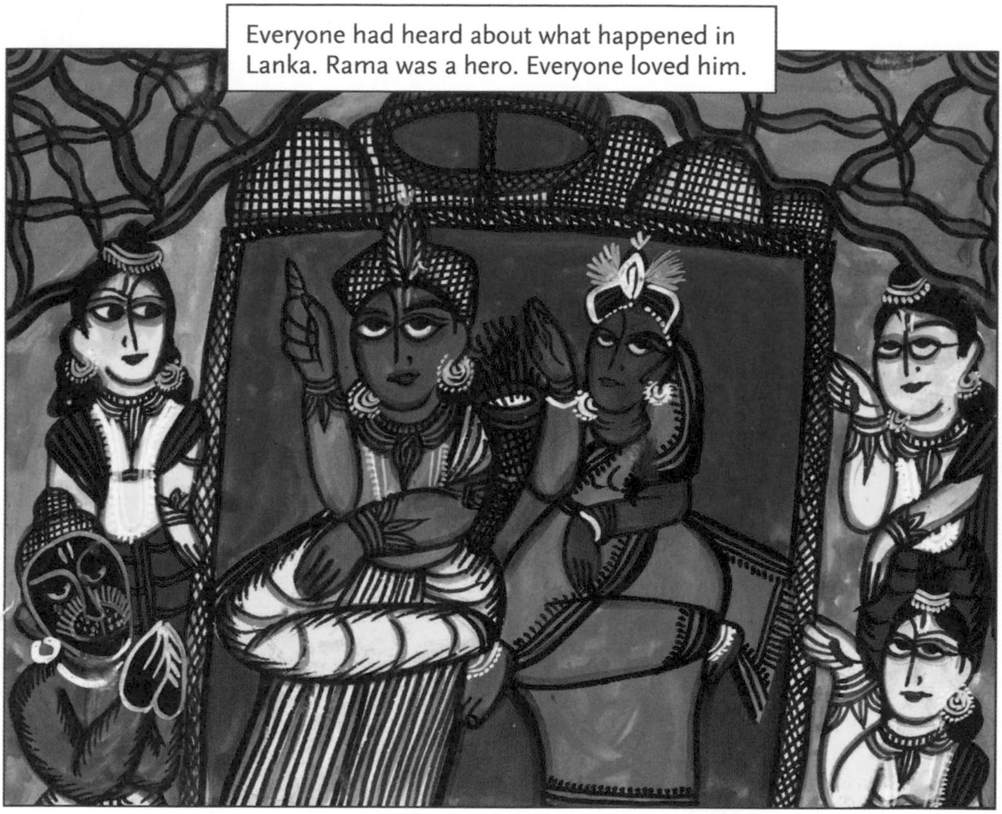
Everyone had heard about what happened in Lanka. Rama was a hero. Everyone loved him.

AND I?

WELL, SOON I WAS PREGNANT.

IN AYODHYA, WHISPERS AND RUMOURS SURROUNDED ME. THE PEOPLE OF AYODHYA DIDN'T KNOW THE ENTIRE STORY – OF MY SOJOURN IN LANKA, HOW I HAD SPURNED RAVANA, THE FIRE-TEST...

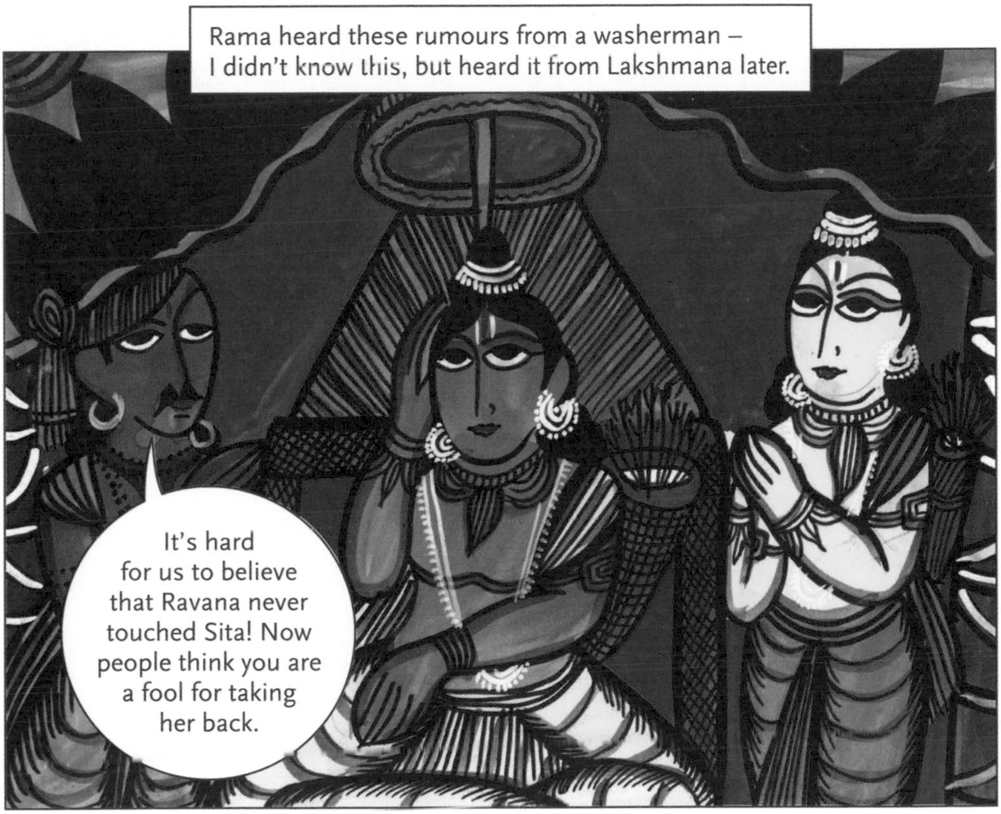
Rama heard these rumours from a washerman – I didn't know this, but heard it from Lakshmana later.
It's hard for us to believe that Ravana never touched Sita! Now people think you are a fool for taking her back.

RAMA WAS TROUBLED.

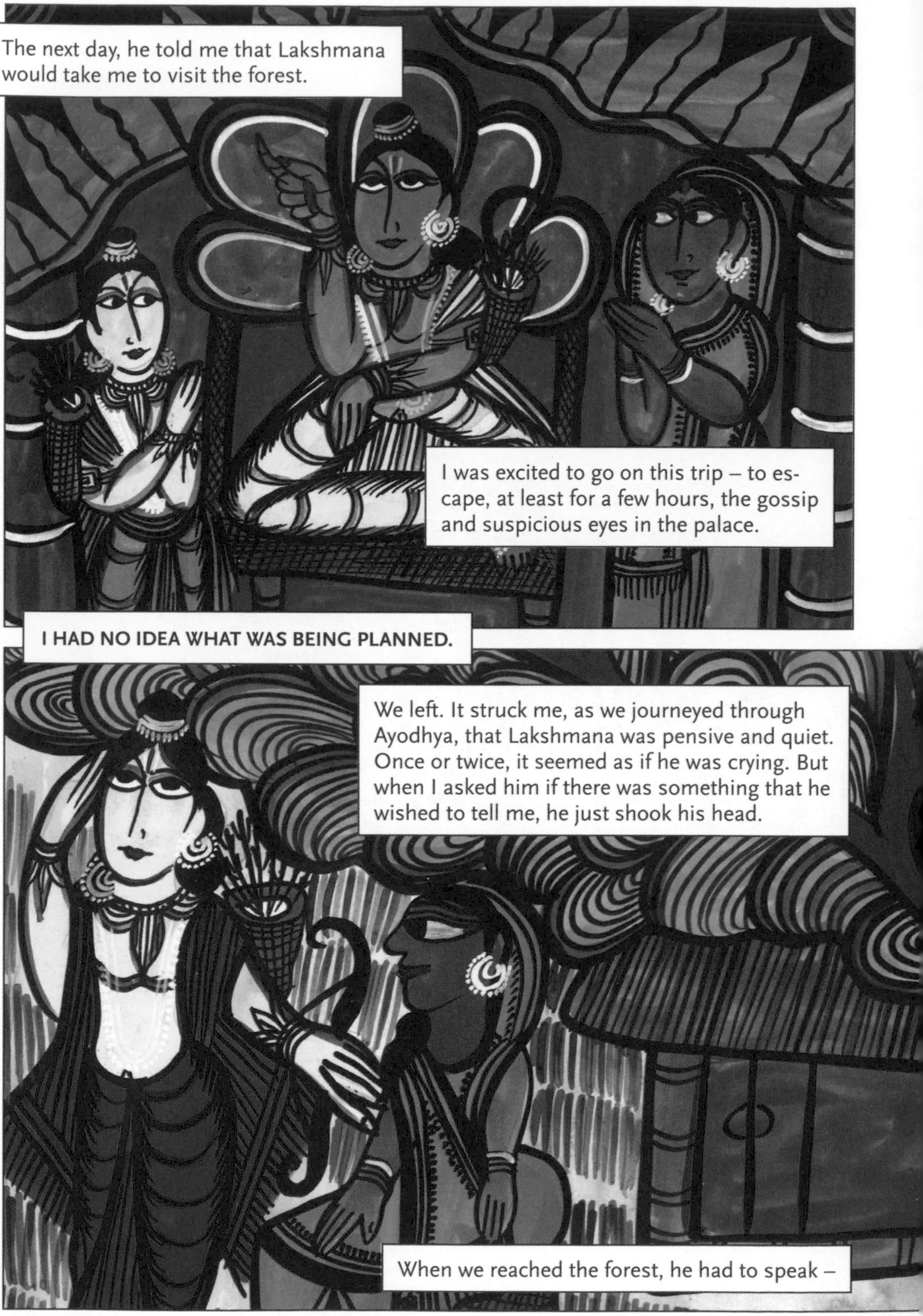
The next day, he told me that Lakshmana would take me to visit the forest.
I was excited to go on this trip – to escape, at least for a few hours, the gossip and suspicious eyes in the palace.
I HAD NO IDEA WHAT WAS BEING PLANNED.
We left. It struck me, as we journeyed through Ayodhya, that Lakshmana was pensive and quiet. Once or twice, it seemed as if he was crying. But when I asked him if there was something that he wished to tell me, he just shook his head.
When we reached the forest, he had to speak –

HE TOLD ME THAT RAMA HAD INSTRUCTED HIM TO ABANDON ME IN THE FOREST.

ABANDON?

The same accusation. The same doubts.

I wish I had died in Lanka.

Now I am pregnant, and alone.

My belly is huge, and I cannot see the ground under my feet. How will I avoid the poisonous snakes that slither across this earth? How will I, with my heavy belly and swollen ankles, outrun beasts of prey?

And when my hour draws close, when my child is to be born, who will calm my fears and assist me in my labour?

How will I, alone, raise a child, born to be king, in this forest?

The forest heard Sita's story.

Her tale was passed from tree to tree, leaf to leaf. The birds flew high into the sky, promising to spread her tale across the forest.

The snakes, hearing of her loss, vowed to stay free of her feet, and the lions and tigers swore to leave her in peace.

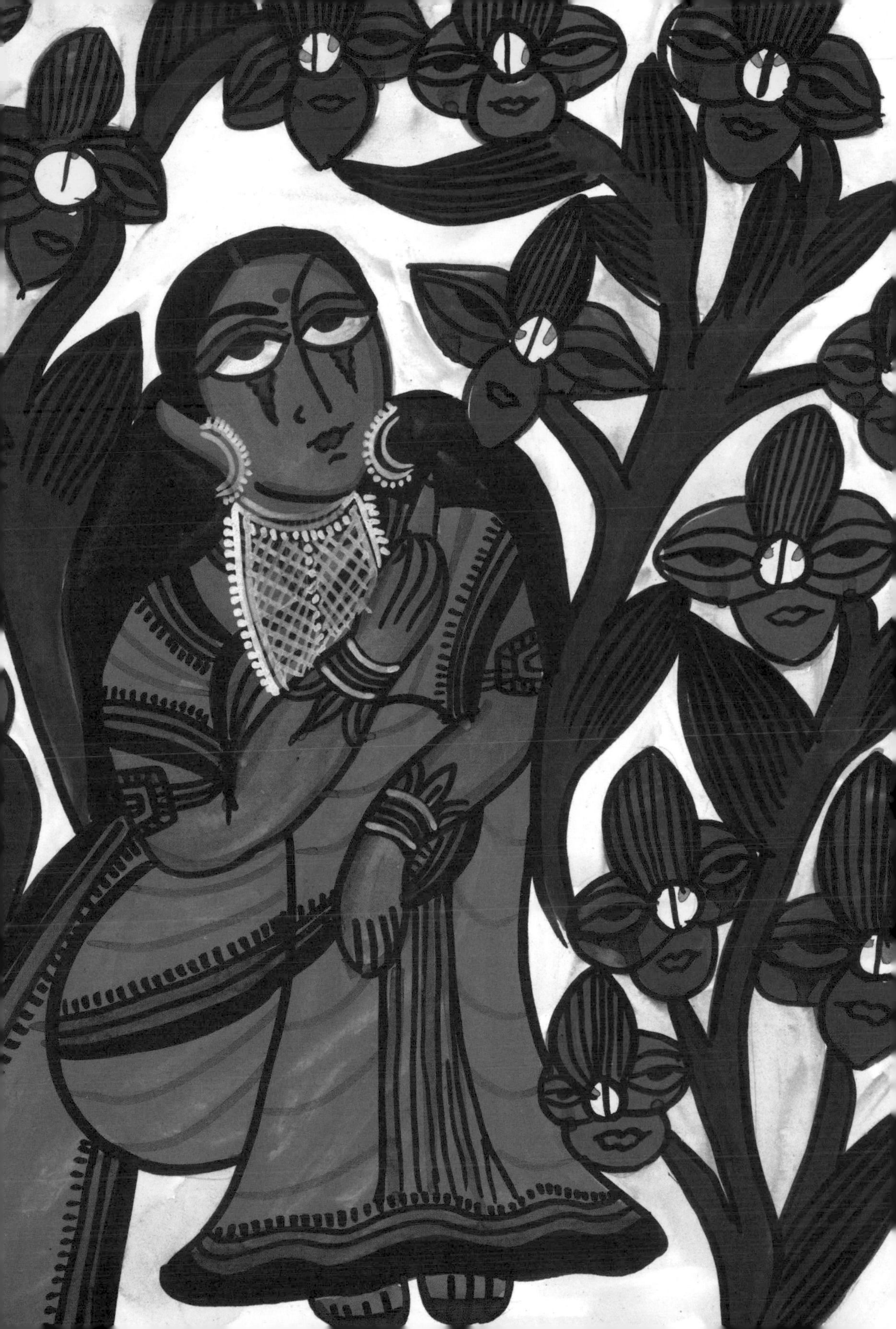

And the whispers of the forest were borne by the breeze to the hermitage of Valmiki, a sage who lived deep in the heart of the forest. He heard the forest and offered Sita a home. She was grateful.

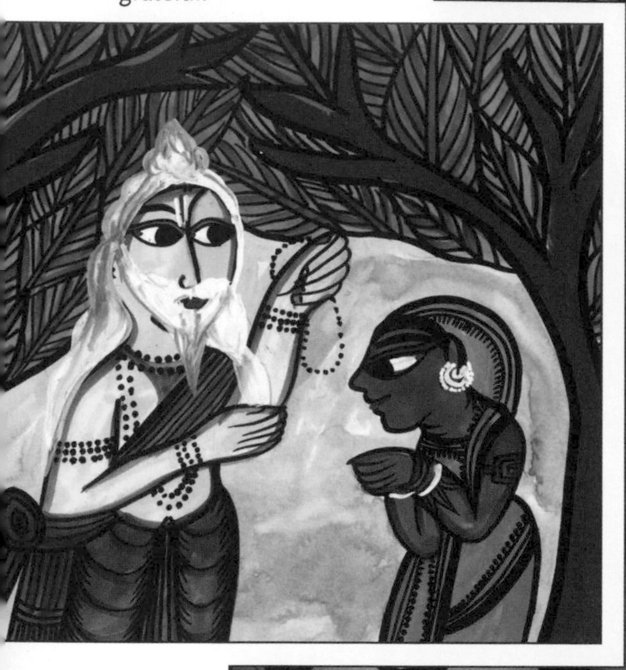

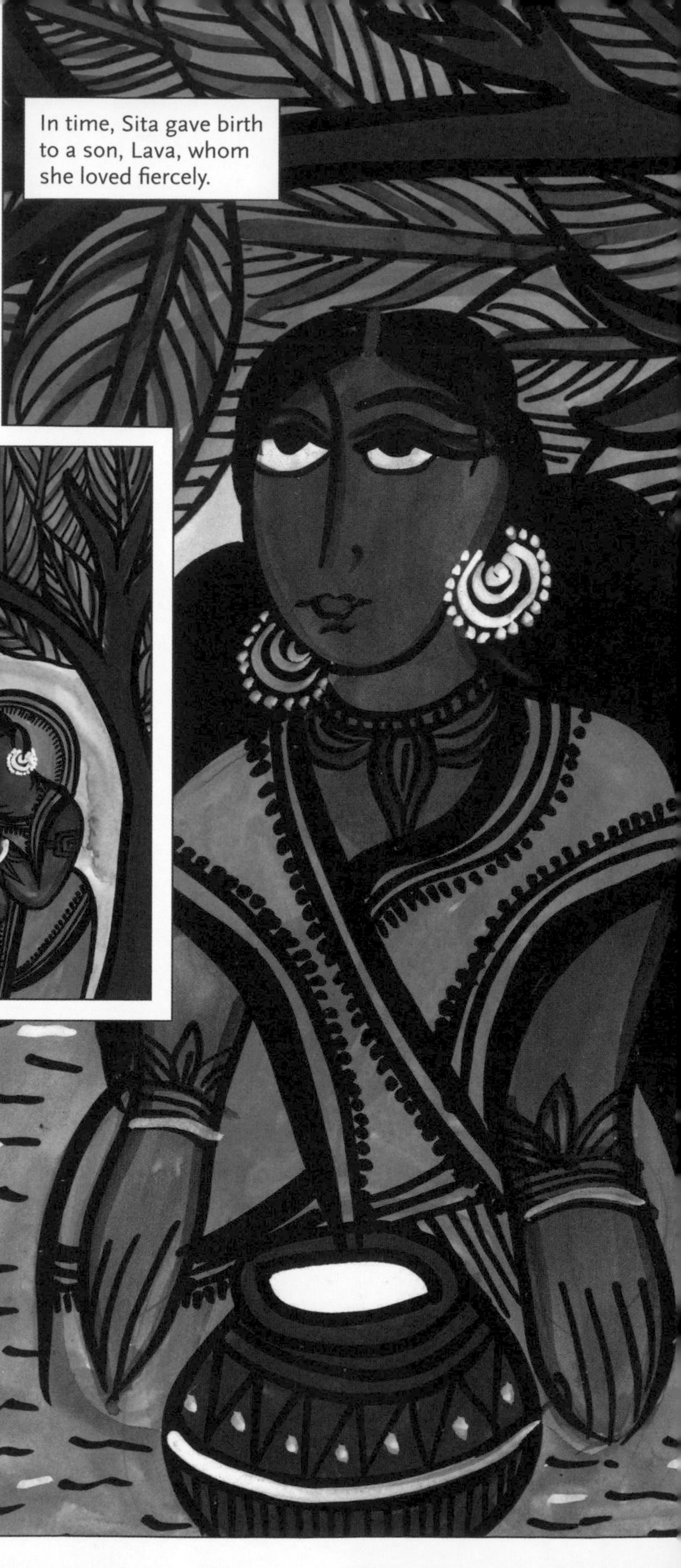
In time, Sita gave birth to a son, Lava, whom she loved fiercely.

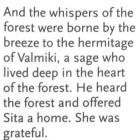

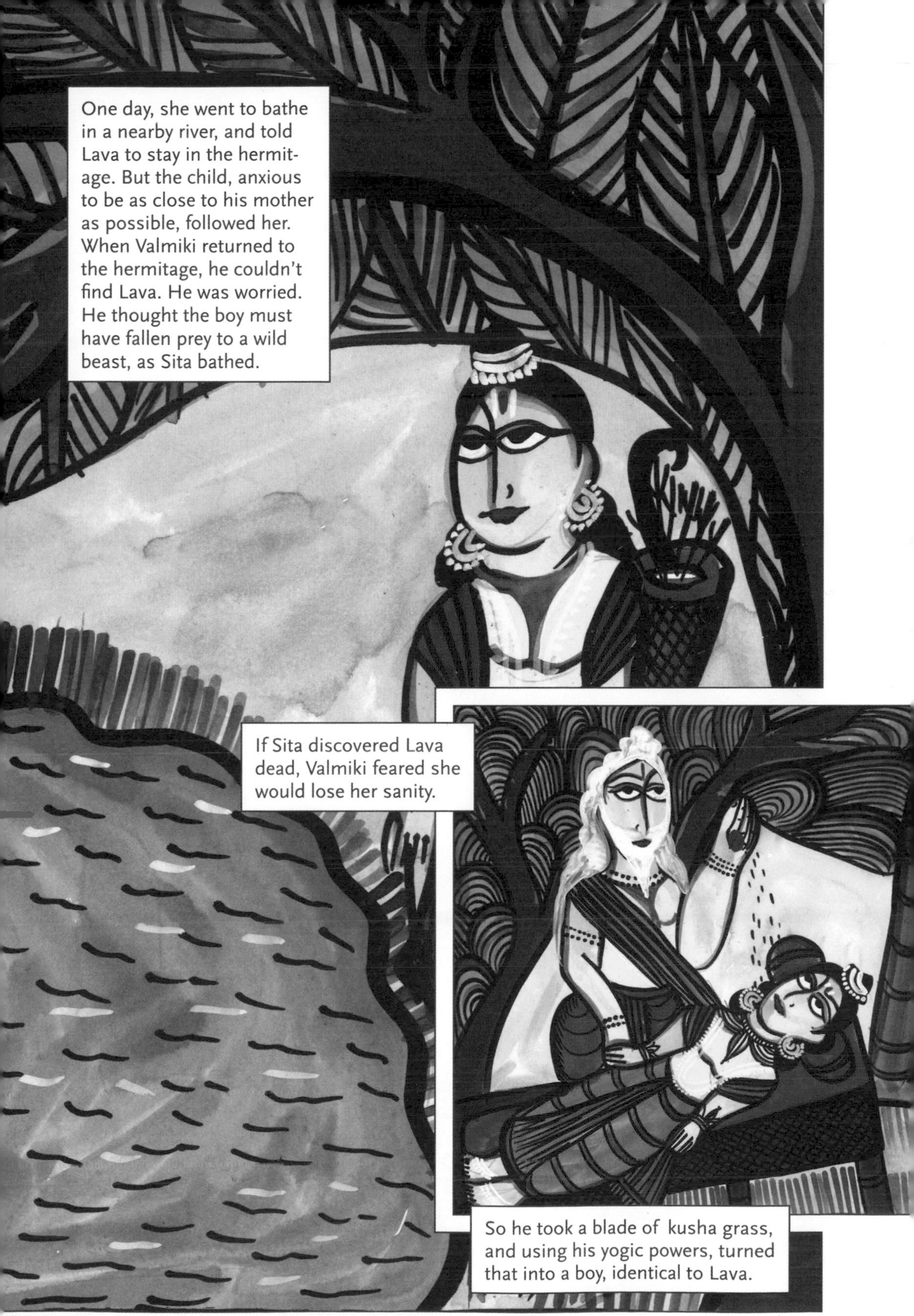
One day, she went to bathe in a nearby river, and told Lava to stay in the hermitage. But the child, anxious to be as close to his mother as possible, followed her. When Valmiki returned to the hermitage, he couldn't find Lava. He was worried. He thought the boy must have fallen prey to a wild beast, as Sita bathed.
If Sita discovered Lava dead, Valmiki feared she would lose her sanity.
So he took a blade of kusha grass, and using his yogic powers, turned that into a boy, identical to Lava.

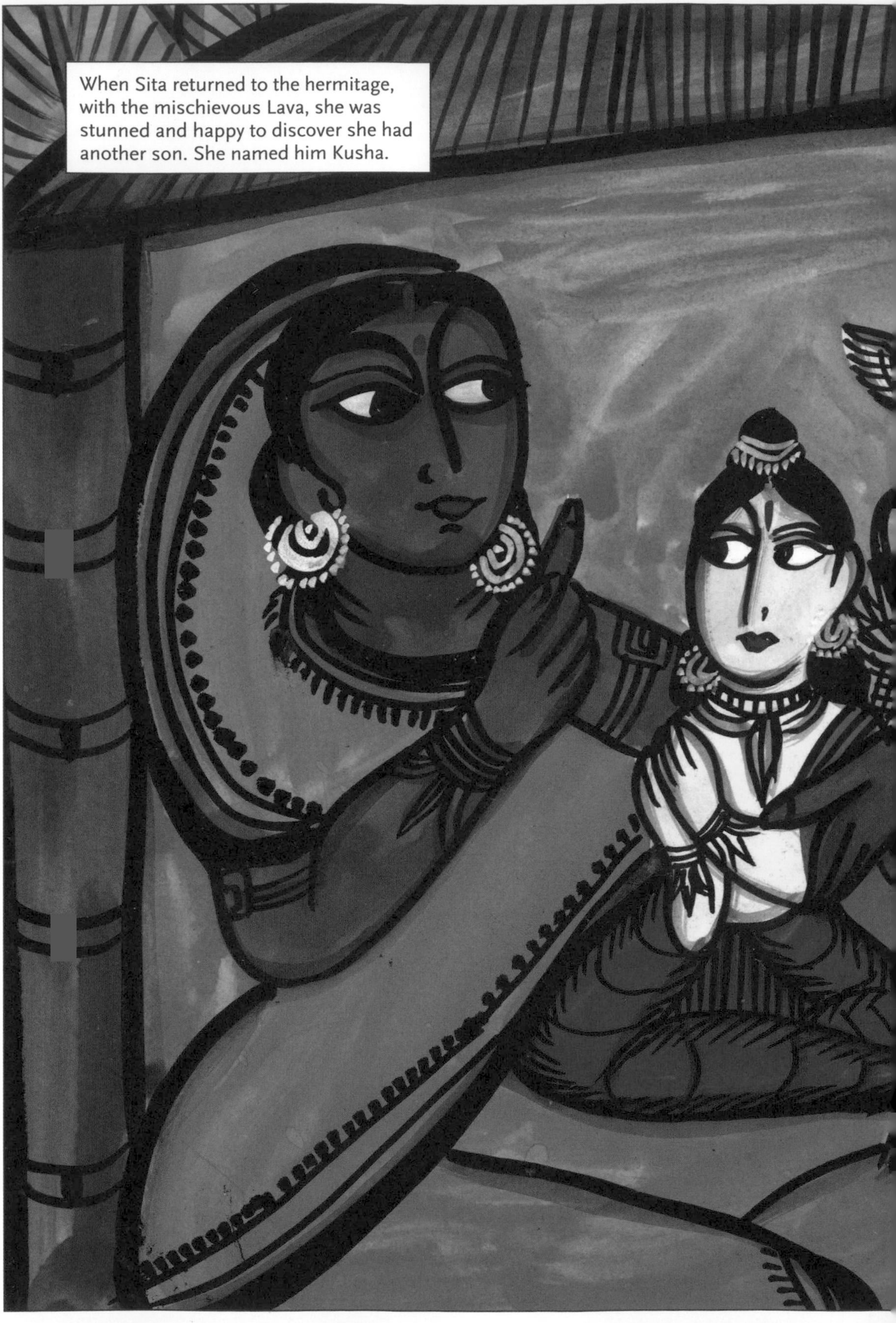
When Sita returned to the hermitage, with the mischievous Lava, she was stunned and happy to discover she had another son. She named him Kusha.

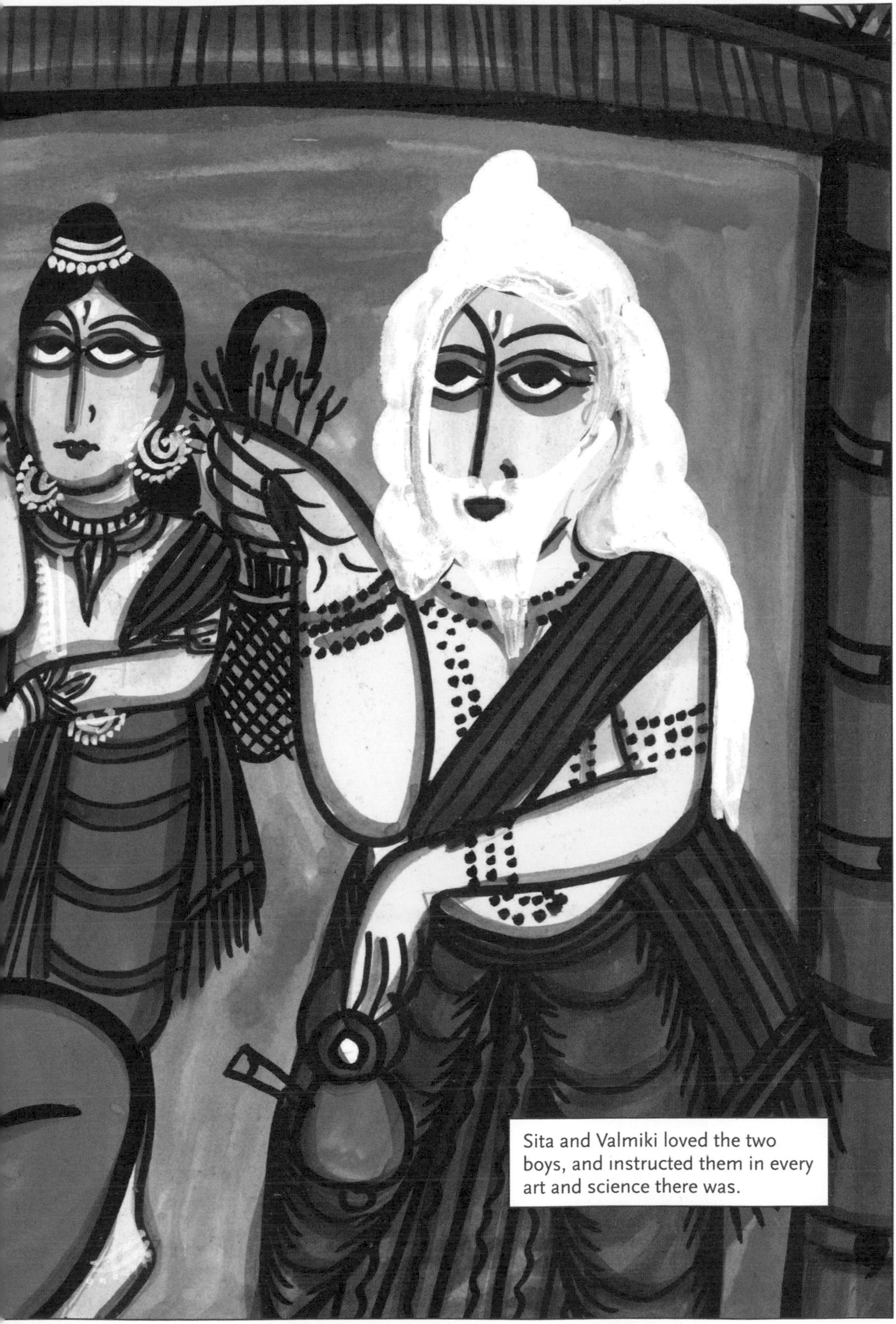
Sita and Valmiki loved the two boys, and instructed them in every art and science there was.

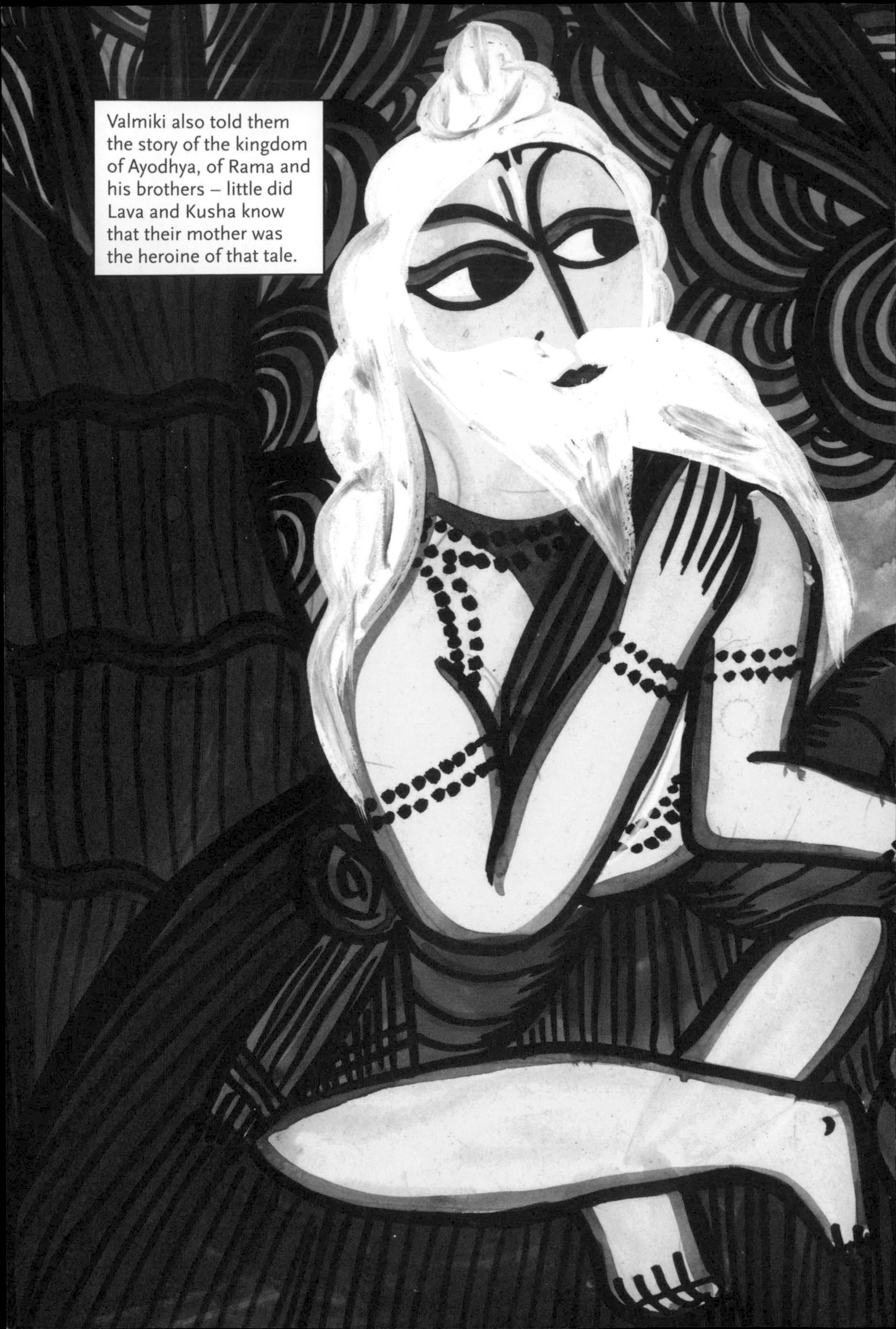
Valmiki also told them the story of the kingdom of Ayodhya, of Rama and his brothers – little did Lava and Kusha know that their mother was the heroine of that tale.

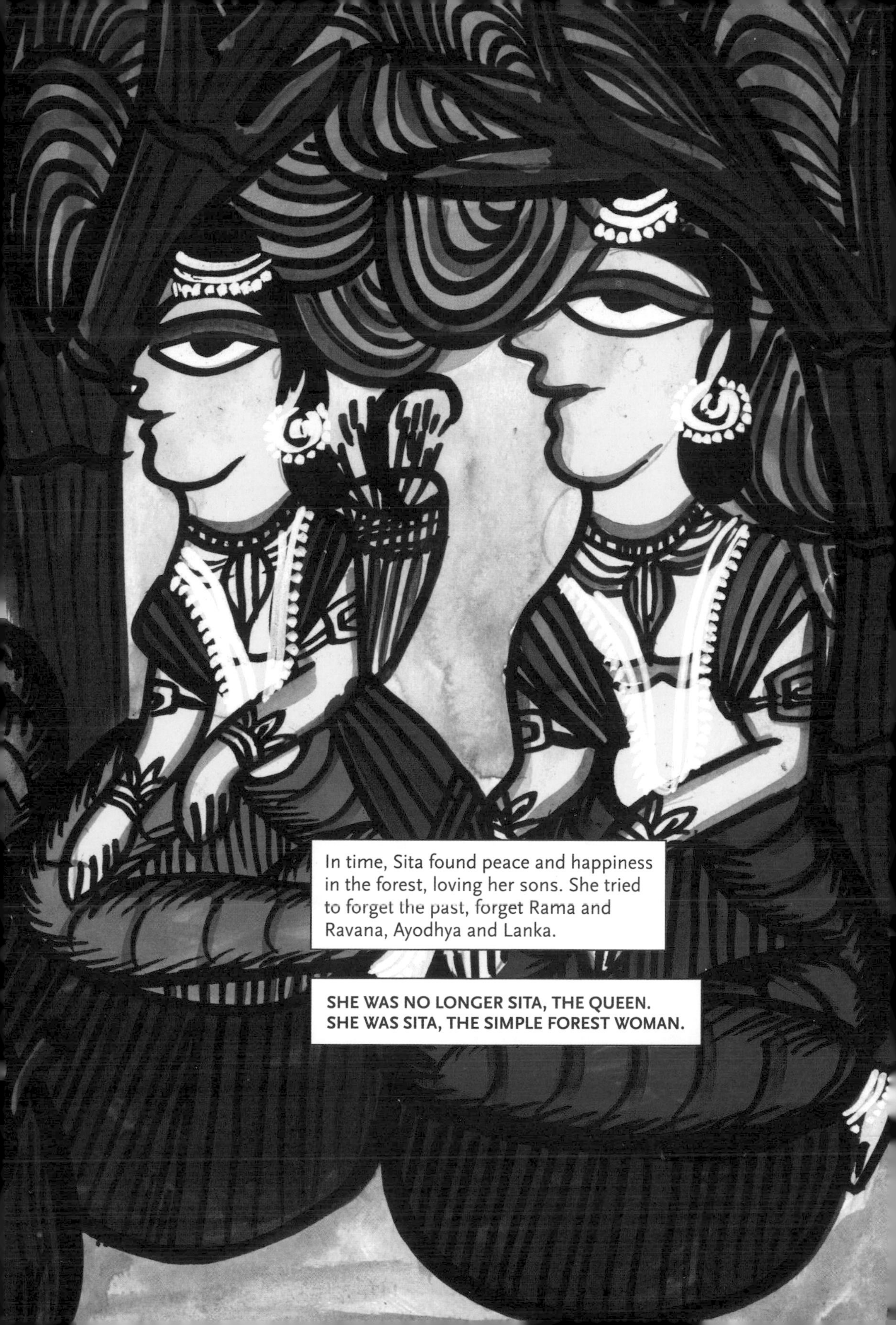
In time, Sita found peace and happiness in the forest, loving her sons. She tried to forget the past, forget Rama and Ravana, Ayodhya and Lanka.
SHE WAS NO LONGER SITA, THE QUEEN. SHE WAS SITA, THE SIMPLE FOREST WOMAN.

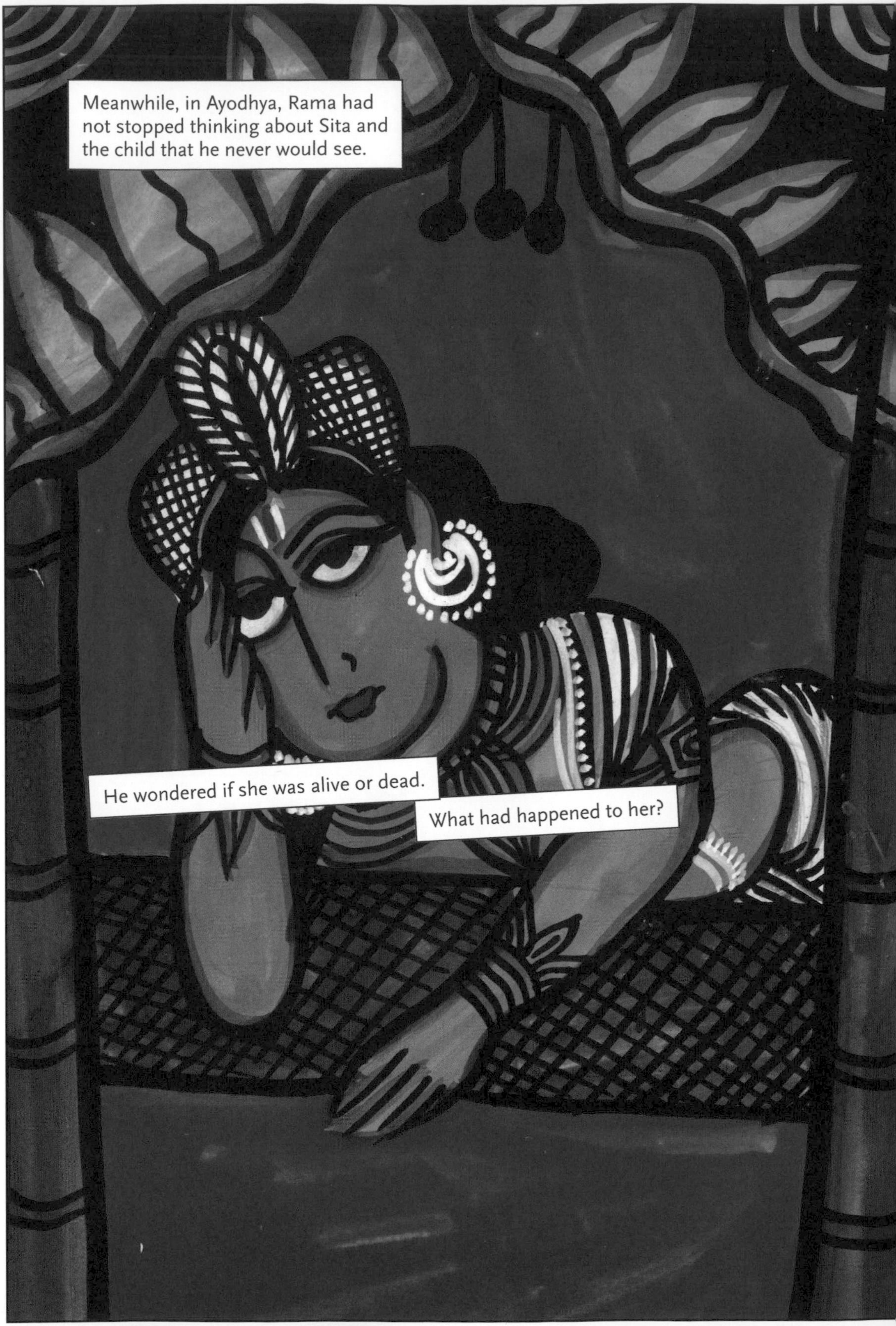
Meanwhile, in Ayodhya, Rama had not stopped thinking about Sita and the child that he never would see.
He wondered if she was alive or dead.
What had happened to her?

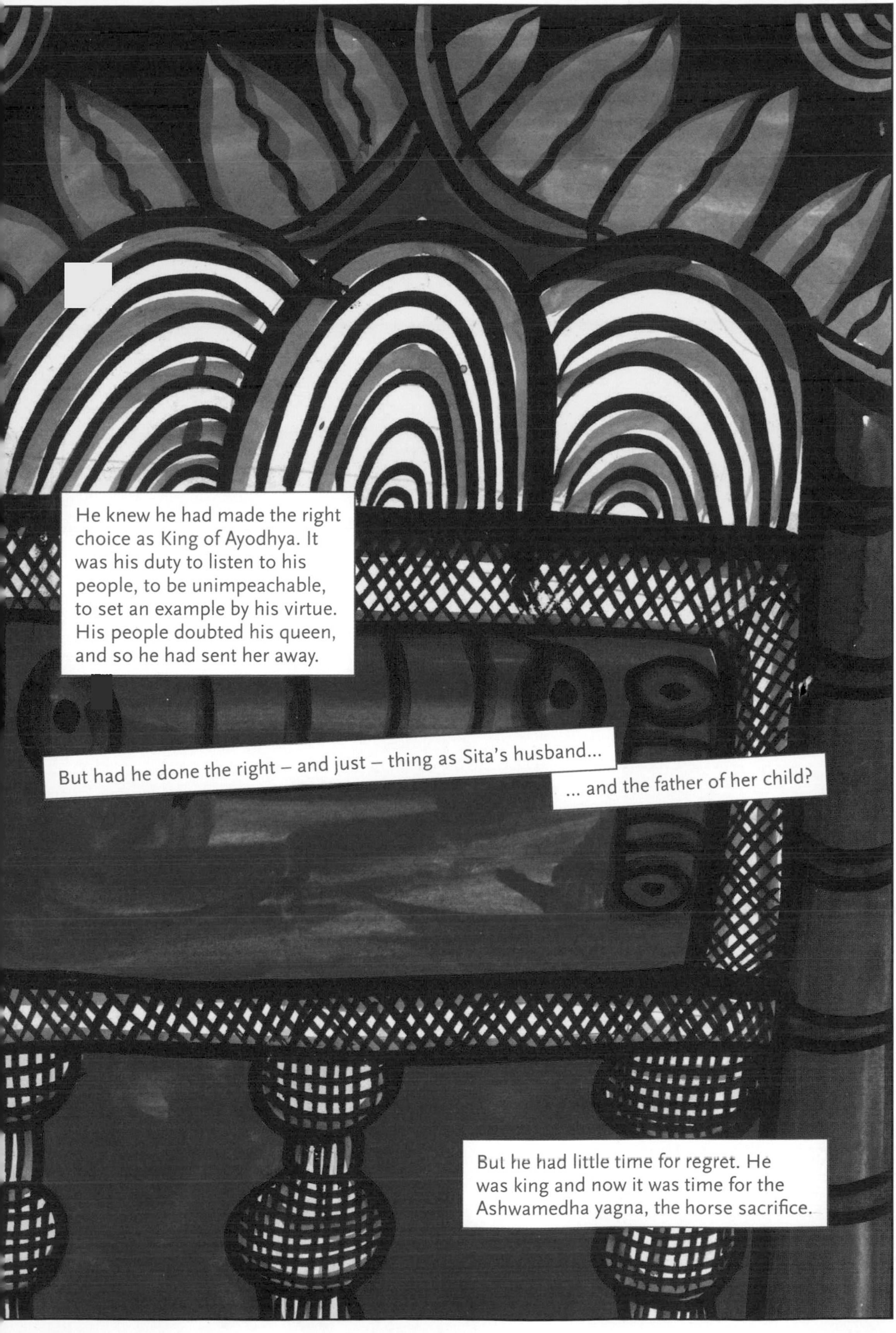
He knew he had made the right choice as King of Ayodhya. It was his duty to listen to his people, to be unimpeachable, to set an example by his virtue. His people doubted his queen, and so he had sent her away.
But had he done the right – and just – thing as Sita's husband...
... and the father of her child?
But he had little time for regret. He was king and now it was time for the Ashwamedha yagna, the horse sacrifice.

As King of Ayodhya, Rama would release a white horse. The horse could take any path, travel anywhere it chose. If anyone stopped it – it meant they had challenged Rama's authority and rule. An army would follow the horse, ready to spurn such challenges.

IF THE HORSE WENT ABOUT LARGE SWATHES OF LAND UNCHALLENGED, RAMA'S ARMY WOULD CLAIM THAT TERRITORY FOR THEIR KING.

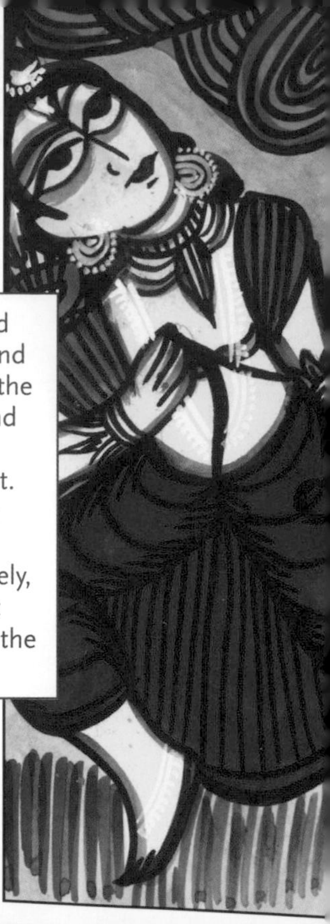

As the horse roamed the wilderness beyond Ayodhya, it entered the Dandaka forest – and sure enough Lava and Kusha spotted it. Surprised at finding such a beautiful animal, roaming freely, they captured it, not realizing that it was the king's horse.

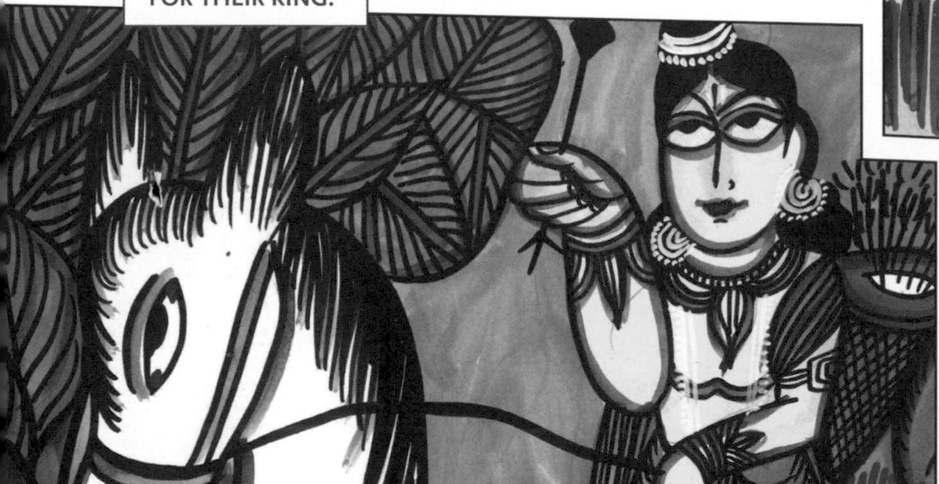

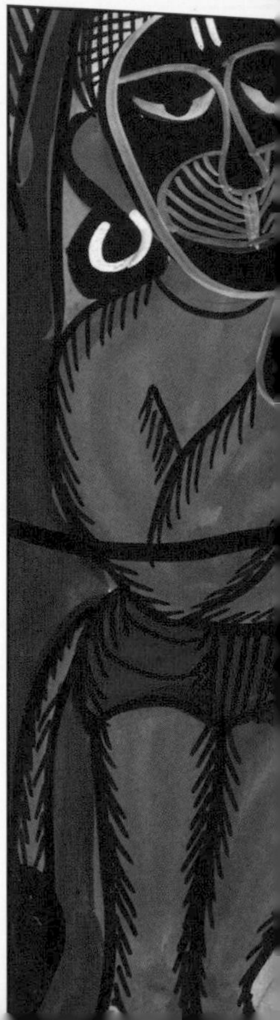

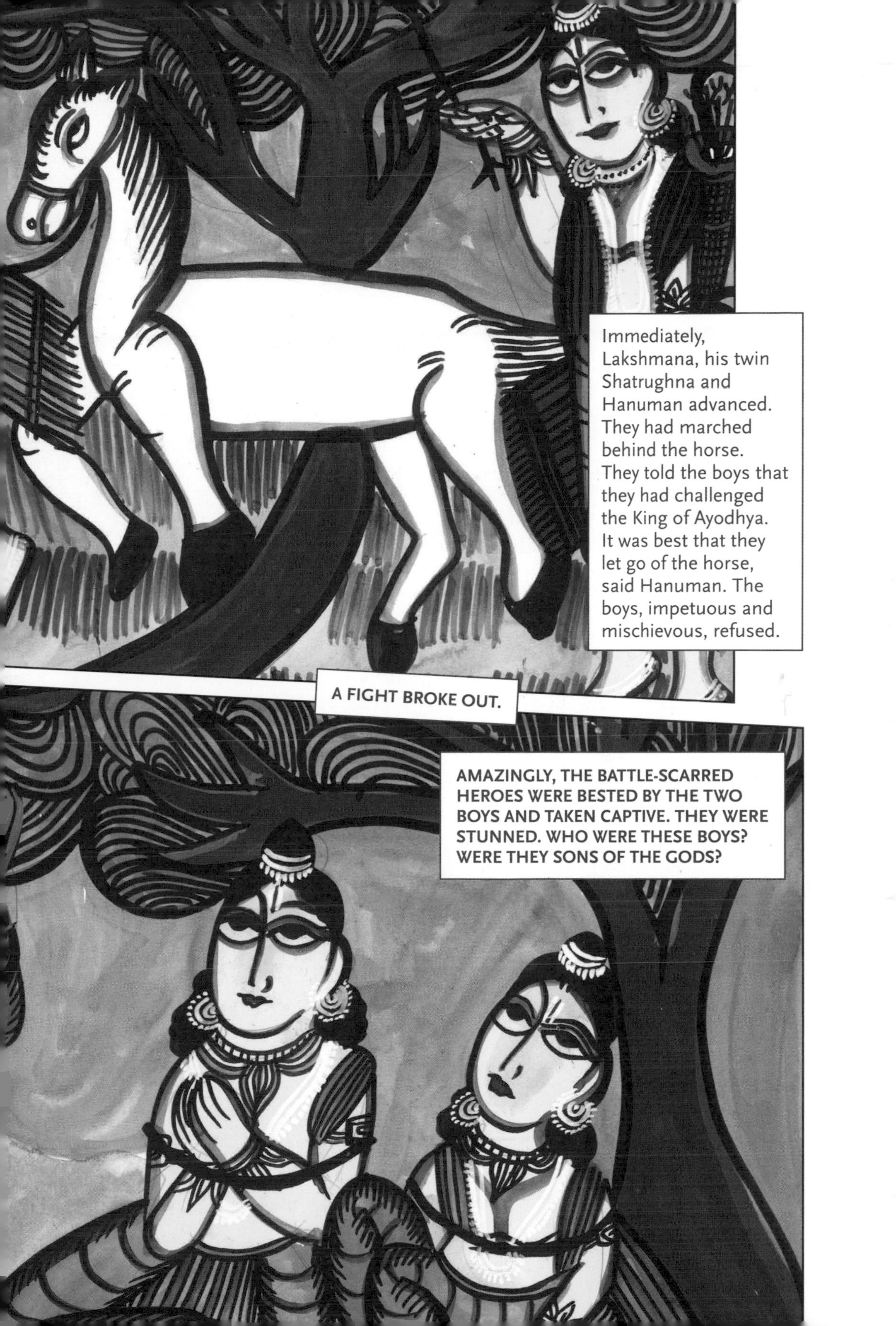
Immediately, Lakshmana, his twin Shatrughna and Hanuman advanced. They had marched behind the horse. They told the boys that they had challenged the King of Ayodhya. It was best that they let go of the horse, said Hanuman. The boys, impetuous and mischievous, refused.
A FIGHT BROKE OUT.
AMAZINGLY, THE BATTLE-SCARRED HEROES WERE BESTED BY THE TWO BOYS AND TAKEN CAPTIVE. THEY WERE STUNNED. WHO WERE THESE BOYS? WERE THEY SONS OF THE GODS?

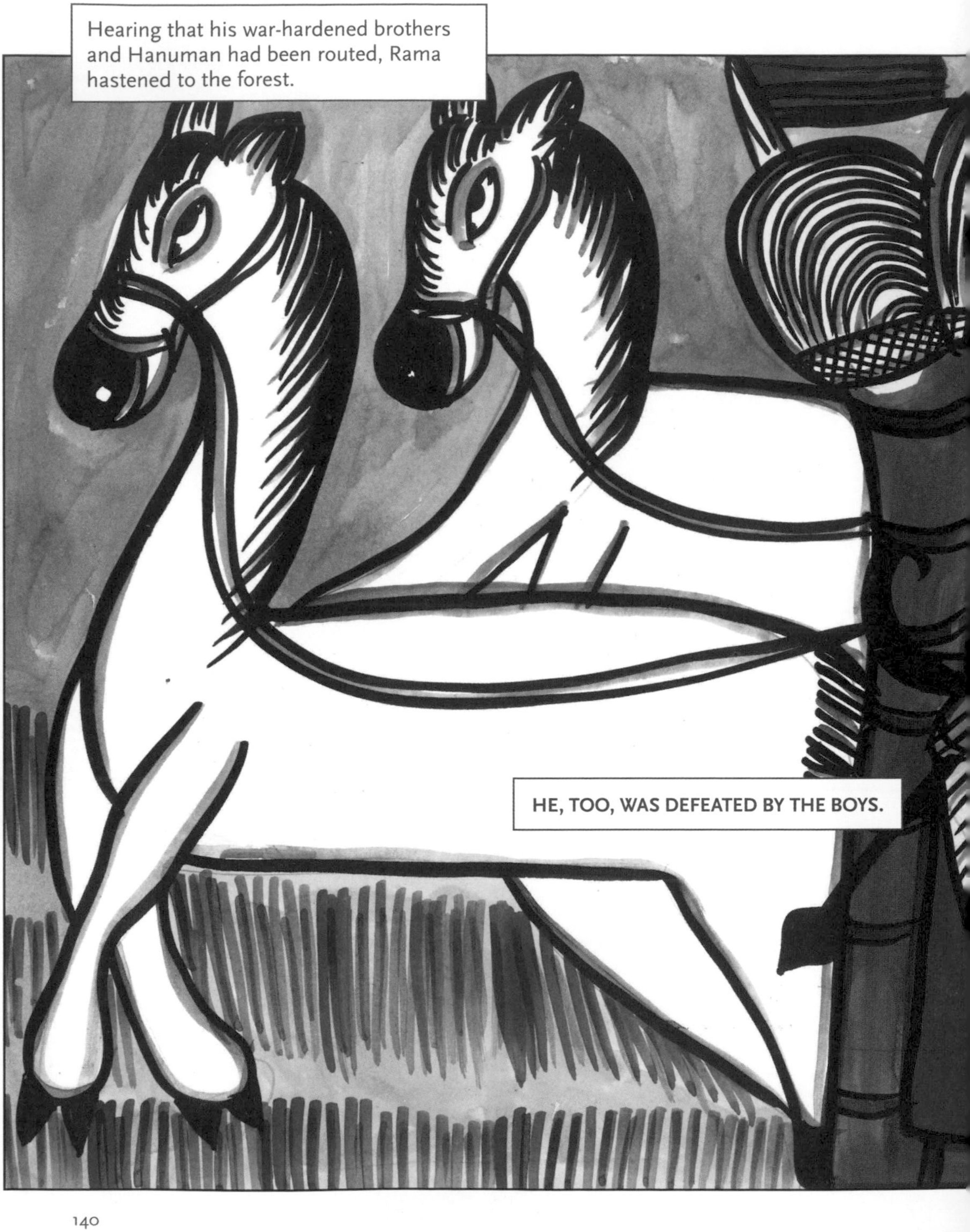
Hearing that his war-hardened brothers and Hanuman had been routed, Rama hastened to the forest.
HE, TOO, WAS DEFEATED BY THE BOYS.

Meanwhile, ingenious as ever, Hanuman escaped his captors and found his way into the deep woods. He found Sita in Valmiki's hermitage –

AND REALIZED THAT THE TWO GIFTED BOYS WHO HAD DEFEATED HIM WERE HER SONS.

He told her what happened, and how her sons had taken Rama captive.

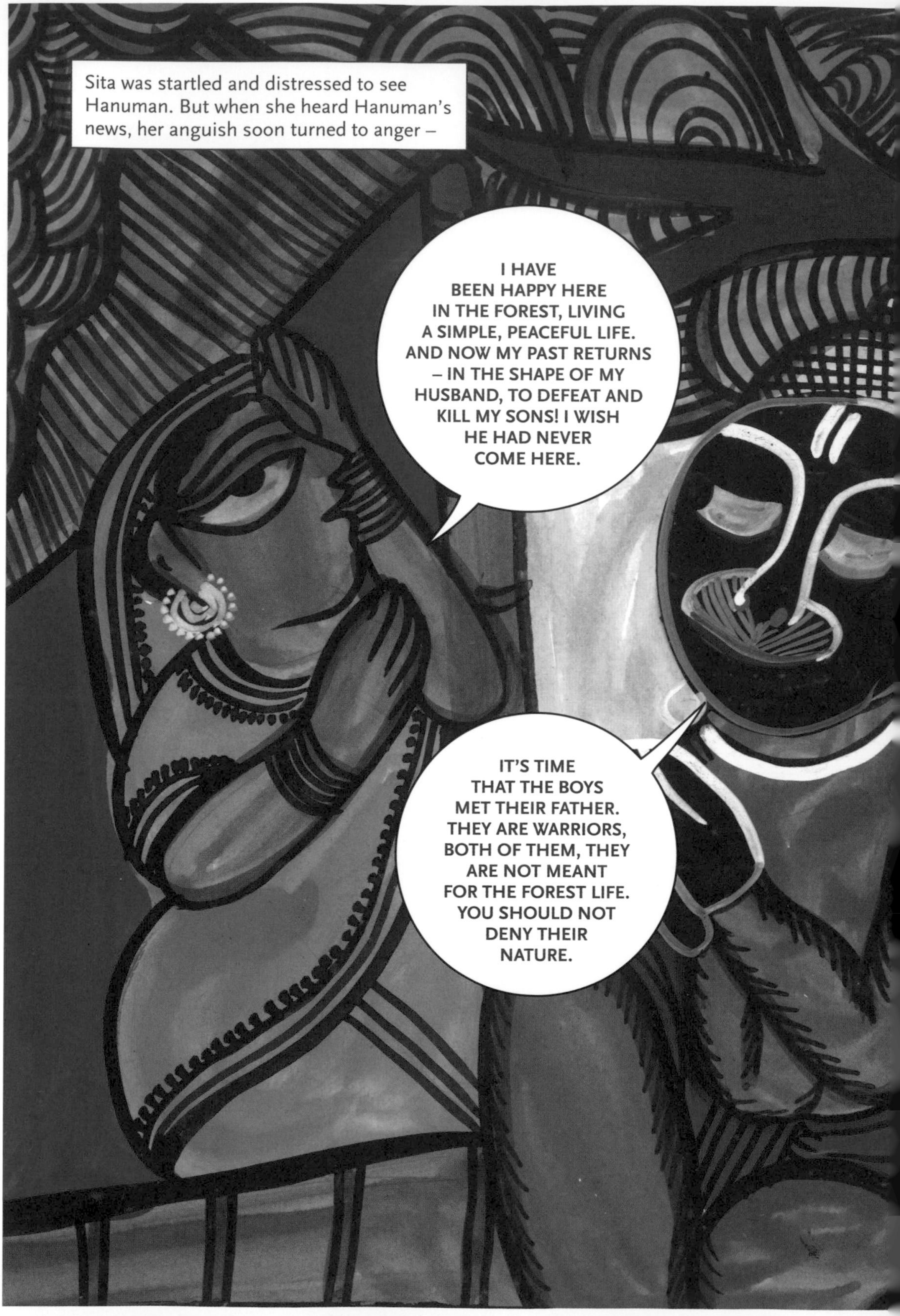
Sita was startled and distressed to see Hanuman. But when she heard Hanuman's news, her anguish soon turned to anger –
I HAVE BEEN HAPPY HERE IN THE FOREST, LIVING A SIMPLE, PEACEFUL LIFE. AND NOW MY PAST RETURNS – IN THE SHAPE OF MY HUSBAND, TO DEFEAT AND KILL MY SONS! I WISH HE HAD NEVER COME HERE.
IT'S TIME THAT THE BOYS MET THEIR FATHER. THEY ARE WARRIORS, BOTH OF THEM, THEY ARE NOT MEANT FOR THE FOREST LIFE. YOU SHOULD NOT DENY THEIR NATURE.

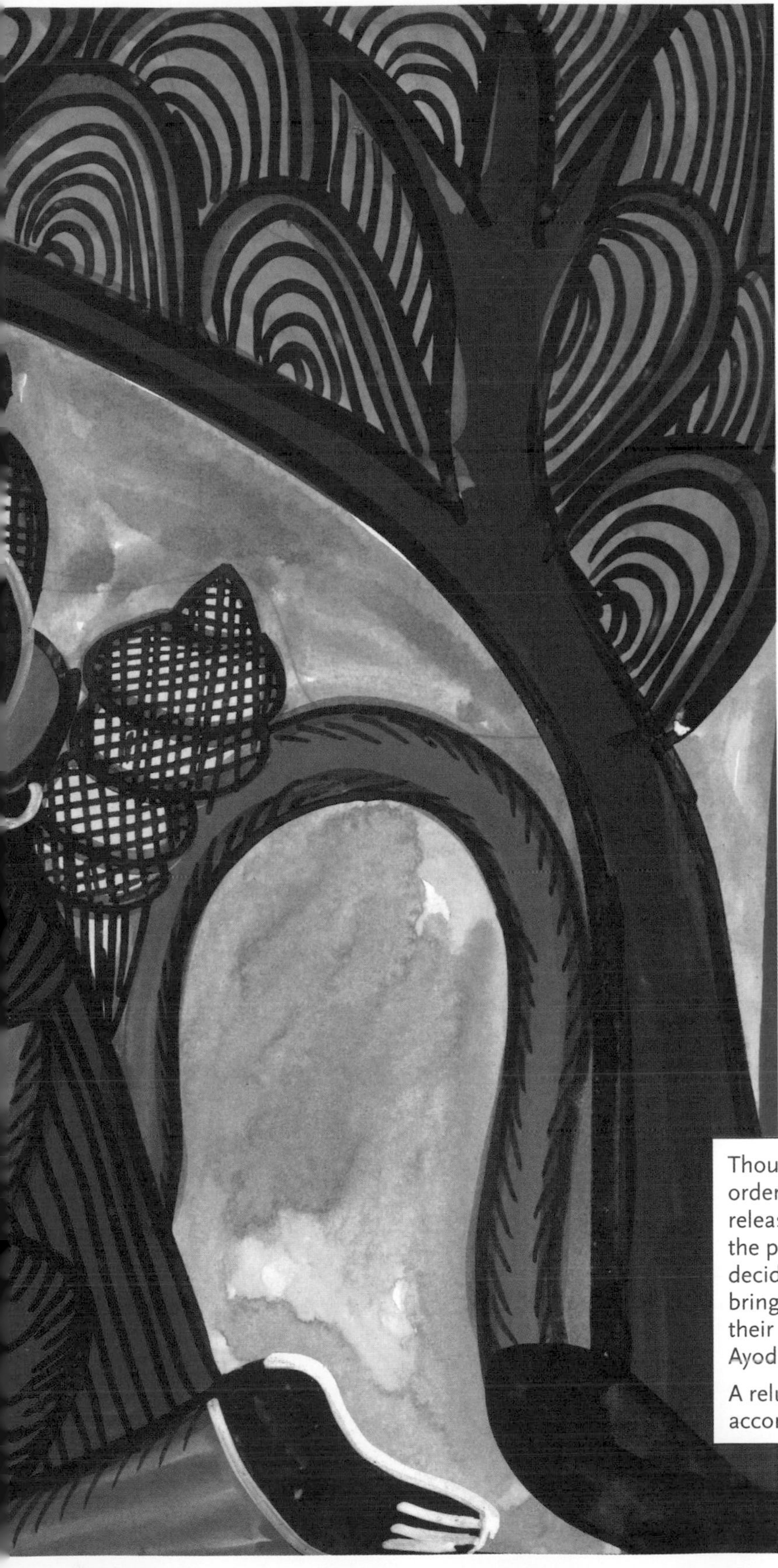

Though outraged, Sita ordered her sons to release the horse and the prisoners. Valmiki decided that he would bring Sita's sons to their father at the Ayodhya court.

A reluctant Sita accompanied them.

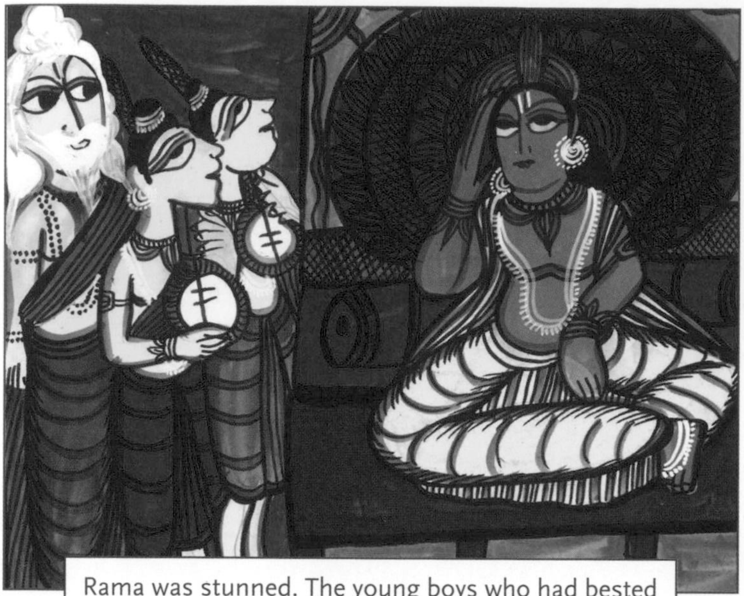

Rama was stunned. The young boys who had bested him in the forest were none other than his sons.

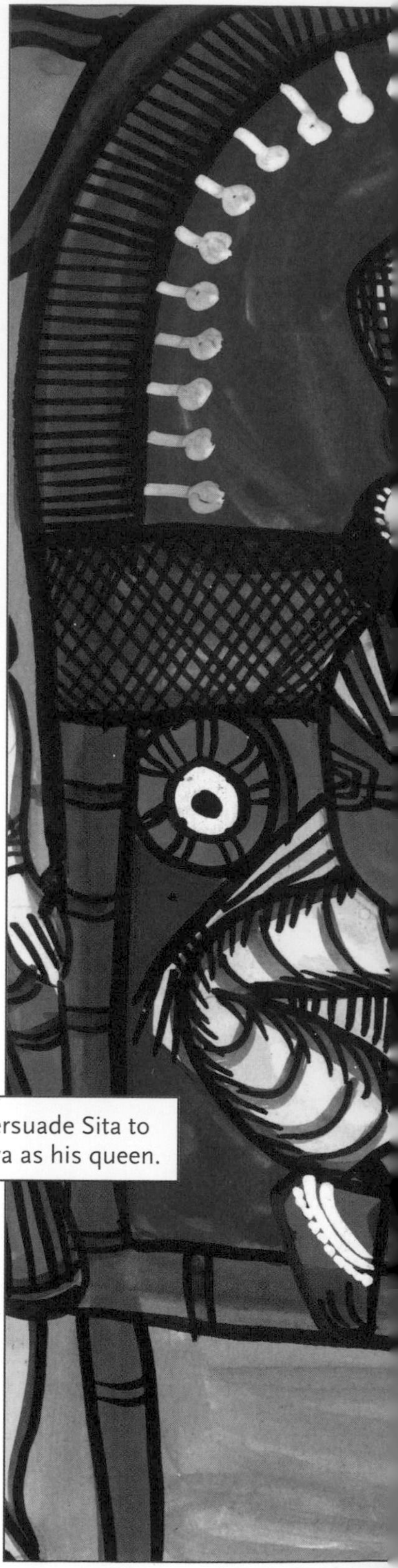

Rama tried to persuade Sita to return to Ayodhya as his queen.

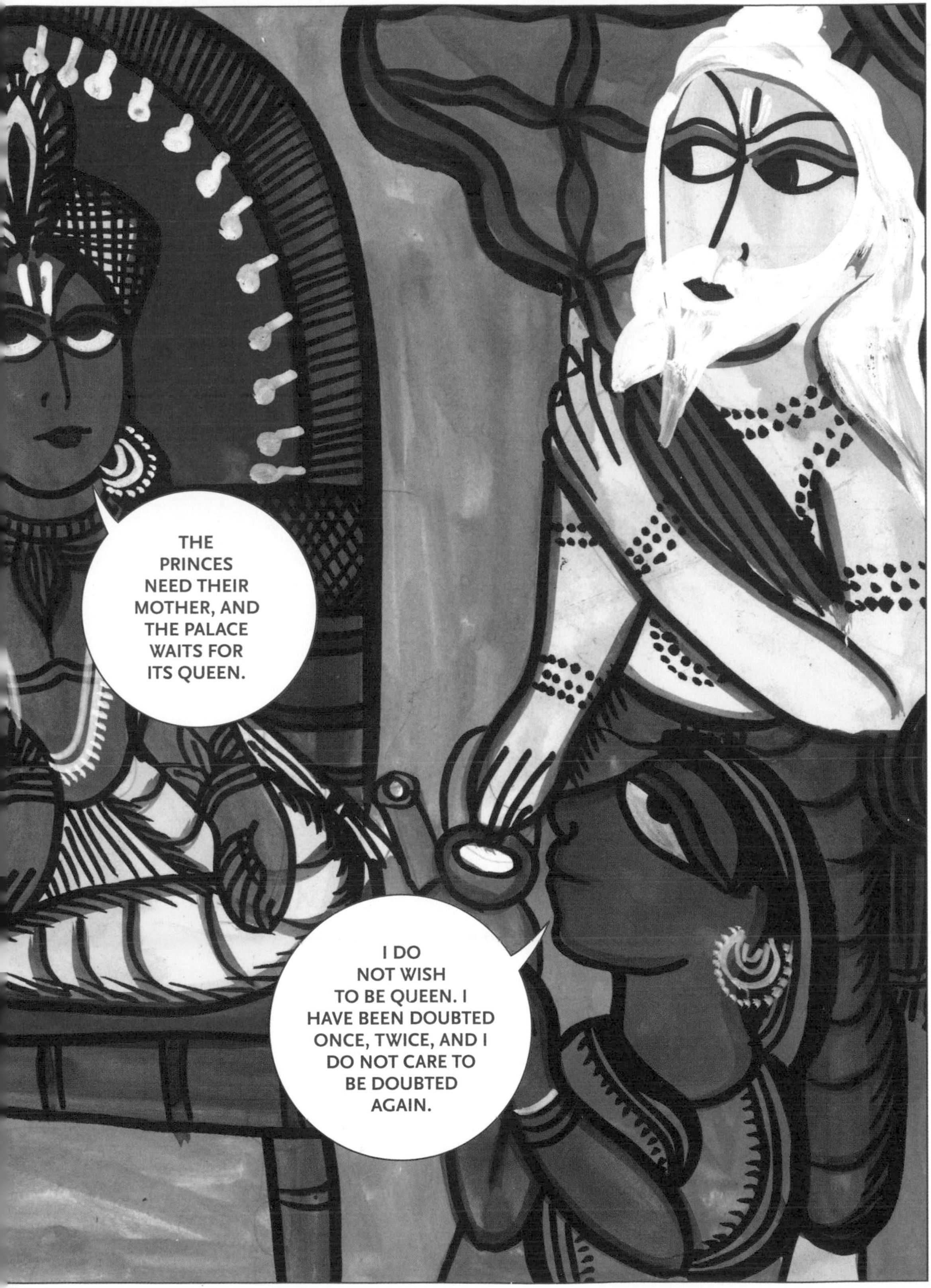
THE PRINCES NEED THEIR MOTHER, AND THE PALACE WAITS FOR ITS QUEEN.
I DO NOT WISH TO BE QUEEN. I HAVE BEEN DOUBTED ONCE, TWICE, AND I DO NOT CARE TO BE DOUBTED AGAIN.

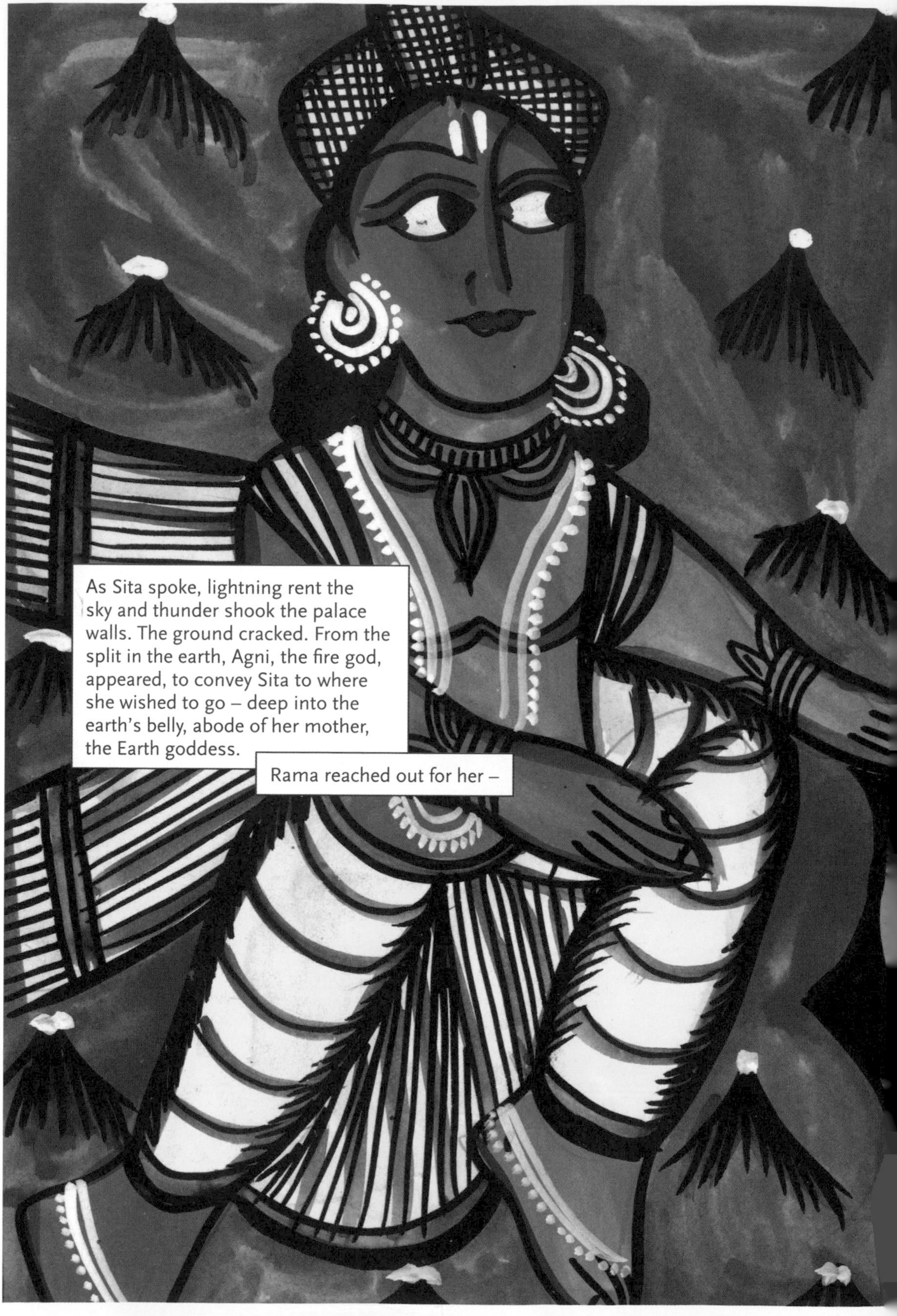
As Sita spoke, lightning rent the sky and thunder shook the palace walls. The ground cracked. From the split in the earth, Agni, the fire god, appeared, to convey Sita to where she wished to go – deep into the earth's belly, abode of her mother, the Earth goddess.
Rama reached out for her –

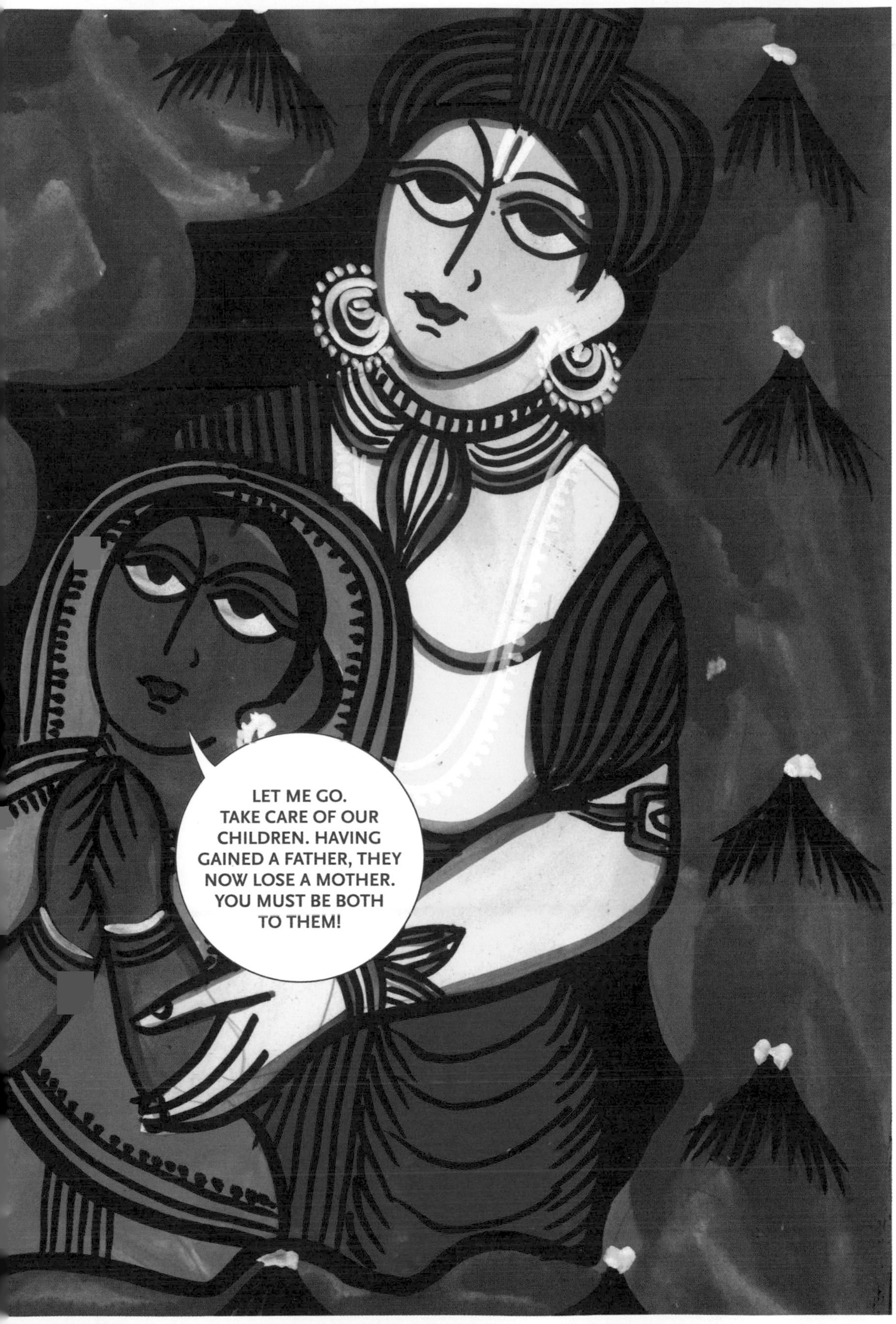
LET ME GO. TAKE CARE OF OUR CHILDREN. HAVING GAINED A FATHER, THEY NOW LOSE A MOTHER. YOU MUST BE BOTH TO THEM!

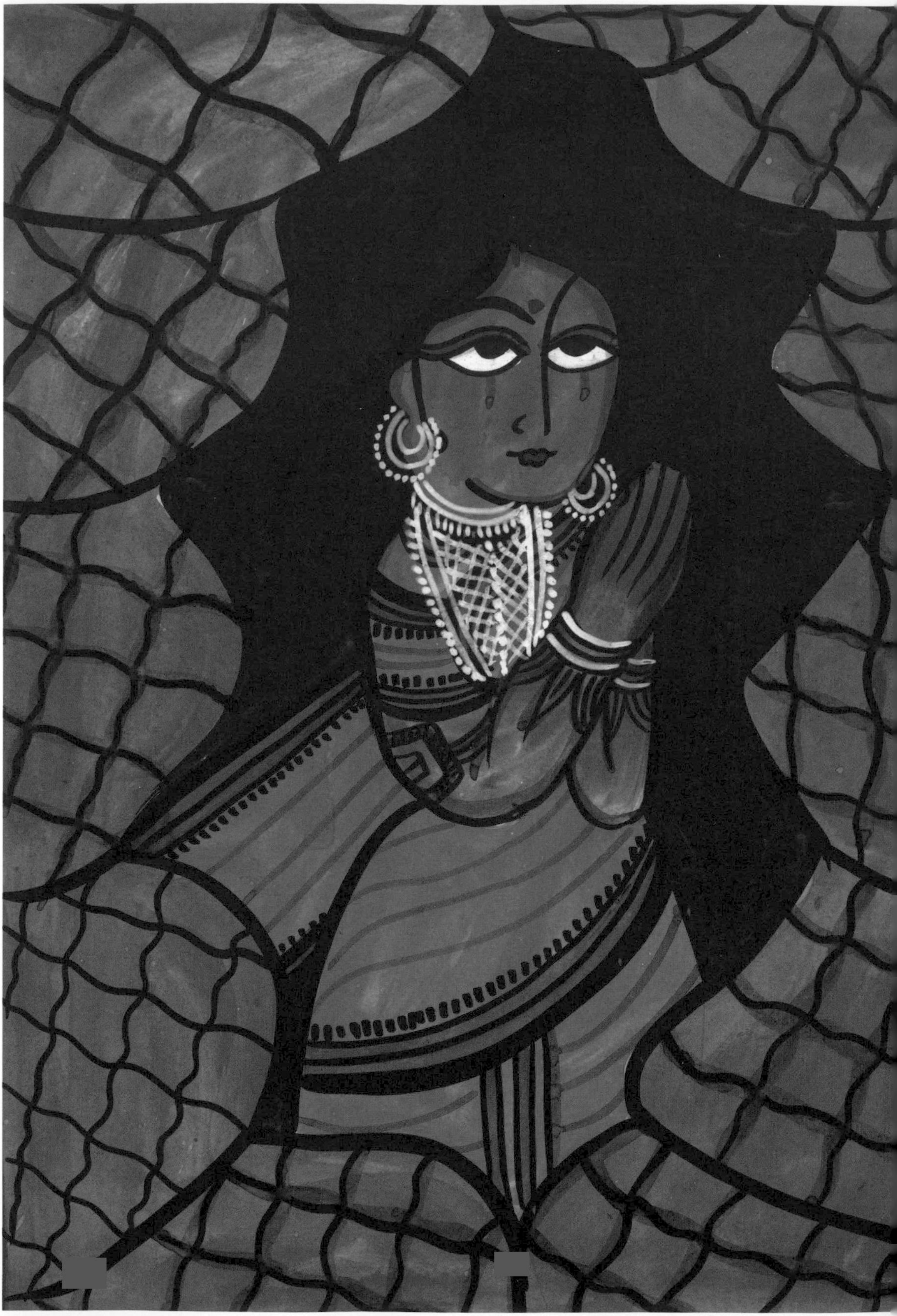

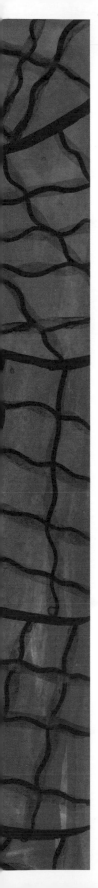

She disappeared, and was never seen again.

FEMALE
RE-TELLINGS
OF THE
RAMAYANA

Sita's Ramayana was painted before it was written. Patua artist Moyna Chitrakar, from Bengal in eastern India, adapted her scroll-version to the form of a fast-paced graphic narrative. Once the drawings were complete, it became clear that her version of the tale was a crisp and terse summary of the original *Ramayana*. It starts in the middle of the action, as it were – the exiled princes, Rama and Lakshmana, are visited in the forest by a beautiful demoness who desires Rama. And, before we know it, we are in the thick of an uncertain and intriguing tale of sorcery, abduction and kingly pride.

Moyna's version remains faithful to the Sanskrit original of the poet Valmiki for the most part, but there are differences as well. There is more magic and wizardry than in the Sanskrit text, and this version features characters such as Mahiravana and the goddess Chandi, who do not appear in the original.

However, this manner of re-telling is not unusual. While Valmiki's version is considered to be the primary text, there exist several regional variations, each taking its colour from local culture, legend and custom. Bengal has its own versions, of which the *Chandrabati Ramayana* is justly famous. Chandrabati, who lived in the 16th century and was one of the few female re-tellers of the epic, appears to have been inspired by existing oral traditions of the *Ramayana*. These songs and ballads were perhaps the creations of women, who sang as they worked at home and outside, and who identified no doubt with this tale of womanly suffering and fortitude.

Chandrabati synthesized these oral stories into a narrative she never quite finished. Significantly, she is less interested in the epic hero Rama's glory, or his courage and kingly prowess. Instead, she takes the part of his bride and queen, the brooding and sorrowful Sita, who is abducted, rescued, doubted and returned to the forest by her devoted but suspicious husband. Moyna's art captures this Sita for us – wide-eyed, soulful and enduring – as she muses on her fate.

Samhita Arni, who has written to Moyna's art, builds on the feminist possibilities of Chandrabati's *Ramayana*. For one, she narrates the epic in Sita's voice, and it is Sita's gaze that guides the reader through its many events and moments. Thus we see things as a wronged woman would, and feel along with her – for the sheer waste and violence that wrongful pride and war bring about. Secondly, as we follow Sita in her recounting of her life and times, we realize that she is essentially empathetic. Her sense of what has befallen her renders her open to what other women endure. And rather than divide the world up into good and bad, right and wrong, Sita's vision encompasses all those who suffer, endure and ultimately bear the consequences of what kings and wars do – and this includes not only women, children and ordinary people, but also animals and birds.

Sita leaves the world as she finds it, but she is changed as a result of what she has gone through – and it is this image of Sita that abides by us, dignified, calm and self-possessed, as she goes to meet her chosen fate.

Sita's Ramayana belongs then to a distinctive female narrative tradition. Kept alive by folk songs and memories, this tradition continues to leaven the epic world of heroes and war with the virtues of nurture, compassion and tolerance.

V. Geetha, Tara Books
Chennai

PATUA
GRAPHICS

This graphic novel has been created by one of the best Patua scroll painters from Bengal, in collaboration with a fine writer and an innovative designer.

Sita's Ramayana was conceived by Tara Books, a publisher with an ongoing interest in connecting Indian picture storytelling traditions with a contemporary reader's sensibility. One of Tara's most exciting dialogues has been with Patua artists – the Patua is a folk-art form that combines performance, storytelling and art. The story is recited or sung as the narrator holds up a painted scroll, pointing to the image that goes with the words.

The narrator tailors her rendering to suit the audience, and her repertoire ranges from traditional myths to current news stories. The Patua is a living tradition whose roots stretch back in time, but these talented artists and storytellers are our contemporaries. With energetic art and an intuitive grasp of narrative sequence, they are constantly looking for ways to take their work forward.

This was the basis of Tara's project: to nudge their work into exciting, more contemporary contexts. The process was a long and adventurous one, but it was apparent right away that the unfolding of the sequence of images in a Patua scroll – the manner in which the images are 'read', one after the other – was more than halfway towards the structure of a modern graphic narrative. The art would have to be divided into panels, read sequentially from left to right rather than top to bottom, and the story would have to be written down, not just recited. To work at creating a graphic novel of a respectable length with a Patua artist involved a range of people and skills – from researcher to author to translator and designer. That is another story. But Tara Books and Groundwood are delighted that the months of intensive – and pleasurable – work with the artist has now materialised from a vision of possibility to this exciting book.

Original edition copyright © 2011 by Tara Books Pvt. Ltd., India
(www.tarabooks.com)
Published in Canada and the USA in 2011 by Groundwood Books

Groundwood Books / House of Anansi Press
110 Spadina Avenue, Suite 801, Toronto, Ontario M5V 2K4
or c/o Publishers Group West
1700 Fourth Street, Berkeley, CA 94710

We acknowledge for their financial support of our publishing program
the Government of Canada through the Canada Book Fund (CBF).

Library and Archives Canada Cataloguing in Publication
Arni, Samhita
Sita's Ramayana / Samhita Arni ; Moyna Chitrakar, illustrator.
ISBN 978-1-55498-145-8
1. Valmiki--Adaptations--Juvenile fiction. 2. Graphic
novels. I. Chitrakar, Moyna II. Valmiki. Ramayana III. Title.
PZ7.7.A76Sit 2011   j741.5'954   C2011-900464-X

The illustrations were made using homemade natural dyes on paper.
Design: Jonathan Yamakami
Production: C. Arumugam
Printed and bound in China

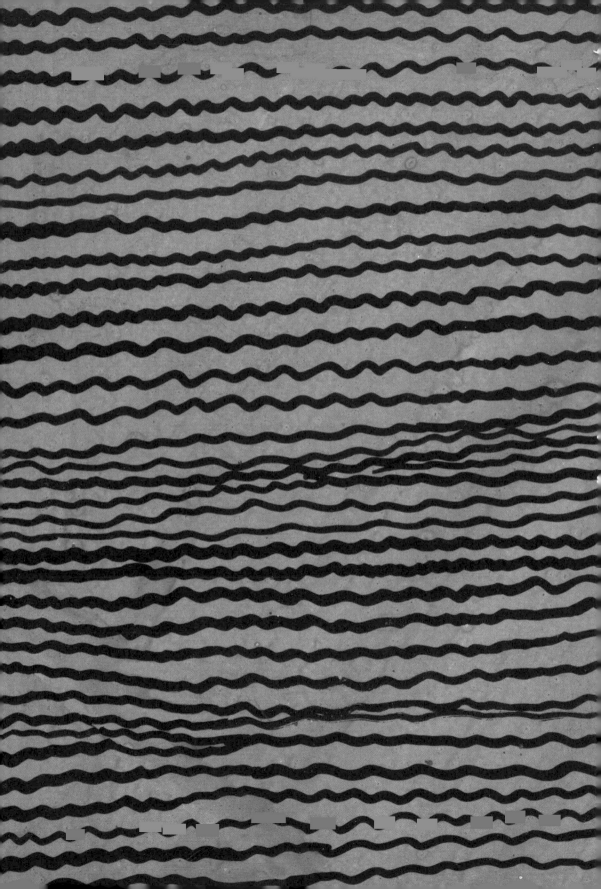